The Brokenhearted Leprechaun

Skip Into Trouble

The Brokenhearted Leprechaun
Skip Into Trouble

L. S. WOOD

Cover Sheet

When Skip turned sixteen, he inherently received a limited portion of his magical powers. Sneaking out of his grandparents' tree home, he went in search of his missing parents who had disappeared a few years earlier. Warned not to partake in any evil brew, he magically partook in some at a pub in Dublin Town. He became drunk and fell asleep in a mortal's trunk in search of gold, and became a stowaway aboard a sailing vessel heading to America. His tomfoolery aboard the ship almost cost him and the others their lives. With sorrow, death and leprechaun magic the adventure in his search for his missing parents begins, through trial and error. Skip finds his full leprechaunic powers along with finding his parents held captive in the New Land by an evil man using them for display in his traveling medicine show. Skip befriends two mortals, a leprechaun's most dreaded enemy, who somehow helps him at different times in this adventure, to save his parents. He returns their favors by making them both wealthy. He saves the returning ship they were on from pirates attacking them on the open sea, and dealing with his difficult-acting father. He proudly was able to return his loving mother back home to his grandparents' tree home, and reuniting her with her worried aging parents.

Dedication

I dedicate this and my many other books, to two dear wonderful friends Simone St. Arnaud and Evangeline Rugg who enjoyed reading my many books before they passed away. To a most wonderful and understanding wife Rebecca, who loves to help people in general, in so many ways? To our wonderful children, son Scott, daughter Jennifer, our five wonderful grandchildren, Amber, Sarah, Stacey, Stephen, and Kendrick (who is pictured on the front cover when he was small).

ARPress
45 Dan Road Suite 5
Canton MA 02021

Hotline: 1(888) 821-0229
Fax: 1(508) 545-7580

Ordering Information:
Quantity sales. Special discounts are available on quantity purchases by corporations, associations, and others. For details, contact the publisher at the address above.

Printed in the United States of America.

ISBN-13:   Softcover   979-8-89356-848-6
               eBook   979-8-89356-849-3

Library of Congress Control Number: 2024908981

Table Of Contents

CHAPTER ONE

Dublin Town, Ireland

With daylight gradually disappearing, Skip watchfully extended his wee head out around the wet dripping cornerstones by Mrs. Mosher's busy tavern.

He carelessly exercised trying not to have himself seen by anyone or worse caught by a Mortal. Skip stood at the corner mentally drained and soaked to the skin. Skip felt abandoned, all alone in a world without love, he thought with misty eyes and a deeply broken heart. He found himself in an alleyway at the corner of a busy pub pitifully searching through the hard misty rains of the day daydreaming. He stood anxiously staring down a busy side street of Dublin Town, seeking out the ones who loved him and who he in return had loved and lost. They just had to be here in or around Dublin Town. They were probably lost in the hectic bustling Main Street sections of storefronts and taverns.

He had come a very long way all by his lonesome along back roads hiding in the camouflage of shrubbery and the foggy rain of the day. He began his day searching every cranny along the desolate roadway nervously looking for his lost mother and father. His life was becoming more difficult for him to deal with each, and every passing day of his life, especially without the love of his mother and friendship of his father to help him through the hard times growing up in the world as a leprechaun.

The mortals around Dublin Town appeared to be terribly busy, according to Skip's laid-back way of life, quickly moving to, and fro along the rain swept streets and alleyways following a long day of work in the city. The mortals looked more than fretfully busy to Skip with each trying frantically in their own special way of thinking to beat the ticking of the clock that stood in the middle of the city common.

A strong brisk north wind was howling throughout the city. Black stormy rain clouds raged in the canopy above the city with an occasional bright bolt of lightning flashing as hard rains drove the light of day into a blurred shroud of darkness cast down from the murky clouds that hovered like huge mushrooms in the sky above. It was raining harder than normal for this time of year in Ireland, more like a monsoon season in the tropics, spattering down heavy rains on everyone by the bucketful.

Oh, how Skip hated nature's hard driving rains that soaked his little frame and chilling every-last inch of his young leprechaun body. Being very limited in the miniscule amount of his leprechaun magic irritated Skip to no end, for he wanted to use them all right away. He needed to exercise great care in the simplest of little hooligan-airy trickery when he performed them, otherwise he might possibly become incarcerated by the leprechaun's most dreaded enemies, the wicked mortals of the world.

Once detained by a mortal Skip knew he would be doomed, and have to spend the rest of his living days in captivity without the slimmest chance of ever escaping himself. He would be a prisoner of theirs for life, feverishly slaving for them day after day until the day he died for the lucky mortal that might catch him. He would become a slave just like his grandparents suspected of his unlucky parents who were probably now enslaved at the present Skip figured it was time to take his chances even if he couldn't save his parents from their captors, but he would at least try. He just had to see his loving mother one last time, feel her soft loving hands on him along with her warm tender arms wrapped snugly around him before he died an orphan.

Skip spotted a rather tall slender but very strong muscular looking young man who had just gotten off a wagon walking slowly down the cobbled stone street toward the corner where Skip was standing out of sight, he thought. "Who was this happy go lucky bloke?" Skipped thought miserably to himself. It seemed rather strange to Skip that such a strong, good looking young bloke was so tranquilly happy on a damp rainy day like this. The man seemed joyful and content singing away and trying to whistle a merry tune. Between millions of tiny raindrops falling on him as he strode along the street with a slaphappy smile on his very damp, face. Other mortals were running frantically in all directions, and did not look too cheerful about the rain that was bucketing down on them, but he did. "He must be out of his bloody wits," Skipped thought strangely to himself. "No one in their right mind could possibly be this happy on such a dank day as this."

Skip continued to conceal himself with his wrap at the corner as he wiped away more raindrops from his face diligently staring down the busy street at this slaphappy bloke.

CHAPTER TWO

Parting of Friends

"Why Vinnie McDougall, you old landlubber, what brings you all the way down here to Dublin Town on this depressing rainy day of ours?" Now there was a man Skip could relate to for he had his bloody wits about himself. This bloke was someone like himself who thought the blasted rain was extremely annoying and dreadfully gloomy.

The stranger, hollering out to the other bloke, sounded faintly familiar to Skip all wrapped up in his raingear, but he could not quite place where he had seen the likes of this mortal before, if ever? Vinnie stopped dead in his tracks when he heard his name being called out from behind. He quickly turned to see who had called out to him. "Timothy you old landlubber, I have come to Dublin Town following the selling off, of my parent's farm. I wanted to give my last respects to this good old city of ours, mind you. Leave for the new world on the fresh morning high tide, at dawn. I will be sailing on her out of Ireland on the newly built tall ship moored in the harbor ready to set sail on her maiden voyage. I am going off to America to live, and am heading out on a new adventure in life. Going to America, the land of opportunity, to make my fortune in gold and walk the gold lined streets of Boston Town!"

Skip's tiny ears perked up straight away when he heard mention the word of gold. "Why, I could give that disillusioned bloke who likes to walk in the rain gold, wealth and more. I could give him all the gold in the world he would ever need if he were to catch me, or could I. I don't have all of my magical powers yet" Skip thought briefly to himself, "nor any of my

4

gold for that matter." The very thought of not having his satchel of magical gold yet irritated Skip to no end. He was very anxious to receive his gold no matter how he came by it. He heard in rumor when not listening properly to his grandparent's instructions to him that it would be in his very own gold where his magical powers would be complete. He would no doubt have powers almost equal to those of the king of the leprechauns.

"It was late day now, and he had better be getting on back home, soaked as he may be," Skip thought briefly to himself. "Sooner than later no doubt as he knew he was in trouble for being gone so long, and would catch the dickens as he usually did from his Granny Broom and his Grandpa Hair when he returned home late again." Granny and Grandpa were Skip's only grandparents still alive. He was fortunate to be living with them ever since his loving mother and foolish stubborn father disappeared a few years back.

Granny Broom acquired her nickname from Skip because she would chase his littleness around the house, out through the tree trunk back door, and into the backyard switching at him all the while with her thatched broomstick in hand. She occasionally landed a few good hard whacks to his hind end with her broom when he did not mind her as he acted up quite often or if he just did not move fast enough when she politely asked him to do a simple chore around the treehouse. Grandpa Hair acquired his nickname from Skip in a similar way. When Skip paid no attention to his grandmother requesting him to do something or just doing something he was not supposed to does, Grandpa Hair would pull Skip around by the thick locks of his hair to teach him manners and respect.

Grandpa had little patience when it came to Skip! He thought he was about as useless a leprechaun as he had ever seen, as was his useless father. Skip's father, according to his grandfather, had led their daughter astray. His father and mother were lost because of him, said Grampa. They lost their freedom to some evil mortal's trickery or to a wild beast of prey for food, a catastrophe caused by Skip's, foolish father's mindless, senseless, and inconsiderate actions for the want of more evil tonic.

Skip, being the young inquisitive leprechaun he was, was too busy daydreaming about shenanigans and tomfoolery his grandfather thought. He was always playing dirty pranks of trickery on the farm animals around the countryside and wild animals of the fields. Skip was too mischievous by his grandfather's strict standards, for Skip did not take his young leprechaun life serious enough to be a good learning leprechaun. His grandfather seemed to have forgotten his own youthful tomfoolery acts of his childhood years growing up as a young leprechaun.

Skip loved tormenting the old bull down in his neighboring farmer's field. The big bull grazing there belonged to his hard-working neighbor, Farmer Prendergast and his two very hard-working boys. Time, and time again, Skip could be heard out in the field, his tiny voice laughing hard as could be like the buzzing of a tiny bug in the breeze. He loved to torment the old animal until blinding tears of joy filled his tiny eyes. Sometimes in the early morning hour's he would laugh utterly loud while walking down the path leading to the pasture where the bull grazed. He was thinking about the Witless Old Bovine what he was going to do to him, when he got to the field.

He would cause, the Old Bull to be anxiously all fired up, by jumping up and down in front of him as he yelled out to get his attention and to irritate him. He always kept the big tall shade tree growing in the field directly behind him for safety. When the old bull became enraged with his shenanigans, it would lift its head from grazing and start pawing at the ground before charging at the annoying gnome. The bull would run at him and tried to crush the life out of him flat up against the large tree trunk behind the little imp. Skip always timed it before the raging bull's large head would reach him and would transpose himself onto the tree branch above the bull's head. He loved looking down from his safe perch as the bull ran headlong full force into the tree trunk, knocking itself out sometimes. Occasionally the old bull would just fall flat on the ground from the wicked blow it took to its head, and Skip would laugh wholeheartedly. He loved tormenting the old bull day after day until the dizzy animal could move no more, laying on the ground below as Skip watched its big round eyes roll back up into its head. When the bull could walk no more, Skip would go on his merry way looking for another animal in the field or forest to play his silly tricks on.

CHAPTER THREE

The Nickname

It was bound to happen one day. Skip being too brave for his own good, waited a second too long before transposing to the safety of the tree behind him. When the mighty bull came charging after him one of its large horns brushed scantly up against Skip as he transposed to the safety of a branch. His magic took the big bull right along with him up to the tiny branch above. The weight of the bull along with Skip's own weight was too much for the tiny limb to bear and snapped like a twig. Both Skip and the mighty bull came crashing down to the ground in a thrashing heap. The bull, as startled as Skip was, flailed its legs all the way to the ground. They landed beside each other with the bull barely landing on top of Skip's left foot. The hefty weight of the huge animal caused great pain for him, making him think his wee foot crushed flat. The bull quickly rose to its feet, walked a short distance away from the tree and Skip, and turned back toward them. Its hooves pawed the ground standing ready to charge with its massive head swaying back and forth, and let out an immense angry snort from his nostrils and charged.

At that very moment, Skip felt the hair atop his head yanked up hard, thinking every, last strand of hair would be pulled out by its roots. The harsh yank pulled him up into the tree and out of harm's way of the bull ready to kill him. The mighty bull crashed headlong into the tree trunk with an enormous loud thud. The bull, so angered with Skip, was going to rid itself of this annoying little creature, once, and for all and had put all of its strength into the charge. Lucky for Skip that his Grandpa had been there watching him play his tomfoolery by taunting and tormenting the old bull from a distance as he stood atop the fence on the side of the field.

Being too busy jumping up, and then down thinking about his painful foot, he had not seen the bull charging after him. Grandpa could have easily used his magic to transport Skip to safety, but wanted to teach him a lesson. Grandma was not any too happy with Skip either, for tormenting the old bull and what had happened. She forbade him from ever tormenting another of Farmer Prendergast's animals after that, but he would for Skip enjoyed his fun of tomfoolery.

CHAPTER FOUR

Mrs. Mosher's Pub
A Drink for Old Times' Sake

Skip snapped out of his daydreaming as Timothy began to speak. "Buy you a drink, Vinnie my old friend, for old time's sake? One for our friendship, one for prosperity and health, and one for the gold you are seeking in the new world." "I would like that Timothy, I really would. Thank you!" Timothy opened the side door of the pub for Vinnie allowing his old friend to pass in front of him out of the rain. He went in and they sat down at the far end of the bar to have their merry conversation about childhood days and Vinnie's adventure in the new world.

Skip curiously watched from the corner of the pub as the two mortal friends disappeared through the side door and into Mrs. Mosher's Tavern. He stood daydreaming again, wondering if the wacky bloke would give his friend Timothy information on how to make gold. He wondered if this Vinnie fellow had any magical ways about him for making gold by using fairy dust, or mortal dust, if there was such a thing! He had never heard mention of mortal dust before, but wondered if it was possible that there might be such a magical dust somewhere in the world.

CHAPTER FIVE

The Spittoon

With a pinch of an ear and a blink of an eye, Skip transposed inside the pub out of the torrential rains. He intended to find perch on a small stool he had seen partially hidden beneath the front part of the bar he magically envisioned in his mind, but instead he found himself teeter tottering back and forth off balance on the top rim of a sparkling brand new unused spittoon on the floor beside the bar.

He had never seen one of these shiny basins before and had confused it for a stool. Spittoons were new to Ireland with the discovery of tobacco products from the new world. Looking up from his precarious perch, Skip sat staring up into a set of eyes of a leathery looking weather beaten old sailor. He was getting ready to spit out a very large slimy chewed up wad of tobacco from his overfilled half toothless mouth down into the spittoon. Catching a once in a lifetime glimpse of a real live leprechaun caught the old sailor off guard, and he could not believe his eyes! Maybe he was becoming a little senile and his mind was playing tricks on him like a shipwrecked sailor adrift on the open sea without food or water for days. He swallowed hard and saw Skip atop the spittoon looking up at him. He swallowed the entire wad of tobacco and its juices as it slid down his throat burning all the way, causing him to gag, cough, and sputter.

He said some not so very nice words as the tobacco and its rancid juices went burning down his throat. "A #@? Leper-man. A real *@%*-* leper can. I mean a real live leprechaun! I saw myself a real live leprechaun, sitting right there." He pointed toward the spittoon sitting on the floor hoping someone in the pub might take a quick look to where he was pointing. "He was sitting right there, he was, sitting on the rim of the spittoon looking right up at me. Did anyone of you bloody fools see him?" He was yelling out to all in the pub as loud he could as his stomach felt a little queasy and he turned a slight shade of green.

Skip knew trouble was brewing and was about to come his way soon as the ghostly mortals' eyes glared down at him. He didn't want to get snared in this position especially by this old wrinkly looking mortal who was about to spit whatever that greenish brown goo was that was dripping out his mouth and onto his chin. He looked a sickly mess to Skip.

Without-delay, Skip transposed to the top of the glasses' wooden shelving rack suspended above the bar. This quickly placed him out of sight and out of imminent danger. He transposed to the far end of the shelf as close he could to Vinnie and Timothy who were sitting at the far end of the bar below. This way he could listen in on every word spoken by them without being seen, or discovered. He wanted to learn firsthand about Vinnie's gold and how he proposed to go about making it along with all the gold lined streets in the new world.

"What are you going to be doing in the new world, Vinnie?" asked Timothy. Just as Vinnie was about to answer Timothy, the coughing, gagging, sickly looking sailor grabbed hold of him by the right shoulder and yanked hard on his sleeve to get his attention. Vinnie prepared to defend himself from attack by a drunk, who he thought had taken hold of him, and about to swing at him as he held up his right arm to fend off the attacker.

"Mate," the old man stammered out of control explaining the situation with very bad breath. "I just saw myself a real live leprechaun, mate." The old sailor was overwhelmed and beside himself. "Right there", pointing towards the shiny spittoon sitting half under the bar. The old sailor was a bundle of nerves, incredibly excited and loud as he went on with his story about the leprechaun. His hand waved wildly shaking more and more as he went on, "I saw myself a real live one I swear mates," he was sitting right there on the spittoon. I tell you mates, it is the truth. He was just sitting there with a frightened looking smile on his smug face, staring right up. The Leprechaun was just about the same size as the dang jug, I mean the spittoon. What am I supposed to do mates? What am I supposed to do?"

Vinnie took a good hard look at the troubled old sailor, trying very hard not to, but could not help laughing right out loud in the poor old gent's face. "That's an old wives' tale, pops. There are no such things as fairylike rascals, leprechauns, or imps in this world. There are no pixies, no leprechauns, not even the tooth fairy for that matter! You have had way to much ale to drink today, pops! How much ale have you had to drink?"

The old man looked a bit put out with Vinnie as he rattled on about there being no such things as leprechauns or fairies in the world. "I do not drink liquor or ale for that matter. All I have had to drink today is a couple of glasses of sarsaparilla sugar water and a cup of hot black tea. I tell you, it is the truth mates! I saw myself a real-life leprechaun right here and now, this very instant. Plain as day, I tell you. Plain as the noses on your faces, I truly saw one."

Seeing the anguish in the old man's face, Vinnie made one last effort to show a little compassion to the babbling old fool. He tried very hard this time to look more serious with him and try not to laugh out loud again for what he thought was a very drunken, very disillusioned old tattered sailor from the sea.

"Well, pops, you had better start drinking something much harder than tea or sarsaparilla then if you really saw a real-life leprechaun without the ale!" Timothy sarcastically roared out mimicking and laughing. "Just think," he said not able to control his laughter," just think how many imps and leprechauns you can see when you start drinking the good stuff." Both Timothy and Vinnie bellowed out in uncontrollable laughter, turning away from the babbling old sailor, to continue-on with their conversation. They did not want to listen to him tell stories about old wives' tales gone to his disillusioned drunkard's mind in a dither of fantasy. The two had important things to converse about before Vinnie left Ireland.

The exasperated old sailor's face turned a crimson red and became instantly disgruntled with the smart aleck blokes for not believing a word of his story. He grumbled exceptionally loud so others in the pub might hear him as he hurried across the tavern floor looking for the vanished imp. He stammered on complaining louder and louder about Vinnie and Timothy the bloody blokes who had just made fun of him for seeing a genuine leprechaun. He would show those two bloody smart aleck fools that he was not just imagining one when he found him and claimed his prize.

He searched every place he could think of in the pub for the missing leprechaun. He looked under every table, pulling out every chair from beneath them except the ones patrons were sitting on. He looked behind the bar where the barmaid was busy preparing drinks. Everyone had heard him talking to Vinnie and Timothy as he was so loud, and they too thought the old gent had had too much ale to drink for one day. He clumsily jumped over the spittoon and fell down on its other side. He thought he could surprise the leprechaun if he was quick enough to find him hiding there. He even looked quickly inside the spittoon, and then lifted it up off the floor and looked beneath it.

One patron laughed to his friend sitting at the table with him when the old man glanced at the bottom of the spittoon to look for the lost leprechaun. The old gent was becoming ever the more dismayed in his frantic search for the legendary imp. Had the tactless old sailor just looked up occasionally, instead of always looking down, he may have caught a glimpse of Skip or have caught him, as Skip was sitting nonchalantly in a lost trance sitting cross-legged gawking down listening to Timothy and Vinnie reminiscing over childhood times. Skip was so absorbed in what Vinnie and Timothy were saying to one another that he paid little attention to what was taking place around him. Skip without thinking could have been caught by a quick thinking mortal, if one had seen him sitting there in his trance listening for some magical words from Vinnie about making gold. His over eager desire for this magical metal might well be his demise in the near future.

"A little rum, lass, a pint of your favorite tonic here to please my taste buds, and a glass of your best bourbon for my good friend Vinnie here to chase away the leprechauns, hey Vinnie," laughed Timothy out loud again. The old man, ignored Timothy's rude remarks and would show them along with the rest of the patrons in the pub they were the real fools for not listening to him when he claimed his prize.

Skip sat motionlessly quiet listening to the conversation take place below him with the greatest of interest! He did not want to miss a word spoken by Vinnie about the possibility of making some gold, since he did not have any of the precious metal to call his own yet. He was extremely curious about how to make some for himself or how he might come by it by some mysterious or devious way that he had not thought of yet.

CHAPTER SIX

The Evil Brew

Rum, scotch, whiskey, and ale, all the evil brews told to him by his grandfather were freely flowing from the kegs and bottles from behind the bar to the patrons in the pub by the barmaid. Every alcohol drink, Grandpa Hair would not allow Skip to taste was being served below. "Take notes, Skip," his grandpa would say over, and over to him. "The evil tonic is what happened to your precious mom and to your foolish father." Skip remembered the words his grandfather preached to him so many times. "You cannot drink the forbidden tonic, Skip, for we leprechauns cannot deal with such evil drinks. They are nothing but evil potions that make you do things you would not ordinarily do."

"Your pa came home real late one night", his grandfather told him, "from Dublin Town drunk from drinking too much evil tonic, and insisted on going back for more. He went off singing his made-up song about mortals being too stupid and weak of mind to catch him." "Now look what happened to him Skip. The drunken fool took your precious mother away from you too when he didn't listen to me. He just had to go back to Dublin Town one last time to get more of that evil witches brew. Your mother, the sweet lass, went chasing after him, she did! She went running off down the road after he had already left and tried to stop him and talk some sense into that thick skull of his and persuade the drunken fool not to go."

"I guess she wasn't very successful as neither of them returned home thanks to that dang fool pa of yours and that evil witches' brew.

The two of them, your Mother and your Father, may been eaten by roving jackals, a pack of hungry dogs, or by some other wild beasts of prey for all I know. "I do know this as a fact, I do your pa was rendered unable to use the special magical powers he inherited from his mother at birth to protect him and your mother because the forbidden magic in the evil tonic he drank made him powerless. All I know for sure, Skip, is this, that they never returned home after your father partook in that evil witches brew." "Skip, your foolish father took our only child daughter, and the only mother you will ever have away, just like that, because the dang fool just did not want to listen to me! It was not fair of him to do that to your grandmother and me!"

"You know, Skip, I once took too many evil drinks at a party held by the King of the Leprechauns. That blasted O'Brien anyway. He and his dang humbug guests all laughed because of the stupidity when I tried to use my special powers to do a simple little trick of retrieving a small apple from the banquet table. It was useless for me to try to tell your father anything what the evil brew did to me, but he did not want to listen. Your father went straight off like a proud old rooster in a barnyard full of free walking hens to prove he was better than me."

Remembering his grandfather's words of wisdom, he sat on the mezzanine impatiently listening to Vinnie and Timothy reminiscing. They were not getting to that very important part in the conversation about how Vinnie was going to make his gold, and the slowness of the conversation irritated Skip considerably. The two below were drinking way-too many evil tonics, as were the other patrons in the pub according to his Grandpa Hair. Vinnie and Timothy both took one drink right after another it seemed as he anxiously listened. He wondered why these mysterious evil potions did not seem to affect the many mortals sitting below him. Might the reason be they were mortals? Vinnie and Timothy had already had a couple of drinks a piece of the evil tonic but they were not acting the least bit silly or loud like Grandpa had explained they should be acting. The mortals seemed to be enjoying themselves more and more with every evil drink they had.

"I wonder how the evil tonics smell or what they taste like," Skip thought to himself. Finally, it became just too great a chore for Skip to handle just sitting patiently and watching the two mortals below him along with the other patrons in the pub enjoy every kind of evil brew they consumed. Concentrating on a glass sitting on a shelf across the bar, Skip found a clean empty glass resting comfortably in his from the bar's glass rack suspended above the barmaid. This new sort of magic of making objects come to him from a distance was still very new to him but a whole lot of fun.

CHAPTER SEVEN

Throwing Stones

Not long ago, Skip recalled how he practiced day after day on tiny pebbles resting on the ground near the roadway near his grandparent's tree home until finally, he was able to make them come to him without getting-hurt by them anymore thanks to his Grandma Broom. When he first tried summoning stones from off the ground, they would fly at him. It was not until Grandma Broom taught him the proper way of concentration in retrieving objects that he was able to make objects disappear and instantly appear in his hands without hurting himself. It was helpful that he first used tiny pebbles to practice with because if he had used larger objects like pumpkins or larger objects, he could have seriously hurt himself.

The first time Skip summoned something to his hand was truly by accident. When Skip first learned he possessed such magical powers, he summoned a large red ripe apple from his neighbor, Farmer Prendergast's apple orchard. The apple appeared like magic in his hand and it tasted good. Ever since then he had tried feverishly hard to repeat the magic trick by retrieving tiny pebbles from the ground.

Grandma was absolutely no help to him at first, as she would laugh every time a tiny stone flew up off the ground similar a speeding bullet shot from a musket. Knowing he was going to get-hit by the stone, Skip performed all sorts of crazy antics like jumping, falling over sideways, and sometimes running off like a surprised jackrabbit away from a pursuing predator. He became annoyed with his Grandma and said to her, "If you can do a better job of retrieving these stones, then why don't you come over here and show me the right way then". Skip thought only the boy and men leprechauns possessed such magic. He tilted his little green leprechaun hat forward and sideways in a sarcastic manner, and placed his hands on his hips as he stood there yelling at her. "Which stone would you like me to make disappear for you and retrieve in my hand?" said Grandma Broom. "Let me see," said Skip, the little one beside the root of that old tree over yonder by the big wagon wheel." He pointed to a small stone sitting flat on the ground by the root of the old shade tree and it instantly disappeared from the ground by the wheel before his eyes. "You mean this stone, Skip?" "Yes, Grandma, that is the one. How do you do that"? "Just a wee bit of good concentration does the trick. It is all in the proper concentration on the object that matters when you want to move it into your hand. When you use the correct concentration, the magic will always work. Do not imagine the objects flying in the air at you as that is exactly what will happen. You have to imagine them snugly held in your hand.

She laughed at him a couple more times until he learned how to concentrate. Next feeling quite self-confident in his new magic, he summoned a larger rock from the side of the road. It proved way-too heavy for him to hold onto and he dropped it down to the side of his foot, making him jump in pain while holding onto his throbbing toes.

"Remember what I told you, Skip, summon only the things you are capable of holding onto. Remember that much bigger things you have the abilities to move from place to place, but never, and I do mean never, think larger objects into your hands unless you are confident you can hold onto them or you will hurt yourself real bad!" Way across the barnyard where Grandma had retrieved her first pebble of the day, sat a large wagon full of hay. She surprised Skip by lifting it with her magic and placing it gently down beside them. One moment the wagon was sitting far across the yard, the next like a flash of lightning it was floating down softly to rest on the ground beside them.

"How did you do that Grandma? How did you move that big wagon of hay from across the yard to here?" Skip asked with the greatest of enthusiasm echoing in his voice, which his Grandma had never heard come out of Skip's mouth before. It appeared now that he was taking in the knowledge everyone had offered him with a little more seriously than just brushing it off with sarcasm. "The same way you move pebbles from the ground, or anything else that you want to move, Skip. We leprechauns concentrate on moving many objects vigilantly from here to there and back again by just thinking carefully and using our powers. Try concentrating on small objects first. Then you can move on to bigger objects like the wagon as your skills get better with age. It will take you a good long time, maybe many years to develop the necessary skill of moving larger objects properly." "Do not try to go rushing your powers for they will all come to you in proper time boy. There will be a special time in your wee young life Ship, when you will cry out for your gold and powers, and magically they will all come to you like magic, a wee little bit at a time, I promise you.

Skip was way-too anxious for his full use of his magical powers to develop and wanted them all that very moment. He felt as if he was a brand new man now even with his very limited powers. He felt that all young leprechauns needed their special powers when they were first born, then they might go out into the world and prove themselves worthy to all the other leprechauns and teach the mortals around Ireland and the world who the bosses really were. The time was rapidly approaching sooner than Skip knew when he would have to prove himself a brave young leprechaun man without the full knowledge of his magical leprechaun powers. He would feel very helpless at times, in the new adventure that he was about to enter into so unexpectedly.

CHAPTER EIGHT

A Drink for the Road

Skip sat there thinking about the many new learning experiences in his young life as Vinnie spoke below and brought Skip out of his daydreaming thoughts. "Let me buy you one last drink for the road, Timothy my old friend. This may be the last drink I am ever able to buy for you Timothy, I think. Well, I should really be leaving for the farm Vinnie, but seeing you put it that way, I guess one more drink for the road would be a nice gesture in sealing together the good lifelong friendship we share." Skip watched the barmaid pour out a full glass of rum for Timothy from a small keg sitting above her behind the main bar, and set it down on the main bar. When she turned back around to pour out a small glass of scotch for Vinnie, the glass in Skip's right hand became full of rum from Timothy's now empty glass sitting alone on the bar. When the barmaid turned back around to retrieve the mug of rum for Timothy, and deliver the two glasses to her customers, she found the mug was completely dry. She glanced quickly from side to side, looking for the smart aleck bloke who had just taken advantage of her good personality. She turned her back on the mug for a wee-bit minute and he helped himself to some free rum. How could someone have drank it down so quickly? The glass on the bar was completely dry and empty as if someone had just exchanged the full glass of rum for a clean dry one from off the rack and ran off with the full one. There was no one sitting or standing near enough to the bar to have taken it in such short order that it had taken her to turn around and pour out the small glass of scotch for Vinnie, she thought.

She flung herself halfway up and across the main bar to see if a bloke or young lass were hiding under the shelf overhang on the other side of the bar. She was disappointed to find no one hiding there. She took the empty glass from the bar and proceeded to pour out yet another one from the small keg behind her, constantly looking over her shoulder glancing from side to side, keeping a keen eye on Vinnie's small glass of scotch. She wanted to make sure nobody would take advantage again by taking another free glass of liquor from behind her as she poured out a second mug of rum.

CHAPTER NINE

The Taste and Smell of Brew

Skip put the glass of rum up to his lips and drank it down like water from a fresh running stream. He noticed a slightly mild tingling taking place as it made its way across his lips as they quivered a smidgen as his taste buds came instantly alive when the rum crossed over his tongue and trickled down his gullet to his tummy below. He felt an almost instant feeling as if he had just drank a cup of warm lemon tea when the rum hit his stomach. It gave him a warm soothing feeling all over. The smell and taste of this evil tonic intrigued him by the strange taste it had left in his mouth and the funny warm feeling it gave him. He was so intrigued that he concentrated his limited powers on Vinnie's small glass of scotch sitting unprotected behind the barmaid on the main bar.

Poof, the small glass of scotch on the bar was empty, as he had made the rum in the mug disappear! He summoned the contents of the scotch glass when the barmaid turned around to pour out the second mug of rum for Timothy. Although she glanced constantly from time to time over her shoulder while pouring out the rum, when she turned around she was astonished to find the small glass of scotch totally empty, just as she had found the mug of rum before. Furiously, she yelled out into the once quiet pub, "Okay, okay which one of you scoundrels took the two drinks from my bar? Come on now, one of you had better fess up to this mean trick now! Which one of you took the two drinks from the bar?"

Everyone in the pub turned toward the bar to see why the barmaid was so sizzling mad, for who she was yelling at the top of her lungs. Everyone in the pub except Skip thought there would surely be a scuffle between the barmaid and a patron if she could only get her bloody hands on the thief. Skip laughed quietly on the shelf as she sounded infuriated, mad enough in fact that she might well have whipped the daylights out of the dreaded banshee with her own hands had she had the opportunity.

Vinnie and Timothy were sitting way-too far away from the barmaid to have taken the drinks from her. All the other patrons in the pub were also sitting too far away to have been able to reach the drinks, and no one was walking around the pub that was close enough at the time to have taken the drinks from off the bar and run.

She thought for sure she was losing her bloody wits about herself, extremely worn out from the long hard day of work without having a single break. She did not have time to eat her lunch. She began to think she might have tried to fill both glasses by using an empty container of scotch and an empty keg of rum. Perhaps she had imagined the glasses been filled and they had not actually been filled at all. She thought maybe she had opened the keg and bottle, and had actually left them closed.

It had been an exceptionally long exhausting very busy day at the pub because of the extreme weather outside. It seemed every one of the pub's patrons had come in off the wet street from the driving rain bringing a friend or two inside to purchase drinks for them. A couple of local trader blokes set up the bar for everyone to have a free drink on the house a couple of times apiece to keep everyone warm and happy and take the cold chill of the day away.

The Lady tending the Pub was not going to take any chances this time, she made certain no bloody-bloke, or lass would be able to steal another one of her drinks from behind her this time. She placed the full mug of rum on the little back shelf in front of her before she poured Vinnie's second glass of scotch. She knew this way no one in the pub could possibly be close enough to reach the drinks without her first noticing him or her. She would be able to reach down and catch them red handed from behind the bar by grabbing their bloody little hands.

Picking up the two refilled glasses, the barmaid quickly turned to deliver the scotch to Vinnie and the rum to Timothy, still looking for the bloody bloke whoever it was who had stolen the two drinks from her. She thought for a split second as she turned to deliver the drinks, she had heard some kind of commotion taking place above her head, but didn't bother to look up to see what it was. She too darn worn out and tired, from the long exhausting day, to even-care if the ceiling was actually falling down.

The day had begun at an early eight o'clock in the morning for her at the pub. She started the day off by having to wash the leftover drink glasses from the night before that the night girl neglected to wash, pick up the place, too Sweep and mop the dirty floors before opening for the day. She usually came into a nice clean establishment, but not this day. After getting her several children all fed, washed and ready for the long day at home, she had to work at the pub for yet another along several unsuspecting hours. The lass, who was supposed to have relieved her for the day, had sent a message by her husband that she had been dreadfully sick at work the night before, and wouldn't be making it into work this day. The poor girl would have to stay until closing. If she had not needed the money so desperately, she would have loved to close the doors to the pub early and gone home. The pub's owner Mr. Harris, was off too London on vacation, and would probably fire her if she had. Her loving husband, the poor dear, had been lost in a severe storm out to sea, leaving her in need of money to raise and care for her several children and to pay for the family home.

Skip enjoyed the incredibly different taste of the rum along with the extraordinary, sweet aroma it gave off from the glass he had just summoned from the bar. He enjoyed the funny tingling sensations that quickly followed its drinking. He enjoyed everything about the rum so well, he decided to try the scotch the same way from the second glass he summoned from the bar, and drank it down in a single gulp. This time he experienced a total different number of flaming sensations. These new sensations became more a feeling of liquefied fire flowing like red-hot lava over his tongue. The scotch seemed to burn every taste bud as it ran rampart down his throat. When it landed in Skip's stomach, the liquefied fire felt like a red-hot firebomb exploding. The trembling muscles in his throat and the explosion in his stomach caused him to gasp for air. A torrent of white steam shot out his little ears, vibrating his wee little head like a steam kettle whistling and blowing off steam. Billions of chills commenced running up and down his tiny spine with the fury of angry fire ants marching wildly through the jungle. With his mouth on fire and his body vibrating from the chilling effects of the scotch, Skip flipped over and over in midair doing somersaults all across the mezzanine above the barmaid till the sudden effects of the scotch subsided.

The noise above the bar had been the commotion the weary barmaid had heard when she turned to deliver the drinks to Timothy and Vinnie was Skip's wee little feet hitting the shelf above her head several times, as he flipped back and forth across it. Wow! Skip reflected on what had just happened to him. No wonder his Grandpa called these tonics potent, potentially dangerous drinks, the forbidden tonics of the world! The strong scotch instantly caused immense tears to well up in his tiny eyes and instantly sweat began to form in large droplets on his tiny forehead. His scalp commenced to get feverishly hot and his head felt as though someone had just placed a large bucket of warm peat moss on top of it as a joke.

CHAPTER TEN

Good Luck Vinnie

"Good luck to you, Vinnie, on your new adventure to America and your quest for your gold! Take care of yourself, lad, and do not forget your old friend Timothy when you become all rich and famous! Come back to Ireland someday Vinnie so we can have another one of them rounds for the road at Mrs. Mosher's pub. Good luck to you and take care." With saying that, Timothy shook Vinnie's hand a hearty handshake and out the side door of the pub, he went into the bucketing down rain of the day. He headed back home to his father's farm that was a good distance outside of Dublin Town.

"May I have a leather of your best scotch to go, Lass?" Vinnie made his pleasant request to the busy barmaid. She grabbed a bottle of the pub's best scotch off the rear shelf placing it into a leather pouch, then wrapped it up in paper. Vinnie put on his nearly dry jacket and placed his leather of scotch into its inner pocket to protect it from the hard-driving rains. Pleasant thoughts of Timothy filled Vinnie's mind as he exited out the side door into the rain. He was off and heading across town toward the wharf to the hotel to the boarding house to spend his last night in Ireland. The covered livery wagon, with all his worldly belongings on it, was outside the pub with its driver just a short distance down the street waiting for him to return to take the short ride to the rooming house.

Skip pondered greedily about Vinnie's fortune of gold, that bright shiny metal that glittered bright in the sunlight of the day which he had none of as of yet. All his thinking was becoming fuzzily unclear with Skip's tonic blurred mind. He had become slightly blurry-eyed and unable to focus correctly. He sat on the mezzanine for a moment contemplating whether to go straight home as he should, but had second thoughts about what Vinnie might say in his travels to another mortal friend or stranger he might run into and talk about making his fortune in gold. That dumb bloke Vinnie had neglected to mention to his friend Timothy just how he was to come by his fortune or how he was going too magically, produce the gold.

Quicker than scat, Skip transposed outside the pub in search of this bloke Vinnie, and see where he was off too. He thought he had safely transposed back out to the security of the corner by Mrs. Mosher's Tavern but instead he found himself right smack dab in the middle of a frothy foam covered mud puddle in the middle of the street just outside the door leading into the pub. The ghostly light of the day had changed drastically into wet drenched frightful foggy night, with only a small number of dim lit oil lamps lighting up the poorly lit streets and darkened alleyways. He quickly picked himself up off the wet cobblestones as he watched Vinnie board the livery wagon a short distance away. In a flash, Skip was beneath the livery wagon, sitting on its rear axle sling as the wagon slowly moved away from the side of the road.

The rain from the storm caused mud and water to splash wildly up and around him from the puddles on the cobblestones roadway as he went along for the ride to wherever the wagon was transporting Vinnie. He sat bouncing along in deep thought as he rode along beneath the wagon. He marveled at the thought of riding along and getting drenched and muddy. Could he possibly one day put an end to the misery caused by the rain when he received all of his superpowers as a grown-up leprechaun?

The livery wagon pulled up to a bed and breakfast. Skip was drenched and completely covered from head to toe with mud, muck, and sand. He watched Vinnie disembark the wagon and quickly head up the walkway toward the front door covering his head with his jacket, protecting himself and his leather of scotch from the torrential rains.

Quickly transposing from beneath the wagon to inside the bed-and-breakfast, he positioned himself behind a long curtain hung by the window beside the main desk where Vinnie was paying for a room to stay for the night. Learning Vinnie's room number when the night clerk spoke and handed Vinnie the key, Skip immediately transposed to Vinnie's room and hid beneath the bed in the corner of the room before Vinnie had the chance to climb the stairs to his room.

Vinnie began wondering, as he climbed the stairs to his rented room, if his choice of leaving Ireland was a good one for him to have made. It was too darn late for him to turn back now. He had nowhere to go back to, for he had sold off the family farm. He quickly put his foolish doubt of a bad idea in his head to rest, and looked forward to his new adventure abroad. This was a one in a million chance in one's lifetime that his friends had hounded at him to do to start a new life in a new land. Possibly he could have a new life with someone he could love, have children with, and have a new family all his own.

CHAPTER ELEVEN

The Nice Warm Bath

The instant Vinnie came waltzing into his room, Skip somehow knew he was about to take a nice warm relaxing bath before retiring to his bed for the night. Skip did not quite know how he knew all this, but somehow, he did. He immediate transposed down the hall to the bathing room before Vinnie had a chance to venture there. He jumped right into the warm soapy hot bath water in the large round bathing tub, filled-ready for Vinnie to enjoy clothes and all. Oh, how welcomed the warm tub of bathwater felt to him. He washed off all the mud that had sprayed and splashed on him and his clothes while beneath the rear of the wagon. He quickly turned the clean warm soapy water into a dark brown filthy tub with the dirt, silt, and sand. A thick brown silty foam floated disgustingly on top the surface of the water after Skip had finally washed and rinsed. He could have easily blinked an eye or pinched an ear to clean himself up, but once in a great while, a nice warm bath soothes the soul of even that of a leprechaun.

Hearing the doorknob to the bathing room squeak as it began to turn, Skip speedily transposed back to the safety of Vinnie's quiet room, knowing he was coming into the bathing room to enjoy his warm bath. He placed himself smack dab in the middle of Vinnie's room, soaking wet. He stood there looking around the room still feeling quite funny from the evil tonic, especially after having soaked in the almost too hot water. Vinnie's two trunks were nowhere around. Skip wondered if there was some mortal dust, or better than that, some of Vinnie's gold he had mentioned to his friend Timothy in one of his trunks. Skip was determined, to seek out Vinnie's gold. He left a huge puddle of water from his dripping wet clothes in the middle of Vinnie's room.

Meanwhile, Vinnie became instantly enraged as he entered his dirty bathing room finding his supposedly clean warm bathing water a total calamity of filthy dark froth. The water in the tub was covered with brown silt that made his stomach churn and was not the tub of clean soapy water he planned soaking his tired body in his last night in Ireland. The dirty water looked as though the proprietor of the boarding house expected all his guest to share their bathing water together, not only with all the other guest of the house, but also with a couple of homeless hobos who might just happen along as well.

Skip heard Vinny loudly ranting and raving in the quiet of the little bathing room, as his loud voice rattled the windowpanes. He immediately went storming off stomping mad out the door and down the hallway toward the night clerk's desk. He complained so loud that everyone in the entire boardinghouse must have heard him yelling about how filthy dirty and disgusting the bathing water was that had left for him to bathe in. The chamber-made wondered who might have been so mean to a play such a dirty trick on her for no good reason, or had sabotaged the clean tub of their new guest Mr. Vinnie McDougall. After preparing a fresh bathtub full of clean water, she called out to Vinnie in the lobby that his tub was ready and went off down the hallway.

Vinnie relaxed in the warmth of the fresh clean tub of warm water enjoying his nice warm bath. He knew that it would be a very long time before he was able to enjoy another soothing tub of warm water as there would be none onboard the ship. He lay in the quiet of the warm soothing water relaxing and thinking about the next day, the next month, and a lifetime of years to follow. He was hoping he was making the right choice for the rest of his life by stepping onto the ship in the morning.

While Vinnie was taking pleasure in his nice warm bath, Skip jumped toward the softness of Vinnie's bed, drying himself off in midair, leaving a huge puddle of water in the middle of the room on the floor. He landed near the headboard and his head hit something very hard lying hidden beneath the softness of the pillow. He found Vinnie's leather of scotch still wrapped neatly in its brown paper wrapper. Vinnie had placed his scotch safely under the pillow, hoping no one would find it while he took his long warm bath.

Just as Skip curiously pulled the bottle of scotch out from beneath, the pillow there came a loud knock at the door that startled him. He quickly transposed out of sight and hid beneath Vinnie's bed uptight against the wall hoping no one would see him there. The door slowly opened, and in walked two very large husky looking blokes meandering slowly in. They were carrying a massive looking handmade travel trunk Vinnie had handcrafted all by himself. They placed the heavy trunk down on the floor at the foot of Vinnie's bed and left, closing the door behind them. Skip inquisitively concentrated on the trunk's lock, thinking it might open, and to his amazement the lock, popped open as if someone unlocked it with a key. This was yet another magical trick that occurred for Skip, when all he had to do was concentrate very hard, and it happened. He did not quite know what he had just done to make the lock open, but it worked like magic and he was glad for it. Inside the trunk, Skip found several clothes of Vinnies neatly ironed and folded up just right in a compact stack. They were placed one on top of the other, carefully packed away not to get wrinkled for the long voyage across the sea to the new world.

Suddenly there came another loud knock at the door. He quickly closed the trunk and hid beneath the bed again. The same two large men came in again carrying another of Vinnie's handmade trunks and this particular trunk made the two strong men moan and groan. They carefully place the second trunk down on the floor beside the first, trying not to drop it. This must be the trunk with all of Vinnie's gold in it, Skip thought to himself. Now he knew how he was going to get his gold. In unison, the two men took handkerchiefs from their breast pockets and proceeded to wipe the dew of sweat and raindrops from their wet foreheads. They took a quick glance around the empty room and then left.

Curious to see what was in the second trunk, Skip opened it by concentrating on the lock as he had the first trunk. Peering into both trunks, he found that neither of them held any gold that Vinnie had previously talked about to Timothy. What the trunks did contain was all of Vinnie's valued possessions, everything he would need to start his new life within the new world. The first trunk contained all of Vinnie's clothes, blankets' and linens. The second trunk contained all his mother's old cooking utensils and most of the working tools of his profession. Sitting on top of the first trunk, Skip slid the paper wrapper off from the leather, and opened up Vinnie's prized bottle of scotch. Tipping the bottle up, he took a large swig of evil tonic and swallowed. He shuddered intently from the instant effects it had on him like his first taste of scotch similar to hot molting lava shooting from an erupting volcano. The scotch lit up Skip's tender mouth again as it flamed all the way down his throat until it hit his stomach, which made Skip feel as though a hot cannonball of fire had just landed there. He wondered just how anyone could drink and enjoy such evil tonic.

Suddenly he sensed Vinnie outside the room returning from his bath. Again, something strange was happening to Skip. He was practically able to anticipate Vinnies every move. He sensed Vinnie reaching for the doorknob and heard the doorknob suddenly squeak as it turned. He quickly closed the two trunks and returned the bottle of scotch back to its original location hidden beneath the pillow. He hid under the bed again, hoping Vinnie would not bend down to find him hiding there. He at first tried transposing back downstairs to the lobby behind the curtain by the desk, but could not, so he opted for beneath the bed to hide instead, which worked.

When Vinnie entered the room, he hung his wet washed shirt and trousers by the window to dry. He turned around to go to his bed, and stepped right into the big puddle Skip had left there in the middle of the floor. He then looked up at the ceiling in despair, thinking the roof above had sprung a leak and was leaking into his room. He found no stains of water nor any signs of a leak, so he figured the two strong blokes he had hired to carry his trunks in must have left the puddle in the middle of the room for him to step in. He was not pleased with the two men at that very moment as his bare feet were wet, and he had to use his fresh dry hand towel to dry them.

As Vinnie reached to light the spare oil lamp on the nightstand, he discovered the paper wrapper from his leathered bottle of scotch stretched out and all crumpled up in a heap on the floor beside his bed and the trunks. "Why those no good for nothing bloody hooligans." Vinnie shouted. "If one of them dang blasted broods didn't find my bottle of scotch hidden beneath my pillow and took a swig of it. They even had the nerve to leave the bloody rapper right out in plain sight for me to find. Oh, the nerve of those two thugs anyway," he thought. He could almost see red fire bolts flowing freely from his eyes he was so infuriated with the two hired liverymen. Skip watched with a smile on his face as Vinnie went ranting and raving around the room complaining all the while about his bottle of scotch having been opened and the privacy of his life having been violated, when another loud knock came banging at his door.

Then, the two men came back to Vinnie's room to retrieve their fare for the work of delivering his trunks to the rooming house. "Come on in gents". Vinnie said with an anchor-deep, low-tone echoing in his baritone voice. "Okay, which one of you to bloody blokes went and took a swig from my bottle of scotch, and then had the nerve to leave the paper wrapper from it out in the open on the floor for me to find?"

Then two men very puzzled looked at one another, and then spoke with a wee bit of perplexity written all across their very stunned faces. "We do not drink Mr. McDougall, sir! We never touch the bloody stuff. We cannot stand the bloody taste or the smell of it, sir. You can go ahead and smell my breath and his too, to prove it to yourself if you don't believe us!"

Skip began to laugh quietly beneath his breath, trying desperately not to make any unnecessary noise by laughing out-loud, coughing, or sneezing. He would not want to be caught in this precarious position, hiding beneath the bed by one of these three bloody blokes. What would he do?

"Well, some no good for nothing scoundrel has bloody well taken a good swig of my scotch, even if it wasn't one of you two blokes. Did either of you two notice anyone in the hall or on the stairs leading up here when you carried the two trunks up where? What about that puddle of water in the middle of the floor over yonder, I suppose neither of you two blokes put that puddle of water there either?"

"No sir. Sorry sir, we did not make that puddle of water in the middle of your room either. We had to take our boots off at the main door entrance. We did not want to get the night manager downstairs all upset with us now did we. He gets right down mean and vicious, he does, if anyone around messes up his nice clean house, especially if it's one of the livery folk from around town come here trying to make a living for themselves like us."

"Sorry gents, I guess I may have caused the puddle myself once I first came into the room from the rain while checking it out. This here new adventure of mine going off to the New World to America is starting to get the best of me, I guess." "Well, sir, if I were as young and single such as yourself, I would certainly be jumping at the chance of starting a new life in the New World just as ye are doing. The crack of dawn first daylight we will be here, to pick you and your trunks up. We'll load them onto our wagon for you early to make sure you get to the docks on time before your ship sails."

"Here are two silver pieces for your labor's gents. Thank you again for your speedy assistance. Sorry to have accused one of you two gents before you head out?" Vinnie was trying desperately hard to catch one or both of them in an out and out lie about his missing scotch before they left his room.

"Sorry, Mr. McDougall, sir, but like we said, neither one of us drinks the stuff. We shall see you bright and early in the morning before the cock crows." She sails on the morning tide, and I cannot be late or she shall sail without me. "Right-oh sir, right oh! Be here right at the crack of dawn like we promised you, we will be, sir."

Closing the door behind the two men, Vinnie turned and took the stopper out of his bottle of scotch. He took one mighty swig of his brew before getting ready for bed. He returned the cork stopper to the bottleneck of his bottle securing it tight, and placed the bottle inside his clothing trunk between the two top blankets for its security. It would not be opened again until he was well underway sailing westward on the tall ship across the Atlantic. Vinnie wanted to save the rest of his special scotch for the long voyage to America, for there would be none on board the ship that he could buy.

Closing his trunk and locking it, he thought by offering the blokes a drink of his scotch he might catch one or both of them in a lie, but it did not work. He would go off to bed tonight wondering who might have drank his scotch and had escaped from his room without being seen or caught in the act. He next headed out the bedroom door to go out back to the outhouse bathroom.

Almost immediately, Skip came out of hiding from beneath the bed as Vinnie closed the bedroom door and had a rather sly grin spread across his cunning little face. He wanted just one last teensy weensy little drink of Vinnie's special scotch before he headed back home to Grandma Broom and Grandpa Hair's house in the pouring rain. A wee drink was all he wanted, just to keep him warm on his long trek home. Quick as scat, Skip opened up Vinnie's linens trunk and found the bottle of scotch hidden between the first and second blanket. He quickly pulled the cork stopper out of its neck and proceeded to have one more very large mouthful of the forbidden tonic. Rivers of shivers flowed again up and down his tiny spine. The brawny sharp flavor of alcohol in Vinnie's special scotch made Skip cringe as the forbidden fires from the tonic flowed over his tiny lips burning every inch of his mouth and gullet, all the way down to his wee stomach. The large mouthful Skip took made him feel quite dizzy and very lightheaded. He was becoming extremely sleepy as he tried to balance on the edge of Vinnie's trunk. "One more good old drink for the road," Skip thought laughing all the while to himself remembering what Vinnie had said to Timothy before their last drink together. He tipped up the bottle one more time as he sat there teeter tottering back and forth on the edge of Vinnie's trunk then took a second large swig of the firewater. Losing his balance, he fell over backwards landing on his back in the middle of the linens' trunk on Vinnie's blankets. He began to laugh out-loud this time, feeling more, and more tired and a lot sillier than ever before. He sat his little tired body up in the middle of the trunk before taken his second swig of scotch, or was it his third or his fourth? He could not quite remember which number he was having. Finally, with great difficulty, Skip put the cork stopper back into the bottle. He was ready to go home now to face the harsh scolding he knew he would surely receive from his Grandma and his not so understanding Grandpa.

Unexpectedly, he heard the doorknob to Vinnie's room squeak as it started to turn. Quickly Skip laid down flat on the blankets of the trunk and closed the lid to hide himself. He thought he would lie there safely for a while hidden until after Vinnie fell fast asleep. He would then sneak out of Vinnie's room and head back home to his grandparent's house. Skip figured he would be able to leave soon, knowing Vinnie was readying himself for bed. When the coast was clear, he would be off again out into the bucketing down rains of the night for home. Gosh! Did he not just think those same words, he thought. He had to keep himself awake just a wee bit longer.

CHAPTER TWELVE

The Morning After

Rising early unable to sleep, Vinnie shaved, splashed water on his face, and readied himself for the day. He was growing nervous with every passing second worried about not getting down to the tall ship before she sailed. It seemed to him that he had not slept a wink all night. He paced back and forth across the room as a tiger held captive in a cage as he waited impatiently for the two livery chaps to show back up. He felt more at ease when there came that firm soft knock at his bedroom door by the two brothers. "Come right in gents". Vinnie beckoned anxiously to the two chaps outside his door. They entered with fruitfully happy smiles spread across their tired looking faces.

"Good morning to you, Mr. McDougall, sir. A grand and pleasant one it be, too", said the older of the two brothers. "Not one blimey cloud anywhere in the sky to be seen, just a few stars fading away to make way for the new dawning of daylight."

Vinnie nodded with a weary smile on his tired looking face. The brothers took away his heavy trunks one at a time, the heaviest one first to their waiting wagon. Had Vinnie not been in such a hurry when he threw his straight razor, soap, and other belongings into his clothing trunk, he would have seen Skip all curled up barely hidden beneath one of his several blankets and towels in the trunk. Had he taken a wee bit more time in straightened out the top wrinkled up bulging blanket and looked just a wee more closely, he would have surely noticed Skip sound asleep passed out cold from the evil tonic in his trunk.

The short trip to the dock seemed a very long slow boring journey for Vinnie with his built-up excitement and anticipation of this choice he had made with his life. It was so early in the day there were merely a couple of men wandering around, the street. Some lucky blokes were heading home from a long work night, while others were just getting to the docks to work. Vinnie could never remember a time in Dublin Town when he had seen it quite this quiet.

Once at the docks, the scene quickly changed. There were many dock-workmen hustling about doing their jobs. Some were busy pushing carts, others lifted sacks, and some busied themselves rolling barrels of rum, water and whiskey up the gangplanks of a couple of the ships.

There were some on the ship right in front of him lowering drum after drum of supplies down into the hold of the huge sleek ship preparing her to sail. This beauty of a ship Vinnie was standing before on the dock named the Shamrock, the ship he was to sail to America onboard. It had beautiful Shamrock carved into the two front sides of her bow planking, proudly displaying a bright glistening shade of the grand isle's emerald green in the early morning sun's rays coming up over the horizon. This proud emblem of luck displayed her Irish legacy brilliantly. The ship stood four main masts tall in her midsection; having a small forward jib mounted on her bow, and a more superior square jib mounted to her aft.

Her captain, a former captain of Her Majesties Royal Navy, stood stern faced, carefully watching over his ship from the poop deck, overseeing his busy crew of sailors from England and other surrounding countries preparing their ship to sail. There were Dutch sailors from the Netherlands, homeland born Irish lads, and a few older English sailors that made up her crew. All seemed extremely busy preparing the Shamrock for her long maiden voyage across the open sea to the New World in North America.

Vinnie looked very happy standing on the dock looking up in awe at the majestic size and beauty of the Shamrock. He stood there pondering about what had taken place in his short lifetime that took him to this important decision in his life. What swayed him to make this decision to leave Ireland in the first place? First, he sold off the family farm left to him by his parents who had both most recently passed away.

He was now an orphan, an only child without the solace of any cousins, nephews, nieces, uncles, brothers, or sisters. He was an only child left all alone in the world with the exception of a most miserable old-made of an aunt who lived across the channel in Liverpool, England. He would never forgive the old beast or forget that dreadful scene she made when he first arrived in England to pay his last hurtful respects to console his only aging aunt, whom he thought he had loved and she loved him, after her sister (his mother) had passed away from a very slow hurtful lung disease. The detestable old witch of an aunt wanted absolutely nothing to do with Vinnie when he went to grieve with her for his mother's loss. She showed no remorse to Vinnie over the death of his mother or father, her brother-in-law, who had just died days prior to his mother's death.

With absolutely no one left on Irish soil or in England in need of his love or attention, Vinnie became extremely motivated for a change in his life to make a good go of it as a blacksmith in the New World. His friends persistently time and time again urged him to change his ways in life, encouraging him to marry a local lass or seek out a new way of life across the open sea in the new world of plenty…America. They would blurt out in friendly unison at the local pub to Vinnie, "Vinnie take charge of your life lad. Get yourself out of here and get yourself off to America where people become instantly rich for just going there to live."

Vinnie had thought long and hard about making such a drastic change in his life, and finally one day he convinced himself to sell off the family farm. He would travel to America as his friends had suggested he give it a good old hard honest tries it to make a good go of it. He was now past that ripe young age of 25, never married, and no longer a spring chicken by anyone's standards. He considered himself a fair, too moderately good-looking older young chap, healthy, single, and maybe, just maybe, he might be fortunate enough to find a-lass in the New World, one that might fall in love with him for who he was and want him as her husband. He had not found a wife in Ireland for he was too busy taking care of his aging parents and the family farm. Vinnie felt that this was a grand dream to hold on tight to, a dream he honestly felt achievable with a wee bit of good Irish luck and a lot, lot, lot of hard work to justify the cause.

CHAPTER THIRTEEN

Settling In

"Which cabin be yours, mate?" asked a pleasant looking older sailor at the top of the gangplank. Reaching into his pocket, Vinnie pulled out the folded up piece of parchment he had received from the harbormaster when he first paid his fair at the dock the day before, and saw his cabin number marked down on it. "Cabin number four, sir", Vinny replied to the sailor standing before him. He knew what number it was, but wanted to make sure of it.

"Down through the scully way hatch, sir", as the sailor pointed towards the passageway in the mid-rear section of the ship. "Down rear mid-ship mate, first door down the scully way on the right to your cabin." "Ah, thank you, sir", Vinnie replied with a grand smile spread pleasantly across his face. "Down the passageway," he thought, setting off across the main deck with the brothers two in tow on his heels, carrying one of his two very heavy trunks.

Opening the first door to the right in the scully way, Vinnie observed his new accommodations that would be his home for the next several weeks. He slowly stepped inside the dim lit cabin and lit the only whale oil lamp in there with a match he took from the tray on the desk. He blew out the match and placed it into a round tin cup provided in the cabin for just that purpose. The oil lamp was a small round glass goblet attached there with mostly water in its base with a small amount of whale oil floating atop the water. A waxed cotton wick floated in an upright position in the middle of the liquid with the wick ablaze. The small lamp gave off a splendid low warm glow inside the cabin. The cabin seemed small yet comfortable. There would be plenty of room for Vinnie to move about if he was to store his two large trunks beneath the bunk. The cabin furnishings included a long narrow high hung divan looking bunk, a small desk, and an accompanying stool. Attached to the cabin wall were a couple of short tapered shelves to store some clothing, and a wooden coat hook mounted in the wall next to the door to hang his jacket.

Vinnie assumed the cabin would serve his needs quite well during the long voyage. There would be ample room on the small desk to spread out all his papers as he enjoyed drawing, one of his several childhood hobbies. He loved it, and hoped to draw portraits of the crew and perhaps one or more ocean scenes. His immediate plan was to unpack some of his packed clothes, not enough to crowd the cabin, but simply the bare necessities he might need. Vinny reached down to unlock his trunk of clothes and linens, a loud knock came thumping at his open cabin door.

"Wicks and whale oil for your lamp, sir", came a young voice from behind him. Turning around, Vinnie observed a young lad of about 14 or 15 years of age standing in the hallway just outside the cabin door. Vinnie noticed right away that the young lad had a big half-frowning and half-forced pleasant smile on his young face. He held a jug of lamp oil in one hand and a packet of short fat stubby oil wicks in the other.

"Ah, sure, lad, and might it be possible for you to fetch me another oil lamp to go above my desk, too? I would very much appreciate that very much young man: for I want to make very good use of time aboard this ship on her maiden-voyage, by writing about it and doing some sketches. A bit more light above the desk would surely come in handy for all of my endeavors." "Another lamp right away, sir, as soon as the captain gets the Shamrock underway, I shall forage through the main storage supplies for a spare lamp for you, sir." "Thank you, son", Vinnie said with a pleasant smile, studying the sober smiling look on the young lad's face. "I will surely appreciate every effort you can make for me."

The cabin boy carefully poured out more whale oil into the almost empty lamp, and filled the lamp to the full mark etched in the side of the glass. He then exited the cabin door and went to the next cabin in the scully way to carry on with his duties.

The Shamrock was the latest of new luxury cargo ships built in Norway for both cargo and passengers. She stood gallantly tall at her mooring, tied up tight against the Dublin docks, and looked majestically beautiful with a backdrop to her side of an early morning sunrise as she waited ready to sail on the inward bound tide. Her cargo hold was-filled to her pinnacles for her maiden voyage to America, and she had a full list of passengers on board who had reserved passage in one of her many specially made cabins. Vinnie had never seen the likes of such a streamlined ship before. She made the other sailing vessels in the harbor look puffy in width, small in length, and stunted in height.

CHAPTER FOURTEEN

The Open Sea

"Cast off her bow tie lines from the dock, mates. Lift up her forward jib and clear the main gangplank. We are coming about," bellowed the captain to his crew. With the sea to her back, Captain Drake turned the Shamrock about in the small narrows of the harbor to enable his ship to head out to see. "Hold Steady her aft lines mates, till she swings on the inward tide and catches her breath. Lower her center sails, now release the aft ties, the Shamrock is now coming about men on her own. Finish lowering her main sails straight away, mates, and hoist up her rear jib. She is catching the strong currents like a seagull floating high on a soft gentle breeze."

Vinny hearing the captain shouting out the commands to his crew above, Vinnie scampered out of his cabin door through the scully way and up the hall stairs to the main deck above. He yearned to watch the spectacular departure of the Shamrock take place with his own eyes not just hear it through his ears as it took place from inside his cabin below deck and wanted to hear every commanding word given out between the captain and his crew. He wished to memorize this spectacular scene to enable him to draw the seen down on parchment paper when they were out to sea. He had nothing better to do while confined to the ship other than draw, write, and laze around until the end of the voyage. Vinnie wanted to draw the onboard working scenes of the departure down as a remembrance of the voyage, and someday in the wishful days of his future show his children how he traveled to America. The Shamrock maneuvered flawlessly upon the water's surface, gracefully turning on the rising tide. Slowly she floated out of her berth and turned with a gentle breeze toward the open sea beyond the breakwaters of the harbor, continually picking up speed as she set sail across the calm blue water on her maiden voyage.

A gentle early morning breeze blew harder and harder in Vinnie's face as the Shamrock slowly and steadily picked up her pace across the water giving him an enormous feeling of freedom. The strangest feeling suddenly came over Vinnie as he looked out over the horizon. It was a feeling he had never experienced before and could not quite explain it to himself. Could it possibly be excitement, or was it seasickness. He had heard so many horrific stories about seasickness and strong young healthy sailors jumping overboard to avoid being dreadfully sick out at sea for another day. Some men would rather die in the rough waters of a storm than face another long day of being deathly seasick on board a ship being pitched up and down continually on the water. Vinnie was not green, nor did he feel sick to his stomach. It was evident to him that he was not experiencing sick sickness but rather his own excitement.

With a strong gentle breeze blowing at her back, the Shamrock gracefully sailed out of sight of land. In no time at all, she had steadily picked up speed to go as fast as the wind would allow her to sail out across the open waters. The funny sensations Vinnie had felt in his stomach soon left. He was becoming more comfortable with the steady swaying of the ship as he stood observing everybody on deck and felt the cheerful warm rays of the sun beating gently down on his back. He soon learned to enjoy the rhythmic sounds of the sea's cold water splashing gently along the sides of the ship as they made their way westward.

The cabin boy approached Vinnie as he stood watching the ship on her main deck. "Here is another oil lamp for your cabin, sir," the cabin boy said with a half friendly and half-forced smile on his face, glancing back over his shoulder toward Ireland. He was holding a brand new oil lamp for above Vinny's desk. It looked more like a small octopus to Vinnie then an oil lamp. "I'll have to hook this special lamp up for you, sir. It is the Captain's direct orders, sir". They immediately returned to Vinnie's cabin where the cabin boy took out a very special looking screw hook from his pocket, and drove it deep into the wood of the ceiling above his desk. He took out another screw hook and drove this one deep into the sidewall of the cabin just above the desk and another one deep into the ceiling a short distance from the first screw. "This will hold the lamp in place, sir, allowing it to sway and keep it upright when the ship rolls from side to side in rough water. It will prevent the lamp from smashing against the wall and possibly causing a fire, sir."

"You are pretty clever with your hands, lad, and seem to be very talented at what you do. How long do you have to serve onboard the Shamrock son?" "Well sir. I have to serve two long very lonely years onboard the ship sir, to help-out my poor mother with money to help-out bring up the kids back home. Father the poor soul, never came home from the sea one day, God rest his lonely soul. He went down with his fishing vessel out in the straights in a very bad storm one day better than a couple of years this last Season. She was a small fishing vessel he served upon sir, the Dolphin, from Dublin, and she was lost to King Neptune's terrifying fury. The only one to survive the sinking of the vessel was her captain. He survived by clinging tight to a small floating section of her mainmast, and drinking rum from a half keg that floated alongside him. He was the only lucky one discovered by another fishing vessel. None of the other men ever spotted and all presumed lost. If it wasn't for the broken mast and half keg of rum, he would have surely drowned or died of dehydration along with the rest of the crew."

"Well, sir, I must be getting along and get back to my duties. If you find you should be in need of anything else sir, anything at all, just give a shout. I will do my very best in pleasing you, sir. I will be around again in the morning if you need some more oil and wicks for your lamps." With that said, the cabin boy turned toward the open cabin door and left.

Vinnie felt extremely sorry for the lad being so young and separated from his family. It was a shame, thought Vinnie, a downright dirty shame for the young lad. No wonder he walks around with a half-smile forced on his very lonely looking face. While the cabin boy was closing the cabin door behind him, Vinnie thought he heard the ship's new timbers moaning and groaning. The new planks of the ship sounded to him like they were settling themselves in one against the other, swelling together to keep out the wet of the ocean. Vinny heard a clanking sound coming from one of the two trunks he had just placed beneath his bunk. He thought it sounded more like an empty bottle rolling around up against the wall of one of the trunks in time with the rolling of the ship. He knew he had not yet emptied either of the trunks, so he bent down be to pull them out from under the bunk to have a look. He would now take out his bottle of scotch for a hearty toast, a wee little swig to congratulate himself for making such a huge choice to move on to a newer and better life

Before his hand ever reached the first trunk, there came another knocking at his cabin door. "Whale off the starboard side of the ship, sir, and she is a beauty! I just thought you might like to take a wee look so you might draw her out on one of your parchment papers." Vinnie immediately went topside, forgetting all about the noise he had just heard come from one of his trunks, to take a good look at the whale for himself. The cabin boy was right, for she was a beautiful specimen of a whale. She was a long splendid looking sperm whale, coming right up out of the water beside the ship and slamming herself down sideways on the surface of the water. She splashed water everywhere. She blew air out of her blowhole blasting water and air high up into the early morning sky, higher than the tallest mast of the Shamrock. Vinnie marveled at the Whale's every move, the friendliness she showed, and how she swam so close to the ship. She put on a splendid show for the crew and passengers for over an hour. He also watched a small pod of different whales swimming along the ship.

CHAPTER FIFTEEN

The Stowaway

Down in Vinnie's cabin, Skip was trying to open up the cover to the trunk he was in to get out, but the lid of the trunk kept hitting something very hard about it. He peaked out into the room through the tiny gap the partially lifted cover made, and blurrily saw an oil lamp swaying back and forth as the ship rolled. He could not remember the room at that Inn being so small, or having two small oil lamps in it.

Oh, what an awful throbbing headache he was experiencing. He held his poor pounding head firm with one hand while making a gallant effort to hold up the cover to the trunk with the other. "What happened to the two big, shaded windows on the wall? Where did that weird door come from?" Oh, what a dreadful throbbing headache Skip was experiencing!

Picking up the bottle of scotch that lay there beside him, he could barely make out that it had half vanished. "What happened to all of the scotch," he wondered while gazing at the bottle. He vaguely remembered the night before chuckling to himself, which made his head hurt more. Last night had been fun, but today waking up was not so funny. His head hurt like the dickens, worse than the day Grandpa Hair pulled him up into the tree. To make matters worse, he did not know where he was. "They must have moved Vinnie to another room during the night," Skip thought.

The problem at hand now was to get himself out of the trunk, so he concentrated on transposing out of the trunk and into the middle of Vinnie's room. He needed to get out of the boarding house, safely back to the street, and then soon as possible back home again. He knew he was in great trouble with his grandparents, for having been gone so very long. He concentrated as hard as possible on opening the lid of the trunk. Suddenly the whole trunk slid out into the middle of the room, and the lid above him popped up wide open. Although it was not quite, what Skip had in mind, at least the lid was up off his poor pounding head.

Slowly he eased one foot at a time out over the edge of the trunk and stepped easily out into the tiny room. He felt so dizzy that he thought he might pass out or fall over onto the floor, which seemed at the time to be moving beneath his feet. Where was he? Slowly reaching up, he took hold of his throbbing head and held it soothingly. He expected at any moment for it to fall off his wee little shoulders down onto the floor and burst into a million pieces. Oh, how it hurt, oh how it hurt so bad! His head hurt worse than his foot did when the bull fell out of the tree with him and landed on it. Skip had never experienced such pain, especially a headache, like this ever before.

Skip was extremely parched, but no more scotch! No wonder his father never came home from Dublin Town that night after drinking the forbidden tonic! Skip thought for sure his father must have just up and died from the evil tonic he drank if it made him feel this dreadful. He wondered why he was not dead from it himself. He knew he should be heading straight away home now. He was now in deeper trouble with his grandparents than he had ever been before, as he had never been gone overnight before. Grandma would be the one most worried sick about him and would want to switch him hard with her thatched broomstick for making her worry so. He felt she had every right in the world to be mad at him this time. Grandpa would be downright mad and cantankerously out of control that he would probably yank out every-last strand of hair from Skip's already throbbing head, one strand at a time, to teach him a lesson.

He knew he had to concentrate on getting back to Vinnie's first room of the evening so he might get his bearings on where he was. If he tried to transpose from this room without knowing where he was, he might end up beneath the hooves of a horse, or beneath the rolling wheels of a heavily loaded livery-wagon, which would surely squash him to death. No matter how hard Skip tried concentrating on the other rooms in the boarding room house nothing of familiarity came to his very blurred mind. The Cabin ceiling lamp wanted to sway back and forth in front of him no matter how hard he tried to adjust his throbbing eyes to make it stop.

Suddenly, without warning, the situation at hand struck Skip like a ton of flying bricks. The reason he could not get his immediate bearings on the other rooms was that he was no longer at the inn! While he was fast asleep in the trunk, the two big men from the livery wagon must have moved him and Vinnie out of the inn, down to the pier, and onboard one of the ships in the harbor. This meant Skip was now a runaway, a stowaway onboard a ship heading toward the new world! He had really done it to himself this time. How would he ever get his bearings to do anything now? If he tried to transpose without knowing his precise location onboard the ship, he might find himself in grave danger. He might transpose overboard, and be left floating and sinking in the salty brine of the sea. The ship would just sail away from him, leaving his wee body to end up as food for the hungry Sharks, fish and other creatures of the deep blue sea. No one on board the ship would know he had gone missing. No more transposing here or there, at least not until he knew exactly where he is on board the ship.

Gently holding his throbbing head, Skip slowly moved toward the small cabin door. He gently turned the door's wooden door handle, trying not to make any noise, and cautiously peeked out into the small hall. Skip knew right away he was in trouble, more trouble than he had ever been in before in his entire life, Vinnie was in the hallway returning down the scully way back towards his cabin, and poor sick Skip had nowhere to run or hide. He could not transpose somewhere else aboard the ship without being caught by someone, or possibly drowning himself overboard if he tried. As Vinnie approached his cabin, he thought it was curious that the door he knew he had closed was-left ajar. When he entered his cabin, he was surprised to find one of his two trunks laid wide open in the middle of the room. This sudden surprise turned instantly to anger as he spotted his half-empty bottle of scotch lying on top of his wrinkled up linens. Having just noticed the cabin boy working in the hall as he was returning to his room, Vinnie went straight to the open door of his cabin and called out to him, "Cabin boy! Have you observed any sailors or useless scallywags in or about my cabin while I was topside?"

"No, sir, not a one, sir, no one except for yourself has come or gone from your cabin since you left. I have been standing right here sir right along cleaning and sweeping up ever since you went topside to watch the whales. No one has come or gone along through here since you left, sir."

"Well, someone or something has gone into my cabin, young man. Did you go in my cabin for any reason, lad, any reason at all?" "No sir, I am only allowed to go into a guest quarters, only when our guest are in them. I assure you, I have not taken any of your Scotch sir. I am not allowed to drink any booze of any kind because of my age. Besides the terrible smell of it, never mind the horrible taste of booze. Once took a wee sip of father's horrid scotch with his permission of course, and it made me sicker than an old dog who just got finished eating a sick dead fish. Cannot stomach the stuff, sir. I do not drink anything stronger than tea or water while out here to sea, I swear to it, sir. No one has come or gone from your cabin since you left to go topside. I would have seen them with my own two eyes if they had, sir."

Vinnie half closed the door behind him as he popped back into his cabin. He next pulled out the cork stopper from his partially drank bottle of scotch. He was disgruntled about the trunk left out in the middle of the floor, the top lid to it opened wide, and more serious than that, more than half of his precious scotch had gone missing. He tipped the bottle of scotch up to his lips and took a hearty drink. "I think I shall drink the remainder of this bottle all by myself, right here and now. No one else on board and I do mean no one else on board this ship shall steal another drop of my scotch from me," Vinnie thought to himself.

"Would you like a wee cut of cheese from the ship's galley to go along with your scotch, Sir", asked the cabin boy who was poking his head back in through Vinnies' partially opened cabin door. "I can get you a small wedge from the galley if you would like one, sir." "Would you do that favor for me lad? I surely would appreciate it. A wee cut of mild cheese to go along with this scotch would taste mighty fine right now. Thank you, son, I would appreciate that very much!"

As soon as the cabin boy went running off down the scully way, Skip wondered where the galley was, and how the young lad was going to get there. He wondered if he could transpose in the same direction to a safe place to hide. As he peered out from behind the tool trunk, Vinnie's loud voice startled him. "Bloke, if I find you hiding under my bunk, I'll surely skin you alive!" Vinnie stood before the bed bending down to have a look beneath his bunk as he shouted, thinking he would surely find the miserable scoundrel who had helped himself to his scotch hiding there. Skip quickly transposed to the top of the desk. He knew there would be nothing beneath the bunk for Vinnie to see except for his tool trunk, and he would be surprised. With no one under there, who could have possibly taken this scotch. The cork stopper in the bottle was still secure, the clothes beneath the bottle dry, but some of his precious scotch had gone missing.

Giving the swaying of the ship, he could only imagine his trunk must have slid out from under the bunk on its own, but how did it manage to get unlocked and opened? "Blimey," he thought to himself out-loud, "I must be losing my bloody mind. I just cannot remember drinking so much of my scotch." As Vinnie stood up, Skip quickly transposed back to the confines beneath Vinnie's bunk and watched Vinnie take another healthy swig of scotch from his bottle. The cabin boy quickly returned to Vinnie's cabin with the cheese wedge he had promised. He had a larger than wee wedge of cheese on a tray and handed it to Vinnie. In return, Vinnie tossed him a silver coin from his pocket for his trouble. "That, will-not be necessary, sir" exclaimed the boy as he admired the bright shiny coin in his hand. "It is my job to help out all the passengers on board the Shamrock in any way that I can, sir." "You have earned it, son," said Vinnie. You do a right good job on board the Shamrock, and you should take any coins offered you from the other passengers if there are any. You just never know when an extra coin might come in very handy. Who knows, some day it may help get your mother and the kids out of a tight fix." "Why, thank you, sir," said the cabin boy appreciatively. Keeping the silver coin in hand, he left Vinnie to enjoy the cheese with his scotch.

Skip stared at the wedge of cheese the cabin boy had brought to Vinnie with great hunger in his tummy. The grand fragrance of the mild cheese made his mouth water. He knew a wee piece of cheese might be just what the doctor ordered to put an end to the hunger he was experiencing in the pit of his stomach, the result of drinking too much scotch.

Vinnie cut a couple of small slices of cheese from the medium-size wedge with his knife from out of his trousers' pocket. He ate one cheese wedge, and so did Skip. He figured Vinnie was sharing the extra cut of cheese with him or he would not have cut two pieces from the wedge. "Oh boy was this cheese good!" Skip thought to himself, letting it slowly melt in his watery mouth as he took great pleasure in its taste. The cheese was not too sharp yet not too mild and just pleasantly delectable. Slowly chewing the melting mass, Skip enjoyed every last little melting morsel. His stomach was so empty he could have easily eaten the entire wedge.

Vinnie could not believe his faltering eyes when he reached down for the second piece of cheese. Did he not just cut two pieces from the wedge of cheese? Where did the other piece get off too? He looked down on the floor, thinking he may have dropped it there, but the slice was not there nor was it on his lap. It just was not anywhere to be-found! Meanwhile, Skip's throbbing headache was slowly on the mend for the pain was beginning to ease just a wee bit.

"Concentrate on the cabin boy," Skip thought to himself. "Where on board is he now?" A slightly blurred vision of the cabin boy came to Skip as he concentrated on the boy's whereabouts with all his strength. He saw the boy in the galley of the ship putting some small pieces of dry kindling wood into the galley's wood burning stove so the ship's cook might have a fire and prepare the day's big meal for the ship's crew and passengers. Soon the image of the cabin boy faded as Skip's headache returned. He swore right there and then that he would never drink another drop of the forbidden tonic ever again. It must have been the wicked scotch that made his head hurt so, and if he never drank another drop of scotch in his entire lifetime, it would be too soon!

Skip was still extremely famished as he stared more absorbedly at what remained of the cheese on the tray. "Concentrate on only half of the wedge," he thought quickly to himself. He figured if he concentrated on only half the cheese that that is exactly what would end up in his hand. To his surprise, the entire wedge of cheese flew at him like a hawk in deadly pursuit of its fleeing victim. He hurriedly broke the cheese wedge in half and sent the remaining half back to Vinnie's tray.

Vinnie could not believe his eyes again! His hand quickly stopped just short of the ragged wedge of cheese when he reached over to cut another thin piece. The cheese had been an evenly cut wedge of cheese, not broken in half the way it now appeared, and it had been a much larger piece. He thought very hard, but could not remember breaking the cheese in half. This was the last straw! He picked up his bottle of scotch and drank down as large a swallow that he possibly could and returned the stopper back into the bottleneck to save the rest of the scotch for later. He could not ever remember having a bottle of scotch that tasted any finer, and hoped there would still be a wee smidgen left in the bottle when he returned for it later on in the voyage. He quickly put the bottle back into the trunk under the blankets, closed the cover, and slid the trunk back beneath the bunk, but it stopped shy of reaching the back wall like his tool chest did. Both trunks were the same size so it should have gone all the way to the back wall, but it did not. He thought it must be stuck on part of the floor, so he pushed hard trying to free it and secure it to the back wall. He tried several times without any success, so he stood up frustrated.

Annoyingly he turned, picked up the remainder of the cheese wedge from the tray, and headed out the cabin door to go topside and enjoy the warmth of the bright sunny day. He wanted to bask in the warm sun and watch the activities taking place on deck. He did not want to stay hidden down in his dim lit cabin all the time missing the special activities might be taking place above.

The sun was shining bright and lighting up the bright sky above as Vinnie emerged into the daylight from the stairway. A few fair weather clouds peppered the blue horizon beyond the Shamrock. A warm gentle breeze was steadily blowing out of the southeast while the crew of the Shamrock navigated her gently across the smooth rolling aqua blue water. It amazed Vinnie that a ship of this magnitude could be as graceful as she glided from the crest of one huge rolling wave down into the trough between two, then up the next rolling wave of water. She sailed over the waves like a downy feather floating softly on a gentle breeze. He marveled at the majestic huge sails filled with air and wind and wanted to memorize the scene and transfer his imagery down onto parchment paper. He found himself daydreaming and imagining if all else failed him in the new world that a life on the open sea might possibly be his next adventure. He envied the crew of the Shamrock as some were whistling out toons while others were singing along with them as they went happily about their many chores. He thought he might very well enjoy being a part of this type of family out on the open sea.

While Vinnie was enjoying his time topside, poor Skip laid all crumpled up beneath the cabin bunk feeling if stuffed down the bore a very small cannon. He tried hard not to moan out in agony as Vinnie pushed harder and harder on the trunk up against Skip tight against the wall. He knew that anywhere he tried to transpose would have been dangerous. If he had aimed for the bunk above him, Vinnie would surely see him. If Skip tried to transpose to the hallway in daylight out from under Vinny's bunk, he easily would have, been recognized as a leprechaun, on the loose by a passenger or a crewmember with no place to go on the ship without his being caught, by someone. Skip decided to stay hidden safe where he was, wedged between the trunk and the inner outer wall of the ship until Vinnie gave up on the trunk and left the cabin with his cheese.

When Skip was finally able to crawl out from hiding, his green outfit was a mass of wrinkles. He stood up carefully, concentrating on his clothing, and poof his clothes went from a dirty wrinkled up mess to a clean splendid freshly ironed outfit. Looking down at his clothing, Skip felt much better, but mostly relieved to be out from under the bunk.

CHAPTER SIXTEEN

Thirsty

Skip felt all dried out and extremely parched. He was almost ready to try a teensy weensy swig of Vinnie's special scotch to see if it might possibly ease the growing thirst inside of him. The very thought of it sent shivers up and down his tiny spine, remembering well what it had done to him the night before. Skip needed a drink of water desperately before he became totally dehydrated, and died. He opened the cabin door just enough to peek out into the hallway to get his bearings. Seeking a good place to hide, he quickly concentrated on a crossbeam down the hallway. His timing was impeccable as he was able to transpose to the beam just in, the nick of time as the cabin boy with a bucket of clean water in one hand and a swabbing mop in the other came meandering down the stairs and into the scully way preparing to wash the floor of the passageway. Skip sat atop the crossbeam cross-legged, looking down at the bucket of clean water in the boy's hand as he passed beneath him. The mop looked new, and had not yet been put into the clean looking bucket of water, so Skip was quite sure the cabin boy would not miss just one tiny little mouthful or two of fresh water taken from the bucket magically. The water looked extremely tempting! Concentrating hard, Skip suddenly found a large mouthful of rancid, salty seawater puckering up his tongue and burning his mouth. Thankfully, Skip did not swallow the seawater the instant it reached his mouth as it made his tongue burn, his eyes water, and caused him to gag and cough! He spat the foul tasting water out of his mouth and transposed back to the safety of Vinnie's cabin immediately.

As the salt water from Skip's mouth rained down on the floor, the cabin boy quickly looked up, to see what had caused the gagging noise and who had caused the puddle of water on the floor. Now was definitely the time for a little swig of Vinnie's scotch to rid him of the rancid effects of the salty water. Skip took one wee little swig and then another one to wash more of the salt brine from his mouth. The scotch did not taste quite as bad or rancid as the seawater, but darn near as unpleasant as it mixed with the salty brine.

"Should I take another wee swig?" Skip questioned himself, and then took one. He put the cork stopper back into the bottle and returned it to where Vinnie had lastly hidden it. Without making a sound, Skip quickly transposed back to the crossbeam in the scully way. "Concentrate, Skip concentrate, where is Vinnie now. See what Vinnie sees," he thought strongly to himself. Over, and over, and over, he was hoping the new magic he was slowly acquiring would show him a vision of Vinnie, but it did not. All he could see now was the dimly lit scully way he was sitting in. Why had he not paid more attention to detail when Grandma and Grandpa tried to teach him the simple rules of magic that they performed so easily? They must both be worried sick by now wondering where he might be and what trouble he might have gotten himself in too. He made it a practice to frequently come in late at night just to annoy the two of them, but was never late a whole day before, or could it be two or three days late by now. He had no idea or sense of time nor how long he had either been asleep or passed out in Vinnie's trunk.

Skip could see a small amount of sunlight beaming its way down in through a grate in the ship's deck, reflecting sunlight up off the scully way floor giving light to the hallway. He transposed beneath the grate, and looked up through it. From this position onboard, he could see the bright blue sky above with a small number of fair weather and whispery clouds floating high above the Shamrock.

Above the ship's tallest mast, he saw a seagull flying toward the rear of the ship. The ship's great sails were full of wind and air stretching them round as they pushed the Shamrock swiftly forward. He could see the ship's crow's nest attached to the tallest main mast in the middle of the ship. The crow's nest built there to give a sailor a most-excellent view of the surrounding ocean around the ship. "Now that is where I should be," Skip thought. He figured sitting up there in the crow's nest would give him a better view of the ship and enable him to see where Vinnie might be on the deck below.

Without giving any nautical thought to it, Skip transposed above the ship's deck to the crow's nest, so he thought. When he stopped, the crow's nest was not there! He found himself in midair just alongside the crow's nest, looking at it from an arm's reach away. Skip floated in air shortly before reaching out frantically towards the crow's nest, as he tried to grab hold of its ring. He managed lastly to grasp hold of the cannabis rope ring, just in time before plummeting to the wooden deck below, possibly taking his life. With both feet thrashing and flailing at the netting around the mast, he managed to scramble into the swaying crow's nest atop the tall mast as his heart raced up into his throat. While he was catching his breath, he realized he had not allowed for the swaying of the ship when he transposed to the nest. At that moment, he knew leprechauns were-not intended to be sailors and were better suited to reside on good old solid land. From high above in the crow's nest, Skip could see the entire ship just as he had imagined it and could see for hundreds of miles around. He spotted a pod of whales swimming not too far away from the ship as well as a couple of fishing vessels pulling in their nets full of fish hand over fist.

He could see what looked like the outline of land, possibly Ireland, quickly vanishing behind them. The world around the Shamrock looked beautifully peaceful to him. This new experience surrounded him with water and a quietness he had never experienced before on dry land, and the shape of the ocean looked like a gigantic ball painted against a canvas of bright blue sky. Skip did not quite understand how that might be as he had always thought the world was flat.

Far below, Skip saw Vinnie standing mid-ship looking out to sea, trying to catch sight of another whale to use as a mental model for a drawing he had in mind. The site of a whale blowing air and water from its blowhole high into the air intrigued Vinnie, as did their wonderful ability to stay hidden beneath the waves for such a long time. Suddenly without warning a blast of misty saltwater came blowing skyward beside Skip and the wetness drifted over onto him. The sudden cloud was a combination of saltwater and wet misty air from the blowhole of a whale that had just surfaced alongside the Shamrock. Several more whales appeared from the far-off depths of the sea. He heard several more blowholes blast out from below and felt the watery mist from each. The entire pod of whales began blowing out there blowholes almost simultaneously and put on quite a display on each side of the ship.

"Wouldn't it be fun," Skip thought, to play a trick on one of these big old whales just as he had done to the dumb old bull down in farmer Prendergast's field. What could he possibly do to one of them that would be as funny as teasing the old bull to charge after him. Nothing immediately came to mind that could possibly match the old bull ramming its head headlong into the tree and knocking itself silly.

A sudden feeling of homesickness struck Skip hard as he thought about home. He became very lonely for his grandparents, knowing he had no immediate way of getting back home to them, at least not for the moment. Skip didn't care at that point is Grandpa Hair pulled out every last strand of hair on his head or if Grandma Broom listed his tiny hind end with her heavy thatched broom, as he missed the two of them so much it hurt worse than having a bad toothache. Grandpa and Grandma were his only family left now since his parents disappeared. What if the two of them were glad he had gone missing, and pleased them both never having to worry about him coming home late at night ever again. Oh, how Skip wished he had never tasted the likes of those darned evil brews, and had the full use of his very special powers so he might go back home that very instant.

Why had he been so darn stubborn? Why did not he listen to his grandparents when they were trying diligently to help him? No, he had to act up as if a big old know it all, all of the time because he missed his mother and father so much. Now he wished he had listened to his loving grandparents instead of sulking foolishly. "Maybe, just maybe," he thought, this is what may have happened to his own mother and father in years past. Maybe they too ended up in the new world. No, if they had been stowaways on board a ship, they could have easily used their powers to return back home to Ireland on the very-next vessel heading that way. If still alive, they were most likely held captive in England, France, Norway, or Africa. It did not really matter to Skip where they were now but he missed everyone back home including the dimwitted old bull.

"Maybe it would be possible to ride back home to Ireland on the back of a big whale. After all, it couldn't be all that far back to land could it?" Suddenly the whole pod of whales dove straight down beneath the surface of the water and out of sight. They did not resurface for at least 20 minutes or so later. Skip knew he could not hold his breath for that long. He thought back to his first underwater experience not that long ago it seemed. He was perhaps three or four years old and his parents had taken him on a picnic to a lake. It was a beautiful cloudless day with a warm breeze gently blowing across the countryside, making the flowers in the field sway back and forth in a peaceful motion. He had played joyfully by the water's edge where a fallen log laid suspended out over the water's edge, as his parents sat quietly on a blanket nearby watching him play. He had been full of energy and climbed out onto a log that had fallen. He continued to slip and slide on his way out to the end of the log, until suddenly he found himself down in the murky, ice-cold water. Luckily, he had taken a deep breath of air before he submerged under the water. Down he sank in the chilly water becoming more and more terrified the deeper he went. He felt the prickly branches of the following tree rubbing against him as he sank, as though he, being sucked down into a giant water spider's web. The thought of it, being-eaten by a big black spider with sharp teeth scared him half to death. Fortunate for Skip, his mother, and his father were nearby before Skip's feet had the chance to hit the bottom of the lake, for he was out of the water standing dripping wet beside his worried parents. It was a horrific experience almost drowning and not being able to breath underwater.

Oh, how homesick Skip was becoming by the minute thinking of his past. As usual, he was at fault one more time for not listening and brought this predicament on himself. He had taken himself away from his only loving grandparents, away from Ireland, and lost his only remaining family due to his own stupidity. What in the world, would it take to drive some good old common sense through this very thick skull of his? If only he could go back home, he would surely change his ways and act more like a good young leprechaun should. He would listen to their every quip, every word spoken as gospel, and try to absorb every instruction they offered him. He would happily do every chore Grandma Broom would give him without her having to ask him more than once, and listen to every instruction they presented him about properly using his magical talents.

The pod of whales soon resurfaced from their long dive beneath the water's surface and swam alongside the ship once again. Skip was still feeling very homesick and depressed. He decided he and the busy shipmates and passengers on board the Shamrock needed a real good laugh. He concentrated very hard on one of the huge blue whales swimming alongside the ship, until at last he was able to transport one of them onto the front bow of the Shamrock.

Again, Skip had not anticipated what might happen when the enormous weight of the whale landed on the bow of the ship. The whale's length was also longer than the ship was wide, so as it laid there dangling over each side of the ship crossways on the forward deck, it almost sank the bow of the ship beneath the surface of the water. The whale's heavy weight crushed the handrails on either side of the deck sending them into the drink. The thrashing of its mighty tail forced its huge body forward up against the forward jib's mast, relentlessly hammering at it until it snapped in two. The thrashing Whale's tail hurled part of the shattered jib shaft halfway across the deck, hitting the cabin boy unsuspecting in the forehead. He had been standing by the first large mast gazing stupefied at the scene on the forward deck. The broken sail's shaft knocked the poor cabin boy unconscious.

What Skip thought was going to be a funny prank actually turned out to be anything but funny. The whale was finally able to thrash its way forward across the front deck and back into the open sea, taking along with it many of the broken pieces of the ship's side railings. The crew busied themselves gathering what pieces of rail remained and piled them beside the broken mast.

Meanwhile, Captain Drake was standing there trying his best to sort out what had just happened. The captain of the Shamrock had heard stories once or twice about an injured harpooned whale attacking a ship. He had heard a Whale or two having turned on the smaller vessels that were in pursuit of them after harpooning them, but never had he heard in his lifetime of a whale jumping straight up out of the water and onto a ship's deck before! What possible circumstances could have caused such a phenomenon to take place? Was there a killer whale after it somewhere beneath the surface of the water? He just did not know.

Skip watched from the crow's nest feeling extremely guilty about the unpleasant event he had just caused. Vinnie rushed to the boy's side, bent down trying to help the injured cabin boy, who had already developed a large hematoma on the top of his four head. He carefully picked the young lad up off the deck, held him in his arms, and carried him swiftly down to Vinnie's cabin.

Skip thought hard about what he had just done to cause such injuries to the boy and more than likely to the whale. What he thought would turn out to be a laughable friendly prank designed to give everybody on board the ship a good laugh, had actually caused very serious injury to someone, not to mention what he had done to the ship with his thoughtlessness. He felt extremely guilty for what he had just done and wanted to rush off to Vinnie's cabin to apologize to all for his foolish actions and make the poor cabin boy well again, but he knew he could not do that. While his powers might possibly fix the mast and the splintered handrails, he knew he was truly unable to heal bruises or make a person healthy again. Pixies, not leprechauns, were the only ones he knew of that possessed these kinds of special powers. He now recognized yet another blunder in his already complicated life, and questioned if he would ever think of the consequences before he pulled yet another foolish prank again.

Skip used his limited powers to fetch the hundreds of splintered pieces of fragmented handrails and mast floating in the ocean behind the Shamrock. While the crewmembers were busy and not looking, Skip placed the pile of broken pieces of ship down on the deck beside the broken mast. Under the cover of night, he would return to the crow's nest to begin the rigorous task of repairing the damage he had cause to the ship. He did not dare perform the obvious suspicious looking whirlwind task in broad daylight. The passengers and crew on deck would surely think the Shamrock haunted by evil spirits and spooks. It would be difficult enough for Skip to fetch all the hundreds of wooden splinters out of the water without them seeing him do so. He certainly wouldn't expect anyone on board not to notice a whirlwind of broken pieces of ship coming back together above the ship and returning back down in their same exact shape as they once were.

As soon as Skip completed his rigorous task of collecting the splintered wood, he tried to transpose back to the wooden beam just outside of Vinnie's cabin door in the scully way. The swaying of the ship again tricked his better judgment, rather than landing on the beam he had intended to, he stopped in mid-air beside it, and then landed in a heap on the floor beneath the beam. He hit his head up hard against the wall of the passageway and almost knocked himself out cold. "Serves me right, you bloody fool," he thought harshly to himself. "Why didn't you think about what could have happened with the big old whale on deck before you did that? I should have remembered what good old Grandma Broom always said about large objects, "Never pick up anything heavier than you can hold onto in your hands or safely put in your lap". The Shamrock was a lap, and the whale was too big for it to hold. I should have never attempted such a foolish stunt."

The poor injured cabin boy laid still just inside the door on the bunk in Vinnie's cabin moaning in pain as he held his swollen aching forehead tight. He wondered why it hurts so, for he could not remember being hit by anything. He had a vague recollection of a whale being on board the ship's deck, but it was very unclear to him. Skip watched as Vinnie knelt down beside his bunk to pull out his special bottle of scotch from the trunk beneath the bunk. "Just a wee sip of my scotch, my boy, and you shall feel much better in about a minute or two. The scotch should help ease the pain a little."

Skip shook his head in disbelief, as Vinnie was about to serve the young boy scotch from his bottle to ease his pain. Skip held his stomach tight as it churned from the thought of drinking more scotch. "Ye cannot give that devils brew to that poor lad, you dumb bloke," Skip thought to himself. "His head will hurt worse than it does right now. Think of his poor stomach, too, will you? Don't you know that his head will hurt worse in the morning?" Skip was thinking back to the morning when he first awoke to find himself stuck in Vinnie's trunk. His head was throbbing as if a big brass drum was thumped upon by hundreds of angry drumsticks, and his poor stomach too, it felt like curdled up milk and sour butter down there. He concentrated hard on the cargo hold below deck to see what might be stored down there that the boy might drink to rid him of his pain instead of the rancid scotch Vinnie was about to poison him with.

He saw kegs stacked four rows deep below under the floor. Concentrating hard, Skip transposed below deck onto a keg of rum. Magically he popped open a stopper from the top of one of the kegs and filled his hat to its brim. He then replaced the stopper and returned to the empty scully way where he had just been standing. Peeking in through the open door, he found Vinnie getting ready to serve the ailing cabin boy a drink of scotch from the mouth of the bottle. Vinnie was gently lifting the injured boys head up from the pillow and slowly putting the bottle of scotch up to the young lad's trembling mouth. "What is your name, lad?" Vinnie asked the cabin boy softly. "Billy," replied the weak speaking boy. "Drink this scotch, Billy. I know you told me you don't like it, but it will help you relax and relieve a wee bit of the throbbing pain in your head, too." Skip concentrated hard on taking some of the rum from his hat into Vinnie's bottle of scotch, and the scotch out of the bottle. It was astonishing, the scotch from the bottle soaked the front of Skip's garments like it had been thrown at him, and it had been, by him! Skip never did like getting wet, so he stomped his feet in an instant tantrum. Realizing what he had just done, he laughed out-loud for a second and then remembered where he was.

Seeing Vinnie's head begin to turn in his direction, along with the others in the room, Skip quickly transposed out of sight and onto the crossbeam in the hallway. Quietly chuckling to himself, he reminisced back to the first time he had tried to magically transport something to himself. He recalled standing with Grandma Broom beside the road when he tried to fetch small stones. It was amazing that nobody in the cabin had seen the scotch stream flow out from the bottleneck and toward him. Still thirsty, he took a wee sip of rum from his hat. The flavor was mild as before, causing a light tingly sensation as he swallowed it. It neither burned nor caused him to gasp for air, as the scotch did. With his thirst somewhat quenched, Skip peaked again through the cabin door to see Vinnie take what he thought was the last swallow of his very special scotch from his bottle. Rum Vinny yelled. "Who broke into my cabin again and swapped my good scotch for this bloody rum?" Vinnie seemed beside himself.

"Now that was funny," Skip thought to himself. His face broke out into an enormous grin, as he laughed wholeheartedly under his breath holding a hand to his mouth so no one could hear him. Skip thought this is what being a prankster is about, and best of all, not hurting anyone in the process!

He finally realized that things were not as bad as he first thought they were, and suddenly had a new clear outlook on life a good leprechaun should have. Still vey thirsty, he transposed back to the keg of rum in the ship's hold and drank his fill.

Skip violently awakened, by several loud horrifying explosions echoing off the hull of the ship rocking the many kegs of rum lying around him. The thunderous noise scared the daylights out of him. He could scarcely hear the captain and sailors on deck screaming and yelling at one another as another loud round of explosions vibrated the Shamrock's hull. Skip, in much confusion, was not sure where he was. The ship was swaying back and forth on the water's surface as if they were in a violent storm, and then something hard hit the hull of the ship as if they had run aground. He immediately transposed to the crossbeam in the scully way hearing the captain frantically shouting out orders to uncover the cannons and prepare to fire. "We will blast those heathens out of the water, mates. They will not take over ship! Secure your positions and make ready to protect our Lady!"

Skip transposed beneath the grate in the scully way and peered up through the latticework to the crow's nest high above on the main mast. The crow's nest was empty. He transposed to the crow's nest taking the swaying of the ship into consideration before transposing this time. He looked to see a waring ship heading towards the Shamrock. Her sails were full of wind as she bore down on them, and the cannons on her deck roared as they fired another round and another round of hot iron balls flying through the air at the Shamrock. The color of the flag on her mast was black against a white background. She flew a skull and cross bones on the canvas flag on her mast. Skip at first thought he must have been daydreaming.

The Shamrock's main sails all been lowered to half-mast to slow the Shamrock down in order for her crew to repair the damage the whale had caused to the front jib mast. The crew had not quite finished their work on the jib when the pirate ship surprisingly came out from the misty fog after them.

"What can I do to help the Shamrock?" Skip questioned himself. While the crew was busy loading their cannons, Skip looked around to make sure nobody was watching him. Using his limited leprechaunic powers, he repaired the front jib mast. He took the piece of metal strapping Vinnie had just finished forging in the galley stove, and placed it snuggly around the broken sections of mast, and secured the repaired sail to the repaired mast. Carefully making sure he was still unobserved, he loosened the main sail tie lines, dropping the sails down while hoisting others up to their fullest position. He secured the loose tie lines of them as the sails filled with wind, as the crew readied their cannons to return fire toward the approaching pirate ship. Most of the Shamrock's crew were unfamiliar with using cannons to defend themselves, and fumbled with the kegs of black powder, cannonballs packing felt, and the cannonballs themselves. Their inexperience caused great difficulty in preparing the cannons to fire toward the swiftly advancing enemy.

Skip witnessed cannon fire-erupt from the pirate ship. Six of her cannons roared spewing smoke and fire, sending six large burning fireballs flying high in the air toward the Shamrock. "Concentrate real hard on them", Skip thought quickly to himself. His magical powers enabled him to send all six cannonballs into the sea short of their intended target. The narrow miss sprayed salt water all over the Shamrock's deck and crew who were frantically busy trying to ready their cannons. Fortunately, for Skip everything below was too hectically busy for anyone below to notice one small leprechaun helping from above in the crow's-nest.

Captain Drake and his first mate aggressively tried to educate the crew on how to load and shoot the cannons. The captain never thought the Shamrock would be in a crippled state or position to be attacked therefore he never showed his crew how to fire the cannons. A volley of cannon fire eventually rang out from the Shamrock's crew. Four cannonballs flashed out of her cannons flying toward the approaching ship. The first volley fired fell far short of their intended target. The pirate ship was closing fast. They had been monitoring the Shamrock for a long time, and watched her crew repair the front jib mast. They knew she was heavy with cargo in her hold and could easily outrun their ship if she was under full power. The scoundrel Pirates were taking advantage of the Shamrock in her state of repair, and tried to catch her off guard with her sails at half-mast and underinflated. The pirate ship sailed in as close they could, without the crew of the Shamrock seeing them before they began to fire their cannons. Seeing all the Shamrock's sails suddenly go from half inflated to fully open, gave the pirates great concern, for they saw no sailors on any of her riggings doing their jobs. They could not believe their eyes. Now they had to rush to catch up to her in order to block the air from reaching her sails as she slowly began to pick up speed. If they could prevent the wind from filling her sails by sailing in directly behind her, she would become bobbing dead in the water like a cork tied to a fishing line.

Without any cargo in their hold, the pirate ship drafted much less water than the heavy Shamrock. This allowed their vessel to float much higher and lighter on the surface of the sea. With their Sails wide open and full of wind gave them an advantage over the slowed Shamrock. The Shamrock had not yet collected enough wind in her sails or momentum to get her up to full speed against the enormous drag of water on her hull. The pirates were hastily trying to block the Shamrock's air supply of wind from reaching her sails just for one minute. This would allow the pirates to maneuver their vessel into position to board the Shamrock. Then the heathens could take control of the Shamrock for their own use and make the crew and passengers walk the gangplank to their death.

The Shamrock's crew continued to fumble with the kegs of black powder and cannonballs as Skip looked down on them from above. The crew finally set off another round of cannon fire, and their balls were flying low toward the fast approaching pirate ship. This next round of cannonballs fired was going to fall way far short of their intended target as did the first round fired. Skip concentrated his entire strength on a single one of the four cannonballs flying through the air toward its target. The other three cannonballs fell far short of their intended target again. With more ease than he had imagined, Skip sent the fourth cannonball skipping across the water's surface. This cannonball skipped from wave to wave until it soared high up into the air across the ship's deck, catching the Pirate ship's main mast at its base. He watched as the main mast splintered in two at its base. The mast with its riggings of sails and rope fell over the side of the ship. It was a beautiful scene to behold, Skip thought. The sail and its riggings quickly filled with water causing the ship to sway dangerously from side to side in trouble as it turned away from the Shamrock, allowing the Shamrock to get up to speed and flee. The main sails of the Shamrock filled to capacity with wind when Skip released the tie ropes. The repaired jib sail also filled with wind allowing it to pull its own fair share. With her sails filled, the Shamrock thrust forward leaving the crippled pirate ship listing wildly on large swells of the sea behind her. Crew and passengers aboard the Shamrock were ecstatic with joy as they jumped up and down in jubilation, hollering and screaming joyfully, celebrating their remarkable yet unbelievable defeat of the pursuing pirate ship.

Billy, the cabin boy, watched the fight between the two ships in terrifying horror. He kept his eyes glued, as did the others on the one last lonely cannonball prancing magically across the water's surface, jumping up off the last wave before the cannonball struck the ship. Billy was extremely frightened that the pirate ship and its outlaw crew would catch up to them and board her. He was fearful that he and the others would become fish food just as his father had told him and his siblings what pirates do with prisoners they capture. Every vessel on the waters of the world, that is, except for fishing vessels. Fishing men around the world not considered enemies, to the pirates, for they carried no cannons, no silver, and were friendly to the wretched scoundrels. The fishing men of the sea were always willing to give up free fish to the pirates to supply their warring vessels with food, and whatever water they might have left onboard. The pirates left the vessels alone to do their fishing and hopefully, be able return back home to port safely.

Skip stood proud as a peacock up in the crow's nest of the Shamrock as he looked down on the jubilation-taking place, with the crew of the Shamrock hooting and hollering with joy down on her deck. He stood there feeling worthy of himself and his feeble abilities. He had in the last several hours, now performed good deeds with his special powers instead of a cluster of awful pranks. Every member of the crew, along with the many passengers, thought it was one of the other sailors or passengers aboard who had lastly finished the job of repairing the small jib, then let down the main sails from half raised or half lowered so the ship could get away from the advancing pirate ship. Skip noticed a sailor climbing up the hemp ladder leading up to the crow's nest to have a look at the ailing pirate ship. He quickly transposed back to the scully way beam, then back down into the cavity of the ship's hold to the keg to hide. The hold would be Skip's home for the remainder of the voyage.

The next several hours passed away very slowly for Skip, as he was a prisoner, self-held in the hold of the ship to protect himself. When nighttime finally fell over the Shamrock, he began the difficult task of piecing back together the countless tiny splinters of the wooden side rail, and check on the repair job he did to the jib mast. It took enormous concentration on his part, especially on the splintered pile of wood on the ship's main deck; in order for him to piece them, all back together as one along the front sides of the ship's bow.

This new task turned out to be tremendously trying and a very exhausting process for him. He had only seen his Grandma Broom perform such a magic procedure once before. She repaired a small antique glass vase her mother had given to her as a gift. Skip had broken it by accident when it fell off the mantle in the living room while he was skipping and prancing around the room. (This is how Skip received his nickname by skipping around the house all of the time. His given name at birth by his mother was David). He had to make sure in his mind each fragment of wood had to fit absolutely positively back into its proper place and position or the splintered handrail would have quills sticking out of it like a porcupine. Then what would he do?

Skip matched each fragment of splintered wood gathered back together in its original place, as a finished would do in the repairs. No one, not even Skip, could detect a blemish or a scratch on the handrail that had not already been there or that a whale had ever been onboard the Shamrock. The only telltale sign of the mishap aboard her was the black metal strap Vinnie had forged in the Ship's-Stove for the mast of the jib to hold the two broken sections of mast together. The forged ban made by Vinny was not necessary to be on the mast after Skip had repaired the mast with his magic. Using his incredible mental superglue, but he did not want anyone on board being suspicious of him being there, so, he placed the metal strap around the mast just for show so no one would ever suspect anything strange had taken place.

After having completed his exhausting mission, he transposed down inside the ship's galley with care, to a safe location out of site. He wanted to scrounge up something to eat, for he was famished. He observed Billy with his very large welt still very visible on top of his forehead helping the ship's cook clean up the dreadful mess left behind in the ship's galley from the encounter with the dreaded pirates. Along with the mess on the floor, he saw stacks of dirty dishes, pots, and pans from the last meal of the day. The floor looked a mess with food scattered. The crew and passengers must have caused the mess as they scrambled top side when the pirate ship came out of nowhere firing its cannons at them.

Billy had a bucket of seawater warming on the galley stove to wash down the slick floor along with enough water to wash the dirty dishes, pots, and pans. He noticed a couple of pieces of dried beef in a frying pan on top of the rear shelf of the ship's wood-burning stove. The sight of food made Skip's mouth instantly water. His wee stomach had been hurting while performing his magic from not having any real food in it for a very long time, except for the tiny wedge of cheese earlier that morning, or was it the day before? With all the excitement of the day, he could not remember! Skip used extreme care as he cautiously and anxiously selected a clean dinner plate from a stack of clean dishes on the counter.

With more caution than ever before, Skip magically called the beef to his plate from the stove along with a large piece of bread. He took a clean mug hanging on a hook for some water or rum he might find to drink. Seeing no freshwater except for the bucket of seawater, Skip summoned a mug of rum from a carafe sitting on a table. He took silverware from the silverware chest to eat his meal. He was learning the caution his grandparents had been trying to educate him in all along.

He would cautiously take his time to enjoy eating his first meal aboard the Shamrock while watching Billy and the cook. Later on, he would look for some fresh water to drink stored somewhere aboard the ship, but right now, he was famished and needed food to rebuild his failing strength. When he was finished eating, he magically cleaned his plate, mug, and eating utensils and returned them to their proper places before retiring back down to the hole of the ship for a good night's sleep.

Skip knew to exercise greater care on board not to demonstrate his very existence and get himself caught especially after fixing the ship's forward damage. Someone had to think it was very strange waking up to a ship in total repair. He knew it would not afford him any good to play mean tricks or pranks on anyone that might give his presence away. He had nowhere to run or transpose to if everyone on board was looking for him all at the very same time. The ship just was not big enough to hide in like Dublin Town where he could at least transpose atop the many buildings or behind a wagon to make his escape.

Skip's homesickness grew in intensity with each, and every passing day. He stayed too long out of sight of everyone down in the dark hold of the ship. The only trusted friends Skip managed to make on board were a couple of dark gray rats that had snuck aboard in Dublin Town, who now call the cavity of the Shamrock their home right along with Skip. The days passed by very slowly for him with nothing to do while the Shamrock sailed her course westward.

Vinnie could hardly wait for the ship to sail into Boston so he could set foot again on good old solid earth especially in the new world. Here he planned to start his new life as a blacksmith, a trade well taught him by his father back home on the old sod in Ireland.

In the meantime, Vinnie made good use of the mass amounts of time he had on his hands. He sat for hours on end quietly drawing at his desk. He would be found sitting there writing down his memoirs of the joyful and not so joyful events that he had while on board the ship. During the day in good and bad weather, he would study the captain and his crew, their every move. He would sometimes join in with the crew as they were doing their work and liked to keep busy. He grew to enjoy the life aboard the ship by the sailors especially how everyone on board appeared to be forever getting along with one another like one big happy family.

Vinnie mentally recorded all the events of the day leading up to and including the aggressive attack of the pirate ship on them. He drew several beautiful sketches at his desk of the whale thrashing on the forward deck of the Shamrock. He drew an assortment of exaggerated drawings of their ship being-attacked by the pirate ship. One drawing fascinated Captain Drake. The drawing illustrated the heartless pirates trying to board the Shamrock with their weapons drawn, and the crew of the Shamrock standing firm fending off the grubby devils from her decks.

CHAPTER SEVENTEEN

A Time to Play

After spending countless lonely days all cooped up in the hold of the ship, Skip decided it was time to pass the remaining time of the voyage away by playing harmless pranks and trickery on the passengers and crew. Perhaps picking selectively the more content looking mortals who would probably take his shenanigans more than others would. He transposed to the galley of the ship taking cover as a few of the crew and passengers sat down to eat their meal at the first sitting of the day. He positioned himself on a beam behind a swinging oil lantern. Here no one could see him or suspect he was even there. From his safe location, he marveled at everyone's happiness while he played his pranks. He included Captain Drake along with his first mate David. He took a real liking to the ship's first mate, as Skip's real name was David, given to him by his mother, but he liked his nickname Skip, also. On the odd days of the week, the crew and passengers would reverse their order of sitting at the mealtime schedule. Time seemed to pass more quickly by for him keeping a little busier held captive by himself, down in the hold of the ship.

Skip's most favorite trick was to place their drinks back into the carafe they had just used after barely pouring out a drink from it into their mug. The funny looks they gave to one another tickled Skip so. He used his magic with care, taking wee morsels of food from everyone's plates around the galley. Most everyone had cut up two pieces of meat from off their plates for themselves, and the second piece just up and vanished as they went to retrieve it.

Skip had an extremely difficult time holding his mouth shut, not wanting to burst out in laughter at the mortals as they searched their laps and the floor for their missing food. He would sometimes double over on the beam quietly laughing so hard and holding his belly. He would wait for the surprised looks on their faces before he ate their food, and then enjoy it all the much more when he did eat it.

By no means did Skip ever leave the ship's galley hungry or thirsty. At the end of the day when he retired back down to the hold of the ship to sleep on his keg, he was tired and happier than before. The pranks he played never hurt anyone except for their pride. Not all on board thought Skip's silly antics were all-that funny. After a short time, Skip could see it in their faces wondering whom the bloody bloke was that was driving them crazy.

Over, and over again Skip would play the same foolish prank on the same people, and would return their rum, wine, or water back into its original carafe. As more time lapsed, Skip grew even more homesick. Even with his time filled with funny pranks, time for him seemed to pass ever the more slowly. The passengers and crewmembers did not act lonely at all, as they had bonded quite nicely together like one big happy family and had made friends amongst themselves. Watching all this take place in front of him made Skip feel all the more homesick for Ireland, his Grandma Broom, Grampa Hair, not to mention his old friend the bull down in farmer Prendergast's field. He had not met one single solitary sole, not one on board the Shamrock he could honestly call friend or family.

It appeared to Skip that Billy he knew, if he tried to befriend anyone, anyone at all on board the ship, he would be found a leprechaun, and captured someone. The cabin boy Billy, looked as if he might possibly be trusted as a friend for Skip to bond to, but how would he go about telling him how very sorry he was for what he had cause to happen. Surely, Billy would not understand Skip.

CHAPTER EIGHTEEN

Home Sick and Lonely

Feeling tremendously homesick, Skip abandoned his customary fun of trickery and dining with the others. He decided to keep to his lonely self by staying down in the hold of the ship and grieve alone. There on his bed atop the keg he partook in rum from the keg for his main course of dinner. He drank rum for his drink, and rum for his bread and butter, and rum for his dessert. He drank rum for a toast to the king of the leprechauns, and more rum just to have more rum.

Not quite knowing where he was or how we got there, Skip found himself high atop the main mast of the Shamrock sitting slouched down in the crow's nest beneath a star-studded canopy of bright dazzling glitter. He found himself sitting there in a stupor. His eyes glazed as he stared up at the brilliant canopy of stars shining bright above him and looked out over the massive Moon lit sea surrounded the Shamrock. He watched the smooth rolling waves of the sea come rolling toward the ship from afar by the bright light of the moon. He began to scream and holler out into the cool night air at the top of his tiny lungs and began drunkenly singing away feeling extremely sorry for himself for the predicament he had gotten into. He carried on singing like an opera singer at the top of this tiny voice with slurred words. He tried to whistle an old Irish folklore, but was unable to whistle. He was trying his best to make jolly music to cheer up and make himself happy. Suddenly Skip stopped his loud singing when he heard a voice hollering up to him from far down below on deck.

CHAPTER NINETEEN

In Mortal Trouble

"Ahoy crow's nest, ahoy up there crow's nest! What in tarnation are you hollering and shouting about up there? I cannot understand a single word you are saying."

Skip knew he was in very serious trouble the instant he heard the loud voice call up to him from down below. He laughed a hardy panicky laugh and without-delay, Skip took another drink of rum from his lambskin canteen. He fearfully laughed out-loud again and looked out over the rope ring to see who might be hollering up at him.

"Ahoy crow's nest, who are you? What is your name? What in tarnation are you doing up there tonight?" Trying to sound as sober as he possibly could, Skip hollered back down to the young sounding voice below. "It is my night watch tonight mate! Watching the stars in the heaven twinkle in the pure of darkness as Skip began laughing a hearty laugh "am up here looking for land ho. Singing a song up here toasting a hearty toast to the Queen's honor". "You had better come down from there at once, mate! If you do not come down right now it will be my duty to fetch out the captain on you straight away". "I am watching for land ho".

The slim figure cast a long narrow shadow on the deck below from the light of the moon as he swiftly ran away. He was running toward the aft of the ship in search of Captain Drake who was in his quarters. Skip knew he was going to bring him back to the mast where he was perched, so he tried desperately unsuccessfully to concentrate on getting out of the quandary he had put himself. He tried to transpose back to the crossbeam in the hallway and then back to his bed on the keg of rum, but to no avail. He could barely move, never mind transpose anywhere. He was drunk, as never a drunken leprechaun should ever become. His magical power suddenly been rendered useless, and he could sense it. It was a pure sense of helplessness, he had never experienced before.

What was Skip to do, and not get himself caught? Quick as a drunken leprechaun might possibly maneuver, over the edge of the crow's nest's rope ring Skip hurriedly departed. He carefully tried balancing his very drunken self, tottering, and holding the flimsy roped ring surrounding the crow's nest. He tried not to fall out of the crow's nest as he slithered like a nervous snake out over the ring to the cross pole of the mast. He was trying to scurry down from the crow's nest to the deck below, and back to the safety of the ship's hold before anyone could possibly recognize him. He was especially afraid the one whose shadow cast on the deck below would perhaps come back with the captain of the Shamrock. Surely, he would have no mercy on him, and would have him thrown overboard to the sharks. Skip's unsteadiness proved way-too slow in trying to descend the rope ladder. On the aft deck, he noticed two ghost like shadows approaching the mast of the ship. He could hear them talking loudly about him being drunk as a skunk up in the crow's nest. He quickly shimmied out onto one of the yard longs holding tight to the main sail's rings as he slithered there along. He laid his body flat along the round slippery top of the yard long, and somehow managed to avoid being-seen by them in the moonlight.

"Sorry, sir," Billy said. "The mate must have crawled down from the crow's nest in quite a hurry when I went to fetch you." "That's okay, Billy, my lad. It is better that he is down here safe on the deck than in danger up there in the crow's nest drunker than an old sailor as you say he was. Should the bloke fall from up there, it would surely be the end of him, and anyone he might fall upon also, it is hard enough to be climbing way up there when you are sober, never mind when you are drunk. I shall have a few stern words with the crew and passengers in the morning about this foolish act tonight. Everyone on board knows the rules! Being Captain of the Shamrock, he did not allow anyone onboard the vessel, to get drunk. If they do get drunk, they shall be locked-up, locked up in their cabin in their cabin, for the remainder of the voyage, or be placed down in the hold of the ship in shackles and chains if they cannot follow my rules. These are my orders, Captain's orders, Billy, the rules aboard my ship when I am in charge." The captain slowly turned from Billy as he slowly walked back toward his cabin. He looked about the deck to see if he might recognize a drunken sailor hiding somewhere.

Watching as the captain disappeared into the darkness, Skip tried to turn around on the yard long so he might start his long slow descent back down the roped ladder as soon as the other shadow disappeared. He had not quite turned halfway around when he slipped from the yard long and fell feet first straight down toward the deck below. Dropping from the yard long, he began screaming at the top of his tiny lungs, trying to concentrate to no avail on stopping his rapid descent. Hearing Skip scream out in panic, Billy looked up to watch in awe as Skip fell from the tallest yard long of the ship down toward the hardwood deck below screaming and kicking all the way. He observed Skip's arms and legs flailing in midair in the moonlight, and saw his feet hit the roped ladder, causing him to somersault two or three times as he plummeted downward from the mast. Suddenly the slack ropes of the hemp ladder grasped Skip snugly, affixing themselves to his little crotch and stopped him from tumbling down.

Billy watched in slow motion as Skip slowly flipped upside down, hanging and dangling there, intertwined in the heavy ropes of the ladder by his feet and legs. Skip's head barely missed the hardwood decking of the ship as he swung upside down swaying back and forth, moaning and groaning and holding his poor aching crotch. Blurry eyed and hanging upside down in great pain, Skip saw Billy come running over to him. He stood there above him looking down in pure amazement.

"Does your mama or papa know where you are, boy? Do they know you are out here in the dark all by yourself and not with anyone?" Skip did not say a word. He knew he was in serious trouble, and did not feel like talking to anyone, especially at a time like this while he was hanging upside down in extreme pain. He felt like a very large great white shark had just clamped its mighty jaws tight to his groin. He would have felt better he thought if he had hit the deck and died. He knew now he was in the worst kind of trouble he had ever been in before in his entire life.

"Are you all right, boy? Are you all right?" Billy yelled out at Skip when he first did not respond quickly enough. Suddenly a quantity of rancid sour rum Skip had earlier in the evening for his meal, drink, and dessert came gushing out his mouth and nose like a fountain. He flooded the deck below with sour vomit, filling the night air with stench of rum and stomach acid. Skip had never been so sick in all of his life.

Smelling the stench and seeing the vomit, Billy blurted out, "I am fetching the captain straight away, mate". He immediately ran off toward the aft of the ship to gather up the captain from his quarters and to bring him back to where Skip hung upside down entangled in the ropes of the ladder this time showing the captain he had not been imagining someone he had heard singing and hollering drunk up in the crow's nest. Smelling the rum and rancid stench of the stomach acid, Billy knew he had the right culprit who was the drunk and had been up in the sails above.

"Wait," Skip yelled out after Billy in a panicked response. "I shall die if you do not get me down from here straight away before you leave! I will be dead before you can return. Billy stopped short in his tracks. Billy quickly turned his head staring over at the pathetic looking person pleading for his life as he hung upside down in trouble and begging him to return. Billy filled with compassion turned around and walked quickly back toward Skip. "Help me down, please, or I shall surely die in my own vomit." Skip pleaded as he threw up again and gagged on some more of his vomit. Feeling dreadfully sorry for Skip, Billy bent down to assist the poor lad. Quickly as possible, Billy helped to untangle Skip's wrapped up feet from the hemp ladder rungs and let him gently down to the deck below his head. He sat there trying to stand up on the wet deck while slipping and sliding, but was able to stand up by holding the ship's railing.

Billy stared down at Skip and instantly started to stammer. He was so excited he could not quite talk properly as he was having a real hard time trying to get the correct words to come out of his mouth. "Why, you are not a sailor or a dumb old drunken bloke, are you, you are a leprechaun." "I am not." "Are you sure you are not a real leprechaun?" "Nope, I do not have any gold and I don't know how to make it either." Skip spoke slurring his words as he stood there weaving back and forth in front of Billy who was looking at him in total disbelief and bewilderment. He tried to stand steady by holding onto the rail in a prim and proper upright position with extremely blurred vision. His stomach began churning again and made him feel as if he would be sick again at any moment.

"I have not seen you on board the Shamrock before have I? What room are you staying in?" "If I tell you a really big secret, Billy, can you promise to keep it a secret between me and you?" "How do you know my name is Billy? You are a leprechaun, aren't you?" "Do not say that. Ah you did."

A sudden feeling of despair came over Skip. He knew the rules of the leprechauns well enough to know that Billy had saved his life by untying him. Skip, having been saved by Billy; he was now obliged by the rules of the leprechaun order to offer Billy his precious pot of gold, to repay him for his good deed in saving his life. "I am not a leprechaun, Billy, I am, but I do not have any of my powers. I mean I am not a leprechaun, because I do not have all of my powers. I mean, I do not know what I do mean. I mean." Skip was confused to the point that what he said made no sense at all. Being alone onboard a ship he didn't want to be on so far away from home, homesick, and being saved by Billy. The perplexity of the moment caused Skip to slide back down from the handrail and sit back down on the deck. He held his whimpering face with his two little trembling hands, and started to cry like a baby in front of Billy.

"Are you all right, bubs? What's your name, anyway?" "No, I am not all right Billy, and my name's not bubs, either! I cannot tell you my real name, Billy. Oh, all right then you can call me Henry, ok Billy?" "Well, Henry, are you all right then?" "No, I am not all right. I got myself stuck in a trunk. Well, I became sleepy drunk on some evil tonic of scotch and rum, and then I fell into a trunk and fell fast asleep. I nearly got everyone killed with that stupid whale I put onboard the deck as a prank, and I am homesick. I am really sorry, Billy."

"I am fetching the captain straight away and am telling him all about you, Henry, and that whale trick, too." "No, Billy, I beg of you please don't because I helped save the ship, too. I fixed the main jib's sail and all of the handrails. I was the one who made the cannonballs hop across the water and hit the pirate ship's main mast, and saved the Shamrock from being captured by the pirates". "You did all that, Henry?" "Yep, Billy, I did all that, and I am very sorry about your head". "You saved the Shamrock from the pirates so you do have the powers of a leprechaun, don't you, Henry". "Some powers yes, but I am yet a young lad like yourself, Billy. I have some very limited powers but not all of them. I probably will never have all of my powers now that I have left Ireland. I should have listened to my Granny Broom." "Hey, I had a Grandma Broom once too, Henry. She used to chase me all about the house and out into the yard at home with her old broomstick wailing away at me, especially if I didn't listen to her and do what she wanted me to do right away or when my mother asked me to do something and I wasn't quick enough about it. God rest her soul." They both laughed.

"Where have you been sleeping aboard the ship, Henry?" "I have been staying down in the hold of the ship on a rum keg along with a couple of the ship's rats at night." "Oh, don't the rats bother you?" "Nah, I just put them into an empty keg for the night so they don't bother me while I sleep and keeps them from running around my head at night. In the morning, I let the two of them out so they can run around the ship again and play. I think that they think I am their long lost mother because I bring them scraps from the galley when I return to the hold to sleep. I have not had a good night's sleep in a real bed ever since we sailed. Oh, how I miss my bed back home in Ireland, Billy."

"What is your grandpa's name, Billy? It is not Grandpa Hair by any chance is it"? "I never knew my Grandpa, Henry. He was lost at sea one day just as my pa was and never came home that stormy day from his fishing boat. Old King Neptune took both my Pa and my Grandpa from me. That is why I am out here. Someone had to step in for my pa's lost wages and help out my poor mother and put food on the table for my brothers and sisters". "You have brothers and sisters, Billy?" "Yes sir, I have several brothers and sisters and a real nice special mom, too!" "Sorry to hear about your pa and your Grandpa, Billy." "That's okay, Henry." "Do you miss your mama and your brothers and sisters?" "I miss them more than food itself. I have no desire to eat most of the time, anymore Billy. I think about my poor loving family all of the time, and cannot wait for my two years to be up serving on the Shamrock. Then I might be able to go back home to live and stay or I will have to sign up again for another two years just to keep the family fed and the little ones in school. It is up to me to keep my family going so they will not be kicked out of our house. My mother works at Mrs. Mosher's pub, but doesn't make enough there in pounds to support everything."

"Hey, how would you like my bunk to sleep on for the night, seeing you haven't slept in a real bed for such a long time? I hear there is only a couple more days left before we arrive in Boston." "No, Billy, I could not do that to you, but I thank you for the generous offer just the same though." "Really, I can get a sleeping roll out of the ship's storeroom for me to sleep on, that way you can have my bunk for the night, Henry." "I cannot afford to be seen by anyone or I will be shanghaied, and then I shall never see Ireland or my family again." Billy made sure the path to his cabin was clear. There was no one on the deck or in the scully way, so the two ran swiftly across the deck. Skip teeter tottering unsteady on his feet as they scampered across the deck with Billy in the lead through the mid-ship doorway, down the scully way to Billy's cabin. Quick as scat, they entered and quickly closed the door firmly, locking it behind them.

No sooner had they settled down on Billy's bunk to talk about themselves and families, then, suddenly someone knocked at Billy's door calling out his name. It was Mr. Vinnie McDougall and he was looking for some more whale oil for his lanterns. Vinnie had been having a grand time drawing events of the ocean battle between the Shamrock and the pirate ship. He had also spent time writing a story to follow along with each of the pictures he was drawing. "I am writing a book about the battle we had with the pirates and the ship the scoundrels were on. I want the book to sound authentic, and want everyone whoever reads it to think we did a real good job defending ourselves out there against them who act as pirates there pirates. You are one of the main characters in the book Billy. There is a chapter in there telling how you helped save the Shamrock all by yourself from the pirates, for you were the one who fired the cannon that blew the heathens out of the water. If you have time tomorrow, can you help me out with a couple of special details, Billy?" "Happy to be of service to you, I shall fetch your Whales oil straight away, for you sir." Vinny is going to America to make his fortune in gold". "He is how you know so much about him Henry?" "It was Vinnie's, I mean Mr. McDougall's trunk that I fell into and fell fast asleep in back at the Inn in Ireland. He is the one who put me here onboard the Shamrock by mistake, without him or me ever knowing about it. He does not even know I exist. You are the only one onboard the ship that knows about me. Can you please help this lonely Leprechaun get back home to Ireland, Billy? Can I hide out here in your cabin on the return trip to Ireland, please? I promise you that I will not be any bother to you Billy. I promise, I will even sleep under your bunk on the hard deck wooden floor if you just let me stay with you. I won't be any bother to you, and when we get back home to Ireland, I will grant you a great big wish if my powers let me!"

"Sorry Henry, we are not sailing back home to Ireland. I hear we are sailing south towards the continent of Africa and then off again to the land of kangaroos to Australia. Then we are going to other ports before we head back home to Ireland. We may not see Ireland again for over a year or maybe two. With poor luck Henry, we probably will not see Ireland again until it is time for lonely old me to sign back on the Shamrock for another two years. The only way we might see Ireland again soon as we get a cargo of goods heading back home there. Otherwise, we will go wherever the cargo we pick up takes us around the world."

"Around the world, Billy, I always thought the world was flat. I never knew we lived on a round ball, no one has ever told me that." "Round as round can be. The captain has a whole bunch of nautical maps in his cabin that shows how the world is round like a ball and has a few islands of land scattered about it. I wish we were going straight back home to Ireland, Henry. I would quit this job Henry but I cannot. It sure gets awfully lonely out here all by my lonesome, especially without any friends my own age or family to talk with. The captain is an all right kind of chap in his own way, for most of the crew are real good blokes who watch out for each other, too. Some of the men have very funny ways about the men they stuck out here all alone without girlfriends or family. The crew do not have much in common with me as I am so young and all. It surely would be a nice thing to have someone my own age out here to talk to once in a while even if he is a leprechaun whom I cannot tell anyone about."

Billy left his cabin to fetch Mr. McDougall some oil for his lanterns while Skip sat patiently alone on his bunk. While he was gone, he cleaned up Skip's vomit from the deck so the ones on board would not slip or see the offensiveness spread out all over in the morning. Billy also grabbed a spare sleeping role from out of the ship's storage cabin for him to sleep on.

An hour had passed before Billy had the time to return to his cabin. When he unlocked and opened the cabin door, he thought Skip had disappeared from his bed and cabin. "Henry, Henry, where are you?" He asked quietly. Skip spoke not a word in return as he had hidden beneath Billy's bunk and stayed purposely hidden out of sight in the scant lit room, cautiously peeking out from under the bunk to see if Billy had kept his word and not brought anyone back. Billy seemed filled with regret by not finding his new friend waiting for him when he returned, especially after cleaning up Skip's putrid mess he had sprayed out all over the deck. Sadly, Billy sat down on his bunk without peering beneath it to take a quick look, then called out to Skip, hoping he would hear him from somewhere aboard the ship as he was a magical leprechaun.

"If you can hear me, Henry, you are welcome to my bunk for the night or to sleep on the sleeping role I have brought back with me from the ship's storage room. You can do whatever you like. I would certainly like to have you stay with me for the rest of the voyage and sleep in my room to just keep me company. I promise I will keep your secret safe while you stay with me in my cabin. I also promise not tell the captain you are on board the Shamrock. I promise you, and all I can do is give you my word and promise you I will not tell anyone. Even if you do not want to come back to stay, I sure hope you find your way back home to Ireland soon. Please don't drink anymore of that bad rum, stay sober, and out of trouble so you can go back home to Ireland to see your grandparents again."

When Skip made sure Billy had not brought anyone back with him and had listened to what Billy had said to him, he slowly crawled out from his hiding place beneath the bunk. Billy had thought he had magically disappeared from him because of had been told many stories about leprechauns that do that sort of thing. Seeing Skip crawl out from beneath his bunk beside his legs, made Billy have reservations about him being a real bona fide live leprechaun.

"Are you sure you are a real leprechaun, Henry?" "Sure and be gory, Billy, I am what I say I am. I am a real live genuine leprechaun. I will prove it to you tomorrow evening at the second meal sitting when everyone sits down to eat their meals with the captain and his first mate in the galley." With a blink of an eye, and a wee twitch of his nose, Skip's clothes became clean and smoothly pressed like they had never been dirty or wrinkled. His little wrinkled up hat became straight lace smooth, without a sign of unwanted creases or wrinkles in it.

"How did you do that, Henry," Billy asked nervously. "I don't really know how, I do not understand just how it happens, it just does. When I concentrate hard about something, it just happens. I wish I had all of my special leprechaun powers right now because then I would sincerely show you just what a real good leprechaun can do with them."

"What do you want from me, Billy? You know, for all the help you have provided me along the way, helping me out of this predicament, I put myself into, and that I must present you with something. A wish or something of value for all of your kind and generous help you have provided. It is the law of the leprechauns you know. I do not really know what I can give you, but I must give you something". "I do not want anything from you, Henry. All I really want from you is". "I knew it! I just knew it", Skip whispered out. "All you really want from me is my precious gold isn't that right?" "No, no, Henry that is not right, I do not want your precious gold. What I do want from you is for you to be my lifelong friend." "That is all you want from me, Billy?" "Yes, that is all I want from you." "Then your wish is granted" Skip said with a sincere smile on his face. "I will always be your friend."

Skip really liked Billy so his requested wish was as easy as pie for him to grant, a wish without having to use any his special leprechaunic powers. It would have been much more difficult to grant a special wish if he had disliked Billy and had to grant him a lifelong wish if he requested it in a selfish way.

Billy slept feeling safe and sound for the night. This was the first time in a long time that he could remember sleeping so well all curled up on the floor of his cabin in a sleeping role. He laid it down next to Skip who fell fast asleep on his bunk. Billy insisted Skip sleep on his bunk, for he was his invited guest. The next morning Billy went straight about the ship doing his many odd jobs, and all day long thought delightful thoughts about what Henry might be up to that night at mealtime. That night, Billy went quickly down to the galley to dine with the captain, feeling better about being onboard the Shamrock. He wondered what Henry had in store for him and was going to do to prove to Billy, he really was a leprechaun. Billy already knew Henry was a leprechaun or a very good and gifted magician when he straightened out his clothes right in front of him. He had a very warm feeling in his heart about Henry being a true friend by using his abilities to fend off pirates.

Skip had instructed Billy to keep his eyes wide open and pay particular attention to the captain and his actions as he ate his meal. Billy watched Captain Drake closely with great interest in what Henry was up to, as the captain filled his mug of rum from the carafe sitting in the center of the table. When the captain returned the partially filled carafe of rum back to the center of the table, quicker than scat the carafe became full again, and the captain's mug became empty. When the captain reached to take a drink, a most surprised look appeared across his face. The mug he thought he had just filled was empty. He remembered this strange phenomenon happening to him before, taking place once or twice at the table and blamed it mostly on fatigue. He poured out another mug of rum as the captain took a quick drink from it before Skip had a chance to place the rum back into the carafe.

Billy tried very hard not to look too suspicious as he watched every one's mug and carafe out the corner of his eye. The contents of the captain's mug swiftly disappeared and reappeared back into the carafe again magically. When the captain lifted his mug a second time, he lifted an empty mug to his lips. He looked visibly frustrated as he looked from side to side to see who was playing the trick on him. First, he looked towards Vinnie who was sitting quietly at the table to his right eating, and then towards his first mate David who sat directly across the table from Vinnie. They were both were in reaching distance of his mug, so he wondered which one of the two culprits was playing such a dirty trick on him, or had he been out to sea too long.

Skip was finally having a whole lot of fun with his trickery, and had finally found a true friend onboard the Shamrock, as had the others aboard. He was happy to know that someone else could enjoy watching the fun take place as he played his silly pranks on the others. Seeing the captain getting hot under the collar and irritated, Skip switched his pranks from the captain to the captain's first mate. At first, he emptied the first mate's mug of rum back into the carafe three times before the first mate looked side to side wondering, as the captain had before, who the silly bloke was who was playing such a grubby little trick on him. He first glanced at Vinnie and then toward the captain. He suspected one or both of them were playing the trick on him. Not wanting to cause a hassle about a silly mug of rum, he began to clasp the carafe of rum before he took his next drink from his mug to make sure his mug would always have some rum left in it. Billy watched in amazement as Skip's silly pranks were taking place right in front of him. Billy tried his best to hide his quivering lips and smiling face from the passengers and crewmembers, sitting at the far end of the table with the captain. He held his pining stomach tight trying hard not to burst out in hysterical laughter, quietly watching everyone make fools of themselves. Henry played his silly little tricks one by one on everyone seated at the table. Skip emptied Billy's glass of water lastly back into its picture on the table, and Billy could not help but to laugh out-loud this time. The others seated at the table wondered what was so funny.

Back in Billy's cabin, he and Skip laughed wholeheartedly late into the wee hours of the very next morning. "Is it true, Henry, that leprechauns really do have gold?" "Oh, yes and no. What I mean is that some of us do have gold and some of us do not have any at all. Someday, if I am lucky enough, I will have all the gold that belongs to me. I am not quite sure how I will come by my goal or from whom I shall get it from, but someday I should have gold to call my very own. I did not pay strict enough attention to my grandparents about how I shall come by it; but yes, someday I shall have some gold, I hope. "Is that what you really want from me, Billy, is my gold?" "No, I do not want your gold. All I really want from you Skip is your friendship as I have said before. I have no desire to have that-which does not belong to me. If someone were to offer some gold to me as a gift that would be different as I would not take it from a friend if it was not given to me as a gift."

Later in the afternoon, of the following day, a sailor was-sent topside to stand guard in the crow's nest. He hollered his signal out loud and clear to the crew standing on the deck below. Land ho, land ho, land ho, off the port side mates!" The outer islands and shoreline of Boston were coming into view on the horizon. The sailors on deck below bellowed out to everyone on board, Land Ho! As they continued doing their many chores aboard the Shamrock getting her ready for the port of Boston for two more hours, the Shamrock would sail into Boston Harbor to unload her stores of cargo and passengers. Billy could not wait to return to his cabin below deck to give Henry the good news. He had overheard Vinnie telling another passenger topside where he was going to be staying for the next day or two before venturing off in the New World to find work as a smithy.

"The Trinity Inn," Billy told Skip that he had heard Vinnie tell someone. It was a large bed-and-breakfast located not far from the waterfront." Skip had informed Billy that he needed someone he might bond to while in the new land. He needed someone to talk to in the future about familiar places from his past, and to stay close to for the meantime, hidden out of sight of course until he was able to find a safe way back home on another ship sailing eastward toward Ireland.

The bright blue light of day was quickly fading to a dark shade of night when the Shamrock finally sailed safely between the Isles of Scholes and into Boston Harbor. Skip sat atop the beam in the scully way as Vinnie made his way topside to have a look at the new world that he was about to make his new home. As soon as Vinnie was out of sight, Skip transposed into Vinnie's cabin and quickly opened up the two locked trunks. He looked inside the clothes and blanket trunk to see if there was room for him to hide again, and lucky for him there was. He wanted to look firsthand and not use his magic vision to guarantee his closeness to Vinnie in his travels. Back to Billy's cabin, Skip went in a flash. He wanted to tell him he was prepared to leave right away with Vinnie by hiding out in one of his trunks, but Billy was nowhere to be-found in or around his cabin. He was off doing his cabin boy chores aboard the ship and helping the crew secure the Shamrock to the dock. All crewmembers were readying the Shamrock to dock at the wharf. Billy was also hard at work helping the ship's cook prepare to entertain the harbormaster of Boston with a great feast.

The Harbormaster's Feast was a tradition started by captains of ships long ago to show their respect for the hospitality of their visit to the many harbors around the world. When the bow and aft lines the crew secured tightly to the Warf, Captain Drake sent for Billy to go ashore to scout out the city for the whereabouts of the harbormaster and his family. He was to bring them back to the Shamrock for a most magnificent harbor feast.

Skip urgently took position in the crow's nest, visually too locate Billy's whereabouts on the wharf or the deck below, but to no avail. He was nowhere to be-found onboard the Shamrock's deck. Skip saw Vinnie walking back toward the ship guiding two very strong looking blokes, that he must've hired, tagging along behind him like puppy dogs on a leash to help him fetch and transport his trunks to the hotel where he would be staying for the night or perhaps several days.

CHAPTER TWENTY

Skip's Cry for Gold

Suddenly Skip's heart filled with instant grief, an unexpected amount of sudden anguish and loneliness took overtook him, as he stared down from the crow's nest at Vinnie. This is the same heart wrenching pain that he had experienced before, when he first heard the terrible news, about his missing parents. His grandfather told him that his parents would most likely never be able to come back home. A large film of sadness immediately swelled up in his tiny eyes for the new friendship he had found in Billy. The sadness caused a couple of beads of moisture to form and fall from his tiny eyes and into his hands. The tiny little beads of water instantly turned into bright shiny new pieces of golden leprechaun coins. Several more tears formed and fell as several more shiny golden pieces fell into Skip's little hands. He was very confused about the teardrops. What was this strange phenomenon taken place to him? Why were these tiny tears of sadness flowing from his eyes and turning into precious pieces of gold? Skip quickly placed the bright new shiny golden pieces of coin into his front pocket for safekeeping and took off back down into the ship.

Quick as lightning, Skip transposed to Billy's cabin where he had been staying with him for the last couple of days. There he decided with a heartfelt conviction to leave a couple of his brand-new golden coin pieces beneath Billy's pillow. He wanted to give these to him for having been a true friend and for not demanding all his gold from him. He left a quick thank you note along with the golden coins saying goodbye to Billy, and wished him the best of luck in his many travels.

It was the least Skip felt he should do for Billy. This newfound mortal friend was like a brother, and a mortal friend who did not want his gold in greed, only to help him and his family out of poverty.

Skip had little time to waste on waiting for Billy, as Vinnie would soon be in his cabin. Focusing quickly, Skip transposed into the tight confines of Vinnie's clothing trunk just in nick of time. Suddenly, he was up in the air roughly bouncing along in the trunk in the hands of the two blokes who Vinnie had hired to carry them and transport him to the Trinity Inn. The two rugged blokes tossed Vinnie's clothing trunk roughly into the wagon without any respect for it. Skip moaned aloud about the roughness he felt while being bounced along in the trunk. "Hey! Take it easy with the trunk, will you mates." The two men just stared at one another shaking their heads and shrugging their shoulders, thinking the other had said it. Neither one of them wanted to think a trunk had just spoken to them. They went back to the Shamrock to fetch the second trunk and returned a short time later. Vinnie climbed aboard the wagon with the two men, and they were off down the road towards the Trinity Inn.

The Lamplighters of the night were busily lighting up the early darkness of night by lighting oil fired street lamps along the many main streets and back alleyways in Boston. Refreshing aromas of fresh baked beans filled the night air along with the pleasant smell of fresh baked breads and pastries. Some of the wonderful aromas of the cool night were quite similar to the ones back in Dublin Town, but the new world had very distinct and different aromas all its own.

Skip watched the magic of the night unfold with his enhanced vision from inside the trunk. Young mortal lasses of Boston were out in numbered force and seemed to be smiling, laughing, and enjoying the warm evening air of their homeland along with its many fragrances. They all looked as if they were joyfully happy, which made Skip feel even more lonely. Vinnie happily watched the nightlife of Boston unfold before him, and took great pleasure in all the new sites of the new world and his new beginning. He felt extremely happy to have finally arrived, and was looking forward to a new life he was about to head out on.

For a split second, Skip made believe he was back home in Dublin Town traveling along beneath a wagon and listening to the pleasant sounds of the night. The enjoyable clicking sounds of horses' hooves mingled with wagon wheels coming together with the cobblestone roads, made Skip experience yet another miserable encounter of homesickness. Sad gloomy tears filled his tiny eyes once again and caused more shiny golden pieces of coin to rain down off his cheeks and into his lap. What was this strange phenomena taking place? Why was this happening to him, in a foreign land, and not when he was back home in Ireland? Every time he drew a sad tear from his lonely heart, a shiny new golden coin would appear. "To be sad is to be rich with your gold," he thought to himself. Why did tears of sadness turn to gold every time he cried? What would happen if there were no more tears left in him to cry? Would there be no more gold left in him to fill his satchel? Would happy tears cause the same results? Would golden pieces clatter down like pouring rain when he laughed and cried out tears of joy, or were gold pieces only produced from the remorse hidden in sad tears? He had no idea what was taking place, and it made him worry.

Oh, how Skip missed his Grandma Broom, especially at a time like this when he had so many unanswered questions he so desperately needed answered. Skip had many questions about being a leprechaun living in a mortals' world. He felt extremely lost by not having anyone around to listen to his every need and to help him with so many unanswered questions he so desperately needed answered just about being himself. The thought of this teary incident revolved around and around in his mind, over, and over again, almost making him sick.

Suddenly, the wagon came to an abrupt stop. The pleasant sounds of the night, which had teased Skip, instantly vanished into the night. The trunk Skip was in they tossed roughly down to the ground, and Vinnie's trunk of tools they hammered down hard on top of the trunk Skip was hiding in. The sudden hard force twisted the cover open to the trunk he was in, allowing him to peek out a wee bit without having to use his special powers.

Just above the door to this Inn, hung a large red, white, and blue sign reading the Trinity House, and not the Trinity Inn, he thought it was supposed to be. The building was a magnificent wooden mansion built right in the middle of many larger tall brick buildings. A large cobblestone walkway extended from the road all the way up to its lovely porch that wrapped around the building with lovely columns supporting its roof and laced with a splendid spindle handrail in between the columns. From its main doublewide French door opening, a red carpet ran all the way across the porch and down the stairs to the cobblestone walkway. The walkway had two rod-iron railings on each side of it and down to the sidewalk beside the road.

Inside the French doors hung a beautiful crystal chandelier lighting up the hall and its entryway. He next observed a short heavy built balding man with a handlebar mustache come quickly waddling down the walkway like a duck trying to run away from a fox. He wore a poorly made toupee half stuck to his balding head had slid halfway off, hanging in disarray up against a cauliflower looking right ear. Dangling from the tip of his nose, he wore a black pair of tiny half-round half-rimmed glasses. He was dressed in an oversized black suit that sat baggy on him like an oversized grain sack instead of a nice clean well pressed fitted suit. He spoke with an annoying high-pitched squeaky voice as he hollered out to the two big strapping men standing beside their wagon waiting for his instructions. Skip just had to mimic him. "This way please gentlemen", he hollered out annoyingly. "This way to Mr. McDougal's room, hurry now, hurry now!" Skip could not help but to chuckle to himself by hearing such a funny voice come out the mouth of such a short fat husky man.

The two big men standing beside their wagon looked around to see where the voice had come from. The little round fat man just glared at the two of them with daggers in his eyes filled with annoyance, thinking one of them had made fun of his voice. Skip quietly chuckled to himself again as he bounced along inside the trunk they carried to Vinnie's new accommodations. When the two men left Vinnie's room, Skip transposed to the top of Vinnie's new bed and looked around Vinnies rented room. "What a splendid room," he thought to himself.

He was sitting on a grand canopy four-poster bed covered with ultra-soft downy filled pillows topped with pillow shams and a wonderful handmade quilted bedspread.

Stretching out his wee body on the soft pillow, Skip sank into the fluffiness of the four-poster bed crossing one leg up over the other, and carelessly enjoyed the quiet of the moment. He placed his hands behind his head staring up into the hollow canopy above his head, thinking back on all the long lonely nights he had spent sleeping in the dark on the keg of rum down in the hold of the Shamrock, with only his two ship rat friends to keep him company. He began to think about Billy who had to work so hard on the ship to support his family.

Quite unexpectedly, the door to Vinnie's room opened wide and in waltzed Vinnie. Back to the safety of the trunk, Skip transposed straightaway. He then put the key from his pocket into the lock of the linens' trunk, and as he turned the lid of the trunk began to lift up. Back to the safety of the bed, Skip shot in a flash. Why did he not pay closer attention to other places in the room where he could have hidden?

"What is this?" Vinnie shockingly spoke out-loud, to himself. He reached down and picked one of several shiny golden coins spread out on his blanket in his trunk. Skip had unknowingly dropped them from his pocket in his haste to transpose out of the trunk and back to the safety of Vinnie's bed. He was infuriated with himself for being so clumsy with his treasured gold. Catching a quick glimpse of two huge sets of draperies hanging artfully on the wall behind Vinnie, Skip transposed behind one to hide from Vinnie's view so he might figure out what to do next.

"My gold, my precious gold you dumb bloke". Skip thought to himself, "You dumb bloke. Make your own darn gold, you bloke head". Feeling hopeless, Skip stood behind the drapes staring out at Vinnie with daggers in his eyes as Vinnie held onto Skip's precious gold coin. "Isn't that why you came all this way in the first place?" Skip thought as he became more and more furious with Vinnie. "Go ahead now Mr. Smarty Pants, show Skip how to make your gold so he will be able to finish making his own pot of gold. You cannot do it, can you? You are not even smart enough to come in out of the bloody rain, are you? You cannot even make a dumb bed, can you?" Then Skip suddenly remembered how Vinnie had made the metal sleeve in the Shamrock's galley stove to repair the small front jib's mast.

"Where did all this gold come from?" Vinnie was so shocked to find Skip's gold that he began to speak out-loud to himself again. Skip's emotions of wanting his precious gold got the best of him that very moment. His eyes began to swell and well up with tears again, but he made his tears stop by pinching himself to quell his sensitive emotions. What were the new bizarre emotions he was having at seeing Vinnie hold onto some of his gold? What was this sudden required sense of need to protect his precious gold and get it all back from Vinnie that instant? The perplexed feeling frightened him. He had no idea what to do next or how to go about retrieving it back without first getting himself caught. He began speculatively wondering how he might go about getting it back when instantly appearing in his tiny hand, he found several new shiny gold pieces of fool's gold that magically appeared. Confused at what had just taken place, Skip stared down at the fool's gold in astonishment. A funny strange feeling told Skip this was not gold in his hand, but fool's gold. Without question, Skip knew exactly what he had to do next with it.

With a blink of an eye, the fool's gold left his hand. The several pieces scattered themselves in and about Vinnie's trunk where the real gold had been resting and laid in his trunk waiting for Vinnie to pick it up and confuse him, while Skip's real gold coins returned to him magically. Picking up the gold coin, he found, for Vinnie was convinced of its authenticity by biting into it with his teeth and found it to be the real McCoy. Putting that piece aside, Vinnie slid out another glimmering piece of shiny gold from under the side of one of his blankets. In his searching the rest of the trunk, he found several more pieces of gold scattered in and around his belongings. He wondered ardently where it had all come from. As soon as he could, Skip took back his precious gold from Vinnie, without Vinnie ever being the wiser including the original piece of gold he had bitten into and had set aside to make a pile of his newfound gold. By holding the precious metal, it gave Skip a wonderful feeling of confidence. It was though he was holding onto a security blanket along with a feeling of home that he had never felt before while he was away from Ireland. The gold also gave him an instant warm feeling of power. What was this magnificent radiant feeling coming from these shiny new pieces of gold? Skip placed all his reclaimed gold back into his front pants pocket, making darn sure this time it would be securely safe from now on.

Vinnie picked up every last piece of fool's gold he found, and bit into every one of them, as he had done to the authentic piece he first picked up. "Fool's gold," Vinnie yelled. "Now where did I put that real piece I found?" Vinnie searched high and low for the original piece of gold that he just knew was real. "Blimey, I know my metals, and that first piece of gold I found was real. Now where did I put it?" Vinnie looked over every piece of fool's gold he found, one by one. Being a blacksmith by trade, he knew his precious metals well, and this was driving him crazy. Real gold was much harder like silver, and not easily dented like fool's gold and lead. He threw the fool's gold down onto the floor of his room in pure disgust. Skip held onto his sides as he laughed very hard but quietly behind the curtain trying not to make any noise.

"I am going down to get a bite to eat!" Vinnie said boldly out-loud. Skip looked around the room to see whom he might be talking to, but there was no one around. Skip thought for sure Vinnie had finally lost any wits he had from the mean trick he had just played on the dumb bloke. Suddenly, Skip could see the layout of the dining room of the Trinity House as a picture in his mind. It happened again just like onboard the Shamrock. Once in a great while, he could see Billy helping out the ship's cook or washing the scully way of the ship. Sometimes he saw Vinnie walking on the deck or down the hallway of the ship without even trying to see him.

All of the sudden a vision, similar to the dining room vision he had earlier in the day, came to him. It was a very bad blurred vision of a little girl sitting on a stool, he first thought. No, she was not sitting on a stool; she was sitting down beside a big old fat blurry looking bloke aboard a shabby covered wagon. The wagon looked to be a canvas covered wagon with many pots and pans hanging, dangling and banging around together from on its sides. The man was relentlessly whipping the little defenseless horse with a heavy long horsewhip. He was really trying to make the poor critter pull the heavy burden he had hooked her up to faster and faster as he lashed out at her already and soar welted up raw looking back with his whip. It looked to be a load that two strong healthy workhorses should be pulling, and not such a little defenseless horse. She whinnied out in pain with every harsh lash of his whip.

In the back of the wagon, Skip could not fittingly make out the blurred vision of a small boy sitting, or lying down in a very large birdcage that surrounded him along with many tonic bottles rolling and rattling about, scattered everywhere across the back of the wagon. The blurred vision made it look as though the boy was trapped like a circus animal confined to the insides of the cage, or was it a small boy at all that he saw? The darkness of the evening made it mostly impossible to distinguish. He was not able to see particularly the children's or the fat bloke's true facial identity, as he could barely make out their very fuzzy outlines. The strange vision soon slipped away into the darkness from Skips' bewildered mind as fast as it had suddenly appeared. This vision made goose bumps the size of small grapes appear all over his body. He could only imagine just how it must feel to be in a cage and not be able to escape from it. He knew it must be the most horrendous feeling a beast or leprechaun might ever experience.

The rumbling sound of his hungry stomach growled and eased Skip's thoughts of the vision he had just experienced. His thoughts quickly went back to his hunger, and the vision of the dining room quickly came back to him. What was the new strange power he had so recently developed? How was he going to be able to control it to his advantage? His stomach growled angrily again at him. Never mind these new powers for the moment, Skip thought to himself, for it was time to eat. He transposed to a small ledge he observed well concealed from the mortals yet out in the open above the dining hall. There on the shelf surrounding the dining hall, he could conceal himself from everyone eating below. What a splendid place to hide and eat his meals without being alone. There would be no better place for the Queen of England or the King of the Leprechauns to sit and eat their meals, he thought. Below he saw a grand smorgasbord spread out before him on the tables just waiting for him to sample! He was proud of his new abilities to see places he had never seen or been to before. Sitting high above everyone, Skip felt like he was King of the Leprechauns at that moment.

He sat there with a happy smile spread across his face, and thought of many ways to which he could please his growing need to play silly pranks on everyone below. Across the hall on the shelf similar to the one he was on, sat a miniature table and chair set above the baby grand piano. It had two miniature mannequins sitting at it as if they were eating. Poof, now Skip was sitting at the little table and chair set. He mentally summoned the small table and chairs from across the hall for his own use. He left the two mannequins sitting side-by-side looking out over the dining hall atop the shelf. Skip would act like a mannequin, so not to be-caught if someone below were to look up at him. He could look stiff with a forced grin on his face, as did the ornamented dolls across the hall. He felt high and mighty sitting there amongst the many mortals of the Trinity House.

He summoned a set of silverware from a table a waiter was setting up for the next guest. The waiter looked dumbfounded when the silverware he had just placed down disappeared from the table right after he turned his back to fetch another setting. The antics the waiter went through looking for the missing silverware caused Skip to chuckle so loud that he had to duck beneath the tiny table on the shelf. He laid there until he could compose himself then righted himself up off the floor and cleaned the dust from his clothing with a blink of an eye. The pleasant music coming from the baby grand piano, the friendly clatter of silverware touching plates, and the ease of conversations taking place in the hall soothed Skip's loneliness for home for the time being.

Soon Vinnie came strolling in through the large dining room's French doors. It was now time to get even with the dumb bloke who had so unjustly taken him away from his homeland of Ireland and his grandparents. He would cause a great scene to happen to this bloody bloke by making his dinner plate land straight away into his lap when he took his first bite of food from it. No, he would have the waiter spill the tray of food he was carrying all over the dumb bloke like it was an accident. Nah, Skip did not want to make Vinnie angry with the waiter or himself, as he did not really know he was there. He did not want to make Vinnie angry for he needed someone perhaps to live with until the right moment of time or opportunity came along for him to return home safely to Ireland.

Suddenly Skip rose to his feet as if he had springs attached to the soles of his shoes. He had a most nervous looking appearance about him as he stared down toward the door leading into the dining hall's kitchen. Vinnie looked to be quickly stepping back toward the dining rooms hall entrance door and away from the waiter, coming out the door from the kitchen. The waiter was carrying the devil himself and was sprawled out lying on the serving tray he was carrying. Neither Skip nor Vinnie could imagine anyone in the world carrying around the devilfish on a serving tray and preparing it to be served to some unsuspecting guests. The waiter was carrying two enormous bright red-hot steamed lobsters that looked like they had just emerged from the volcano of hell on the tray ready to serve. The waiter gracefully placed them down on a table in front of a young couple who were sipping wine and eating bread and cheese. He placed one red devilfish each on their empty plates. Vinnie appeared extremely nervous seated by the host at a table right next to and across from the young couple. He sat nervously watching the young couple break open their lobsters and enjoy eating them.

Lobsters in Ireland, according to legend and old wives' tales, are one of the many devils who live in the vast oceans of the world. Both Vinnie and Skip knew the devilfish was worse than the dreaded banshee herself. The Banshee would howl and sing out her horrifying melodic song of death in the bright of day or in the dark of night, while sailing across the heavens in her chariot of fire to claim her prize of the dying both young and old alike.

The lobster was one of the devils who lived in the vast sea surrounding Ireland. Then there came in another waiter from the kitchen with another devilfish lying red hot on the tray along with a large hearty looking steak served to other guests.

Vinnie watched as the second waiter brought his tray of food to a couple sitting at a table far across the large dining room. Both Skip and Vinnie watched in awe as the waiters delivered their trays. Skip so nervously excited had stood up tall on the shelf nearly hitting his head on the hall ceiling, watching what was going on below without using any precautionary measures at all. If anyone below was vaguely observing the overhead, he or she may have spotted him standing there. The two couples who receive their lobsters looked extremely overjoyed at one another, especially the young lass.

In Ireland, the lobsters from the Sea were the devil from the deep blue depths, except for old King Neptune himself. If a lobster caught by an angler's net, while he was out fishing, it would cause great havoc by destroying the fisherman's gear. One unlucky fishing man had an index finger taken off by a lobster, so the story goes, that the lobster devil smiled at the man as he ate his finger!

Why would anyone in their right mind want to sit down at a nice table in an exclusive inn and eat a gross looking lobster? Then there came another waiter out the kitchen door carrying a platter of food with a rather funny looking new appearing fish on it. It had a very large black stripe painted down along its scaly sides. "Your, stuffed striped bass, sir, and your steamed clams, ma'am," said the waiter to his guest. Neither Vinnie nor Skip was too impressed with the strange looking foods the people of Boston and the new world were eating in the dining hall of the Trinity House. Vinnie tried to be quite safe with what he ordered to eat, steak, fresh vegetables, and a potato. He left the striped fish, clams, and the lobsters to the other people who did not know any better than to be ingesting such things as the devilfish and the other strange fish from the sea.

America was a new land where he would experience many new things he would have to abide to. It had a variety of people, new customs, and many new items of food to eat. Why, would anyone in his or her right mind want to eat a devilfish that is so evil? Vinnie thought they must want to die an early death if not right this night. He shook his head in disbelief as the girl at the table across from him broke off a lobster's claw. The girl sitting to the left of him ordered shrimp. Oh, how small these shrimp were, compared to the ones caught off the grand Ireland coast. These shrimp were baby shrimp compared to the ones he was accustomed to ordering at the pub back home in Dublin. Vinnie carefully cut up his steak and glanced over several times toward the woman who was eating her lobster.

Skip took advantage of this opportune time to help himself to a small portion of Vinnie's meal. He took some potato, squash, and the steak Vinnie had already cut up on his plate. He left behind a funny looking little red stick sticking up out of the remaining steak. Next, he helped himself to half of Vinnie's bread, leaving behind the one piece of bread Vinnie had not yet buttered. Why should he have to butter a piece of bread if Vinnie had already done it for him, Skip thought joyfully and mischievously to himself!

Vinnie reached down to his plate for his buttered piece of bread and began to wonder just how tired he was from his long voyage. The food he was eating, seem to be disappearing right before his very eyes. He thought he had only taken a bite or two of steak and vegetables, but the amount on his plate looked greatly smaller now. The piece of bread he knew he had butted was missing from his plate along with several small pieces of cut up steak. He looked down on the floor under his table to see if he had dropped anything there. Focusing the remainder of his time on his hunger, Vinnie devoured every last crumb of food left on his plate before retiring to his room for a good night's sleep.

Skip sat quietly at his little table on the shelf enjoying the evening. Captivated with the large crowd seated below him, he enjoyed every piece of food he scrounged from Vinnie's dinner plate. Still not quite satisfied with his meal and still feeling hungry, he looked out over the small captain's railing he was sitting behind for more food. Below him on the many tables sat a wonderful smorgasbord. It intrigued him that the devilfish had not killed anybody who ate it. He wondered what it tasted like and if it would make him sick if he tried a piece. He watched a young lass break and pull the meat from out one of its claws, placed the lobster meat in some hot butter, and then ate it. He wondered if the hot butter would kill any of the Lobsters spells, or the hot water the Lobsters had ben boiled in to kill their spells. Skip sat there watching how one would eat a lobster.

A waiter came out from the kitchen door carrying the granddaddy of all devilfish steaming red-hot upon his tray. It looked as big as he was. There could not possibly be another Lobster its size left anywhere in the world. The young waiter carried the huge crustacean to a grumpy looking old sailor sitting in the far corner at a table alone. He looked a mess for he had spilt ale all down the front of himself. He sounded drunkenly gruff as he ordered the young waiter to put his lobster down on the table in front of him with a mean voice, before the young lad had a chance to get to his table. Skip laughed out loud, wishing Billy the cabin boy was able to be there with him to share in what he was about to do next. Then again, he wished to be still on board the Shamrock sharing Billy's cabin with him on a return voyage back home to his beloved Ireland.

Suddenly, the larger lobster stood up on its long tail as if it was still alive, and politely bowed down to the old sailor at the table. His eyes grew the size of sauces at watching the lobster. He shook his head and reached out to grab it before it could get away. Skip fell over backwards in his chair landing on the shelf and bursting out in uncontrollable laughter. Happy tears began streaming down his cheeks like rain drops, and the sound of golden coins clanged about as they hit the shelf floor stopping Skip's laughter instantly. He became as still as a statue after hearing the sound of the many golden coins clanking about his head. He quickly bounced to his feet and picked up the coins before they had the chance to roll off the shelf and placed them snugly into his front pockets which were about to burst at their seams.

By the time it took Skip to compose himself, the drunken old sailor had grabbed his getaway lobster from standing on its tail and placed it back down on his plate. It stood a second time to bow to the old sailor, as Skip performed his magic again. This time the old drunken sailor spit ale out of his mouth as he hollowed to the young waiter to return. When the young waiter returned, the old sailor loudly yelled out, this Lobster not cooked properly, and is still alive. The young waiter assured the old gent that his lobster was cooked, and that it was very much dead because it is very red color, and then turned back towards the kitchen. Skip made the lobster stand again and when the old sailor reached to grab it, he made the lobster's claws snap open and shut several times at the old man. This made the old man fall over backwards out of his seat screaming and yelling for the waiter. Skip fell out of his chair again as he was laughing so hard trying not to make any noise as he rolled back and forth on the shelf with happy tears of joy flowing out his eyes. He could not help but laugh and gather his golden coins until finally he was able to control himself.

The young waiter returned disgruntled with the old sailor, helped him up off the floor, and back into his seat. The waiter then tore off the lobster's head, broke open its tail, and ripped the two claws from off the lobster's body. The old gent said thank you, as the young waiter headed back to the kitchen. Skip watched as the old drunken sailor ate one claw of meat from the lobster very carefully, and then quickly devoured the rich white meat from its tail. When he reached for the second claw to eat, Skip made it snap at him. This was just too much for the old gent to handle. He pushed his chair out and headed for the door. Skip had to laugh, for he heard the old sailor mumbling to himself that he was going to quit drinking. He thought the darn lobster was trying to get even with him for eating it.

Skip summoned the lobster meat from the lobster claw left behind on the table by the old sailor. He summoned only the meat from the claw and left the hard shell on the plate. When he bit into the meat of the claw, he almost broke a tooth. He bit down hard onto the flex bone cartilage of the lobster's claw left in the meat, and thought for sure the devilfish was playing his own prank on him. He chuckled when he realized what he had done and what had happened. The joke was on him this time for not realizing there was a cartilage strip inside a lobster's claw. Eating his fill of assorted foods from the many tables around, Skip finally satisfied his gnawing hunger and fulfilled his curiosity for the taste of the devilfish.

It was getting late when Skip figured it was time for bed and a good night's rest. He wanted his rest in anticipation of what Vinnie might have in store for the next day. Envisioning Vinnie's room, he could see it was dark and quiet and saw Vinnie asleep on the four-poster bed with his head resting comfortably on one of the two very large down filled pillows. Transposing to Vinnie's room, he quietly stood beside the bed with Vinnie fast asleep in it. He took the second pillow off the bed and placed it down beside the four poster bed between the bed and wall for his own bed. He fell fast asleep, keeping a listening ear open just in case Vinnie was to wake up early.

It had been a long night since Skip had left the security of the Trinity House. He had spent most of his time drifting from room to room and out into the hall, seeking people out to play his silly little pranks. He had his best fun the first night at mealtime on the narrow shelf overlooking the dining room playing his tricks on people who were sober. There had not been another drunk around the Trinity House to play a hard serious prank on since the old sailor that first night. Vinnie had come and gone many times on long day trips during those first few days in the new world looking to find a place where he might start or go to work for a business of his trade. Without any luck at all, Vinnie was becoming extremely discouraged.

Skip sat patiently around the Trinity House listening anxiously for word of a ship, a small frigate vessel, or anything that might be sailing back toward Ireland. He heard captains from many different ships in the harbor talk about different destinations around the world, but none going back to Ireland.

Vinnie through conversation heard about many places to the north of Boston where his skilled trade as a blacksmith should be welcomed. Having not heard about any vessels heading back home to Ireland, Skip reluctantly decided to venture forth with Vinnie to find his future. Wherever Vinnie was going, so was Skip, no matter where he went. He felt in his subconscious that he was required to go along and stay as close as possible to him until word came of a ship heading back home to Ireland.

Vinnie ventured north along the coastline of Massachusetts without finding a job, so he ventured further north along the coastline into the state of New Hampshire, and again to no avail for there were no jobs found. Frustrated in not finding any work, he ventured further northward into the state of Maine almost to the Canadian border. Luck in his travels northward, Vinnie did not give up hope, and ventured westward across the state of Maine and through the rugged mountainous interior into the state of New Hampshire. He ventured past the Old Man in the Mountain by way of Crawford Notch, New Hampshire, and over to the Connecticut River Valley. He searched high and low through the small towns and family farms as well as any city along the way. In the end, he began wondering if this new adventure had been a good move for him to take. He did not want to venture out west in the new land to the frontier where he heard of so many people getting all cut up and butchered by the wild savages living there. The story was true, the white man was busy pushing the Indians from their land, and the Indians were fighting back the best they knew how.

From Lunenburg, Vermont, Vinnie ventured south down along the Connecticut River basin through the valley toward Bellows Falls, Vermont. Not finding any promise of work in this area, he cut back across the Connecticut River into the state of New Hampshire again. He traveled down to Keene, New Hampshire. Not finding work there, he went south to Massachusetts to a small town called Winchendon. This would be his last attempt in finding work before heading back home to Ireland.

Skip ventured forth with Vinnie riding on stagecoaches anywhere he could out a sight. When possible, he would ride on top of the coach's roof behind someone's luggage or in Vinnie's trunk. He was becoming as disheartened as Vinnie was to find out just how Vinnie was supposedly going to be making his fortune in gold in this new world.

He had never observed Vinnie crying or shedding any sort of tear before and wondered if Vinnie's tears would turn instantly to gold like his did or if they turned to gold at all. How much gold did Vinnie have? Skip did not see or find any large amounts of gold, only silver, and a few gold coins stored away in his money chest hidden deep in the bottom of his tool trunk made to look like part of the trunk's bottom, and very well camouflaged. Skip kept his eyes and ears wide open to see or hear when Vinnie might start to make his gold. This way he might learn how to make his own gold without tears of sadness or joy. He knew the making of the gold had to do with Vinnie being a blacksmith.

One bed-and-breakfast after another, and farmhouse after farmhouse, Skip went along for the ride with Vinnie in his travels. He laid on hardwood floors in many a bed-and-breakfast, as well as many farmhouses where Vinnie rented a room for the night. He felt extremely lucky when he could lay on pillows or blankets he borrowed from linen closets or would sleep in Vinnie's trunk. He felt more comfortable sleeping out in a barn, and would transpose to its hayloft to get a good night's sleep. Sleeping quietly alone in the barn soothed his ears because he was far enough away from Vinnie's annoyingly loud snoring and breathing.

Massachusetts to New Hampshire, New Hampshire to Maine, and over to Vermont, Vinnie was getting discouraged. From Vermont, back to New Hampshire, and then down to a town named Winchendon in Massachusetts. Vinnie was at his wit's end with the whole idea about making a go of it in the New World. He was ready to throw in the towel and give up this whole ridiculous idea of making his fortune in gold living the good life in the New World, and was getting ready to leave to go back home to Ireland.

Finally, Vinnie found a tiny spark of hope in a small blacksmith shop located on Pleasant Street in the town of Winchendon, Massachusetts. George, the stable smithy and proprietor of the blacksmith shop, was a big tall dark-haired handsome looking man. He had large tan arms of steel, a back as strong as an ox, and a deep laugh as gentle as a wee kitten, had promising news for Vinnie. Luckily for Vinnie, George had an aging uncle living in Greenfield, Massachusetts who was about to take down his shingle of many years in the business. His uncle Charlie wanted to retire from the blacksmithing business altogether, and travel the world with his beloved wife. He was getting ready to sell out his thriving livery stable business, as he did not have any sons or son's in-laws to leave his property and booming business too.

George would have loved his uncle's business, but his family had now sunk their roots and ties deep into the township of Winchendon, and did not want to move away from their friends and acquaintances. He and Vinnie struck up a good friendship right away. George invited Vinnie to stay with him and his family for the night, and had invited Vinnie home with him to partake in a good old New England home-cooked meal as soon as he had time to close up his smithy shop.

In the morning, George would send a letter along with Vinnie introducing his new friend to his Uncle Charlie. He would tell his uncle just what he thought of Vinnie and his credentials from their very short visit that evening. George lived on a small farm just outside town on the outskirts of Winchendon with his wife and children. He had two milking cows, a breeding bull for hire, several laying hens for eggs, a few piglets he was feeding to sell for meat, and a couple of frisky milking goats for making delectable cheese from their milk.

Skip could not help himself from getting extremely excited when he saw George's lone bull out in the pasture behind the barn. He quickly transposed between the large black bull and the tall thick round maple tree growing in the field just a few feet away from the bull, just like back home in Ireland he thought. Looking up into the tree, he looked to see what branch he might want to quickly transpose to after he got the young looking bull all fired up.

"Hey ye bull, hey bull". Skip started yelling at the top of his tiny voice in hope that the mighty bull would take a quick notice of him. He stood his ground jumping up and down in place in front of the massive tree to get the bull's full attention, and it worked. The bull looked up slowly from his grazing and slowly but eagerly began pawing swiftly at the ground beneath his hooves before he charged. The tree shook violently as the bull's massive head came crashing headlong into the tree's trunk. Skip let out a mighty roar just as the old bull back home did, he thought. Again and again, he proceeded to get the mammoth bull all fired up by jumping up and down in front of it, yelling at it, and carrying on until the huge bull came charging after him time after time crashing itself into the tree below.

The harebrained incident made Skip roar with laughter. Finally, the old bull had had enough of this foolish game of punishment he was putting himself through for one day of trying to crush this menacing little annoying creature dead flat up against the tree. The last time the bull's head hit the tree, its strong legs went weak and wobbly beneath him. He stood up after a minute and almost knocked himself out cold on the tree's trunk. He shook his mighty head from side to side to clear the cobwebs, and walked away slowly to continue his grazing in the pasture.

Skip had finally found a smart bull, smart enough to walk away from him and his foolish punishment. Great memories from the past came to his mind that short time while he was teasing the bull out in the field. He could almost feel the deep pain in the roots of hair atop his head when Grandpa Hair pulled him out of harm's way back home when he almost met his doom. Oh, how he wished his grandfather could be there to pull his hair.

He slept out in the hayloft of George's small barn that night. He ate his fill of goat's cheese from the kitchen table, ate some potatoes, and partook in his fill of all the milk he wanted to drink. He sat relaxed on the hay in the hayloft and listened to the quiet of the night on a farm out in the wilderness of the new world. Skip left Vinnie and George alone to converse that evening as he tried to play with the bull outback, the goats, and slept up in the hayloft of the barn.

Skip laid there in the fresh green cut hay, comfortably enjoying the tantalizing aroma it gave off, daydreaming of Ireland and the wonderful smells of fresh cut grass until a cock in the barnyard crowed early the next morning with the coming of daylight. He took his fill of fresh scrambled and fried eggs, cooked potatoes, bacon, cheese, hotcakes, and fresh biscuits straight from the oven magically from the kitchen for his breakfast. He managed a wee morsel from everyone's plate as everyone ate, so no one would be anymore the wiser of his presence.

Early that morning after breakfast, Vinnie caught a ride on a wares-fare wagon at George's smithy shop heading west. The wagon brought an assortment of hardware and needed supplies to the small town stores along the path of the Millers River and points west to Greenfield. The day passed along very slowly for Skip, for the trip to Greenfield was slow, long, and boring. Vinnie, on the other hand, enjoyed the trip along the river and over the countryside, as the wagon crisscrossed along different roads from small town to small town. The teamster driving the wagon dropped off his wares and much needed supplies to the town hardware stores and farms along the way. Vinnie really enjoyed himself by relaxing, sitting back, and taking in all the wonderful scenery along the way. He conversed with the teamster at the reins of the wagon about the area, its people, and their customs. He wanted to get to know the traditions of the people in the new world, their ways of their living, and what they might expect of him being a newcomer to their country.

Skip tried his hardest to ride along under the wares wagon by sitting on a bar strung across between its two large wheels just hanging there. He found it excessively dusty, and he almost choked to death. He tried riding in the back of the wares wagon with its pots, pans, tools, sugar, flour, and cooking wares. The noise of the wares clattering and banging together drove him bonkers. He stuck his fingers into his ears while riding in the back of the wagon all the way to Greenfield, getting ready to transpose to a hiding place when they stopped to unload its wares. It would have been a whole lot nicer for him if he could have ridden right up front with Vinnie and Darrell on the long trek to Greenfield. There he could have enjoyed the beauty of the land instead of concealing himself out of sight most of the time.

George looked almost like a twin to his late father's brother, his uncle Charles, except for a few less wrinkles and countless weary years' difference in age. Charles was a tall dark bronze skinned, handsome looking man, who was a softspoken man just like his nephew George. He had powerful large arms of steel, but unlike his nephew George, he had very graying hair. There were many deep wrinkles scattered about his hard weather trodden face just like a sailor who had been out to sea for so many long hard years.

Charles's wife Bernice on the other hand was a beautiful younger looking older woman. She was a tiny framed woman, the size of a monarch butterfly and just as pretty as one. Charles and Bernice had been happily married for many years, and were as happy as a bushel of sea clams in seawater with their long lives spent together. They were both extremely happy when they found out Vinnie had a sincere interest in purchasing their thriving business. The special letter George sent with Vinnie to his uncle, introducing Vinny to him, pleased his Uncle Charles and Aunt Bernice more than hearing the story from Vinnie himself. Reading the informal introduction about Vinnie pleased them both. George was more a son to his uncle and aunt because they had a chance to raise him after his mother and father both perished in a fire in their barn trying to save their livestock.

George had lived with them for a short two years before striking out on his own at a very young age. Whatever George put pen to paper on in his letter must have been gospel to them both and taken with the utmost of sincerity of their wishes. Vinnie looked to be as good a prospect of any they had ever talked to about taking over their livery business and inn. Charles and Bernice had worked many exhausting days, weeks, months, and years to build their pride livery business and lodging inn. It had taken their precious blood, sweat, and tears of many a blue moon to build such a thriving business, and neither one of them wanted to give it away to any unworthy stranger. They especially did not want to sell it to the stagecoach company for which they contracted to, knowing the way that company conducted their business. The small amount of money the stagecoach company had offered them to buy out their thriving business was an insult to them.

Vinnie did not know Charles and Bernice would soon become a brand-new family to him. Bernice would become a mother to him, and Charles his father that he had lost. Charles taught Vinnie many new things and schooled him in ways he never knew by working with fine metals. He showed him a method of how to melt gold bars down to the thickness of tissue paper in order to cover a dome on a building. He showed him how to mix beeswax and linseed oil for rubbing down and protecting the harnesses they used. In addition, Charles showed him how to make Babbitt bearings using bronze and graphite for the stagecoaches, and many more tricks he had learned over the years.

Bernice taught Vinnie the art of beekeeping for honey to supplement their need for cane sugar when it was in short supply. She had a special knack of cooking, the likes Vinnie had never seen before. To his amazement, she could make several meals for the three out of a single chicken. She amazed him with her many special dishes, bakery compliments, and confectionery goodies. She enjoyed making candy out of the excess honey they did not need and hard rock candy out of cane sugar. She did this to hand it out to the children who frequented the stagecoach inn and stable, and the two made it a practice to hand it out to all the children in the area, even if they were just riding by on a pony with their parents. She and Charles both loved to see the pleasant smiles generated on the children's faces when they ate her candy. They would have made wonderful parents and grandparents, unfortunately the two were not blessed, unable to have children of their own.

At night, Bernice kept herself pleasantly busy darning socks, repairing clothing, or making new garments for both she and Charles as she rocked in her favorite chair beside the fireplace. Charles would sit by the window near her, reading his books about Africa and the many species of wild animals that freely roamed its plains. In another year or two, after Vinnie purchases the stable business from him and Bernice, he would like to take her on a safari to Africa to see all the wonderful animals.

After a fantastic meal prepared by Bernice, the three of them sat at the kitchen table going over what they expected of him before they sold their business to him. Vinny would have to train running the stable in their full presence for the next two years. Learning how to operate the boarding house business to their fullest expectations, and then, only then would they be willing to sell the Inn and Stable business to him after proving himself. With a firm as steel strong handshake and a smile on his face, Vinnie agreed to their hard stringent terms. He had a tranquil feeling in his stomach and a warm feeling in his heart that this arrangement between the three of them was the correct thing for him to be doing.

Skip listened very carefully to the seriousness of the conversation, taking place between Vinnie, Bernice, and Charles in the kitchen as he hid out of sight in the parlor ready to transpose out to the barn if necessary as he sat quietly in Bernice's rocker. He took into account the seriousness of the conversation between the three of them that the stagecoach inn was now going to be his new home for quite some time.

He immediately responded by transposing from site to site around the land while there was still a flicker of daylight remaining. First, he transposed to the top of the big red barn's cupola outback of the inn, and then to the confines of the hayloft inside the barn. He was like a little mad man leprechaun transposing from site to site in and around the boundaries of the inn and stables. He transposed all around the grounds looking to see what he might find of interest to pass his time away during his long stay at the stable. Finally, he transposed back to the front porch roof of the inn.

Next, Skip found a nice warm comfortable safe haven hidden quietly away in the spacious confines of the attic of the inn. This would be his own special place to call home for the time of his stay, and a place to hang his hat until one day he might safely return back home to Ireland. He found an old bed there, many soft blankets, and a couple of old pillows neatly stacked in a cubbyhole closet in the attic. There were extra linens and things put there by Bernice to accommodate any guest who would have to stay at the inn in case of bad weather or to rest themselves between stagecoach stops on their long journey across the state and country. The inn was an old farmhouse been converted into an Inn, had several very large bedrooms for families and weary travelers to stay in, and had a very cozy attic room with an old bed for Skip to sleep on.

Charles's large barn outback was equipped with a stable to house 25 horses, 10 stanchion stalls for cows, a pigpen to house several large pigs and piglets. It also housed a smaller cradle for a few goats to live in so Bernice would have their milk to make her special goat cheese, and a big long attached henhouse with a countless number of nests for free-walking hens to lay their eggs in for her to gather, cook, and sell for a profit.

Skip felt slighted because there was no place for a bull in or around the stable. Without having a bull to play his pranks on, he would have to find other ways to pass his time by playing his pranks on other animals around the farm or wild ones in the field, while he waited for word to come about a ship sailing back to Ireland. He had a strong deep feeling of need inside him that he had to stick close to Vinnie's side no matter what the reason might be until the right time came for him to leave. He did not understand why he had this special need, but he did and knew he had too desperately stick close to him. Maybe it was just common sense that Vinnie would become all melancholy about Ireland and want to return, back to his homeland very soon. If so, Skip wanted to be right there beside him and ready to go along for the ride back home to his beloved Ireland. He only wished his melancholy about missing Ireland would happen to him sooner than later, as he was becoming more and more homesick with each, and every passing day.

CHAPTER TWENTY-ONE

The Long Stay

The adventure to the new world was becoming monotonous. All he could think about was going back to Ireland. He soon realized Vinnie did not need to go back home to Ireland because he did not have any family left back there as he had. He only had a few friends scattered here and there about the countryside. He knew the most important thing next to living was to protect his precious gold made from all the happy and sad tears he had shed. He knew there would be more gold to come, for his satchel was nowhere near as full as his Grandpa Hairs' or other leprechaun's satchels were. The second most important thing for him to do was to stay out of trouble and not carelessly get himself caught by a sinister mortal. If that were to happen, he would never go back home to Ireland and never see his grandparents ever again. That would kill him and probably them too, if they had not already gone to the other side of life by the wicked banshee.

Several more weeks passed away before Skip built up enough courage to try his ever-growing need to use his magical powers. Skip becoming overly brave one day, too comfortable in this new environment, Skip transposed to the top of the big red barn out back of the Inn in broad daylight. Like a yo-yo on a string transposing up and down from the rooftop to the ground several times in quick succession, he should have known better for there were many mortals standing around the stable grounds moseying in and around waiting for Vinnie and Charles to exchange one tired team of horses for another to pull the newly arrived stagecoach.

With more courage than brains at times, Skip was bored out of his wits, so he placed himself on top of the ice chest in the inn's kitchen. Bernice was standing at the counter preparing lunch for Vinnie and Charles at the time. He was feeling courageously brash atop the ice chest and crossed his legs one flung up over the other, with his arms neatly folded up tight against his chest. He daringly sat there with a devilish smile painted wildly across his young aging face and stared at her with confidence because she had her back turned toward him. He thought he was quite the cat's meow, sitting up there in the wide-open spaces of the kitchen without someone seeing him. He was ready to transpose back to the protection of the attic ifs Vinnie, Charles, or Bernice began to turn around, or someone surprised him by coming in through the side door of the kitchen.

He frequently found himself outdoors sitting down and hiding beside the roadway near and close to town or hiding behind a very large old oak tree close to the one room schoolhouse. Hiding there, he would make the sounds of angry bears and wild boars ready to attack their prey. His silly antics scared the dickens out of several school aged children returning home on their long walks from school. He laughed when the children screamed and ran away home as fast their little legs could carry them. One day, one of the bigger boys in the group picked up a big rock and flung it as hard he possibly could in the direction of the loud noise. It almost hit Skip directly in the head only, tipping his hat up and surprising him for not paying more strict attention. Skip, deciding after the large rock came quickly whizzing by next to his head that this kind of foolhardiness was not worth losing his head over. He decided never to try that prank again or ever to scare the children, at least not for a little while.

Skip found it very hard to stay out of mischievous trouble. He did not want to jeopardize his freedom captured by a quick acting mortal. The harder he tried to stay out of trouble and keep to himself, the more mischievous things rambled throughout his itchy mind. He wanted to play more silly pranks on the farm animals at the inn and the rabbits, squirrels, deer, and other wild animals of the forest and fields.

CHAPTER TWENTY-TWO

Vinnie's Hard Work

Vinnie did not have the time or need to get into any more trouble than he already was in. He had his own sort of trouble brewing trying to manage his way through life in and around Hampshire County visiting the many farms there. He kept extremely busy repairing farmer's broken down equipment he had taken back to the smithy shop, and returning it back to them as a service to the farmers in the area. When he was not out at a farm shoeing horses, he was busy back at the forge in the blacksmith shop in front of the barn making more horseshoes. He had to make different horseshoes for the many different sized workhorses, carriage driving horses, pleasure horses, and stagecoach teams.

Early one bright sunny morning while Vinnie was out in the barn doing one of his many chores milking the cows, Skip transposed to the loft of the barn above him and wondered what he might do to entertain himself for the day. Feeling very mischievous, he made a fresh cup of milk that Vinnie had just scooped out the bucket from milking the cow turn sour. He spat the sour milk out of his mouth and made a surprised funny face. He could not believe the milk had gone sour that quickly. The funny look on Vinnie's face caused Skip to laugh quietly while covering his mouth. Vinnie immediately picked up the whole bucket of milk to smell it to make sure the entire bucket had not gone sour.

Skip could not stop playing his silly pranks of tomfoolery on unsuspecting people and the animals around the inn, for the nature of it flowed freely in his veins. He kept the promise he made to himself and played no more serious pranks on mortals or the animals that would seriously hurt them. He played mostly simple little harmless pranks to make himself laugh so he would not go totally out of his mind. He never did anything to those who came along by stage or horseback who looked as though they might have word of a ship ready to take him back home.

One day, a young new mother came by the inn. She was extremely proud of her brand-new baby girl and went out of her way to show Bernice her pride and joy of the day held in a basket in her arms. Skip, for a split second, changed places with the newborn baby girl as Bernice glanced down to take a look at the child with a friendly smile on her face. He made the blanket in the basket fluff up so the baby's mother could not see him and winked at Bernice. Oh, how the horrific look that developed upon Bernice's face tickled Skip when he winked up at her when she was looking down. Her face distorted into a weird frown and tried not to scream out in total surprise.

Skip was becoming annoyed with the passing of every day, as he grew beyond patience with Vinnie and the main reason he had followed him into Mrs. Mosher's pub in the first place. Vinnie was not making gold the way Skip had imagined he would. He thought for sure he was going to make his gold using magic with a potion made from pixie dust. He thought he would mix water with dirt and a pinch of fairy dust or by some other special exotic way that only Vinnie would know how to do, and he was going to use it to make his own gold.

He was so angry with Vinnie that he thought he would make all of his wealth disappear from the hidden compartment in the bottom of his trunk. This way Vinnie would have to make some gold to replenish that which he made disappear. Skip was sure leprechauns made their wealth in gold by other means, and not by making shoes all of the time either, although Grandpa Hair was a very good shoe cobbler.

Skip felt time had finally arrived for him to take charge of his own life's destiny. He would no longer have to rely on the help of the mortals who surrounded him for his security and well-being. Maybe it was time for Skip to grow up and venture back to Boston where he would take his chances on hearing about a merchant ship or other vessel leaving for his homeland. No one, not one solitary soul, since he had arrived at the Inn and stable, ever mentioned a word about any type of vessel in Boston Harbor. He felt he stood a better chance by living in Boston than just sitting around lollygagging to himself at the inn.

The accommodations at the Trinity House were more attractive than at the inn, as was the greater variety of foods he had ever tasted or seen prepared in its enormous kitchen, but he would miss most of Bernice's special meals and desserts. He had been amazed at how the chefs at the Trinity House cooked the devilfish by placing it into a big pot of boiling seawater, still alive and squirming. He thought that any type of water was suitable for the devilfish to survive in, and was thankful the legends and old wives' tales were not true, but was it the hot water that drove away all of its wickedness.

He reminisced over the thought of leaving for Boston for yet another several more days. Finally, one night after thinking hard and long, Skip made up his mind to leave the security of Greenfield and Vinnie. He had finally concluded that the time was right in his life to venture back home to Ireland before anything terrible was to happen here in the New World or back home.

He did not want to end up like Vinnie, with no family left alive back in Ireland. He was not going to let this happen to him if there was anything he could possibly do to prevent it. The loneliness growing deep in his lonely heart caused him to have nightmares about missing his grandparents as he had missed his mother for years.

Would it be possible, Skip wondered, to transpose such a great distance all the way back to the Trinity House in Boston from Greenfield? He had transposed all the way across the large field several times with ease and transposed another greater distance down the road toward town to scare the dickens out of the schoolchildren, but all the way to Boston? He wondered if it would be possible for any leprechaun even the chosen King of the Leprechauns for that matter to transpose such a great distance. Skip concentrated with all his might and using his newly acquired powers, he felt coming from his gold, and focused it all on transposing back to Boston, placing himself atop the decorative ledge, which overlooked the large dining hall in the Trinity House. He caused himself a throbbing headache the likes of which he had never experienced before, even worse than from the scotch. He transposed back to the safety of the attic to rest his thumping head and think of another less painful way to get back to Boston.

With eyes, half shut and half open, resting his sick throbbing head down on his soft pillow, Skip experienced another vision. It was of the big man again in the wagon with the two small children. He tried concentrating hard, very hard on the meaning of the vision. It showed the little girl dancing an Irish jig around the cage with the small boy securely locked inside like a wild animal held prisoner. The vision came to him between the loud strong beating pulses of his heart. His headache did not help matters as it blurred his vision well beyond intelligibility. The harder he tried to make the vision more clear the harder his head would throb. The vision slowly vanished as it had appeared. He laid there on his bed wondering what the vision was all about, and what it might mean to him, as his stomach churned from his throbbing headache. Why did the same vision of this ugly looking bloke and the two children keep popping back up in his mind to haunt him? What bearing did this mental picture have to do with him anyway, and what if anything did it all mean to the world? Bad boys put into metal cages because they are unruly and naughty, while good little girls can dance around freely. The whole scene did not help his headache and he finally fell asleep on the softness of the blankets on his bed.

He woke to his clear panic-stricken voice, "Mother, where are you? Where are you, Mother?" The commotion and loud sound of Skip's yelling caught the attention of Charles who was sitting and relaxing downstairs in his favorite soft chair. He had been sitting there lost in his own little world reading a book about the many wild animals roaming the plains of Africa. As soon as he heard the loud yelling, he jumped to his feet and scrambled up the stairs to the second floor of the inn, rounding the corner in the hall and up the attic stairs in a hurry to open the attic door to see who might be making such a loud screaming racket up there.

Skip heard Charles come running up the attic stairs and quickly transposed to the weathervane atop the big red barn outback. He found the light of day had suddenly turned to the pitch-dark blackness of night as he had napped for so long. He tried yelling out to his mother once again without so much as a faint whisper in reply. Could he have been dreaming? He had just heard her sweet soft voice strong and clear as he awoke from a deep sound sleep, or did he? "Mother, where you", he yelled out loud again from atop the weathervane's roof. "Please mother, please answer me." Not a sound could be heard, nothing but pure silence in the dark of night, which surrounded him, and the countryside. The sound of a lone wolf from far in the distance suddenly broke the still quiet of the night. It had begun to howl at the shallow crest of the bright new moon. The lone wolf broke the quiet of the night first, and then an old night owl hooted out softly in a tree not far away from Skip and the barn.

Suddenly to his unwelcomed surprise, Skip heard the dreaded screaming laughter and sorrowful happy crying song of evil from the dreaded banshee in the far-off hills. He was sure she was singing her deathly song and crying out in jubilation and celebration about something. He could hear her singing away at the top of her devilish lungs, singing her song of death in the distant hills and forests surrounding the inn and stable. She scared Skip blind with alarm filling him with fear. Fearing in his heart for himself and others, Skip lost his perch atop the weathervane's small roof on the barn, and went tumbling off the cupola and down onto the big barn's steep slanted roof and tumbled to its end. He rolled off the roof in the still darkness of the night and landed in the wet sloppy mess of the muddy pigpen. The many pigs big and small scattered in different directions trying to avoid and get away from the loud screaming object falling from the sky that landed in the midst of their quiet haven, making all sorts of noises before it hit the wet muddy patch of earth.

The howling banshee continued to sing her song of death as Skip laid there in the slop of the pigpen. Her voice was much louder now than it had been just moments before, and she must be much closer now than she had been. He knew from all the old wives' tales told to him back home in Ireland that he was in grave danger. He was in trouble if she appeared before him. He knew from tales of old, that it might not be him, but someone very near or close to him that may be in grave danger of death lingering not very far away. It may be as close as a family member, a distant relative, or even a very close friend. The displeasing song of the banshee sent rivers of shivers up and down Skip's tiny spine.

He remembered his Grandfather once told him the banshee would lie in quiet wait for her victims, and would only sing her song of death with her screaming screechy voice when she was on the prowl to take her next victim away to the land of no return. She could be heard loudly laughing, and singing her song of death all the way across the heavens to the other side of death in her flaming chariot of thunderous fire, especially when she had a firm hold of her victim in her clutches, and had them securely trapped aboard her flaming chariot.

The situation was much worse than Skip had first imagined as loud screams of many banshees singing suddenly filled the quiet moonlit night. Skip's blood turned hot boiling cold, cold as the melting snows of spring filling a mountain stream, making him feel all the more frightened deep down inside. He thought there was only one banshee in the world, but he could hear the screaming songs of many of them singing in the distant hills. He thought instantly of his poor missing mother as she had called out to him in desperation and fear of the banshee. She must be one the banshees were after. He thought for sure it must be her, and that must be why she was calling out to him. "Where are you, Mother, show me where you are, please!" He felt more helpless now than he had ever felt before. He knew he was too far away from Ireland to do her any good and be able to protect her from the banshee. He had no way of helping her, especially now that he was an ocean's distance away. Even if he was lucky enough to find a ship to transport him back home to Ireland, it would be too late for him to save her by the time he would arrive back there.

Skip slumped over in the middle of the smelly slop behind the barn crying a river of tears in anguish over his lost mother. Before long, he realized his lap had many glittering coins reflecting the light of the moon up into his eyes. There were too many gold pieces in his lap to carry in his front pockets now, so he took his hat from off his head and filled it with his golden coins. He retrieved all the gold from his lap and from the slop, and with the blink of an eye, Skip cleaned himself up and was standing outside the pigpen.

With the ever-growing power he just received from his new gold, he could see with his inner mind's eye, whomever it was who opened the attic door in such a rush had gone back downstairs and satisfied there was no one there except for the storage in the attic. Charles thought for sure his wild imagination must have been playing tricks on him by reading too much about the laughing hyenas of Africa. Holding his precious wealth of gold firmly, Skip transposed back to the comforts of the attic. He sat there lonely as a church mouse on a cold winters' night, all alone on his bed sulking.

Bernice had just filled the inn with a wonderful aroma of her cooking for the evening meal, along with her specialty breads and pastry goodies. Skip never missed out, on any of Bernice's cooking especially her desserts, but tonight he had no desire for them. He was extremely sad and very concerned over his mother's well-being. Why were so many banshees screaming and singing all at the very same time? Was it his mother they were after or could it possibly be the crew of the Shamrock going to meet their doom like his father and grandfather did when they were aboard their vessels and never returned home to port? Maybe it was the she-devil, the most dreaded pirate of all after the Shamrock. She was a heartless half woman half monster without mercy for anyone including small children, and had found a way to attack the Shamrock. Oh, how it bothered Skip thinking Billy might have to walk the gangplank. Seeing they were so close, maybe it was Vinnie, Charles, Bernice, or himself. Skip had been so concerned about his family and Billy that he had forgotten all about his newfound family of mortals and hadn't given any of them any thought at all.

"Leave them all alone you wicked witch of death, pain, and agony. Go away from them. Be gone with you. You she devil of death." Skip laid dreadfully awake all night listening and shivering with fright, wondering who the banshees were after. The dreaded devils had no enemies that he knew of, so he was sure he had no control over their powers, only the ones she was after. A transparent vision of Vinnie's future happiness came somehow to his searching mind in a half vision that night. Vinnie's future looked both full and bright to Skip, but wait. There was a dark side to this happy half vision, a dimness of some sort, a ghost-like silhouette of sadness shadowing Vinnie's happy heart. Oh, how Skip wished at that very moment that he had full use of his new magical powers. He needed a true working knowledge of them, at least to know how to use them properly. How exasperating it all seemed to him, and it was just not fair.

He had to lie perfectly still on his bed to enable him to see and observe tiny fragmented pieces of the future. Many visions came to Skip at different times of day and night. They would briefly appear in a haze, and then vanish instantly so quickly they did not let poor bewildered Skip see the worst of life to come or life's happiest times. Why could he not control the new special powers he was slowly receiving, one little tiny slice of power at a time. Oh, how he wished he were back home in Ireland so his grandparents would be able to take this heavy burden of confusion off his shoulders. He knew they would be able to explain how he should go about using his new special powers, and possibly help him solve the mysterious disappearance of his mother.

He stayed strictly to himself like a lonely hermit, hidden away up in the attic of the inn and totally depressed. He had no desire to play any tricks or pranks on the goats, pigs, or cows around the stable by moving their feed bins on them or their water buckets, which Skip usually thought was fun to watch. He speculated about the safety of his missing mother, and the health and well-being of his grandparents back home in Ireland. He did not want to leave the inn and was afraid he might miss the mention of a vessel sailing back to Ireland from a passing wagon, rider, or stagecoach. He did not care who brought the word, he just wanted to hear it. He had ventured away from the inn too many times in the past, and he may have already missed one or two mentions of a ship sailing back home.

He tried to listen in on Charles and Bernice's conversations they had with all the people on carriages and stagecoaches traveling past the inn that stopped for a moment. They loved to pass out Bernice's homemade candy to all the children who frequent their establishment. Vinnie was no help to Skip as he was always working long hours learning the business of running a stagecoach inn and a blacksmith shop. He did not care about the old sod anymore it seemed to Skip, as he was always busy absorbing information from Charles and Bernice about the inn. He enjoyed sitting in the parlor in the evening while Charles read his books and Bernice rocked back and forth in her rocker mending socks or other clothing. On occasion, they would sing a song or two as Bernice played the standup piano in the corner, singing along with her splendid melodious voice.

CHAPTER TWENTY-THREE

Winter in the New Land

The cold snow of winter grew deeper and deeper as winter pressed on, in and around Greenfield and New England. Skip slowly lost most of his precious need for getting into mischievous trouble because it was so cold and raw outside. He concentrated more in the attic on his self-inflicted loss of family back home in Ireland. He searched the far depth of his young curious mind looking for the unanswered questions to the strength of his still partial powers.

Time passed even more slowly for Skip as the snow became even deeper outside. The powdery snow reminded him of fairy dust and how he wished he had run into a magical fairy in the new world who would be able to conjure up a beautiful flying sailing ship for him to sail back home to Ireland aboard, just like the ones he had heard about that took young leprechauns away. The inn in winter was a very busy place in the early evening with all its guests who stayed over for the night to rest and warm themselves up from the bitter cold.

Bernice kept herself extremely busy by preparing food out in the kitchen for the guests, as Charles and Vinnie were busy entertaining the guests in the power of conversation about things including the wild animals of Africa. While they were keeping busy, Skip kept to himself tucked away up in the attic concentrating on the power of thought, and too busy to notice how full the inn was with its many guests. He was lost in his own little world of quiet concentration, and every once in a great while he would eat his fill from the kitchen, but was never too hungry these days to partake in any deserts. All he wanted to do was use his special powers to search for the answers to life. He did not realize he would never find the answers to life no matter if he had all of the powers of every leprechaun in the entire world at his disposal all at the very same time. Even when his powers all come together for Skip, he will not be able to see his own destination in life, only the small fragmented happenings of others.

As soon as the first snow of winter began to float to the ground that fall, the hair on Skip's young face began to grow. Stubbly little bits of soft hair began to form on his chin and then the rest of his face. It was time in Skip's young leprechaun life to grow a full beard and take on the responsible values of being a full grown up leprechaun, whatever that might mean. He knew from listening to his grandparents that when his beard grew out that he was supposed to be all grown up and grown up leprechauns were supposed to have their full use of all their powers. Skip did not believe, however, that he had all his special powers as of yet, but tried in vain to use them in his search for answers about himself. He felt very sad knowing something very special about his powers was still missing.

CHAPTER TWENTY-FOUR

Springtime in Greenfield

The very first sighting of the first robin of spring brought along with it longer days and warmer weather. It brought along with it the fresh smell of clean air, and a special pleasant cheerfulness to Vinnie, Charles, and Bernice. The three of them seemed extremely happy, and cheerful, as the long hard cold months of winter had finally come to its end. Skip could see and feel just how happy they were, but deep down within himself, there was something very special missing in his life. Skip was as cheerful for spring as the others were, because now he could venture outdoors in the warmth of the sun's delightful rays, but sad with his ever-growing need of Ireland. Skips broken heart for his Grandma Broom, and his Grampa Hair was becoming a great burden for him to carry. It weighed him down with sadness when thinking about them and Ireland all winter, while trying hard to use his special powers to find his own niche and purpose in life. He was becoming extremely homesick when seeing the new green shoots of grass growing up in the meadow. He was homesick for his Grandma Broom to hug him and for his Grandpa Hair to twinge at his hair, along with a thought or two about his missing mother and father. It had been a long, long time since he had last seen his parents. Skips wonderful memories, of the two was becoming shallow and not as vivid as Skip would have liked them to be. With the freshness of spring hanging pleasantly in the air, Skip felt the extreme need to cause mischievous pranks getting greater and greater inside of him with each, and every passing breath of air he took.

CHAPTER TWENTY-FIVE

Sadness Filled the Air

The sad half-mixed vision Skip had one winter's night of Vinnie's happiness and pure sadness came to fruition for everyone in and around Greenfield. Charles and Vinnie had just harnessed up a fresh team of horses for the Stagecoach, which had just arrived. As Charles was leading the fresh team of horses out around to the awaiting stagecoach, he twisted his foot on a loose stone kicked up by one of the horses in the yard. Losing his balance, Charles fell to the ground spooking the horses, and they ran off entangling his feet in their reins. The team of horses dragged him to his death as Charles hit his head on a protruding rock embedded in the roadway before anyone had a chance to stop the runaway team of horses. Broken hearts from around the county spilled with love for Charles at his funeral when they buried him on the small hill just above the inn. Tears fell from everyone's eyes like on an autumn day when trees shed their leaves from their canopy for the long winter months ahead.

Skip hid out of sight from the mortals on the hill and cried himself. He cried watching two big men cry like babies, as Vinnie and George both wept profusely for a man they both loved, as did all the other mortals who came from miles around to grieve Charles' passing at his funeral. Vinnie stood half-strong, and half child-like standing next to Bernice both sobbing with their broken hearts. The world had taken yet another father image away from Vinnie in less than three years. Charles had taken Vinnie under his arm of care that only a father would do to his own son. He had taught him how to heat treat and roll out precious bars of gold into as thin a sheet of bright shiny metal the thickness of thin tissue paper to cover the state's capitol building dome. It had been a good thing at the time Skip hidden away up in the confines of the attic grieving over himself and Ireland, when Vinnie and Charles were busy out in the blacksmith shop with gold bars, for the gold bars may have surely disappeared.

Skip shed many tears of grief, along with all the other mortals, having a strange heartfelt bond with yet another mortal, filling his pot of gold even more. Why had he not been out back of the inn when this dreadful thing happened to Charles? He could have saved Charles life, but no, he was too busy selflessly hiding like an old hermit up in the solitude of the attic. What would happen if that had been Vinnie instead of Charles, then what would he do? Where would he go? The banshees had told him some time ago someone close to him was going to die. Skip had refused to listen to her gruesome song of death, so too protect his loved ones around him from her grasp. It grieved Skip so that it made him sick at heart.

Bernice was devastated with the sudden unexpected passing of her precious soulmate, Charles. She worried that she was getting along in years and without family around, she had no one to take care of her in her later years. The only exception was Charles's nephew George, who lived in Winchendon a great distance away. She knew he had all he could handle with the very large family he had to take care of. Vinnie told Bernice that she would-forever and always, have a home at the Inn with him, even after he purchased the Inn from her. The Inn he said would always be her home, until the time came when she wanted to leave on her own, or when that special time in life came when she would leave this world to be with Charles, above in heaven. She then would be buried with her precious Charles on the hill, and meet him on the other side of life.

The happy part of Skip's vision for Vinnie had already come true for him before Charles' sudden death. Vinnie found himself a beautiful female friend to court, and he helped-out this precious jewel of a person Becky, attractive young lass she was, one day while he was in town fetching supplies. One of the wheels on her carriage became loose and fell off due to a broken wooden cotter pin while he was in Greenfield picking up supplies for the inn. He was just coming out the general store when Becky's wheel came off her carriage and went rolling down the street. Losing the wheel dropped her carriage suddenly to the ground and spooked her horse. The horse started running off down the road with her, as Vinnie dropped everything, running as fast he could stopping the horse before Becky could get hurt. With a little help from a couple of strong young men and a lever, he put the wheel back on her buggy's axle and struck up a pleasant conversation with her. She asked him where he was from because of his strong Irish brogue and where he lived. Somehow, they started seeing one another just before Charles met his dreadful fate that early spring day with the runaway horse team.

Becky grew fond of both Charles and Bernice in the short time she knew the two of them, and they too thought the world of her. What nice friendships can form out of a simple act of kindness between two strangers! Vinnie fell head over heels in love with Becky almost immediately at first sight. He went home that day knowing she was the one miracle in his life that he had been waiting for. One day in the not too far off future, Vinnie hoped she would become his bride. If Vinny, ever built enough courage to spring the question of marriage to Becky, she would probably say yes

Enjoying the softness of his blankets up in the attic and ready to go off to sleep several days after Charles's funeral, Skip experienced another one of his fretted mystifying visions of the mean looking old disgusting bloke and the two little children he seemed to have been holding captive in his company. The vision was as clear a picture as a bright summer's day. Skip had the ability to see all three of them right up close as his vision continued to unveil in his magic psyche. The mean bloke was a flabby fat older looking man with droopy eyes similar to a deadly viper ready to strike out at anything that moved. He looked as if his heart could be made of straight razors and a disposition of an injured grizzly bear tearing wildly through the forest, angry at the world for being born into it.

He was at the reins of his heavy-laden covered wagon rolling along an old dirt road brutally whipping out at his poor horse, as he usually did in all of Skip's previous visions. The poor horse was constantly whinnying in pain trying feverishly hard to please her master. She was struggling with anguish in her cry, and pulling with all her strength at the overburdened wagon hitched to her. This vision showed his true colors of being cruel, despicable, unearthly, and a greedy monster that he was without concern for man or beast. These types of beings somehow seemed to plow their way through life dishonestly. Living off the suffering of other much less fortunate than he and became mixed up in his dreadful dishonest schemes of things. He lived purely for his own satisfaction in life striving to rob the good people of the earth of their worldly possessions of health, wealth, savings, and dignity.

Skip's tiny eyes grew large seeing what he saw with his mind's eye. His tiny chin would have hit the floor of the attic in horror if it could have. He was not only seeing a tiny girl with this beast on the wagon with him, but it was his own true to goodness living mother sitting down beside the cage in the back of the wagon which housed his father. The vision instantly brought back the memory of what they looked like when he was small, and now how they looked today. The two were a lot older and looked very drawn out from the terrible life they were leading as captors of this horrible creature. Skip's father was dressed up in a bright green poorly handmade suit with a green top hat with a tattered shamrock affixed to it for a decoration. He father looked hideous Skip thought.

Skip began yelling out to his mother, in total disbelief to what he was seeing in total disbelief in this appalling vision. He observed her tiny eyes suddenly glance up toward the top of the covered wagon as he called out to her. She tried in vain to see where Skip's wee voice was coming from. Maybe she was just daydreaming and had not heard his voice the first time, and wishing with all her might that it was true. The second time he called out to her, she knew it was real and his voice was clear as a bell ringing pleasantly in her ears. She looked up around the wagon, as a tiny gleeful smile developed on her sad gloomy face. This time Skip's vision of the bloke who was holding his parents prisoner was as strong a vision as it could ever possibly be. He yelled out softly to his mother again, not wanting to make Vinnie or Bernice aware that he was in the attic. This time the expression on her face was grander than it had been the first time.

The cruel monster keeping his parents prisoner did not hear him call out to his mother as she had. He kept right on whipping the poor horse and yelling at her with profanity to make her go faster and faster under the wrath of his torture. Skip's father did not hear his own son's voice calling out to his mother either time. He was a prisoner in a cage made from his own gold, which rendered his powers as a leprechaun useless. The golden cage his father was in, did not allow him the pleasure of escaping, or in hearing his son's caring voice calling out to his mother. The mortal beast used the wish granted him against Skip's father's own powers after the mortal beast captured him. If only his father had first listened to his wife and his in-laws, this whole thing would never have had to happen to any of them. If he had listened, he would not have selfishly ventured back to Dublin Town to partake in more of the forbidden tonic having already consumed too much and he was drunk. Now he was a prisoner of this mortal beast at the reins, due to his own stupidity. Oh, how Skip knew firsthand about the evil forces of the forbidden tonic. If he had only listened to his grandfather, he would not be in the terrible fix he was in now either. Skip's mother felt obligated to stay with his father after the mortal beast captured him. She tried to help him escape from the evil beast, but to no avail. His cage made from his own gold rendering his powers useless, so both his mother and his father stayed captured by this beast of a man until he had no use for them, or until he killed the two.

Skip remembered very well the day his father returned home from Dublin Town stinking of booze and very drunk. Skip was a small-frightened boy when his father demanded to go back to Dublin Town against everyone's wishes. He snuck out the door to get more evil tonic after his mother went out back for the wash. When she came back in, he was gone so she went running off after him, but never returned that horrible night

Without having the use of his magical powers, he walked right up the mortal who was standing by his lonesome beside a street in Dublin Town. Skip's father stupidly reached right into this mortal's pocket and pulled out a nip of evil tonic the mortal had just placed there for a later drink. He was so drunk that he thought he was invisible to this mortal as he laughingly sang out loud and walking up to him before total darkness overtook the town and hid him. The mortal reached out with his right hand and grabbed Skip's father by the nap of his neck causing him to drop his precious satchel of gold from his belt and down onto the ground. The bloke called the Duke reached down and quickly snatched up his father's satchel of gold from off the ground and claimed it for his own. Later on, that evening, he tricked the very drunk leprechaun into telling him some of the precious secrets only a leprechaun would know. The dreadful Duke supplied his drunken father with more and more evil tonic until the drunk leprechaun passed out cold.

The timing of him passing out was the moment Skip's very concerned mother came scurrying onto the scene of her drunken husband who had passed out in his arms. This mortal, the Duke, was climbing in to lay her husband down on a pillow in the back of his covered wagon. Standing in front of her and acting proud, he lied with a slinky forked tongue to his mother. He told her that her husband had granted him several wishes for his thoughtless acts, and for taking his beverages from out of his pants pockets. He had caught him red-handed in the act, of pilfering carelessly through his pants pockets, before he caught this thief.

He then filled her full of lies when he told her how her husband had given him all of his gold out of the kindness of his heart for saving him from a very leathery crowd of extremely angry men. The Duke kept him drunk for the anticipation of a cage made to keep him in, out of his own gold, which would render the poor leprechaun powerless and not able to break out through the powers of his own gold wand powerful magic of the cage built to keep him in.

Afraid to be in deep trouble should he ever break any promise he had made to this mortal while he was drunk, Skip's father went along with him that it was the truth. Not hearing what he had said to the

Duke, Skip's mother stayed with him, as it was her marital obligation to stay with her husband through thick and thin. She would not have full use of her magical powers until her son had all of his gold at hand, and knew that he had not received it all yet due to her lack of being able to use her old powers again.

Display and dismay was their future. They were to live as an attraction in a roadshow against their will. The Duke's medicines were his own non-medical remedies thrown together just to sell to the unsuspecting public. People flocked by the dozens to purchase his healing remedies for themselves and their loved ones expecting miracles. The Duke raked in money hand over fist by using the two leprechauns as an attraction to sell his useless remedies. He would hold up a small satchel of gold at every showing to prove they were truly leprechauns, and they would punish anyone who tried to steal his gold from him. He used scare tactics to make him feel superior to all men.

Skip's vision faded into the dark of blackness leaving him wondering what he could do to free his parents. What could he do to set them free from this evil bloke? He had to tell someone, maybe Vinnie or Bernice, about the very special news he received in the vision without trapping himself. He would have to try to explain to Vinnie why he had to leave Greenfield and travel back to Ireland as soon as he possibly could. He had to act immediately by leaving for home to save his mother and father from their fate of living and traveling around being-exploited by the Duke. Would his Grandma Broom and Grandpa Hair be proud of their little grandson then if he was to find and free their daughter from the likes of this nauseating beast called the Duke? If only he could safely return home to Ireland, and bring them both back with him to his grandparents. Skip felt they would exonerate him for disappearing for such a long time without telling them where he might be off to without informing them first.

Skip made up his mind to leave Vinnie and the safe confines of the inn and stable behind. In the morning, at the very crack of dawn, when Vinnie is out milking the cows, he will personally inform him of his decision. He will be leaving for Ireland on the first stagecoach leaving for Boston. He will go back to the Trinity House and remain there until word of a ship comes to him. Skip sit on the shelf overlooking the dining room and listen to all the people below talk until he hears of one. He will check out all of the ships in the harbor to see if any might be sailing back home to Ireland. On the very same day, at the crack of day, first day light, Skip will be off for home. No matter what happened, soon as the next stagecoach leaving for Boston arrives, he will be on it or in it if it is empty

Transposing to the large mirror hanging on the wall in Bernice's bedroom, he straightened up his jacket, twisted his pants to fit just so, and tilted his hat so that he would look quite debonair. He then tied the fine satchel he made from a piece of cloth from Bernice's sewing room for his gold, and tie the satchel of gold to his new belt that he made of buckskin from an old broken harness. Admiring his suave appearance, Skip was now ready to set out on a new adventure of returning home to Ireland and save his parents from the wicked beast in his vision. His mission was to save his precious mother he loved so much from the tyrant Duke. If his father had to stay left behind as a prisoner of this Duke fellow, he would feel bad, but did not really care. His father's selfishness for himself cost Skip the love of his beloved mother. He felt his powers were strong enough to overcome any bad medicine the Duke might throw at him, and he would be able at least save his mother, from this beast.

CHAPTER TWENTY-SIX

Leaving for Ireland

"Vinnie McDougall, I have to leave Greenfield immediately and must set my feet forward toward home back to Ireland." Vinnie stopped and looked up into the rafters from on the milking stool milking the cow. He looked each side of the cow, around behind him, and then in front of the cow, but to no avail, he did not see anyone. "I am going back to Ireland immediately to try to save my mother and father from that wicked bloke." "Who are you, where are you?" "If I tell you where I am you have to promise me you will not demand a wish from me!" "I promise, I promise. You are a leprechaun no doubt or a good flying fairy with the voice of a ventriloquist hiding way up in the hayloft and trying to play a good trick on my brain."

Suddenly Skip appeared in front of Vinnie from out of thin air and placed himself down beside the milk bucket Vinnie was filling. Vinnie fell unexpectedly over backwards and spilled half the bucket of milk all over himself. The surprised look on his face made Skip smile with pleasure. The cow bolted when she looked back and saw Vinnie lying on the floor beside Skip. She kicked the milk bucket emptying the rest of it all over them, both covered with milk from head to toe. It then headed for the open barn door at the far end of the barn kicking and bellowing out all the way.

Vinnie laid there on the floor looking up at Skip in total disbelief as milk was running down his clothes. With the wink of an eye, Skip cleaned both himself and Vinny up; they looked as if the milk was never been spilt on either one of them. Vinnie could not believe his tired eyes. Skip was chanting at such a fast pace that Vinnie laid there unable to understand a single word he was saying.

"I was as mad as a mad hatter at you Vinnie McDougall because you got me drunk and stuck me in your trunk. Then you put the trunk onboard the Shamrock when I was still fast asleep in your trunk in the middle of the night, and you stole me away and took me here to America. You then had the nerve to try to squash me flat beneath your bunk in your cabin aboard the ship and then, and then the whale jumped up on the ship's deck. Well, I made the whale land on the deck of the Shamrock, breaking down the jib mast, and trashing the ship's side rails."

"Whoa there son, and slow down for me will you so I can understand you?" "Well, I fixed up the front jib sail's mast. What I mean Vinny is this; you made a sleeve for the front jib sail when the pirate ship came sailing toward us firing her cannons. When finished fixing the sail, I mean the mast of the jib sail. Then I let the main sails down to fill them with air so we might have a chance to get away from those bloody pirates. After dark, I went about repairing the broken handrails, and then and then, I managed somehow to get up into the bloody crow's nest, nearly killing myself mind you almost missing the darn thing because of the swaying waves. I transposed up there then, well, well I threw one of the Shamrock's faulty fired cannonballs at the pirate ship's mainmast and knocked it down, and then, well then, I met Billy, the cabin boy. I am sorry he got hurt when that big dumb whale hit him in the head with a piece of the mast. Well then, I fell from the main sail mast one night, drunker than a polecat. Falling, these little feet here suddenly tangled themselves up in the rungs of the crow's nest ladder. While hanging there upside down throwing up all over the deck, Billy helped get me down and out of the tangled mess I was caught up in, and then he brought me back to his cabin to sober me up."

"Then you had the nerve to leave the ship before I could say my final goodbyes to Billy, my new friend. I left him a couple pieces of my golden coins for good luck for a while, until returning for them. I sure hope he didn't spend either of them or give one or both away as I might never get to use my full power as a leprechaun ever if he did."

Unknowingly, you took the two of us to the Trinity House to stay for a spell. The steak you ordered that first night was excellent. Vinny, you should have tried the red cooked devilfish it had a most enjoyable flavor. Do you remember the old drunk sitting at the table all by himself over in the corner? I made the devilfish stand up on its tail and snap its claws at him. It was just the funniest thing to see, as you would have cried your eyes out laughing at him. You took me out of the Trinity House up the coast to Maine and then across the state of New Hampshire over into the state of Vermont. Then we went down the Connecticut River to Bellows Falls, Vermont and then down to the town of Winchendon, Massachusetts to meet George. Then you took u over here to Greenfield to live with you, Charles, and Bernice. I am very sorry about Charles, and the way in which he passed to the other side. I really think Bernice is one of the nicest mortal woman I have ever seen. She reminds me so much of my own grandmother Grandma Broom and she is one of the world's greatest cooks, too. I like your new girlfriend, Becky. I think she is a sweetheart like Bernice and my own mom."

"You see, Vinnie, why I must go then, don't you? I know my mother and father are still alive somewhere back home in Ireland, England, or some other country over there, for I have seen them both together in the visions I have been having. Both my mom and father held against their wishes, by this big fat mean looking old bloke who holds them captive. He has my father locked up in a cage in the back of his wagon like a wild animal, and he makes my mother dance an Irish jig around while he is a trapped prisoner inside a green colored cage. I cannot thank you and Bernice enough for being so nice and generous to me while I have been your guest here at the inn. You see, Vinnie, if there is a stagecoach leaving for Boston, I must be on it. It is a matter of life and death for my parents." Vinnie was speechless, sprawled out on the floor of the barn staring up at Skip in total amazement as he listened to this little elf, gnome, or leprechaun, whatever he was, tell a wild fabled account of his life's journey from Ireland all the way to his new home in Greenfield.

With a nod of his head and a blink of his eye, Skip sat Vinnie back on his milking stool without a drop of milk left on his once milk-soaked clothing. The sudden shock of finding himself sitting upright on the milking stool caught Vinnie off-guard and caused him to catch his balance so he would not fall over. With a total loss for words, he just sat there bewildered and staring over at Skip while he continued to talk. He wondered when he was going to wake up from the incredible daydream he thought he must, be having. Leprechaun's, fairies, elves, the little people of Ireland do not exist, he thought bizarrely to himself, for they are but old wives' tales, he kept telling himself as he sat there staring over at a real-live leprechaun talking to him. Was he not really dreaming?

"Do you remember sitting back at the bar in the pub back in Ireland, Vinnie? When you and your friend Timothy were having a drink together to celebrate your new adventure of coming here to the new world to make your fortune in gold, and that old sailor came storming up to you and your friend stammering and stuttering so loudly, and said he had just seen himself a real live leprechaun? Do you, Vinnie, do you?"

Vinnie just sat there with a blank look on his face staring over at Skip. "Well, Mr. Vinnie McDougall, it was I who was that leprechaun sitting on the rim of that spittoon when he about covered me with his awful tobacco juices running from his mouth." Then Vinnie cracked a smile. He did remember the old sailor come running up to him and Timothy, as they both laughed out-loud at him and made fun about him and his wild tale about a leprechaun. "Now it is time for me, Vinnie, to venture back home to Ireland straightaway. I must leave at once Vinny it is my duty as a son to go. Home and save them both from the likes of that horrible beast of a bloke who calls himself the "Duke". Skip took little time explaining the visions he had had of the beast that held his parents captive. He looked closely into Vinnie's truth-seeking eyes as he tossed him one of his precious golden coins. "This gold piece is for you and your Becky, Vinnie. It will give you both good luck. You must make me a promise though Vinny. You have to promise me you will never spend it or give it away to a stranger. Never give it away to anyone who comes along. I will come back one day for its return and when I do and you hand it back to me, I shall grant you both a special wish." Vinnie reached out to take the gold piece from the little man. He blinked his eyes for a second to clear a sudden blurry vision from them, and when he did, poof, Skip had vanished into the thin air of the barn. He slowly rose to his feet from sitting on the milking stool and finished his chores. He constantly looked at the bright shiny gold piece Skip had left in his possession for good luck.

Vinnie wondered, all the while as he hitched up a fresh team of horses to the stagecoach going to Boston, if he would ever see the little leprechaun again, and if he would see him board the stagecoach leaving for his long journey east. After enjoying a cup of Bernice's fresh brewed coffee with her, he watched carefully as everyone boarded the stagecoach. There was a tall slender man helping his young wife and her mother aboard the stagecoach along with their two small boys, and then the young man boarded the coach himself. He only observed the family and the driver boarding the coach and did not see the likes of the little leprechaun climbing aboard. Had he imagined the earlier visit in the barn, or was there really a leprechaun living in or around the inn somewhere?

Looking up after staring at the bright shiny coin the leprechaun had handed him, he spotted the leprechaun sitting joyfully beneath the stagecoach. Skip was sitting on the cross axle sway bar beneath the rear of the coach, with his tiny little feet dangling down towards the ground and was waving to Vinnie good-bye. He waved back to him and slipped the gold coin back into his front pocket as he continued to watch the stagecoach round the bend and out of sight. The little leprechaun was gone.

He walked around the remainder of the morning in a daze. He acted bewildered doing his chores, and thought about how the leprechaun had wittingly introduced himself to him. He gazed at the many chores he had to do and thought constantly about the little Leprechaun, and what he had said about going back home to Ireland, to save someone. Every time Vinnie hitched up a fresh team of horses to a stagecoach, he would automatically reach into his front pocket and pull out the golden coin. Every time he reached for the coin to see if he was dreaming. This golden coin confirmed he had not had a wild dream about a leprechaun after all.

Sitting at the kitchen table eating his noontime meal, Bernice noticed a funny stare in Vinnie's eyes. "What is it, Vinnie? Are you all right?" He acknowledged he was feeling a wee bit tired. "It is nothing to worry about Bernice, nothing at all. I assure you it is nothing to get overly concerned about; it is just a little something I got from a leprechaun friend of mine". Bernice shrugged her shoulders at Vinnie and shook her head. She thought Vinnie was playing mind games with her. "A leprechaun by golly, a real live leprechaun Vinny, now I have heard just about everything there is" she exclaimed.

Skip's long journey to Boston was a fun filled trip for him. Along the way, Skip saw children playing in the fields that reminded him of home. The lonely feeling of homesickness he had experienced was slowly fading away as he knew he was finally going home. "Home," Skip thought "home, what a splendid place to be, home!" He wondered if Grandma Broom and Grandpa Hair would recognize him being all grown up with his full-grown beard he had grown during his long stay away.

After arriving in Boston, he went straightaway to the docks. He was anxious to explore the harbor for a ship that would be sailing back home to Ireland. He transposed from ship to ship looking recklessly and not paying attention in his searching out every vessel he saw in the harbor. Luckily, for him Skip did not caught, as he tried to find out information on their destinations. He had hoped with all his might one would be heading to Ireland, one that he might immediately stowaway on for a few long weeks on its voyage. From ship to ship, Skip became more depressed. Was not there just one ship he might stowaway on that would fulfill his simple wish? He tried using his special powers to make one of the ships ready to return home to Ireland, but to no avail. He could not change their already made plans.

Sad, depressed, and disappointed, Skip transposed back to shore, and went to the Trinity House to find temporary refuge in his search. Sitting sober faced on the shelf in the Trinity House he sat there overlooking the dining hall. The table and chair set, had been moved from their perch where he had placed them. The kitchen crew must have placed it back across the dining hall to the other shelf that overlooked the baby grand piano. He took back the table and chair set for his own use from across the room, and rearranged the mannequins to side-by-side the way he had placed them on the shelf before.

He sat at his reclaimed table and stared down at the happy faces of people eating their evening meals. He was feeling lonely again, and had no urge to play even the littlest of pranks on anyone. He felt more homesick now than he had when he had his last vision of his mother and father, and was extremely disappointed there were no ships ready to transport him back home. All he could do was sit there looking down at all the happy people as he thought of home, his grandparents, and his poor parents held captive in his visions. He hence taken aback to reality, for he was so certain the first ship he transposed to in the harbor would be the one that would be his safe haven for a wonderful voyage.

He sat on his private shelf watching family after family come and go below. They all looked so happy and full of love sitting together laughing and telling jokes to one another. They all seem to be having a grand old time for themselves, just as Skip used to have with his Grandma Broom and Grandpa Hair back at their kitchen table. Every minute that slipped away seemed more like an eternity to him. Time just could not go by fast enough for Skip until; he found a ship ready to sail home to Ireland.

Finding an empty room to stay in at the Trinity-House, his first night back in Boston was easy. He settled down for a good night's sleep in an empty room after he had taken a wee bit of bread to eat from a table down in the dining room. Maybe the next morning word would come to him at breakfast time by an overheard conversation of a ship arriving in the harbor that would bring good news to Skip's lonely ears. The bed in the empty room was soft, and the pillows filled with soft downy feathers just like his first visit. Skip fell fast asleep and knew no one would enter his room and surprise him because he had placed a large clothing dresser in front of the door for security.

Sleeping only half the night, Skip opened his eyes and thought about the plight of his mother and father back in Ireland. Where were they now, he wondered, where had this monster taken them to now? What could he possibly do all by his lonesome to save them from their horrible fate of living in captivity?

The laws and rules of the leprechauns confused Skip's young mind because he had only half listened to their crucial explanation. He thought he might seek out his grandmother's advice first before setting out alone on this daring mission of mercy. He would not seek help from his grandfather. All Skip would get out of him would be to have all his hair pulled out one strand at a time.

Concentrating as hard he could without giving himself another migraine headache, Skip brought a vision of his mother, father, and the Duke into a blurry vision it was totally distorted as he tried his hardest to clear it up so he might see it better, but to no avail. The cynical monster that led them astray was feeding a fire with some wind-fallen wood he scavenged from the forest floor. Skip saw him waddling towards his wagon like a duck, and began to slam and hammer at the outer steel wrap around the wheel on his wagon with vengeance. The vision was not as clear as the one he had had just three days hence, and suddenly the vision was gone.

Why was he not able to make it more clear as he had previously done, and why had he lost it? Why was he able to have seen everything a few days earlier so clearly, and now not able to control or see the features on any of their faces? What was he doing wrong with his powers? He must see his mother and father one more time. He began concentrating on them as hard he could one more time, but still to no avail. He tried making a vision of them come to him several times in the day that followed but still to no avail. One moment a vision came to him, but it was so blurred Skip could not tell if it was of the three of them, or a pile of rubble piled up out in a field somewhere beside a fire.

CHAPTER TWENTY-SEVEN

Word of a Ship

One night while sitting at his little table sulking, Skip's ears perked up to the sound of a conversation, taking place at a table below him. A young girl with a very strong sweet Irish brogue was talking to someone sitting across the table from her. To Skip, the young lass had the voice of an arc angel, and he had not heard such a lovely Irish accent since he left Vinnie back at the stagecoach inn in Greenfield a week ago. How nice it will be to get back home where most all the people sound alike, and to smell the freshness of her Irish meadows in spring," he thought. The young lass was telling her friend about a ship leaving for Ireland that was sailing into the port of Boston from Africa on her return voyage home to Ireland. He could not believe his ears. The ship she was describing in detail must have been the Shamrock, Skip thought hastily to himself. He could not wait to see her beauty again when she sailed back into the harbor. Had not Billy said the crew of the Shamrock was sailing off to Africa for spices or something like that before they sailed back home to Ireland? He said that it might take a year or better to do. The excitement of the night and joy of her conversation filled Skip's heart with joyful delight.

Skip was astatic, and could not wait to see Billy the cabin boy again. Sharing the cabin onboard the Shamrock with him for the long voyage back home to Ireland would be wonderful. He was exceptionally happy that he was going to see his grandparents again. He did not care if his grandmother chased him all over Ireland, switching him in the hind end with her coarse thatched broomstick repeatedly, for he deserved it after all this time away. He did not care if his grandfather dragged him around by the deep roots of his hair attached to his thick skull to teach him a lesson. A well-deserving one for running off and getting drunk enough to fall asleep in Vinnie's trunk, and for not listening to a single word they both told him about partaking in evil brew. The very thought of holding them both tight in his arms again filled his heart with joy. Now, for the time since he became lost over a year ago, maybe his longing dream of returning back home to Ireland might come true for him!

CHAPTER TWENTY-EIGHT

The Duke

A strong gruff crotchety sounding bold voice, hollering and screeching at the top of his lungs, brought Vinnie out from the barn to see what the commotion was. He was, at the time, making a new set of horseshoes for a waiting horse out in one of the paddocks. Hot and sweltering, Vinnie stood strong and tall in the opening of the half closed barn door. "Are you the smithy, good sir?" The Duke yelled out, "The one I was told about in town to come see at the inn? Are you not the great Mr. Vinnie McDougall everyone in town and all around the countryside are raving about?" "That I am, I guess. I am Mr. McDougall. I don't know of any who are raving about me or my work, but how may I be of service to you?" "I have lost the outer steel ring on a wheel, on my traveling show wagon over yonder, and broke a spindle its hub when it hit a boulder in the roadway. I have a very special engagement to attend that I am late for, I had to make a temporary repair on the road to get the wagon here, but it is in great need of your very special services, I am afraid". "It may take quite some time to repair your wagon wheel along with all my other chores I have to do around here, sir."

"I have no time to waste while you do your other chores, my good man. Money talks louder than chores do, my boy. A splendid tip you shall receive if you hurry along the job right away. I have to make up lot lost time and have a show, to show, sick people to cure, and great medicine to distribute to the needy. I am the Duke! I see all, I hear all, and I cure all sick people!" A very strange, sick wet clammy feeling filled the pit of Vinnie's stomach with a knot the size of an oak tree. There was something noticeably familiar, yet very strangely striking about the man who called himself the Duke, that gave Vinnie a very bad feeling of urgency in his yearning gut.

The poor nag harnessed to his wagon looked half starved to death. She looked to have never seen or experienced the taste or pleasure of a good meal of sweet hay nor experienced a needed feedbag, filled with desperately needed sweet grain to feed on for months, never mind days. She was also in desperate need of shoeing her hooves to help her pull such a heavy wagon. This man who called himself the Duke was nothing better than a jackal in disguise, Vinnie thought quietly to himself as he glanced at the horse's swollen back covered with welts of torn skin and blood.

"Do you have any good horses for sale? I see you have many strong good-looking horses roaming about your paddock here on your farm." Looking how this beast brutalized his poor horse, Vinnie would not be as cruel a man to sell him a horse even if he had one to sell. Far and few were such men as this bloke, who stood brazenly large and boastful before him. He had little use for such conceited men of the world as this duke fellow was, and wished there could be more laws made that would protect critters from beastly men like him. All Vinnie wanted to do that very moment, was to hitch this brute of a bloke up to his own wagon and show him firsthand just what he was making his poor horse do by whipping the daylights out of him the way the marks shown he did on her back.

Vinnie's right front pocket felt much warmer now than normal for the gold piece in it was becoming very hot to its touch on his leg inside his trousers. He thought it must have become hot because he had just been working close to the hot forge in the barn, and it had absorbed the heat of the forge, so he took it out of his pocket to cool it off for a moment.

"A fine gold coin you have there in your hand, my lad. Can I interest you in some of my fine tonics that will help keep you from going bald or getting gout in your older years to come? The Duke recognized the gold coin in Vinnie's hand as that of a leprechaun's gold piece or a very good replica. I am the Duke, I see all, I hear all, and I know all! May I see and feel that special gold coin of yours, my lad?" The Duke reached out his hand to take the gold coin from Vinnies hand, as Vinnie hastily put the gold piece back into the safety of his pocket and out of the reach of such an animal. "I shall start your wagon, sir, as soon as I am finished shoeing this broodmare."

"Time is a wasting, my good fellow! An extra coin or two for you young-man, if you start the job immediately." Just to rid himself of the likes of this beastly pest who called himself the Duke standing before him, he dropped everything he was doing and went straight away to the wagon to begin preparing it to take its poor broken wheel off from the wagon. Vinnie heard a low dainty high-pitched sweet voice of a child come echoing out from within the canvas cover of the wagon as he passed by it. "Skip, Skip, is that you, my son? Where are you, Skip, where are you?" Vinnie listen to her soft voice repeatedly calling out again, and again to this one called Skip. In the meantime, the Duke found himself a nice cool shaded seat on the grass beneath a maple tree. The shade protected him from the hot sun's rays of the early day. Truly, by accident, Vinnie spotted a tiny set of eyes peeking out from the rear canopy of the wagon looking toward him. Then the eyes saw Vinnie standing there behind the wagon staring back at them. The low sweet voice stopped calling out to the one called Skip, and disappeared back into the depths of the covered wagon and out of Vinnie's site. With the sun shining directly into his eyes, he could not tell who', or what was in the wagon, and figured it was none of his business anyway. It may be some lonely child stuck back there by this monster of a beast who looked to be resting beneath the tree.

Returning to the hot forge in the barn with the raggedy looking wheel, Vinnie carefully removed its outer ring of battered steel. He placed the round hoop of metal onto the hot forge and took apart the wooden wagon wheel and its hub to replace the broken spindle. Pumping the bellows of the forge with his right foot, Vinnie began heating the coal-fired forge with extra air to make the coal glow red with hot burning embers. He carefully rotated the wagon's metal wheel ring of steel in the red-hot embers to expand it and then shrink it back down again around the wheel once he had completed his repairs. The wooden structure of the wheel was a mess, in a horrible mess and splintered. If left up to Vinnie, he would have rather just thrown the worn-out wheel away into the trash rather than try to repair it.

Looking out the side door of the barn, he could tell from the looks of this beast that it would be a fruitless waste of time to try to sell the likes of him a new wheel. He could feel it in his gut that this man thought he knew everything. Vinny also felt that he might never be reimbursed for the wheel he would be trying to repair, never mind being paid for a new wagon wheel.

Using great care, Vinnie opened up each joint of the broken wheel, and carefully removed the several severely bruised spindles from the main hub. Upon doing so, he found there were two more badly cracked and damaged spindles that needed replacing as well. He replaced the three broken spindles, and sealed the joints with hot glue and beeswax. Next he placed the cherry red-hot steel wagon wheel's outer rim back down over the outside diameter of the wheel, shrinking the metal back down to fit over the wooden wheel like a tight metal ring that holds together the outer staves on a wooden pickle keg as he placed the wheel in the tub of cold water. Steam rose up from the steel rim shrinking it down snugly around the outer wooden wheel.

He returned to the wagon with the repaired wheel, rolling it along in front of him to finish the job. The gold piece in his front pocket began to heat up again, getting hotter and hotter with each passing moment as he approached the wagon. He thought the occurrence was weird and that he may have to keep the gold piece in his back pocket from now on to keep it away from the heat of the forge. Again, the tiny high-pitched voice began to echo out from within the canopy of the wagon. "Skip, Skip, where are you, where are you, Skip?"

At that very moment, Skip saw a blurred vision of someone putting a wagon wheel on the Duke's wagon, and could see the silhouette of a man that looked like that fat lazy bloke lying beneath a tree fast asleep. He heard the faint voice of his mother calling out to him as well. This vision was so blurred and distorted that he could not tell where in Ireland they might be at this moment, but he knew he had better hurry home to Ireland to save them from their fate of living their life with this beast. He could barely make out his mother's soft voice as she spoke, and her words were not very clear for him to understand. "Skip, where are you? I feel your presence, son? Where are you Skip, where are you?" The gold in his satchel began to make funny groaning noises like expanding metal when it gets hot. He thought it very weird he had never heard his satchel of gold make any sort of noise, before. "Skip, where are you son?" When Vinnie reappeared, the voice stopped as he walked past the slit in the rear canopy of the wagon. Returning to the barn once again to obtain some axle grease for the Duke's wagon wheel, Vinnie put the gold piece in his rear pocket to keep it cool and away from the hot heat of the forge. Returning to the wagon with the grease, the gold piece in his rear pocket again became extremely hot as it had before when in his front pocket. This bewildered him as he was so far away from the hot forge and the gold piece in his rear pocket was now becoming very hot.

The low soft voice came echoing out of the wagon again. "Skip, where are you?" Hearing the low shallow voice come echoing out the wagon again got Vinnie's curiosity up, so he threw back the rear canvas flap of the wagon. He saw a tiny woman, not a child as he had thought he had heard at first, staring back at him. Then he noticed a small man in a cage trying to cover up with a small blanket in order to hide from his view, and the little woman ran to hide behind the cage with the little man who looked held prisoner. Stretching her tiny head out from behind the cage, she began to talk to him. "You are not our son, Skip. Who are you? What have you gone and done with our boy?" Vinnie was puzzled hearing these same words spoken by the little woman in the wagon. He had curiously opened up the rear canopy to share a piece of Bernice's special candy with the child. "I have not seen a small boy get out of the wagon, miss. If I should see one, I will surely return him to you straight away."

Vinnie let the flap of the wagon canopy go flopping back down, closing up the rear of the wagon. Midgets, little people, thought Vinnie. He returned to the barn to get a wooden dowel to secure the wagon wheel to the wagon, as the old dowel was trash. Walking toward the barn, the gold piece in his rear pocket cooled down. This strange experience dazzled Vinnie's mind. Walking toward the wagon with the new dowel in his hand, the gold piece in his rear pocket started to get hot again, making Vinnie wonder what was going on with it.

"Mr. Duke, Sir." Vinnie yelled out to him, "Your wagon is ready for you." c The Duke rolled over onto his big fat belly of jelly using the trunk of the tree to help get himself into a kneeling position and up off the ground. He looked more like a huge whale out of water trying to stand up rather than a man getting ready to do the same thing's the huge beast came waddling towards him like an overgrown pumpkin trying to walk for the first time in a pumpkin patch.

Looking at the repaired wagon wheel with a frown of an angry bear, the Duke hastily made it known he was not very happy with Vinnie. He went on snapping at him sarcastically, referencing the two new spindles Vinnie had inserted into the frame of the wheel's hub in order to put the wheel back together properly.

"All that was required of you to fix that wheel, my boy, was only one new spindle to be inserted into that wheel to make it as good as new, not one plus two more new spindles, for that, make's a grand total of three brand-new spindles. You are nothing but a crook and a swindler. You are a man of mistrust and dishonor to the human race by fraudulently cheating good people like my-self out of their hard-earned money. To cheat people out of their money is shameful and dishonest, boy. You certainly cannot be the honest smithy told about in town. Here is the money for your dishonest work." The Duke did not dare not pay Vinnie as feared he might take offense to being-cheated out of his fare, and beat it out of him instead. "I certainly do not tip swindlers, and what is that feed bag of grain doing on my horse's head? I did not ask for my horse to be grained by you. Swindler, I say, swindler. You will not get paid for the grain in that feed bag because I did not order it, and I shall never employ the likes of you ever again."

Vinnie stood there mortified and feeling dumbfounded. He did not know why he stood for such verbal lashing from this heathen of a man. He had never taken it from anyone before. He instantly turned bright red with anger as his jaw tightened with rage. Vinnie would have at that very moment, liked to have picked this beastly man up off the ground and thrashed the daylights out of his thick skull. It would have pleased him to no end.

He reached out in haste and took his money, took the feedback off the poor mare's head, and gave her a loving pat on her neck. "Sorry girl," Vinnie said with love in his heart and pity in his soul. "I wish I could help you out, but I'm afraid I am not in that position to do so, pretty girl." The horse sensed Vinnie's kindness given to her as soon as she stood there gazing into his caring saddened eyes, as these were the first kind words spoken to her in a very long time. Next came the vicious snap of the Duke's horsewhip right up next to Vinnie's fingers. The poor mare sprang forward and struggled at her hitch as she tried to get the heavy burden moving. "Swindler, you are nothing but a swindler, you are. Nothing but a swindler, I say!" Vinnie sidestepped in order to let the Duke and his wagon pass.

As the wagon passed, the gold piece in Vinnie's rear pocket became tremendously hot and felt more like a red-hot ember lying tight up against his naked skin. He pulled the very hot gold piece from his rear pocket as the wagon pulled away, and saw a reflection in his mind of a little leprechaun who had just befriended him a few days ago waving goodbye to him from beneath the stagecoach that had left for Boston the week before. The story the leprechaun told him was about his returning back home to Ireland to save his parents being held captive by some monster of a bloke, and his father held in a cage. The name "Skip" came to Vinnies mind. Skip was the same name the little woman in the wagon called out every time he approached the wagon. The gold in his front pocket became hotter and hotter as he worked on or around the wagon. The little woman kept repeating her boy's name, Skip, Skip, Skip. He must be off to Ireland not knowing his parents are here in the new country.

Vinnie immediately put the brood mare he had been working on out to pasture. He would finish trimming her hooves and nailing her new shoes on later. There were much more important matters to attend to at that very moment. It seemed more like a life and death situation to Vinnie, and he needed to do something immediately or it would be too late. He ran swiftly toward the house panting out of breath, and was stuttering and stammering half-talking to himself, half shouting at Bernice like a foolish drunken sailor, as he tried to tell her the story as he ran past her up the stairs to his room.

"Tell Becky I love her, and I have to leave for Boston straight away on some very important business that just came up." Vinnie could not tell her why or whom he was going off to Boston to see. I have to tell a leprechaun friend I met the other day about his parents' held prisoner in this country by a man named the Duke I fixed his wagon wheel. That would be a likely story to tell her, and an extremely hard one for her to believe. "I shall be back as soon as possible, in a couple of days or so, I think, I hope, I don't know. Get ahold of Bruce Butterfield, and Bruce's nephew Dick down at the Butterfield Farm to help do the stable jobs around here for us. He owes us a couple of favors, for he would not mind helping us out a bit. I have not a precious moment of time to waste!"

Vinnie grabbed an empty sack from his room, and filled it with some clothes and money and did not even take the time to wash the dust and grease from his sweaty body. He kissed Bernice on her cheek as he swiftly passed her like a small child rearing to go outside to play. Like a hurricane, Vinnie saddled up his mighty steed and was off like a pony express rider. Bernice watched in disbelief and amazement as Vinnie slapped his horse on its rear hindquarters, to get him started and then jumped on her back and galloped away. He was off to Boston as fast as his mighty steed would carry him.

He stopped several times along the way at different stagecoach stops to change his tired out horse for a fresh one each time as he made his long journey east toward Boston. Knowing all the owners of the stagecoach stops along the way helped Vinnie, and he had little trouble borrowing one of their finest and fastest horses to complete his journey. His request was always granted and was never questioned why he needed them. Down deep in his heart, he knew that he had to intercept Skip before he had the chance to sail for Ireland if it was not too late already. He had thought about saving Skip's parents from the Duke before he left for Boston. Being leprechauns and all, scared Vinnie as he had heard so many wild terrifying fables about how leprechauns could turn people into stone, make them into strange animals of the wild, and they too into stone as well. So how did this Duke fellow hold them captive as it seemed, or were they even really Skip's parents to begin with?

The gold piece in Vinnie's front pocket reassured him that Skip was the son of the little people in the wagon. When he passed the Duke's wagon on the road leading away from Greenfield, the gold piece in his pocket became extreme hot as he passed the wagon.

Skip's mother strained to see who was passing the Duke's wagon. Sensing the closeness of her son, she sat up tall in the front seat of the wagon to see who the stranger was riding the horse. At that moment, Skip had a vision of the horse and wagon as Vinnie quickly passed them. His gold groaned at that very moment and then the vision was instantly gone.

CHAPTER TWENTY-NINE

Setting Sail for Ireland

Sitting at his table looking down over the small railing, Skip was extremely happy that he would be going home to Ireland in the morning, which made him a little mischievous. Should he make a devilfish dance for some unsuspecting guest, or simply empty some glasses back into the pitchers on the table? Perhaps make a cooked fish laying ready to be eaten, or have it swim off their dinner plate across the table, and flop down onto the floor. Then Skip laughed. Maybe make the baby grand piano play an old Irish melody. He just sat there with a happy smile on his face and stared down at the many people laughing and having happy times, with thoughts of home. Feeling overly charmed about himself, he did not really care if he played any silly pranks or not because tomorrow he would be setting sail for home back to Ireland.

Skip was more than just a little disappointed in the morning when a couple of tall ships sailed into Boston Harbor he stood looking out to see at every sailing vessel afloat, wishing and hoping, and watching for one particularly important vessel to arrive in port. He was hoping to see the tall slender mast of the Shamrock come sailing gracefully up over the horizon and into the harbor. He knew by seeing her small size sailing into the harbor, that the vessel was not the majestic Shamrock with Billy aboard. She was way too small compared to the large size of the Shamrock. He scouted her out from stem to her stern, transposing from her hold to her crow's nest. She was not the Shamrock, but she would do in getting him back home. He found a nice little nook down inside the hold of the ship, and with a fluffy down-filled pillow he would borrow from the Trinity House he would be very comfortable sleeping onboard her. The voyage back to Ireland would be a soft pleasant ride, he hoped, sleeping soundly on the pillow on the beam and out of sight. He would return the pillow to the Trinity House someday in the future when he would return-back to America, to retrieve the piece of gold he had given to Vinnie for good luck to hold onto. Would it not be his good fortune in the end, as Skip could not wait to tell Grandma Broom and Grandpa Hair all about the remarkable devilfish not being the devil of the sea after all! He would explain how grand the flavor of its meat was to the palate, especially when the pinkish white meat, was stripped out of their shell and dipped into a cup of hot melted butter.

The bright moon lit up the trail for Vinnie as he rode quickly along the road. The skyline of Boston glowed like a million lightning bugs from the many oil lamps and lanterns on the buildings and street posts. Tired and aching, Vinnie hoped to be peacefully resting and getting something good to eat at the Trinity House within the next hour or so. His feet and ankles were throbbing with pain from being tight in the saddle and stirrups for so long. His back felt like he had been out at the woodpile behind the inn chopping wood all day long without taking a single break. His arms felt like huge pork sausages attached to his body and ached from being held up in the air holding the reins of the many horses, he had borrowed. Vinny oh so wished that with every passing moment all of his suffering he was enduring would not be in vain. What if Skip had already sailed east for Ireland and he was already too late to intervene?

Skip ate his fill of fresh cooked lobster meat, steak, and vegetables. He took a tiny morsel of every kind of food there was from everyone's plate sitting below before retiring to his room for the evening. He decided not to play a single prank on anyone that night. Skip was way-too pleased knowing he would be going home to Ireland in the early morning hours. When he finished eating, he transposed to an empty room he had visited before while scouting out the rooms of the Trinity House. He wanted to retrieve the softest pillow there was in the Inn to use for his bed on board the ship. He was not going to be sticking around the dining hall all night long and playing his silly little tricks on mortals. He especially did not want to fall fast asleep from being overly tired and sleep as the ship sailed off to his home in Ireland without him onboard. Tonight, he would get a good night's sleep before boarding the ship going to Ireland waiting ready in the harbor leaving at the crack of dawn to depart. No, wait, that was not a good idea, he thought. He had a better idea. He would board the ship tonight just to be on the safe side. Skip did not want to take a chance of missing the opportunity he had, not knowing how long it would be before another ship would come along heading back to Ireland. With pillow in hand, Skip transposed aboard the moored ship waiting quietly in the still waters of the harbor.

The last vision he had of his folks and the Duke was very weak and was getting weaker with time. He related the strange phenomenon to a distance factor. He figured it out that the closer he moved toward Ireland, the better his visions would become of his mother and father. The large soft pillow he had borrowed from the Trinity House fit the curvature of the ship's planking like a mattress to a box-spring, making Skip's new bed a place of comfort for him. With a blink of an eye, he took off his shoes and laid back down on his new bed. He fell fast asleep dreaming of the woods, meadows, and the very comforts of being back home. A mischievous smile broke out across his face as he slept. In his dream, he saw the old bull just standing there peacefully eating grass in front of the old tree down the pathway from his grandparents' house, and grazing peacefully out in the field in his dream.

Vinnie came charging up the road to the Trinity House on his horse, at a full gallop, and went straight out back of the Trinity House to stable up his borrowed horse. Vinny walked the walked the Mare, rubbing her down to cool her, and wiped the sweat from her neck and made sure she he fed some grain and some hay knowing she must be hungry from the hard ride he made her do. He patted a couple of the other horses stabled there as he passed them bye. Then he walked swiftly in great throbbing pain, straight away from the stable up to the front desk of the Trinity House carrying his dirty dust-covered duffel bag with his change of clothing tucked inside to secure a room to stay while he looked for this mysterious leprechaun called Skip.

Vinnie instantly encountered great inequality from the man standing boldly behind the counter staring at him when he approached the night clerk to register. He surely looked the part of a slithering scummy bomb, and was still all sweaty, smelly, dirty, and unshaven. His clothing looked stained, layered with grease, and looked a real mess. His hair was windblown with grease and dirt in it, and he was carrying a dusty dirt-laden satchel in his hands. "How may I be of service to you, my good man?" The desk clerk's voice reminded Vinnie of the Duke's smart aleck and nasty way of saying things in a quaint challenging and disloyal manner. He almost wanted to reach right over the counter and grab him to bring the little fat balding bloke moron to him, and give him a good word of advice on just how to treat decent people. He could see the little fat beady-eyed night clerk, stand ready to call for some assistance if this great big, huge hobo looking man gave him any trouble. The night clerk did not want to give this filthy looking traveler a room for the night in his majestic abode.

"I need a room for the night, Sir". Vinnie said. The desk clerk interrupted Vinnie before he could finish saying what he wanted to say. "I am dreadfully sorry my good man that we are very crowded here this evening and do not have a single room available." He knew from the sound of this little scoundrel's timid voice that he was lying, and began his speech over again across the counter looking straight into the night clerk's eyes. Vinnie's voice got louder and louder with anger. "I need a room, I need a bath, and I need some good food because I am starving." Vinnie's voice began cracking from the dust of the ride and the cool night air. "I am sorry, sir, but like I said before, we do not have any rooms available this evening." The clerk obviously did not approve of Vinnie's ruffled up looks. "I need some food then. How about a nice table so I might dine on some of your delectably good food? I have come a very long way without eating this evening, and am famished beyond belief and thirsty as a horse out on the desert." "I am terribly sorry sir, but we don't have any tables available either." Vinny then looked with great anger through the open doors leading to the dining room hall before him and saw two empty tables.

"I know I look a mess and smell of a stable because I have just ridden half way across the state from Greenfield without stopping this very afternoon. I own my own stable out in Greenfield, The Greenfield Stagecoach Inn, and Stables. I assure you, sir that I am much more than the bum that I appear to be. I have money and gold in my pocket, but need a bath desperately and a room to sleep." Vinny then reached into his pocket and pulled out the shiny gold piece Skip had given him. It glittered like a star in the heavens above. A small voice from Skip came instantly into Vinnie's subconscious mind. Never spend this coin of gold, Vinnie, or give it away to a stranger. I will be back for it one day and grant you a wish".

The desk clerk's eyes opened as wide as saucers when he saw the shiny gold piece reflecting back at him from the glimmering chandelier that shown on him from above, and without delay returned the shiny gold piece back into his pocket and pulled out another handful of silver. He quietly put his money down on the counter for the desk clerk to see and behold. "Very well, sir, you may have a room for the night and a fine meal once you have freshened up." Seeing Vinnie was not the hobo the night clerk thought he was the night clerk quickly signed Vinnie up for a room. "May I have my old room back for the night for good luck?" "Your old room, sir", the night clerk questioned Vinnie. "Yes, the one I had here when I first came to America, the room at the top of the hall on the left." "Very well then if the room is still available"? The room is the second one on the left at the top of the stairs." "By golly it is available and here is your key." "Can you tell me please if a ship has yet sailed for Ireland in the past few days?" "No not to my knowledge in quite a few weeks, but there is one ready to be leaving in the morning at the crack of dawn. The ship's captain and his First Mate seated at the table next to the baby grand piano over yonder in the corner. The captain of the ship surely looked the part of a sea captain. His face looked well brined and weathered from the misty brine saltwater of the sea, his face looking well wrinkled up with a deep tan from the sun's strong rays and the gale force of the winds he endured while out to sea. The first mate looked half the age of the captain, and well on his way groomed by the sea, the sun, the wind, and by his captain in charge.

The hot bath prepared for him by the staff of the Trinity House felt extremely pleasurable to Vinnie's tired discomforted body. His aching muscles relaxed in the warmth of the soothing heat, practically hypnotized Vinnie into complete relaxation. He became so relaxed that he began to nod off when suddenly a little Chinese man came knocking gently at his door. The pleasant little man was carrying some clothes from Vinnie's satchel all pressed and freshly ironed. Vinnie looked like a new man when he descended down the spiral staircase, from his room. The night clerk quickly jumped to his feet as he came down the stairs trying to assist him in any way possible, hoping for a good tip. Knowing Vinnie was famished, the night clerk seated him at the table where the sea captain and his first mate had been sitting.

Skip's words back at the barn constantly ran through the back of Vinnie's mind over, and over again. Vinnie looked up at the shelf where Skip said he had sat, and there it was. Vinny had not noticed the shelf on the wall before, and if he had, he did not think anything of it at the time. There was not a sign of a leprechaun up there along any of the railed shelf.

Vinnie tried very hard to envision the story the leprechaun had told him about the happenings taking place in the dining hall. Looking off to his right into the far-off corner of the dining room, he recognized the round table where a drunken sailor had been sitting. Looking back above his head, he spotted the two mannequins he had mentioned, but there was definitely no sign of a leprechaun. Was he up there somewhere hiding and looking down on them that very moment? Could it possibly be that the little leprechaun was sitting right there beside him in the next chair? He did not call out to Skip because the ones sitting near him might think he had lost his mind. He at that very moment could not believe he was really sitting there in Boston at the Trinity House eating a meal in its dining hall looking for a mere fragment of his imagination.

Could it actually be true that there was several real live leprechauns living somewhere scattered about the world? He sat there with great skepticism about Skip as he slowly reached into his front pocket for the reassurance of his sanity and pulled out the bright shiny gold piece he had so generously received from the leprechaun. He had taken the gold coin out several times in the last week to assure him that he was still sane and not really going senseless. The people of Boston would surely think he was crazy being there looking for a real, honest to goodness leprechaun. They would surely run him out of town on the first available trash wagon that would take him to the outskirts and drop him off in a ditch. No one would ever really believe his story as he would have had doubts in anyone who might be there looking for a real live leprechaun himself. Just like he and Timothy had doubts about the old sailor's sanity back home at the pub in Dublin.

He thought real hard back to when he and Timothy were happily sitting at the bar reminiscing over old times back in the pub. When the old man first came up to them, they thought for sure he was either drunk or had surely lost his mind. The wild story he told about a real live leprechaun, made the two of them make fun of the old gent. The same would surely happen to him in Boston if he were to mention Skip to anyone. Old wives' tales, they would say to him, just as he and Timothy had said to the old sailor they thought was crazy. Why had he wasted all this precious time and come all this way to Boston anyway. He reached again into his front pocket a second time for the piece of gold to reassure his good reasoning and to find out why he had come.

The gold piece began to feel warm and vibrate a little, and then it stopped. Skip must be close, Vinnie thought to himself. That was definitely why he had journeyed all these eighty some odd miles of rough terrain to talk to a leprechaun. He had to save two very special little people from the fate of held prisoner for the rest of their lives by the likes of that horrendous man who called himself the Duke. He was definitely the most offensive looking and acting bloke Vinnie had ever witnessed, encountered, or had the misfortune of running into in his lifetime. There was his wicked witch of an aunt back in London though who would've surely come in second place to this Duke fellow with her sinister dislike of human beings which included Vinnie's mother, her only loving sister, and his father.

Getting back to reality, Vinnie hoped it was not too late to save the two little people from the likes of the monster named the Duke. "Skip, Skip, where are you, you little bloke of a leprechaun, where are you?" Vinnie whispered out as loud as he dared as Skip hid behind his napkin and covered his face. Not the slightest of a whisper made anywhere in the Dining Hall by Skip, nor a sign of him anywhere in or about the hall. A dancing Devil Fish Vinnie thought to himself. A newly married younger couple, happy at the table across from Vinnie's table, were being served two large bright Red-Hot steaming lobsters. He stared at the couple's plates throughout his entire meal eating his steak, potato, and vegetables. He took one small bite of steak at a time and ate it very slowly. He had hoped to see at least one of the two devil fish act up a little on one of their plates so he would know Skip was somewhere about. Then he would know he was around the dining room causing trouble and having a good old time for himself as all leprechauns were supposed to do.

All through dinner, he did not taste a single bite of his food as he was way too busy looking for signs of Skip. He watched for him to appear out of thin air, but to no avail. There was nothing. Vinnie saw the empty small table above on one side of the hall along with the two mannequins on the other, and then glanced back over toward the couple sitting across from him. If Skip was there in the dining room, he was surely behaving himself tonight, and that was not like a leprechaun.

Maybe Skip never made it all the way back to Boston, Vinnie thought cautiously to himself. Perhaps he just, just, just, well, he did not know what to think any longer. He was just too exhausted to think about the possibilities of the situation at hand any longer. He knew he needed a well overdue snooze to rest his weary body from the long exhausting ride he had just taken all the way from Greenfield to Boston. He decided to go upstairs to his room, lay down for a short spell. When rested a wee bit, he would proceed down to the docks of Boston Harbor to search for this little missing leprechaun. In his room, he took out the shiny gold piece from his pocket that the leprechaun had given to him for safekeeping. Holding it tight in his hand, he began to call out to Skip using the name the wee little woman in the wagon had used. He was hoping it had been his mother in the back of the wagon at the stable. The gold had to have some kind of magical powers he thought, as it had turned very hot when he approached the Duke's wagon. What if this was all a great big ridiculous joke played on him, by this Duke fella and the three little people he now thought were real live leprechauns? He shook his head in disbelief that the little leprechaun would have anything to do with the likes of the Duke, or was this just one great big trick. He was so confused at the time he just laid there on the bed thinking, talking out-loud to himself, and to this wee little imaginary leprechaun called Skip.

Skip, I have found your mother and your father. It is I, Vinnie from the Stagecoach Inn, and I have found your parents, Skip." Vinnie wished the gold piece in his hand had some magical powers he could use and would somehow guide him to Skip's location, or lead Skip to him, as he held the coin in his hand. He again called out to Skip, holding the bright shiny gold coin snuggled tight in his hand until he fell fast asleep on the soft down bed in his room.

The gold pieces in Skip's cloth satchel lying beside him began to moan and groan loudly. The commotion of his gold awakened Skip from a very-deep sound sleep. He opened his small bag of gold carefully, looking inside to see what was in there making his gold grown so. Did he have a nightmare, or did his gold really moan out in pain as he had suspected it had?

Taking out a gold coin from his satchel, it felt extremely warm to the touch, as did the one Vinnie had been holding. What did all this warmth of his gold, and moaning mean too Skip he wondered. Holding the gold piece tight, a vision came to him. There in a very dark room was the shadow of a man lying on a bed. It was extremely clear to him except it was so dark in the room he could only make out the dim lit shadows of objects. Searching the room from side to side, he could not find a single trace of his parents or the cage that his father had been stored in anywhere within the darkness, and wondered what this new vision was about,

Who-ever the shadow of this person was in the dark room was all by his lonesome. "Where are they, you dumb bloke? What have you done with my mother?" Skip did not care where his father was at the time, but he was very concerned for the good health, welfare, and safety of his loving mother. If it had not been for his father's thoughtless acts in the desire for more evil tonic, his loving mother would have still been at home all safe, and sound with him. As Vinnie rolled over, the warm gold piece slid from his limp fingers and slid down to the bedspread, and ended the vision Skip had of him in his room.

In the early part of the next morning, Skip tried to create another vision of his parents. Concentrating as hard he possibly could on his mother and father he hoped he would be able to see them in a vision as clear as he had before, but in the brightness of the daylight hours where he might see them more clearly. If he could recognize any surrounding landmarks where they might be in Ireland, he might stand a better chance of finding them alive and freeing them from the grasp of the monster who held them captive when he returned home to Ireland.

Waking up much later than he wanted to in the middle of the night, Vinnie grabbed a sweater from the chair and went straight away for a walk down to the wharf in search of Skip. The light from the oil lanterns scattered about the city streets lit up the dark of night along his way to the wharf. He was the only one out walking toward the wharf and when reaching the waterfront, he proceeded back and forth along the boardwalk whispering out Skip's name softly every few feet. He hoped with every step he took, Skip might show up in a poof out of nowhere as he had done back at the barn. There at its mooring was the ship lying ready to set sail for Ireland in the morning.

Vinnie hoped in the depth of his mind that Skip had not boarded the wrong ship in the harbor when he first arrived in Boston, and now was heading out off towards Africa, or some other parts of the world. Reaching into his front pocket to retrieve the gold piece, Vinnie found it had vanished. Where was it, where had it gone? Had he dropped it on the ground in his travels back and forth across the boardwalk?

Vinnie was horror struck and worried sick, as he had promised the little leprechaun that he would not spend it or give it away. Now he had gone and lost the precious coin. He immediately began searching back and forth along the massive boardwalk hoping he might spot it shining brightly. He searched frantically near and far along boardwalk before he realized he had fallen fast asleep with the gold piece in his hand back at the Trinity House. It might still be on his bed back in his room safe, and sound, he hoped. Vinny remembered lying down with it grasped tightly in his hand calling out to Skip before he fell asleep. He hoped the magic of the coin would have led him indirectly to Skip when he first came to Boston, but it had not. Vinnie guessed the magic of the gold piece he held in his possession only worked for leprechauns, if there was any magic in it at all. The only thing the gold piece did for him was to get hot and almost burn his hind end.

Vinnie rambled back and forth on the boardwalk for the longest time, constantly calling out to Skip in his same low voice. "Skip. Skip, where are you little fellow? Skip, where ye?" Over, and over again Vinny whispered to Skip until he spotted some sailors heading down the boardwalk in his direction. He instantly stopped calling out to Skip and placed his attention upward toward the bright new moon. He looked at the two sailors nodding his head showing them recognition as they passed him by. Oh, how he urgently wanted to walk up her gangplank and board the Queen Lady with the two sailors in his search for Skip. She was the vessel Skip must be on or was going to be on shortly. He began to wonder how he might possibly go about approaching and boarding her safely.

Oh, hi mates, he would say as he reached the top of the gangplank. I have come all this way here looking for my friend Skip. He is a leprechaun you know! They would surely throw him overboard laughing all the way across the deck carrying him to the rail. Leprechauns, leprechauns surely Mate, well why do you not go and look for your leprechaun friend down in Davy Jones' locker. That is where all good leprechauns belong you know, there are no leprechauns onboard this ship. Over the side rails of the ship, the crew would through him sailing in the air like a seagull without wings down into the water below. Vinnie knew no matter what he would say to the sailors on watch, it would be a wrong thing to mention Skip a leprechaun a friend of his needing some help, and over the side rail, he would go the crew thinking he was a drunk, or a crazy person.

Several more trips back and forth along the boardwalk brought no luck in finding Skip, so Vinnie gave up. Why had he wasted all his valuable time coming all this way, in the first place? He knew he would never be able to find Skip in the city all by himself. It was like looking for a needle in a haystack. Vinnie was becoming more frustrated and very tired. He turned and walked back along the boardwalk toward the Trinity House to go to bed for a while. In the morning, he would give it one last valiant try to find Skip in or about the Trinity House and down by the harbor, and that would be that. If he were to find Skip, it would be wonderful, and if he were not to find him, it would just be too darned bad for Skip and his family.

Finding the gold coin on his bed, Vinnie settled down for two more hours of restless sleep. He awoke a short time later still exhausted. He was ready to try his last and final goal in finding Skip. He slowly without much enthusiasm walked out his room along the quiet halls of the Trinity House softly calling out to Skip. He eventually found himself standing again on the dock beside the Queen Lady watching her crew lift her anchor and set her sail for the open sea. Slowly she turned from her berth and mooring at the dock as her crew dropped more sails from her masts. Slowly she began to pick up speed as she headed out of the harbor toward the sea.

Taking Skip's gold piece from his pocket in one last frantic effort to find him, he had the strangest urge to heave the bright gold coin he held into the salt water behind the Queen Lady. The Queen Lady was leaving the harbor, possibly with Skip onboard her in spite of all his effort in trying to find and save this little mysterious leprechaun, the one whom he thought, named Skip, or was he.

With one last very loud bellow and not caring if, anyone around him heard him or not, Vinnie yelled out to Skip one last courageous time. "Skip, you dumb bloke of a leprechaun, where in tarnation are ye?" He was nowhere, for Skip was still fast asleep upon his down-filled pillow on the beam in the hold of the Queen Lady. When Vinnie yelled out to him holding the gold piece firmly in his hand, the gold in Skip's satchel came instantly to life and made such a racket that it startled Skip instantly awake. It jingled and clattered thunderously like a thousand or more horseshoes clattering simultaneously on a cobblestone street. Skip jumped from his bed and away from the thunderous clattering sound that his gold was making.

Getting his bearings to where he was, Skip picked up his satchel of gold and peered in at it again the way he had earlier in the night when it first moaned out in pain. The gold in his satchel was warm to the touch, almost too hot even for Skip to touch. While picking out a piece of gold from his satchel, another vision of a man came instantly into Skip's mind. He could see Vinnie standing on the dock of Boston Harbor looking out to sea at them sailing away. He could see and hear Vinnie mumbling something to himself about some dumb leprechaun or something of that nature. He could not make out what Vinnie was trying to say because his gold satchel was making so much noise. I tried, Skip, I really did try. I found your mower and father Skip, as the words kept repeating themselves over, and over again in Skip's mind. Then the words came echoing to Skip one more time. I found your mower and fatter, Skip, where are you? He continued to repeatedly toss the jumbled up words of Vinnie's voice around and around in his tired mind. Mower and fatter, I have found. Then again, Skip tried to unscramble the words, and finally the words came clearly to him. "I have found your mother and your father."

Skip could not believe his eyes seeing Vinnie standing there on the dock and hearing him say those wonderful words to him. He quickly jumped to his feet in disbelief and overwhelming joy. He put on his cobbler shoes and silk lined hat knowing he must get back to land and to Vinnie as fast as he possibly could. Fastening his satchel of gold to his waist, he was off to the Queen Lady's crow's nest high on the ship's tallest mast. He shot from the hold of the ship in a flash, like a cannonball, transposing to the tallest mast without checking to see if any sailor was up there looking out for the ship's safe passage out of the harbor. The poor sailor on lookout duty in the crow's nest was watching out for the dangers of small Island rocks and small vessels almost fell to his death. He lost his perch when Skip bumped into him and knocked him out of the crow's nest, grabbing at thin air as he plummeted down to the hardwood deck. Skip seized the falling sailor in midair by using his special powers and softly let him safely down on the deck.

Looking back toward shore, Skip knew from past-experiences, that his powers for transposing great distances would not carry him all the way back to land. The Queen Lady was already too far out to sea for his weak powers to work. Again, he felt trapped by his own stupidity and would have to stay trapped aboard the Queen Lady until she arrived back home in Ireland. Then, maybe, he would be able to convince his Grandma Broom and possibly his Grandpa Hair to come back to the new country and help him save his mother and father from their demise.

The more Skip thought about the situation, the madder he became about his own wrong thinking. He should have been smart enough to realize what was taking place in his visions and taking place right under his own nose. The closer his parents were to him in Greenfield, the stronger his visions were. Skip knew his visions faded at times, but to think they were coming all the way from Ireland in the new land was ludicrous. When would he ever grow up and start thinking for himself as a grown up leprechaun? He had his full growth of beard now, and yet he still had the dim-witted intelligence of a very young child, and not the intelligence of a grown up leprechaun yet. When would he ever learn? Skip's first vision had come to him over a year ago when he first thought there were children on the wagon and not his parents. They must have been real close to Boston or in near proximity of him to visualize them in the first vision.

Oh, how these new magical powers infuriated him half to death by not knowing what he could do with them or what to expect from them the next time he would use them to stay out of trouble. Over the last several months, he had waited impatiently for the fullness of his powers to arrive, and now when he received most of them, he did not know quite how to handle them properly. Surely, Vinnie would not have come all this way if it were not important for him to do so.

Mother and Father may be safe, and sound staying at the stable with Vinny and Bernice. No, Skip, think. Vinnie would not have come all this way if they were safe. They were probably at the stable sick, hurt, or possibly dying and Vinnie come all this way here looking to find me, and bring me back to the Inn too help them. What had that miserable mean fat bloke of a monster done to them?

Skip felt in his heart that he had better get back to shore no matter what. He looked out over the water searching frantically at several vessels afloat between the Queen Lady and the shoreline. Skip saw a couple of fishing vessels heavily loaded down with fish and heading back towards shore. He noticed the sailor, whom he had just saved from dying, scurrying quickly up the hemp rope ladder to claim his prize. Skip did not plan being anybody's prize at that moment, but there was not anywhere aboard this ship he would be safe with everyone looking for him all at once. Splat into a great mound of slimy freshly caught smelly fish, Skip transposed like a rock flying through the air without thinking of the consequences. He was so excited that he pictured himself flying through the air instead of being there, and boy did he fly. The crew looked back toward the pile of fish to see what made the slurping splattering sound like a shark had just jumped onboard to eat their catch, as Skip slid down under the fish so he wouldn't get caught.

CHAPTER THIRTY

The Long Ride Home

Vinnie was almost at the stables of the Trinity House, slowly sauntering along kicking at a small stone, and mumbling to himself. Vinny felt bad, indeed he did, about everything. He had failed the two little people held captive in the Dukes wagon, and he failed the young leprechaun named Skip whom might never see his parents alive ever again. He had failed immensely and it was now time to retrieve his borrowed steed from the stable where he had left her. He was not excited one little bit to start his long slow track back home to Greenfield. His misfortune of this long journey was still not over with yet. He had a lot of explaining to do when he returned home and knew he faced a hard rigorous argumentative task of telling Bernice and Becky why he had left the stable in such a hurry in the first place. The two of them would surely think he had gone insane with such a story. "A real live leprechaun surely now Vinnie said Bernice, a leprechaun?" Bernice would say sarcastically and poor Becky would think the one she had fallen in love with had surely lost a spoke from the lonely once smart wheel in his head.

Slowly Skip peeked his little head out of the pile of slimy fish just barely enough to see if the boat was close enough to shore for him to safely transpose back to land and catch a very much-needed breath. The smell of the fish was making him sick. The slime of the fish covered him from head to toe, and the prickling of the fish's sharp fins and scales poked through his clothing making him experience a sense of seasickness that he had only experienced when he was dead drunk and hanging upside down vomiting from a roped ladder's rung.

The crew onboard her was busy readying their vessel by lowering their sails, and busy getting the boat ready to dock at the pier to unload their precious cargo of fresh caught fish. Closer and closer to shore the boat, and her crew sailed for the crew was busy adjusting her riggings for docking. Was it too soon for him to transpose to land yet? Millions of beady background eyes were staring at him from a thousand different directions all at once, it seemed. He laid there perfectly still amongst the fish that he was hiding in. It gave Skip a very uncomfortable disheartening feeling of claustrophobia. The longer he laid there in the stench the sicker he became. He knew sooner than later he was about to vomit from the rocking of the vessel, the stench of the fish, and the chum they had used to catch all the fish.

Skip had had just about enough with these fish. The vessel had to be close enough to land now for him to transpose himself. He was so anxious about it that he did not care any longer, where he might land. He just knew deep down inside that he needed to get away from this self-imposed prison and get to land no matter what it took as he was becoming desperately ill. "No, not yet, Skip", he thought. He remembered vividly falling off the log down into the murky waters back home when he was a small leprechaun and almost drowned. The frightful thought of drowning in the harbor made Skip even that much more reluctant to transpose too soon to land and end up in the salty brine of the sea. He had never learned how to swim properly, and did not know if these new special powers of his would work in the water or rendered them useless under the water to save him from drowning. He did not know what he could not do with them, and the very thought of it frightened him so.

Oh, how Skip missed his grandparents at times like these when he needed their knowledge of these new very special powers he possessed and of how to use them properly. He looked an awful site and blended in quite well with the fish that were scattered about him. His clothing, his beard, and skin now covered with loose fish scales, and his eyes were barely able to peek out of the big pile of fish to see where the crew of the vessel was taking the boat. The closer, and closer the boat came to shore, Skip had a good feeling about leaving this hideous hideout. They must be close enough to land now for him to transpose without landing in the water. Still looking at the dock, he was ready to act. He looked hard and then transposed behind a wagon waiting at the dock for the boat to bring in the catch of the day.

Next, he transposed to a much closer safer location along the boardwalk, behind another wagon heading he thought toward the Trinity House. It was dangerous for him to be transposing out in broad daylight, as someone might see him and capture him if he was not careful enough. His precious satchel of gold worried Skip as it would be gone if he be caught, and his special powers rendered useless and gone forever. He knew most of his new powers came from his gold. It had taken him a very long time to figure it out and did not know why or how, he just knew.

"Vinnie, where are you?" Skip thought to himself. The gold piece in Vinnie's pocket began to react by getting warm again as he rode along the roadway leading westward toward Greenfield. Vinnie thought for sure that at any moment now he would probably be passing the Duke's wagon on the roadway heading east toward Boston or places east wherever the road might take such a scoundrel as him. This was the only time he could ever remember the gold piece in his pocket getting warm or hot when he was near the Duke's wagon. What, if anything, could Vinnie do for the two little people when he came upon the Duke's wagon? Should he help release the little people? What if they were not Skip's parents to begin with, then what?

The whole idea of leprechauns was starting to haunt Vinnie's very weary mind. He visualized Skip standing in the barn beside the milking stool and talking to him. Then he saw him waving goodbye to him from beneath the stagecoach when it left for Boston. He had a gold piece in his pocket that Skip, or whoever it was, had given him that heated up when a little woman called out to Skip, or was it his name. This all seemed to be a very bad realistic dream to him. Vinnie reached over with his right hand and vigorously pinched himself a good old hard pinch on his naked left arm. "Ouch," he was not dreaming. Darn that hurt! It sure would be a lot easier if he was just daydreaming or having a nightmare. Now he would have to go back home empty handed, asked Bernice and Becky for their forgiveness, and ask them what he should do next. Vinnie was out of ideas for the moment. The harder he tried to think what the right thing to do next was, the more confused he became about the whole idea. Convincing both Bernice and Becky would be as hard a task if not harder than trying to find Skip lost all by his lonesome in Boston.

Transposing to get away from the dock, Skip found himself standing out back of the Trinity House beside the rear door. The staff used this door to bring in the clean linens merchants used to deliver all the food for the kitchen, the staff to take out the trash, and everyone to report to work. He immediately stepped behind a large trash storage bin to hide for a short time until it was possible for him to get a true bearing on where Vinnie might be staying at the inn. Loud clicking sounds of hungry cat jaws snapping, hissing, and snarling caught Skip's immediate attention. Standing only inches away beside and to his left staring at him with dinner on their minds, were two very large mean looking scruffy tomcats licking and snapping their jaws open and shut at him as he was a mouse or rodent or some kind of prey. He had been so busy trying to reach shore to catch up with Vinnie that he had neglected to clean himself up from all the fish scales and stench of the fish. Both large tomcats simultaneously jumped at Skip and tried to attack and eat the largest fishy smelling rodent they thought they had ever set their eyes on!

Poof, instantly Skip transposed up to the room where he had been staying the day before and had borrowed the pillow for his bed on board the ship. There in the room stood a young woman dressing, and having only her underclothing on. Seeing Skip appear out of thin air, looking like a monster from the sea and smelling like fish, the woman surely thought he was a demon from hell. She screamed a loud bloodcurdling scream that deafened Skip's ears. He was as terror stricken as the poor young lass, for he too turned a crimson shade of red from head to toe with embarrassment by seeing her standing there half-naked. The young lass tried to cover herself up the best she could before the strange looking beast as she passed out cold on the floor from fright.

He instantly transposed himself to the ledge in the dining room where just the day before he had been sitting down to eat at the little table he had placed there from across the hall. Calamity struck once again! Skip landed on the shelf overlooking the dining room hall and knocked over an urn the kitchen staff had just placed there that very morning. His unsuspected arrival sent the urn flying over the captain's rail and crashing down to the dining room below. The urn fortunately hit the table's edge and sent the breakfast the older couple at the table were enjoying everywhere about the dining hall. Fortunately, no one was hurt.

The staff had just returned the small table and chair set Skip had borrowed from across the hall to its original setting, and set the two mannequins back in their original seats at the tiny table. It made them both look as if they were enjoying a splendid time together. Skip, not wanting to be seen on the shelf above by a patron, instantly transposed beneath the dining room table down below so as not to be seen on the shelf where the vase had been sitting. When Skip landed beneath the table, Skip was caught off balance by stepping onto a foot belong to the woman sitting at the table with a man. Starting to fall over, he automatically reached out and grabbed her by the outer thigh as he tried to steady himself. The young lass sitting at the table was not very impressed with his hand touching her, and reached far across the table and slapped the unsuspecting man in his face. She thought for sure, it must be he who was touching her with his long lanky arms were both still quite obviously above and on the table at the time. An instant argument erupted between the two of them, and again Skip had to transpose to another vacant room in the inn in hopes of not being-discovered by anyone. He felt his luck as a leprechaun that day had finally run out. There lying on the bed before him were newlyweds. A young man and his new bride frolicking on the bed in joy, seeing Skip standing there, the lovely young woman pushed her new husband off the bed and onto the hardwood floor. She screamed out in fright while the young unsuspecting groom picked himself up off the floor. She was screaming at the top of her lungs and pointing towards Skip who was standing right behind him.

Back to the servants' entrance behind the Trinity House, Skip transposed without thinking about the two tomcats that had just pounced at him. Sure enough, the two huge cats were still out back by the trash bin roaming around the back entrance in search of their food that had suddenly disappeared as it had appeared. Knowing he was next on their dinner menu and at the top of their list, he transposed the two of them with his magic to the tiptop branches of the tallest tree growing out behind the building. With both tomcats out of his way, it gave Skip time to think a little more clearly. He cleaned himself up with a blink of an eye, and transposed himself to the hayloft above the stable outback. Looking down from the loft above the stalls for Vinnie and his mighty steed, there stood not a single horse in the entire barn. He must have already left for home on his horse. Staying in the hayloft to rest, Skip took out his satchel of gold. Holding it tight between his hands, he began to concentrate on Vinnie, and a vision came to him. There he was sitting on the back of a large dark brown Morgan horse, and was slowly riding along a gravel road alone. It was not Vinnie's horse though and Skip wondered why he had a new horse instead of the one he loved so. He knew Vinnie was heading west as the shadow of him and his horse cast down in front of them, and the sun had just come up in the east.

Skip concentrated as hard as he could on the back of Vinnie's saddle trying with all his might to transpose himself and his satchel of gold to be with Vinnie. His special powers would not let him do it, as he had not yet achieved his full knowledge of how to transpose such great distances. The gold piece in Vinnie's pocket began to get warmer and warmer the harder Skip concentrated. The hotter the gold piece became, the more it irritated Vinnie. He finally took it from his pocket and practically burned his fingers. He knew he must be real close to the Duke's wagon, so he placed the gold piece in his saddlebag taken out later that day, after he passed the wagon.

Two shiny gold pieces a thousand miles away aboard the Shamrock was getting warmer and warmer as well. The two gold pieces hidden in Billy's room safely hidden beneath his pillow where he kept them all the time as the ship floated up and down over the rolling waves of the sea inside the Shamrock. They too were getting warm as well as Vinnie's were trying to act in response to Skip's request. The gold in Skip's satchel commenced to sound more like singing whales or porpoises calling out to each other through the hall of a whaling ship, when he was concentrating on transposing himself. He suddenly stopped what he was doing, glanced down at his satchel of gold, and wondered why it was sounding so strange. They seemed to be talking to one another, so he poured the gold from his satchel out onto his lap in a heap. He wanted to understand more about their powers and watch his pile as it sang with great desire. They began to wiggle and move about on his lap and together they formed an arrow pointing westward toward Greenfield, the direction Vinnie was traveling in. Skip knew this must be a sign to him from his gold by giving him some sort of instruction on what he should do next.

He wanted desperately to understand his gold even more now that it was reacting to his wants and needs. Both Grandma Broom and Grandpa Hair had neglected to mention one very important thing to him, how he would come by his gold and wealth not just for its monetary value alone, but for its special powers as well. All Grandma would say to him was that one day he would cry out for his gold, and it would come to him a little bit at a time. He understood now how very important it was to hold onto his precious gold, as it would necessitate his safety in future years. All his grandparents ever told him, was too never let the mortals catch you and take away all your precious gold and wealth away. What they should have said to Skip, was not let any mortal take away your gold from you, for you will lose all of your special powers.

The golden coin for the tip of the arrow on his lap was missing along with two gold coin pieces from its tail. Skip figured out what the missing pieces of gold were from the arrow in his lap. The one coin in front of the arrow must be the one he had given to Vinnie, and the other two missing pieces of gold were the coins he had given to Billy. He suddenly realized what he must have done. No one had ever told him about the special powers and that they would never be complete without his full satchel of gold. This caused great concern for Skip as he wondered if missing these three crucial pieces of gold would cost him the ability to save his mother from the Duke.

He must have shed his last gold tears at Charles' funeral because when he shed happy tears atop the stagecoach heading toward Boston, they never turned to gold. He played a silly trick on a farm boy along the way by making his bicycle ride off without him for a distance, making him cry happy tears while watching him run after it. When he went to catch his tears, they remained wet. He knew then that his satchel of gold and all its powers he was to receive must be complete. What Skip did not realize at the time was that he had given up some of his very special powers and his ability to use them to their fullest degree. Oh, how he wished his grandparents were here to show him the right way to use these special powers. He wondered what the two of them would have done in this predicament!

Skip transposed to the nearest livery stable down the road and onto a wagon going westbound toward Concord, Massachusetts. Mile after slow dusty mile the wagon proceeded west, but at a crossroads the wagon turned north away from where he wanted to be going. He transposed from beneath the wagon to the side of the road, took cover beneath a tall maple tree, and sat for a while in its shade. He hoped sooner than later that another stagecoach would come along heading west that he might hitch a ride on. From there he would catch a ride heading west toward other towns along the way to Greenfield.

A stagecoach went swiftly by heading east as Skip stayed hidden in the shade of the maple tree out of sight. It was the stagecoach he had hitched his ride on to Boston from Greenfield. He felt it would not be too long before another stagecoach would soon come along going in the right direction. Almost an hour later, the stagecoach he was wishing for came along heading west. This time he transposed aboard the top of the stagecoach and hid behind and between two very large strongbox chests and a big duffel bag. Skip hid himself behind the luggage so not seen by the stagecoach driver or the man riding-shotgun with him, holding a long barreled rifle. Sitting peacefully and comfortably on the back of the stagecoach rooftop, Skip went happily along letting his tiny feet and legs dangle over the back of the stagecoach. All along the road, he played harmless tricks and pranks on the children he encountered as the stagecoach drove past them along the way. He would transpose to the quiet of a tree or beneath an abandoned work wagon sitting in the yard of the next stable when the driver stopped the stagecoach for a fresh team of horses.

Vinnie did not quite reach home in Greenfield until just before dusk. After walking his horse for a short time, and rubbing him down, grained him, and quickly put his horse up for the night. He discovered Becky sitting across from Bernice in the living room talking about him and looking worried as he passed by the front window. He could tell Becky had a bad case of trepidation locked firmly in her heart when he first entered the door into the parlor. She was babbling on with concern about why Vinnie had to go off to Boston so suddenly in the early part of the day without giving a very good reason to Bernice. She was concerned that Vinnie had found himself another woman or younger girlfriend. Why else would he have just picked up his things and left several stagecoach drivers to change their own teams of horses all by themselves! Nothing else in this world could have possibly been that important to a man. What would have happened to her if they were to have been married already and possibly had a child or two? Would Vinnie in the middle of the day just pick right up, and leave his family if things were not going just so to please him, or would he. Why else would Vinnie have left without first telling Bernice the importance of why he had to go and place Becky in such an awful fix! She placed her face softly down in her tiny hands as they talked and began to weep profusely as Vinnie closed the door.

Walking in the front door of the inn, Vinnie found Becky weeping and Bernice was very cold to him when he tried to explain why he had to leave in such a hurry to go off to Boston. The story Vinnie told them about a leprechaun was just too much of a fable for either of them to believe. They both thought Vinnie was lying through his teeth and was just making up this harsh wild cruel story about a leprechaun in trouble to cover up some foolish romantic and probably animated love affair with another young woman. This wild story, he was telling looked to be a cover-up story for some scheme he had neatly tucked up his sleeve. The more Vinnie talked of this wee little leprechaun friend his family imprisoned, Becky would weep even more. She wept the more she listened until both she and Bernice totally disbelieved him to the point Bernice almost asked Vinnie to pack up his belongings and leave the inn for good and never return again.

Becky continued to shed massive amounts of tears and demanded to know who this young beautiful woman was every time she spoke. She asked Vinnie who had been on the manifest of the last stagecoach heading for Boston. Who was the woman that had been so important for him to drop everything around the stable in the middle of the day, pack up a few clothes, and leave for a couple of days without a very good reason!

Bernice began giving Vinnie the third degree on just how important being a faithful and truthful husband was to form a good relationship between a husband and his wife. She then gave him a serious tongue lashing about leaving the stable unattended in the middle of the day. "What would Charles have said about you or to you? Gallivanting off after some pompous lass, and then returning home the next night with a wild made up story about some ridiculous leprechaun, and his poor little leprechaun family held captive on a wagon by some mean monstrous man that you had just fixed a wheel for. What a bunch of Blarney! Both Bernice and Becky thought that leprechauns are nothing but old wives' tales and do not exist! Next Bernice fired off at Vinnie by asking seriously if he still intended in good faith to the agreement he had with her about buying the stable business and inn from her as planned from the beginning.

"Charles may have made a grave mistake in trusting you, Mr. Vinnie McDougall." Bernice went lavishly on to him as he stood there in the center of the parlor taking the tongue-lashing from her. Charles may have only seen the good man in Vinnie, which he had demonstrated so many times in the past, and it may have all just been a very talented act to win over someone's vulnerable hearts and a way for Vinnie to embezzle the business from Charles and her. The business which Charles had worked so hard and slaved over with his blood, sweat and tears to create over the years of hard labor. Or did Vinnie just take the money from the safe to go off to Boston to gamble it away, drink, and having a merry good old time on the town with it while everyone else around the stable and the inn tried to make up for his lost time. "What kind of a man are you anyway, Mr. Vinnie McDougall?" Bernice asked him again with anger in her voice.

CHAPTER THIRTY-ONE

The Arrival

Approaching Greenfield on the last stagecoach of the day, Skip concentrated on Vinnie's location to see what he was doing. He found poor Vinnie in his vision in a whole heap of trouble. He was taking a tongue lashing from Bernice, the likes of which he had never heard before except from his Grandma Broom when almost crushed by the charging bull.

He found Vinnie standing in the front of the inn in the parlor and trying to defend himself for having ventured off to Boston to find him. Poor Becky was sobbing steadily and crying her sweet little blue eyes out while she sat on a chair by the window. Bernice was standing in front of Vinnie in a ranting raving rage pointing her finger at Vinnie. Skip had never seen Bernice act like this before when he had stayed in the attic of the inn.

Skip could see the gold coin piece in his vision. Vinnie was taking it from his front pocket to prove his story to the two of them, and began handing it over to Bernice as proof of his story. The shiny gold coin was getting hotter and hotter while Skip concentrated generously on Vinnie's whereabouts. He became instantly furious with Vinnie after seeing him hand his precious gold coin over to Bernice. He had instructed Vinnie never to do this. "You cannot spend it or give it away to anyone, you dumb bloke! I will not grant you the special wish I had promised you and Becky if you do, as I won't be able to." Bernice instantly dropped the hot coin and stared weirdly down at it, and wondered why Vinnie would hand her a coin this hot as a joke. Becky bent down to pick it up and dropped it from her hand, as it was way too hot for her to pick up as well. Vinnie bent down to retrieve it back, and behold, he too drop the hot gold coin back down to the floor. It was as hot as a red-hot glowing ember straight from the forge. It did not look hot just looked like a normal bright shiny gold coin resting on the floor.

The gold in Skip's pouch was moaning like the whales of the ocean anxiously talking to one another beneath a ship. Skip held this pouch of gold in his hands hoping it would talk to him as his Grandma did, and give him some instructions on what to do next. He concentrated hard, very hard on what Bernice, Becky, and Vinnie were all talking about, He wanted to know first-hand what was going on between the three of them as they spoke in heated anger to one another while standing over and looking down at one of his prized special gold pieces.

Suddenly without forewarning, Skip found himself in the front parlor of the inn right in the midst of the three of them standing over his gold piece on the floor. He stared right back up at the three very bewildered looking faces. The four of them stood in the room looking thunderstruck at one another for the longest time before any one of them spoke. He did not know exactly how he got there, but Vinnie sure looked glad to see that he turned up to defend his wild story of going off to Boston and chasing after some mysterious leprechaun!

Now he could back up this story the girls thought Vinnie had made up to hide the truth about some luscious money hungry wrench. The two girls just stood there in dumbstruck awe, looking down at what they thought was a real live leprechaun. Skip looked up at the three of them in disbelief himself and had no idea what to do next. Should he transpose to the quiet of the attic where he would be safe, just stand there and take whatever was about to happen to him next, or just disappear to the safety of the barn before he got caught by one of these mortals? He felt like a prisoner in a world he did not belong.

He looked up toward Vinnie in search of a friend, a smile, and a sign of kindness, or anything about him that might possibly secure his sense of safety. Skip had mixed feelings as to what he should do next.

The gold in his satchel began to moan again. Skip reached down and picked up his gold piece from off the floor, and quickly placed it in amongst the other gold coin pieces in his satchel. The gold coin piece from off the floor made the other gold pieces in his satchel stop their moaning.

"Mr. McDougall, sir," Skip spoke up. "Why did you come all the way to Boston and call out my name? I never told you my name or who I was." Vinnie just stood there staring down at Skip in a daze. "How do you know my name? Did my gold piece I left with you talk to you, Vinnie, and tell you my name?" Vinnie just stood quietly staring down at Skip in disbelief that he was really, there. Then Skip began to jump up and down in a bit of an anger and rage almost yelling out at Vinnie. "Why did you come all the way to Boston, Vinnie McDougall, and call out my name?" Skip yelled louder and louder as he jumped up and down in place now screaming at Vinnie at the top of his tiny lungs. "Why did you come to Boston, Vinnie, and call out my name?"

Vinnie just shook his head from side to side. He tried to shake out the numbness of the situation at hand from his very bewildered mind, as he tried to compose himself while staring down at Skip jumping up and down, and hollering. "Your mother Skip and your father", Vinnie spoke up loudly. "At least I think they were your mother and father. I am not sure of it, but I think it was the two of them. The gold piece you gave to me for its safekeeping and good luck became extremely hot when I approached their wagon to fix its wheel. I could hear this little woman calling out your name when I went by it. I mean, I mean, whispering out this name of someone she called Skip from within the wagon. Calling to you, I suppose! Is your name really Skip?" He shook his head up and down. "Yes, I am Skip, the lady leprechaun's son."

"Well, Skip, this great big mean looking round faced bloke who called himself the Duke had your father in a cage and your mother was in the back of the wagon freely walking around. The Duke is a mean despicable acting creature and not worthy to be called a human being. Then I remembered the story you had told me about going back home to Ireland to save your parents from some mean looking bloke and a covered wagon. Well, I traveled all the way to Boston to tell you that your parents were here in this country and for you not to go back home to Ireland in search of them. "Skip remembered the vision he had had just a couple of days ago when some bloke was fixing a wheel on a wagon. The Duke was lazily lying down under the shade tree looking like a big-beached whale out of water. "That was you, Vinnie, who was fixing the Duke's broken wagon wheel, then that was you Vinnie?" Vinnie agreed and shook his head that he was the one fixing the broken wheel.

A funny feeling filled the pit of Skip's wee stomach and making him feel very ill at that moment. "Where are they now, Vinnie? I must go to them at once as they are in extreme danger. I can feel it in my stomach. The longer they are associated with that monster who calls himself the Duke, the greater the danger and jeopardy of being caught up in the deadly schemes that that evil monster does to the good mortals around him."

The immoral cry of the wicked banshee filled the quiet night air as Skip spoke. He grimaced with pain and fear, and stood there between the three of them holding his pouch of gold tight to his chest. He concentrated hard on the whereabouts of his parents, and a vision of them came to him as clear as daylight itself.

CHAPTER THIRTY-TWO

The Deadly Duke

A large crowd was gathering in the square and packing themselves in and around the Duke's wagon like flies on cattle dung. They were all listening intently to all the false misleading speeches of health and healing from his deceptive tongue. Skip's father was on a stage dancing an Irish jig as usual, and his father held prisoner inside his little green cage. Skip's mother was gracefully waltzing around the outside of the cage doing the same Irish jig as he was inside the cage and drawing the attention of the crowd. The Duke was selling his therapeutic healing medicinal remedies hand over fist to the ones who were gullible and foolish enough to listen to what the worthless tonic would do for their lives and future. He claimed his new and improved medicine would make freckled children's freckles go away. He stood there lying to the good townspeople about how his tonic melted away ugly warts from the inside of one's body. It was a sure cure for rheumatoid arthritis and stiff unyielding joints, loss of hair and the regrowth of hair, and many, many more problems which he made up to sell from his tonic water, herbs, roots of grass, and coloring to give it a pleasing color. He could sell it to most any gullible individual around that would fall for his pitch of blarney.

Suddenly from way deep in the crowd, a loud shaky voice bellowed out from an angered elderly farmer-man, out over the heads of the large gathered crowd. He sounded extremely disgruntled with the Duke. He was screaming at the top of his old shaky voice, "Fake, deceitful witch doctor, monstrous devil from hell, trickster, cheat, con artist, liar, and murderer. The crowd quickly turned, to get a glimpse of the man dressed in his farmer overalls, and making such a loud protest about the Duke's medicine.

The Duke instantly spoke up and asked the disgruntled old man to come forward to the front of the crowd. "Good sir" said the Duke, "please come forward". The crowd parted ways so the old man could come forward to the stage of the wagon and state his case. "You took my money and my life's savings from me, you swindler. You made a potion, a special healing tonic that killed my poor wife, Bonnie!"

The old man heard of this man who healed the dying and the sick, and he had come to him. He had gone to the Duke at his last stop near his home and hoped this man's great magic medicine would cure his ailing wife from her debilitating arthritis and hypersensitivity of her nervous system. The Duke took the old man's life savings in exchange for a useless bottle of foul-tasting water. She died before morning from the poison in it. The Duke left the area in a hurry soon after he closed up his show that day. He cured her illness all right, and he knew what he had done with his poisonous potion.

The large crowd gathered tighter around the covered wagon and its stage and slowly began to grumble angrily over the situation. Some were getting out of hand and becoming unruly as they listened to the old man tells this worthy pathetic story, about his wife and this medicine man's useless tonics. The Duke immediately put the blame of his wife's death on the disgruntled old man for not being able to tell him exactly what the proper name of the disease was that she had. The Duke continued to yell out over the crowd, "If the old man had given me the proper name of his beloved wife's disease," the Duke said, "the lovely woman would be very much well again right now. I am the Duke! The Duke knows all! The Duke sees all! And the Duke hears all!"

Saying his last few words of dishonest encouragement to everyone around the wagon, he tried to buy as much time as possible to save the three of them from what looked like it could be a lynching. The Duke and Skip's mother passed out many free samples of his worthless tonic water that he had prepared at his camp along the road just the night before. He was giving it all away as fast as their four hands could possibly hand it out to lighten the load in his wagon and make their escape. He was trying desperately to appease the rumbling crowd and to ease the ever-growing rage building from within the disgruntled mass. He promised the grueling crowd that he would return to Hubbardston in the near future, prove to them just how good his new modern medicine really worked. Closing up his roadshow as fast as his big fat blobby body would allow, the Duke threw the cage Skip's father was in quickly into the rear of the wagon. He flung it hard, and did not care the least about the consequences it might have caused the poor little individual trapped inside of it.

Skip's mother quickly helped the dastardly Duke, as she knew that she and her husband, could possibly lynched along with the Duke as well. She helped pick up the small stage and closed up the wagon show, readying them to leave immediately for parts unknown. Heaving his monstrous size body up and onto his wagon with difficulty, the Duke made as speedy an exit from Hubbardston as his poor little mare could possibly go. He frantically whipped at his poor little horse, making her whinny out with a cry of pain while she struggled with the wagon and its load as large welts rose instantly on her already raw swollen back. The mean Duke lashed out at the small filly of his again, and again with his Bullwhip over, and over again as tufts of blood soaked hair and flesh flew from her back with every crack and lashing out with his bullwhip in hand.

"What is it, Skip?" Vinnie asked with a loud and sharp concerning tone in his voice. Skip had been staring off into outer space and daydreaming with the strangest blank look on his face Vinnie had ever seen before. It scared him as it looked as if Skip was in some sort of hypnotic trance or going to pass out at any moment. Large beads of sweat were profusely pouring down from his brow, and Skip's small framed body shook as if he was cold and shivering. For several long minutes, he had been just standing there between the three of them without saying a word. He looked off toward the kitchen wall while having his vision of the angry crowd and the trouble his family was in because of the Duke! "Do you know of a small town Vinnie, a small town just up the road from a pond with a church and a steeple in the middle of its common? Where is that town, Vinnie?" Skip asked with great desire and concern in his very trembling voice. "I don't know of a town around here with that description." Bernice or Becky did not know of it either. Skip new he had to use the magic powers of his gold to find the direction the town was, and where his mother and father possibly could be, before it was too late for the two of them. It would only be a matter of time now before the Duke's misgivings got himself and Skip's parents into grave trouble.

"Mr. McDougall, sir, can you help me find my mother and father right away, please? Vinnie first looked toward him, looked over at Becky, and then glanced toward Bernice with great concern written all over his tired face, and the girls knew it. "What can I do, Skip, I have a business to run here." Suddenly the banshee's laughter broke the still of night air as she sang out her song of death as loud as she possibly could, heard for miles, and miles around the surrounding countryside. She sounded as if she was flying close by in circles around closer and closer as she flew above. The banshee's voice continued growing louder and louder in strength, with every breath she took. She sang out yet another harmonic verse of her death-seeking song. Poor Skip was surely afraid that he would never see the likes of his mother or father alive ever again, especially his mother. "Take all of my gold, Mr. McDougall, right now this very instant if you must, but please, please, please help me find and save my mother." Skip begged for mercy from Vinnie for his mother's life with pity written all over his poor little sad frightened face. It must have been the desperate look of heart-felt anguish written all over little Skip with his saddened face that melted the hearts of all three mortals standing there in the room around him. Vinnie, with kindness in his voice, was first to speak out with words of kindness from down deep in his heart to the extremely saddened leprechaun. "I have my chores to perform around the inn, and must accomplish them in the morning, Skip. I also have some other very important work to complete on several very large pieces of farm equipment out in the stable yard. I have other promises to keep as well. I have promised the hard-working farmers around here to have my work completed on their equipment so they might run their farms efficiently. When I have completed my chores, I will be more than happy to venture away with you to help find your mother and father. There will be a couple of stagecoaches to attend to as well when they come rolling in to change their tired out team of horses for a fresh team. When all the work is finished in a couple of days or so, then I promise I will get a helper for Bernice to run the stable and the inn. Then Skip dear friend, I shall be more than happy to help you find your parents. I cannot make any real promises that we can even find your parents, but I will help you out the best I can.

Becky's eyes had dried from crying and said she would stay another night at the inn with Bernice to help her and Vinnie out around the inn and stable as much as she could. Skip, shortly after their first fearful introduction to one another, disappeared from the parlor, poof right into thin air to the safe confines of the attic where he felt the most comfortable and would be safe for the night, as he had so many nights in the past.

None of the four managed to sleep much that night if not even a wink. They all laid down stone cold awake in their beds most the night just thinking of what the new morning might bring. Becky lay awake, as did Bernice thinking of Skip how he appeared in front of them, out of thin air. They tried to fathom the existence of a real live leprechaun in their own presence, each one lying awake wondering if they were having a bad dream that would soon go away when they woke up.

The three of them, Bernice, Becky, and Vinnie, all felt as if they were playing a part in a fable of Alice in Wonderland's story and falling into the looking glass. They now felt as if they were live actors in a child's fable. Vinnie lies awake in bed, stone cold awake wondering what the last few days and months really meant to him. He had traveled all this way across an open sea to the New World of America to discover a real live leprechaun living in his own house. The entire situation felt like an enchanted dream to Vinnie, and he could not sleep a wink all night just thinking how very weird the situation at hand was. Now instead of capturing a real-life leprechaun and taking away all of his gold and money or having him grant him a wish or two, Vinnie was now going out of his way to help a real-live leprechaun to save his parents. How ironic could one's life become?

The early morning hours of the next day found Vinnie in his usual place in his favorite chair at the head of the kitchen table. He was rather quiet and not quite himself as he waited for his breakfast. Bernice and Becky were busy going about the kitchen in their usual manner of preparing the morning meal. There was not a single word mentioned about Skip. They just talked to one another normally as if nothing different had ever taken place. Bernice poured out some tea for Vinnie the way she always did where he sat to eat his breakfast. Becky made the toast as she always did when she stayed overnight or on the weekend. Skip sat impatiently restless in the attic, thinking whether he should join the trio in the kitchen or just take his meals by magic from the kitchen the way he had so many times in the past. He was afraid one of the three mortals might change their minds about helping and would now want to take his gold and fortune from him.

Well, over a year had passed by since Skip was last in Ireland. His gold pouch was now complete except for a couple of pieces of gold he had left with Billy, the cabin boy. He was fearful that someone would try to take his remaining wealth of powers and gold away from him, and Vinnie was his only hope. Skip new this and had to put his full trust into someone else even if it was but a mere mortal. If only Grandma Broom and Grandpa Hair were here to save the day. He knew he would be in severe trouble with his grandfather for putting so much trust in a mere mortal, but he had no other choice now. His loving grandmother would understand. Skip did not really care about the wealth or the use of its very special powers any longer. He only cared for his mother and if she could be saved and returned to him safe and sound. The mortals could have all of his worldly wealth if they would help him save his mother. To suffer the loss of his wealth and the leprechaunic powers would be but a mere inconvenience well worth the trade for his missing mother.

Becky frightfully threw her basket full of ready cooked and buttered toast high up in the kitchen when Skip suddenly appeared out of nowhere. Seeing Becky react that way caused Vinnie to spill his cup of tea all over the kitchen table, himself, and down onto the floor as he jumped back in his chair. Skip began to laugh out-loud when he saw Becky and Vinnie look so tremendously funny, and just could not hold back his sudden feeling of happiness. Becky was so frightened by his sudden appearance that she began to scream, yelling out at Skip in a very high-pitched frightened squeaky voice, "Come through the danged door like normal folk next time, will you Mr. Leprechaun, sir. You scared me half to death." Vinnie began to laugh too as Becky was all flustered over what had just taken place. Bernice jumped frantically, startled, at hearing the explosive commotion behind her as she turned around to see what was taking place. Spotting Skip and hearing the commotion, Bernice dropped the plate of cooked eggs she was holding. He caught them in midair and transported them all the way to the table with his special powers. Becky joked with Skip about Bernice's eggs. "Nice how do you do there, Mr. Skip leprechaun? Save Bernice's eggs will you, but not my toast." Vinnie roared with laughter. Skip just stood there with a puzzled look not knowing if Becky was serious or not. Then she and Bernice both laughed out-loud by seeing Skip sitting there with a bewildered look on his face and wondering what he had done wrong. Poor Skip just sat there at the kitchen table red-faced and embarrassed with the three mortals, all staring at him. His head continually bobbed up and down swaying side to side and in every direction, rapidly keep in an eye out on the kitchen door, the den door, and the three mortals all sitting around. He was so busy that he was neglecting to eat his own breakfast that was on the table before him.

"Will you just stop doing that, Skip? Eat your breakfast for crying out-loud! No one is going to take your food from you," Bernice said harshly. He was not worried about his breakfast as he was not hungry. He was more concerned about the satchel of gold he had tied to his waist than he was about eating at that moment. He was extremely concerned that one of them or someone else might come unexpectedly through the kitchen door, and catch ahold of him and demand his gold before he could use its special powers to free his parents.

Skip ate his breakfast quickly after Bernice yelled at him. He scoffed his food down like a hungry wolf, and finished his breakfast before anyone else in the kitchen had a chance to finish their own. Swiftly rising to his feet, Vinnie pushed his chair back and left the girls sitting there eating at the table by themselves. He turned and headed out the back door to do his chores. He was quickly walking across the backyard to the stables when he yelled, "Skip, if you can find the time to give but a wee helping hand lad, we just might be able to leave a little bit sooner and look for your mama and your pa." Out in the barn, Vinnie was prepared to ask Skip to help him do the small chores of the day because of his small size. "Can you go over yonder by the fence and fetch me that brown brood mare that is grazing in the field? I need to take a good look at her and put these last two horseshoes on her two front hooves. Skip nodded his head that he would fetch her without saying a word. Vinnie turned to fetch the two horseshoes from the shelf then turned back around to see Skip had headed out yet, and magically standing right there beside him in the barn was the brood mare still chewing on the grass from the far-off field. She was as startled as Vinny was at first, wondering what had just happened to her. She had just been eating fresh grass out in the field and then the next moment she was standing in the barn right beside Vinnie. She stood nervous at first, but calmed right down because Vinnie was standing there holding the horseshoes. He hammered the two horseshoes to her front hooves, cut off the extra length of nail with his hammer, and tapped over their sharp edges as Skip watched him do his work.

"Skip, I need you to fetch me that long round wagon wheel stave over yonder on that high shelf next to the door for this wagon wheel." Zip in a flash, the wagon wheel stave was resting in Skip's hand. Vinnie was astonished to see it appear out of nowhere and no longer lying on the shelf. Next, Vinnie gave him several more small chores to do as he worked on finishing the wagon wheel. Just like before in a flash, Skip was back and had accomplished all of the small chores. "Can we go now, Vinnie?" he asked impatiently.

Skip was in a panicked rush for them to get going. He wanted to head out immediately, and try to help save his mother and possibly his father as well from his cage. Vinnie becoming tired trying to finish his heavy workload became the more put out with Skip, and his impatience moments, for he wanted to help Skip out the best he could. "I told you that I have to get all this work all done before we can leave." Skip did a traversing somersault in the air across the barn floor and landed on his two little feet. "There, now, it is done, Vinnie! Now can we possibly leave?" Vinnie looked out the open door of the barn and there he saw the once broken plow lying on its side with its two broken handles replaced. The disassembled garden harrow, which had been lying outside by the fence in a million pieces, was now resting by the fence reassembled and looking brand new and ready to use again. The bent up old stone bolt with its broken wooden skirt appeared to be repaired and ready to go to work, and the many leather harnesses Vinnie had told Skip about earlier were all repaired, saddle soaped, and hanging exactly where they all belonged on their proper racks in the barn. Vinnie could not believe his wandering eyes.

"I still need to repack and grease the wheels on Mr. Bailey's hay wagon over yonder and repack the grease in the stagecoach outback, Skip." Mr. Bailey's wagon in the yard is now up off the ground and settled to a stop in midair. The four wheels of the wagon magically floated off it like feathers in a gentle breeze while hanging there suspended in midair as well. Next, the grease from the grease keg in the barn went sailing through the ear in globs, landing in the hubs of each wagon wheel as the wheel slid slowly back onto the wagon, and the wagon settled back down to the ground with that job completed. Next, he looked out the barn door toward the stagecoach sitting across the yard. Doing his magic again, he did an exact repeat of what he had done to Mr. Bailey's hay wagon by repacking the grease in its wheels, then placing the stagecoach back down on the ground where it belonged. "Now can we leave, Vinnie, now can we leave?" "Okay, Skip, now we can go.

Bernice and Becky were just barely getting up from the morning breakfast table after reminiscing over Skip and Vinnie for a while and sipping on their tea and coffee. They were getting ready to pick up the table and do the dirty dishes of the morning when Skip and Vinnie came happily waltzing back in through the back kitchen door looking all swanked up and pretty self-satisfied. "Well, we are ready to be going," said Vinnie with a big smile across his face. Bernice all at once became furiously hot tempered with the two of them. She figured it was just another one of the leprechaun's dirty little tricks he had played on Vinnie to get him to leave the stable and inn before all the work was completed. "You two cannot leave until the work around here is done." I have guaranteed these hard-working farmer folk around here that the work on their broken equipment would be done by the end of the week!" "It is all done, Bernice," Vinnie said with a smug look on his face. "Mr. Bailey's hay wagon is all packed with grease and ready to go, the stagecoach outback is all packed with grease and ready to be put back into service. Jefferson's stone bolt out back, repaired. The harrow by the fence outback is all-so repaired, reassembled, ready to go back to work again and is resting altogether over by the fence. The harnesses all repaired, all saddle soaped and hanging on the repaired harness rack out in the barn. Skip saddle soaped each and every one of them for me along with the two saddles on the rack that needed sewing as well."

Suddenly, in front of their astonished eyes, all the dirty morning breakfast dishes that were sitting on the table flew across the kitchen in a parade to the sink. A tiny tornado spout of bubbly soapy water whirled swiftly around them in midair and back down into the sink as the dishes passed quickly through it. The dishes then flew to a drying cloth suspended above the counter, which was busy flipping and flapping in the air, drying the clean dishes. Then the dishes flew to the shelves in the pantry to their proper places. The silverware sparkled bright, cleaned the same way as the dishes were. After cleaning, the silverware went swiftly flying through the air to their appropriate silverware bins, along with the dishes. Neither Becky nor Bernice said a single word. They just stood there in awe at the site of dishes and silverware floating through the air and everything being clean, dry, and put away. They both shrugged their shoulders as they looked at each other, turned and walked away into the front parlor room both with smirks on their faces and not saying a word.

CHAPTER THIRTY-THREE

Quick Hitching

An early morning stagecoach came rumbling quickly down the dirt road with dust flying around the bend and swiftly into the yard of the inn. The horses were sweaty, tired, and chewing at their bits. They were ready for a break all being put out into a paddock to rest. Vinnie went quickly through the rear kitchen door outback of the stable to help change the tired team of horses. When Vinny unhitched the tired team of horse from the stagecoach, and was walking them around outback to the stable, he found a fresh team of horses already harnessed up and ready to be hitched up to the stagecoach. The horses he was leading were suddenly all standing in the middle of the paddock all stripped of their harnesses, their harnesses cleaned, and saddle soaped along with their bridles. The bridles all hung up in their proper places along the racks and put away out in the barn. Vinnie just shook his head in disbelief. He then brought the fresh team all harnessed up and ready out front, and hooked them up to the waiting stagecoach.

"Okay, Sam, your horses are all changed. Your old team out in the back paddock grazing and a fresh team all hitched up to the coach and ready to go to work when you are Sam." Sam could not believe this tired eyes, Vinnie must be jawboning him, he thought. He just stood there trying to light up his pipe and just barely had enough time to pull out the tobacco pouch from his coat pocket. He had to take a double look at the fresh team of horses Vinnie had just hitched up to his coach, just to make sure Vinnie was not trying to play an old dirty trick on him. "Fastest unhitch and hookup I have ever seen. Must have a couple of right new real good working stable hands outback, do you Vinnie?" "No Sam, I cannot afford any new help around here ever since Charles has been gone. God rest his soul. Only my-self and Bernice around here Sam, that is all there be. She is as good a helper as ten good men would be." Sam just shook his head in disbelief that anyone could be that fast in hitching up a fresh team and putting the tired team out to graze. He just stood there scratching his head in disbelief and puffing on his pipe until he got it lit.

"Don't mind if I have a fine cup of Bernice's special coffee inside before I leave do you, Vinnie?" "No, Sam, go right along in. Don't mind if I join you for a cup of her tea while you have yours, Sam?" "I would love to have someone sit down with me for a change just to have someone to talk too. It gets pretty dusty and lonely out there all alone most of the time. The only time I have anyone for company on the coach is if we have to haul a large payroll out of Boston. Then they send a guard or two out to ride along with for safety reasons.

Skip stay hidden but sat out in plain sight, on top of the ice chest in the background from Sam, with Sam's back towards him. The more they talked, the angrier Skip became with Vinnie. Skip very anxiously wanted nothing better to do than to get going and stop sitting around reminiscing about nothing. Then he was extremely nervous seeing Skip just sitting there on top of the ice chest out in the open. He did not realize that Vinnie was searching for clues from Sam about the whereabouts of Skip's parents and was just getting prepared to ask him all kinds of questions of where he had been and whom he had seen in his most recent travels. Sam liked to talk to the people at the different stagecoach stops along his route. "Have you seen or heard anything about a show man peddling healing remedies and tonic potions around the countryside, Sam?" "Yes sir-re-bob, Vinnie, I sure have! Seems this medicine man named the Duke you are talking about duped an old farmer over Athol Way. He told the sheriff that he was going out to look for that one just the other day to shoot the no good son of a so-and-so for what he did. The story has it the poor old farmer said he had paid out half of his life savings to this medicine man for some useless supposedly lifesaving remedy he had talked him into to save the life of his awful sick wife. The poor old-guy said his sickly wife gagged on the rancid no good for nothing tonic. The old gent said this Duke medicine man put poison into his wives bottle and not medicine at all. After looking at it, he told the sheriff the bottle contained old axle grease, some beeswax and honey, and some sort of colored water. It was not an hour or two after his wife tried to swallow the poisonous solution that she died gagging, holding onto her throat unable to breathe, and died right there in his arms. Said he was going to go to the ends of the earth if need be to track down the three of them varmints and teach them a real lesson in life about being honest. Said he was going to shoot the no good for nothing man that called himself the Duke, and string up his two little midget accomplices to a big old oak tree. He said he was going to leave them out in the sun to die a horrible death as his wife did. Hearing this sort of news did not make Skip feel any more comfortable about sitting around the kitchen doing nothing to save his parent's from the Duke! "In which direction did they take off to Sam?" "Easterly I reckon towards Winchendon, east of Athol said the farmer.

CHAPTER THIRTY-FOUR

Time to Hit the Road

Skip, after hearing Sam tell his horrific story about the Duke and the farmer, was becoming extremely anxious and wanted to get going immediately down the road to find his parents. With a quick blink of an eye, Skip spilled the remainder of Vinnie's hot tea on the table and making it look as if it was accidentally on purpose. "That Duke fellow, Vinnie, did he ever do you or Bernice any kind of wrong doing?" "No, I was just curious about him, that's all, Sam. I fixed a broken wagon wheel for him about a week ago, and was just wondering if his poor little horse had not yet died. The way the Duke, the cruel monster treats his little horse is downright inhumane." Vinny instantly splattered with his own tea, got the important message Skip passed quite nicely along to him. It was time for them to leave, for Vinny to stop flapping his jaw, and for them to get going. He knew it was time to leave before Skip really showed his anger by whatever leprechauns do to people when they get upset with people. "Well, Sam, it has been real nice talking to you, but it's time to get back to work. Have yourself a nice day. Then he quickly got up from the table, pushed his chair back underneath it, placed his teacup in the base, and was gone. Sam slowly swallowed the remainder of his coffee and headed out the front door to the awaiting stagecoach with his horses ready to go.

The time of day had finally come for Vinny to pack up his saddlebags, and get started with the arduous task of searching for Skip's parents. He knew the different roads leading from Greenfield to Winchendon like the back of his hand after making the long trip so many times in the past few months. He made it a habit to visit George once a month ever since his Uncle Charles had passed away.

CHAPTER THIRTY-FIVE

The Dastardly Duke

A young very upset family came running into the sheriff's office and almost knocked each other over. They were just passing through this quiet little town and had come in to tell the sheriff that they had just found the body of an old man dead lying face down on the dirt road. His body found lying along a stretch of road leading out of the town of Hubbardston, leading towards the city of Gardner. In rolling the old man's body over, one of the men who went out with the sheriff that day, discovered that the deceased body was that of the elderly farmer man from Athol. The one who had just the night before caused the ruckus out in the town square by the church at the Duke's wagon show. He was the same one who had yelled out profound words and accusing criticisms in the midst of the crowd accusing the peddler who called himself the Duke of killing his poor sick wife. There in the roadway alongside of him laid an open bottle of the Dukes, specially marked magic tonic. The strange looking bottle emitted a strange strong sweet aroma of chopped up almonds coming from its open top. Placing a small drop of the sweet smelling tonic water on his tongue, the sheriff instantly frowned, for he knew he shouldn't have done any of it and he began to spit, and spit, and spit. He was trying desperately to rid his tingling tongue of the horrid sweet smelling tonic water. It caused his tongue instantly to start to tingle and swell, and became instantly numb and so did his throat. The sheriff immediately took his canteen of water from his horse's saddlebags and began to rinse his mouth out feverishly. Over, and over, and over again he put water in his mouth swished it around and spitting it out on the ground until his canteen was empty.

One man in the crowd that went out to inspect the body grabbed at his throat indicating to the sheriff that he thought the old man lying there in the road had been strangled by someone. The sheriff knew he was right. The old man had been strangled, but not by someone's strong hands. The old man strangled by the poison, the poison in the bottle of tonic water the Duke had given the old man to shut him up. The Duke had done it to him to put an end to the farmer's life so he would not ever be able to pursue him. The Duke never wanted to ever, endure another scene they had experienced this night. No one noticed the bottle the Duke purposely pulled from his coat pocket and handed over to the old man.

To confirm suspicion that someone poisoned the old man, the sheriff quickly sent for two of the most prominent professionals in town to help confirm the cause of death. He called for the assistance of old Doc Roberts and his friend Henry, the town's undertaker. Their professional views would tell what had really taken place along the roadway the previous night. The sheriff wanted a trusted professional's opinion before he or anyone else could jump to any wild conclusions and calling it murder.

After traveling a great distance, Vinnie and Skip came up the River Roadway and into the town of Athol. Skip stayed safely hidden away while riding along with Vinnie by hiding in one of Vinnie's very large saddlebags attached to the rear of his saddle. In Athol, Vinnie and Skip ran into the same old story that Sam had told them back in the kitchen at the inn. Everyone they inquired information from about the trio had said the same thing. They all said the Duke was heading east toward Winchendon, Gardner, or other towns toward Boston. Unbeknownst to Vinnie and Skip, there were many more people now out looking for the Duke and his two small friends. When they were passing the sheriff's office going up the hill heading out of Athol, a telegram came into his office from the Sheriff's Department in Hubbardston. It was an informative message for the family of the deceased older man. Old man Bristol from the Bristol Farm in Athol, found dead in roadway from poisoning. Be on the lookout for medicine man's wagon, the one who calls himself the Duke, and his two little associates.

The townspeople of Winchendon had never heard of nor seen the Duke passing medicine wagon show. This particular day Vinnie did not take time to stop and visit with George or his family out at the farm nor blacksmith shop. He was on a mission and did not want to waste any precious time held up from the search. Vinnie talked too many people along the way towards the town of Winchendon, and not a soul had seen or heard of him. The trail leading out of Athol had become cold as ice. Vinnie wondered what direction he and Skip should try now. "Skip, what do we do now? What direction do we go in? We can travel back and forth across the state until we exhausted from traveling, and we may never find them at all. I have only a couple of days to spare away from the inn, Skip, before I have to return to the stable and tend to my chores again."

CHAPTER THIRTY-SIX

The Arrow of Gold

Skip had an idea, why not use the powers of his gold to find the direction to his parents. Vinnie found an isolated location along the roadway where he could stop this horse, and Skip could come out from hiding to ask the special powers of his gold. Skip jumped out and down from Vinnie's saddle bag and sat down cross-legged on the ground beside the road. He anxiously took out his gold from its pouch and poured it out on the ground in front of him. Then he concentrated real had on his mother and father with all his might, paying strict attention to his scattered pieces of gold. "Gold of mine, please gold of my powers, show me where to go to find my mother and father." The gold began to wiggle and squirm right before Vinnie and Skip's eyes. Quickly it formed an arrow as it had back in the stable at the Trinity House pointing southeast this time. Vinnie wondered to himself why there were two pieces of gold missing from the back of the arrow, but did not dare ask Skip why. Skip scooped his gold up quickly from the ground and firmly placed it securely back into his satchel for safekeeping. They were off down the road once again looking for his parents. This time they were off toward the south east of the state toward the township of Gardner. They reached Gardner just before dusk and the late afternoon sky was becoming dark with a chance of rain in the air. They could hear large claps of thunder rumbling toward them from off in the distance, and could see the lightning as it lit the sky.

The Duke headed east toward Princeton. He feared for his life and safety from the angry crowd, worried they might follow him to the outskirts of town and beat him to a pulp. The Duke did not dare go back along the good road leading out towards Gardner, or towards Winchendon, for fear the angry crowd might easily catch up to them. He knew it would be easy for them the way they were acting that night to catch up with him and beat him for the type of man he really was. He had good reason to fear for his miserable life, especially for what he had done to the old man's wife, and now what he had hoped he had done to him.

Routing his exhausted mare off the well-groomed beaten path by a hard relentless yank of the reins, the Duke drove his horse and wagon quickly down onto an old abandoned beat-up looking logging road. He did not know where it went, and did not really care. He just figured it would lead him somewhere to safety, away from town deep into the forest, and away from the dangers that were brewing by the ravaged crowd, he just left behind at the square. The people were getting more rowdy all of the time as he was packing up his wagon, and looked to be getting ready to explode into an uprising against him for a lynching, for he was sure of it.

Viciously whipping his poor mare, the Duke made his way in the dark down the poorly lit abandoned logging road. He relentlessly lashed out at her with his bullwhip to make her go as fast as she possibly could over the rough ground and large rocks in the offbeat pathway. With the dark of night upon them, the poor horse had to feel her way for footing in the pitiful road that lay ahead, as she pulled her heavy wagon and oversized blob of a man behind her. He screamed an abusive tongue lashing at his horse all night using words that scorched Skip's parents' little ears. Without remorse, he relentlessly whipped his poor horse and did not care what he was doing to this poor little creature, on the horses back.

The Duke knew he had gone way-too far this time and had really done something very unchristian like to more than just one person. He knew he would be going straight to hell when he died and knew he was in grave danger if caught, for the bad dastardly deeds he had done so foolishly performed back in the small town of Hubbardston. Thinking of the consequences for his foolish actions scared him half to death He had no choice but to run for his life, and get himself to the busy docks of Boston, as fast as he possibly could. He would have to sell off his wagon along with everything else he owned. He would have to rid himself of these two useless imps he had tagging along with him no matter what he had to do with them, no matter what, even if he had to drown them, or set them free in the forest to fend for themselves if they did not get eaten by some wild animal. Then he would sail for England or other parts of the world unknown to his followers where he would not be recognized, and live comfortably off the riches he had already stolen from people in need.

Deeper into the forest, the Duke rolled his wagon and wares, whipping, and whipping is poor little mare half to death. They came to a fork in the logging road, beneath what looked like the shadow of a mountain in the dim lit moon light, and he chose the road less traveled to the right. He was hoping it would discourage anyone who might want to follow them there. Up the hilly road, he pushed on over the rugged terrain, he pushed his worn out exhausted horse, and whipped her continuously over, and over again. The relentless whipping finally shred away all the horse's hair from the middle of her back. With each crack of his bullwhip, he started splattering large drops of pure blood from the horses tattered back at himself. The poor little mare exhausted, finally collapsed deep in the woods from her exhaustion and loss of blood. She could not go on any further under these extreme circumstances, laid perfectly still in the pathway of the road, panting for air. The Duke relentlessly continued to whip the poor creature with more fury than he had ever shown her before as she lie dying there in the woods. He was fearing for his own life now and tried to get the exhausted mare to her feet one more time to make her pull his heavy burden. The harder he whipped her, the more blood he drew from her severely torn tattered back, until there was no more blood taken from her. The Duke became so angry he kept striking out at her until the ill-treated horse tried one last time to get up to please her mad crazed master, pawing frantically at the ground. She whinnied loud one last time in severe pain and gave in to his abusive treatment. She fell one last time to her side, her feet perfectly out straight, and with one last very shallow breath of cool fresh air. She would no longer have to hear the mean wrath of the Duke's inhumane language or feel the sting of his whip. She now laid there on the ground perfectly still, in peace and tranquility with the world.

Far into the night, the Duke began to take his acidic anger of his situation out verbally on Skip's mother and father. "I demand a wish from you at once, you dirty little no good son of a leprechaun, "the Duke yelled and pointed his index finger at Skip's father. "No, I want one from you my dear little Mrs. Leprechaun instead of one from your useless husband." The Duke turned his immediate attention toward Skip's mother, yelling out at her and thinking she had been holding out on him about her own magical powers. "I demand one of you to put some life back into that dead horse of mine. No, I want you to replace her with another good horse even bigger and better than she was." The Duke's ignorance of leprechaunic powers made him more treacherous now for the two leprechauns than it had before his horse died. "I cannot be of any greater value for you Mr. Duke than I already have been. I do not have any leprechaun powers left, nor can I grant you any wishes."

The Duke then turned back toward Skip's father. This time with anger beyond belief, he began demanding him to give him a new horse at once. "I demand of you a new horse right now or you will stay in that blasted bloody cage and rot like the no good scoundrel you really are!" "But Mr. Duke, you have all of my gold and my gold is the power of my magic. Without the gold, we leprechauns are about as vulnerable as you are to the hungry wild beast of the woods. I am no match for any large or small." The Duke turned, focusing his tyrant attention away from Skip's father sitting in his cage, and focused his ever-growing maddening anger toward his mother again. "Then I want you to grant me a simple wish or you shall rot in the cage along with your husband. Where is your Gold wench, I need it now, quickly from you I say, right now, you wicked wench, I want your gold too. I want it now or I will slam you and you're no good for nothing crippled up looking husband in the cage in your heads to teach the two of you a lesson of manners!"

"I have no gold, Mr. Duke. I am sure you would have taken it from me many years ago if I had any at all." "Do not lie you wicked little wench of a leprechaun woman, or I shall teach you a lesson with the Bullwhip as I did that good for nothing horse of mine lying there dead on the ground. I know that all leprechaun's male or female have gold," the Duke bellowed out in anger as he hammered his fist down on the floor of the wagon. "Only when I was a young single Leprechaun girl did I have my own gold and great powers. My powers and Gold all transferred to my son Skip when he was first born in a very special ceremony over me. I am truly sorry that I can do nothing for you, Mr. Duke, as I have no special powers."

The Duke became even more furious with the two little people. He reached across the rear of his wagon, grabbed the cage Skip's father was standing up in, and viciously yanked it toward himself. He knocked Skip's father off his tiny feet and onto the floor of the cage. "Here is your good for nothing magical gold, Mr. Smart Alec leprechaun. Here, use your precious powers now and grant me my horse." The Duke took a coin from his full pocket of silver coins and scraped away at the coating of green paint that colored the whole of the golden cage a bright money color of green. The true gold color of the cage glittered brightly as a ray of moonlight reflected up into Skips, fathers, eyes. "Here, use your special magic powers now leprechaun. I want a new horse now! I demand one from you this instant!" "I cannot grant you a wish this instant, Mr. Duke. You have entrapped me within my own powers. I therefore, cannot use my special powers at all. I have known all about this for a couple of years. If I could have used my special powers, Mr. Duke, believe me I would have used them a long time ago to escape from you and all of your foolish shenanigans."

With all this bad news said and done, the Duke became more serious than he ever was. With a bright red face of volcanic force, the Duke looked down at the leprechaun trap inside his golden cage with a rage about him. He took the cage in his hands and flung it across the back of the wagon. It landed hard on its side with poor Skip's father lying in pain in a heap on the inside of the cage. Skips very concerned mother rushed to her husband's side trying to upright the cage, to make her poor moaning husband as comfortable as she possibly could. Little did the Duke realize when he heaved the golden cage back across the wagon with such force the special lock he had made out of Skip's father's gold became jarred and broken open. If only Skip's mother could upright the cage, she and her husband might free themselves at last by the very hands of the one who had imprisoned them. The cage was resting on the door of it, and they did not realize the lock on the cage had sprung wide open.

The Duke pulled his moneybag out from under the special hiding compartment he had made in the front seat of his wagon. He was off down the road with his wealth to find someone foolish enough to sell him another poor horse for him to kill. He took most of the food from the wagon for himself and left very little for the two leprechauns behind in the wagon. He did not care if they lived or died at that moment, or if the beast of the woods would come along and feast on them. If they did, he would not have to find a way to rid himself of them, and he could melt Skip's fathers golden cage back into wealthy gold for himself. His mind was sick, as he went babbling on down the road talking to himself about how smart he was and how he was going to escape to Europe. The Duke did not fear the little woman leprechaun escaping or leaving him knowing her husband was still locked securely in his cage.

The scary hours of the long lonely night, left all alone out the forest without any protection from its wild beasts, past the leprechauns by slowly. The night became much darker with the bright light of the moon fading rapidly into and behind the back threatening clouds that were quickly approaching. The night soon turned blacker from the angry storm, and the torrential rains heard coming through the trees like angry bees, and began to fall harder and harder onto the canvas cover of the wagon. Their little ears could hear the strong loud claps of thunder echoing off in the distance, as the strong storm quickly approached from the northwest. Lightning flashes were lighting up the blackened sky above the forest everywhere, and the harsh howling winds were picking up strength in the trees outside, making the canvas top of the wagon flap briskly.

Skip took out his satchel of gold again and asked it to show him and Vinnie the way toward his parents' location. When the arrow of gold formed this time, it was pointed in the direction of Westminster, east of Gardner and toward Princeton. The rains of the storm began to fall on them as well. The force of its wind and rain soon became harder and harder as it poured down by the bucketful. Lightning of the approaching storm lit up the blackened sky like a magnificent fireworks display. The same storm also sent wave after wave of thunder echoing around the Duke's head as it lit up the road ahead of him. He found shelter from the storm in a roadside bar and found himself a horse in the barn that he would buy. She would serve him well until he could get himself and his captives to Boston. He decided he would not take no for an answer in buying her. Even if the farmer did not want to sell her to him, he was going to take her anyway even if he had to kill them. She was a strong older horse by signs of her aging teeth. This horse had been put out to pasture for retirement to die, and the poor appearance the barn was in, showed an older farmer must own her. What would be another life on his hands at this time in his useless life, for the Duke knew what he had done, and needed to escape to England or face a hangman's noose around his fat neck.

The song of the dreaded banshee returned and filled the wet night air with a chill to everyone who heard her. She was joyful with rage screaming out, and singing her song of death all around the forest. She sang louder than Skip had ever heard her before. Could it have only been the wind howling through the trees or was it really the Banshee looking for her next victim to take to the other side of life? Large goosebumps grew in welt form all over Vinnie and Skip's body after listening to her horrid screams of joy. Her song of death she played above sounded like an out of tune harp in the trees surrounding them on this very windy, dark, frightful night. Vinnie wanted to stop somewhere to take cover from the storm, but Skip did not want to hear such nonsense and wanted to press on through the storm for fear of the safety and well-being of his parents. Skip knew in his heart he had to reach them before the banshee had time to find them. It would be far too late for the ones he loved if she found them first.

Skip knew very well why the new powers of his were so weak. Two of his very important pieces of gold and power were somewhere aboard the Shamrock floating halfway around the world. Would he be able to ward off the likes of the banshee without them? Could he squelch her mighty power by using all the love he possessed, or would he need them to fend her off should he come face to face with her? Even if he had the use of all his full powers, could she still bring them with her to the other world no matter what he did? Maybe she would be so strong that she could take him right along with her, too. He did not care. He did not know what would happen, or what to expect, but deep in his heart, he knew he would sacrifice his own life trying to save his mother if that was what it took. He was going to send her home to his Grandma Broom as soon as he could.

Suddenly a vivid vision came to him as he was thinking of his parents and rode along with Vinnie. The lightning was flashing above the trees all around them as they slowly proceeded along the darkened roadway. His mother and father were in the wagon. The lightning was flashing around them at the same precise time it was flashing around he and Vinnie. Skip knew at that moment that they could not be too far away from them. The bright light of the electrically energized storm was flashing its deadly light across the sky and lighting up the inside of the Duke's wagon. His mother was sitting down beside the cage and holding his father's hand. Getting nervous with the storm, she got up to try to right the cage one last time to make her husband more comfortable for the night.

Skip could see the dead horse stretched out in front of the wagon, lying on her side still hitched to the staves and harness of the wagon. The water from the torrential rains had filled the deep ruts of the roadway, causing the ruts to look more like tiny streams of water flowing down the mountainside. The Duke was nowhere in or around the wagon. Suddenly, as Skip was trying to help his mother right the cage with his magical powers, when a bright blinding bolt of lightning came blazingly shooting across the dark wet sky over his and Vinnie's heads. It shot toward the mountain that lay right in front of them. He saw in his vision the blinding bolt of lightning strike a significantly large pine tree just above and behind the Duke's wagon. He focused his entire vision on it and watched as the enormous pine tree came crashing down with great force straight across and crushed the Duke's wagon flat to the ground like a pancake. The gold in Skip's pouch moaned loud as if it was in tormented pain. The banshee screamed out with her laughter at the same time above them as she sang out her song of death more briskly than Skip had ever heard her sing it. He slouched like a fallen fool down into a heap in Vinnie's saddlebag and began to cry hysterically.

"What is the matter with you now, Skip?" Vinnie tried yelling out over the howling wind. Skip went right along crying as the gold in his satchel moaned as if it was still in agony. Finally, Skip composed himself long enough to say just a short few words to Vinnie. "They are doomed, as we are way too late, Mr. McDougall, I have just witnessed the doom and gloom of my own parent's right now in front of my own eyes. A large, tall pine-tree just fell down across their wagon and crushed it flat as a piece of paper. They both were trapped and probably dead in the back of the flattened wagon." "Look again, Skip, look again," Vinnie yelled out to Skip over and above the howling of the wind and the splattering stinging of huge ice pellets and raindrops pouring down on them from the horrendous thunderstorm above. Skip brought back a horrific looking vision of the crushed wagon and the poor dead horse. No one could have possibly survived the ravage of the storm as the once strong built wooden wagon having splintered into a million pieces of broken wood the size of toothpicks. Another loud volcanic clap of thunder filled the night air. No, it was the banshee thundering across the sky with her wagon of vengeance to claim her new prize or two.

The lightning of the night flashing wildly above Skip and Vinnie with Banshees wicked smile of her light flashing with her zig-zagged-lee smile spread wildly across her face. The bolts of lightning had to have been the banshee's wagon that she was traveling in across the sky. It sounded like she was getting ready for her two prizes. To take claim of her fare and bring her catch both back across the night sky to that land beyond death of which there is no return. "No," Skip screamed out in excruciating pain "we must hurry, Vinnie, now we must hurry to them."

"I am going as fast as I can, Skip. Use your powers to help. For the love of mighty sake Skip, use your powers now!" Skip tried at once to transpose himself, Vinnie, and the horse they were on to the scene of the crushed wagon, but to no avail. His powers would not do it. His pathetic powers would not bring them to his desperate parents' needy side to try to help them. He knew deep down he could not face the horrific scene all by his lonesome and knew he needed the friendship of Vinnie with him for his kindness, along with the sympathy he might need. Especially if he discovered what he thought he might discover buried within and beneath the rubble of the ruined wagon. He concentrated again as hard as he possibly could. He wanted nothing better than to transpose Vinnie and himself to the crushed wagon where his mother and father lay trapped inside and most probably dead. His special powers were just not doing the magic for him that he requested. No matter how hard he concentrated on them, they just did not work. Had he had only paid more attention to his Grandma Broom, and to his Grandpa Hair when they were trying to teach him what they would when he received them. If only his foolish father had listened to someone, not a one of his family would be in this dreadful fix. The lightning flashed again above them causing the hair on their arms to rise up as it narrowly missed the treetops above them. The wicked loud explosion of its thunder hurt their ears and made it impossible for him to concentrate on transposing to the site of the wagon.

Oh, how Skip hated the rain and now the lightning's light just before the thunder as well. All he could imagine in his tattered mind was the banshee happily smiling and riding wistfully along on the bolts of lightning dancing high above the tree tops in the dark night sky smiling, knowing she was about to fetch her bounty. Suddenly, Skip became more overwhelmed with grief than before as he wept. Vinnie had to finally dismount his horse and lead it with Skip sadly weeping inside a saddlebag along the muddy road until they reached the safe haven of cover in a farmer's barn along the roadway. The weather of the night was too dangerous for the two to continue with wild bolts of lightning dancing above the treetops all around them. When the dark of night in danger of the storm had passed, Vinnie, with the help of Skip's magical powers and his gold's suitability, would bring Skip to the location of the wagon and tragic scene where his parents may have met their doom.

A glimmer of light from an oil lamp was shining through the farmer's kitchen window when Skip and Vinnie finally left the comforts of the barn in the early morning. The unaware farmer would never know he had had visitors staying out the barn for the night. Before they ventured out, Skip emptied his satchel of gold onto the floor of the barn. He asked it for a direction to follow to find his mother, and it pointed them in a direction down the road. Not many miles away, over the crest of the mountain at another farm, the Duke was leaving the shelter of yet another farmer's barn. The early crack of dawn, before they had awakened, the Duke went straight up to the farmhouse back door, and basically pushed himself through the kitchen door and into their home. He almost knocked down the poor old farmer's wife when she went and answered the door. The farmer's wife would have grant him anything he wanted just to rid them of this dastardly evil beast. The Duke demanded a very large morning breakfast as part of his price for the old mare, which the farmer did not want to sell him in the first place. The elderly farmer and his wife were definitely scared to death of this huge non-manageable beast. They both filled with joy, when the Duke finally left them after he had eaten all their eggs, bacon, and apple juice they were going to share for their breakfast. They suddenly filled with grief, especially the old farmer as they watched their mare old Daisy being led down the road by this indignant beast of a stranger. Daisy had been a part of their family for many years of her life, and she was not really for sale. The old farmer had put her out to pasture just to finish out her elder years in peace for helping him run their family farm when she was young and strong.

The Duke had been so hostile toward them is his approach to buying Daisy, that they sold her to him just to rid themselves of this evil creature. They both feared the man and thought he might kill one or both of them if they did not sell her to him. The farmer listened to his wife and let the Duke take the old mare for a mere two-dollar bill. The old farmer wanted to shoot the miserable Duke, but his wife would not let him do it. The Duke, not liking the discomfort of bouncing up and down on a fast-moving horse, let old Daisy stroll leisurely along the road and then down the pathway leading toward his wagon. He knew when they reached his wagon that he would hook her up to his dead horse and pull her out of the way. Then he would hook her up to his wagon and teach her how to move it at a much greater pace by beating some sense into her lazy thick skull for being so slow.

Shortly after leaving the comforts of the barn, Vinnie and Skip came upon crossroads in the middle of the woods. They both looked for a sign of a wagon's wheel in the muddy trail, but to no avail. There weren't any kind of marks in the mud not even a dog print, a deer print, or any other kind of animal print or mark in it.

Skip used his gold for directions to the wagon as the arrow pointed easterly off into the thicket of the woods. It did not point down any one of the four roads they were on at the crossroads. "What does it mean, Skip?" Vinnie asked quite confused. "I don't know, Vinnie?" Skip made a vision come to him. "All I see in my vision is an old road not much traveled and covered thick with leaves. The Duke's dead horse was lying partly covered in some leaves, mud, and the muck with the crushed wagon laying sprawled out behind the horse." Skip's eyes filled up instantly with large tears of sadness. It surprised him because he did not think it was possible to have more tears left in his tiny eyes. His only thoughts were to give his lost parents the respectable burial they both deserved. They were not in a land not their own, but in a land far away from their beloved Ireland, unless the banshee had already taken them far away to the land of no return. Skip knew too well in his heart that he might, never see his parents alive ever again. After he and Vinnie bury the two, he would like to somehow return back home to Ireland and bring the sad news back with him to his Grandma Broom and Grandpa Hair of their lost daughter.

Vinnie took the road bearing off to the right as Skip's golden arrow pointed somewhere between it and the road to the left. "The road must connect to this one somewhere up ahead, Skip. I believe they will connect somewhere beneath the mountain on the other side with the road less traveled will appear again." After a couple of miles, the road turned into more of a path than a road. His gold again pointed into the woods and not down the path, they were on. After another mile, they came across the old logging road they had been so anxiously looking for. A set of wagon wheel marks plainly seen half filled with mud, muck and the leaves from the devastating storm of the night before. Skip's golden arrow pointed them in the direction to the left and up the road.

CHAPTER THIRTY-SEVEN

Finding the Wagon

Skip rode up front of Vinnie behind the post, and riding as a child would do on the saddle in front of his father on a trail ride, out in the woods. He felt that he would be safe and not seen by any mortals other than Vinnie, and he could hide like a child behind. Just up the road ahead of them laid, the crushed wagon beneath the mighty pine tree, and the Duke's dead horse still harnessed, to the wagon. Vinnie quickly jumped down from his horse and started feverishly tearing away at the crushed canvas top that was covering the top of the ravaged wagon. Skip began hysterically yelling out to his mother and father who looked to be beneath the crumpled up rubble. "Mother, mother, are you all right?" Skip began screaming while frantically helping Vinnie tear away at the inflexible cloth of the canvas top. He tried to help Vinnie pick up the tree from the wagon to set it aside and to get inside the wagon. He was so excited that he was not thinking clearly about his very special powers.

"Skip," yelled Vinnie, "pick the tree up and off the wagon with your magical powers". Skip suddenly came to his senses and immediately the tree floated up into the dry air and off the crushed wagon. He placed it down beside the wagon along the roadway. Tearing away the top of the wagon, Vinnie saw a most horrible site inside. The cage crushed beyond recognition and a small green jacket was sticking out from the side of the crushed wire mesh. "You do not want to look inside here, Skip. I shall take care of this problem for you by myself."

"What have you gone and done to my wagon? Get out of there, get away from that wagon you scoundrel. The law shall have you hung, strung up from the tallest tree for destroying the wagon, the medicine, and all of the belongings inside. What have you done with the two little friends on the wagon? What, have you done with them? What have you done? Thief, get away from the wagon. You, you have killed the horse too, by whipping the poor little thing to death you beast. Hey, are you not that scoundrel of a smithy, the thief I met back in Greenfield, the one who cheated me out of my hard-earned money, you are, are you not? You are that dishonest smithy, that smithy is who you are? You friend, will be put behind bars for the rest of your life, for what you have done to the horse, destroying the Duke's wagon, and killing his horse. You shall pay dearly, smithy. What have you gone and done with my two little friends, you scoundrel. I demand to know immediately! What you have done with them, and where are they off to?" Vinnie could not get a word in edgewise as the Duke continued hollering and screaming at him. He just stood there looking dumbfounded listening to this arrogant individual of mad man talk on and on, as the Duke picked up the crushed up cage, from the wagon without anyone inside of it.

Turning to Vinnie with the look of a viper in his eyes, the Duke immediately exploded into an even greater outrage. "You, you let him out didn't you? You let him out to get away, did you not? You had no business letting him out of his cage!" Vinnie then yelled back at the Duke. "Let who out of what cage? At this very moment just barely arriving here on the scene, trying to assist anyone still trapped if not a miracle, inside or under this crushed wagon. That is most that I have done since, and nothing else. What else, do you think I have done to your foolish flea circus if you had one, if there was one inside? I have been here but a few minutes, a few mere seconds looking inside to see if anyone including yourself trapped inside, and in need of some immediate medical assistance. A nice thanks, a man gives to a stranger who just happened bye to assist in helping someone.

Skip immediately transposed back into Vinnie's saddlebag when he first heard the Duke's voice hollering from afar. He stayed safely hidden there listening to the verbal battle going on between the Duke and Vinnie. "Who removed the tree from the wagon then, you? How did you move that monster pine tree that fell on my wagon, all by yourself then, might I ask?" "I did not move any pine tree from your wagon."

"Why that little wrenched twit of a liar. She said she did not have any powers left. She lied to me, why that little liar". "Mr. Duke, sir, that is your name I presume is it or not. Whom are you flapping your jar about anyway?" "Leprechauns you fool man, leprechauns is what I am talking about, you, you, fool! Leprechauns, I caught one. Then I caught his wife, and well that little mendacious twit!" The Duke used big words to baffle the ones around him. "She waited for me to leave she did, and well, sir, you are in real big trouble now for destroying this man's wagon and killing his sick defenseless horse. You good for nothing, I will own your livery stable back in Greenfield my good man, for all you have done to me this day! You are nothing but a horse thief, a crook, a butcher of animals, and I don't know what else!"

CHAPTER THIRTY-EIGHT

Lost Reality

The Duke lost all thought of the dire situation he had placed himself in just the day before. He pulled out a handgun from his pocket and quickly pointed it at Vinnie and gave him orders. "Pull the rest of that canvas off the top from the wagon. I want to see for myself what if anything still left intact of my worldly belongings that you have not managed to destroy inside with that tree you felled on it. I want to see if he or she is still not alive somewhere inside, hiding in a corner somehow beneath all that rubble. Vinnie began slowly taking pieces of splintered boards from off the top of the crushed wagon, and pulled as hard as he could on the canvas covering until it moved. They found much torn clothing and smashed tonic bottles everywhere. Nothing could have survived the wrath of the huge pine tree coming down on it. Vinnie pulled out many broken glass bottles, big pots for making the Duke's brew that were all squashed flats and other debris from within, but there was no sign of Skip's parents anywhere.

"Stealing another man's personal property in this country, my good man, is strictly against the law. I have caught you red-handed, right in the act of it steeling, if I might say so, myself. Doing such a horrendous deed to another human being's property is unchristian like, you know, for I know it was you who let the two of them get away, didn't you? You will pay dearly for the maliciously and dastardly deeds you did sir".

"I let the two of who get away?" "You know perfectly well, who I am talking about. You and that leprechaun's gold coin you are carrying around in your front pocket." Vinny pulled out the two of his front pockets to show the Duke he had nothing in them. "Letting them escape is the same as stealing one's money. You are nothing but a bad crook at that, and a scoundrel in the eyes of the law in this country. Mount your horse you scoundrel, you are going along to face justice, you are. Do not make any sudden moves sir, or try to make a run for it, as I am a good shot with my little friend Betsy that I have in my hand. I my good sir would like nothing better than to shoot right now you for killing the horse, especially after you have beaten her to death while trying to steal her along with all the worldly belongings in the wagon. You are nothing but a horse thief, murderer, and a useless dishonest s

CHAPTER THIRTY-NINE

The Duke's Ride to Justice

The Duke's ride to justice was a long slow one from the crushed wagon to the sheriff's office in the town of Westminster, and took most of the forenoon to do it. He would not stop his insane senseless talking to Vinnie. All he managed to talk about or ramble on about over, and over again was how he was going to own Vinnie's home and business. "I am the Duke! I see all, I hear all, and I know all!"

Vinnie softly talked to Skip along the way to the Duke's so-called justice. He kept telling him in a soft voice to stay calm and not to worry about his parents. They could not find a trace of them inside or outside the destroyed wagon. Soon they would return to the scene of the crushed up wagon and find his parents safe, and sound around the wagon somewhere he hoped. It was a good thing they were not in the wagon when the huge tree came crashing down on it. Then he told him beneath his breath that all he had to do was think what he wanted to tell Skip, and he could hear him. The same true experience was also occurring to Vinnie, for Skip would answer him without making any sort of noise. Vinnie did not quite understand what was happening, but he was glad they could talk without making a sound. It must have been Skip's leprechaunic mental telepathic abilities, Vinnie thought to himself. Skip was quite content for the moment knowing his parents were not dead in the debris of the wagon, or held prisoner any longer in the company of this mad man lunatic, the Duke. Even though he seemed very concerned for their welfare for his own benefit, he was very much concerned they were out in the woods all alone and much in another type of danger of wild animals who live there. Without his father's magical powers with them to protect themselves, anything imaginable might happen to the two of them, at any one given moment.

They arrived at the sheriff's office in Westminster after a very long tension-filled ride. With a gun still pointed at his back, Vinnie hoped the Duke was not really holding his finger on the trigger being the mad man he really was. "Dismount your stead, you good for nothing scoundrel. Dismount it now I say, now!" He screamed getting the attention of a couple of passing woman just to show them he was a big hotshot with a gun. Get off your horse and tie him to that hitching post over there, and then tie this horse to the hitching post over beside yours. I still have my faithful friend here in the palm of my hand, and it is pointed directly at your heart!" The Duke flopped down to the ground half falling over and almost landing flat on his face when dismounting his horse after being in the saddle for so long. The passing woman snickered at him the way he looked like a fish out of water, and it made the Duke even the more madder. After catching himself, he ordered Vinnie straight away into the sheriff's office.

"Good day to you my good young sir, sheriff. Here for you I have a criminal sir, a scoundrel of a beast just for you, so-as to serves justice, my good sheriff sir. I have come all this way here for your good legal system of this fine country to serve justice for handing over to me immediate restitution that I am so well deserving of, for all the sadness, the lonely inconveniences, along with all the losses this scoundrel of a man has caused me. You see my good sir sheriff this here is a crook I say to you as well as a horrific horse thief! My, good sir sheriff, I have brought him here before you for you to serve justice to me, and to restore my good deeds owed me by your wonderful government as a pleasant reward. Thankfully, I came up on this thief when he was trying to steal my horse and all of my belongings. He had already beaten my poor horse to death with my own whip after he had already stolen some of my most valuable and precious belongings from my wagon. Then good sir, after he killed my horse and pilfered through my belongings from within my wagon, he had the audaciousness to drop a very big pine tree down upon my wagon, destroying it along with the remainder of my precious goods. I demand justice immediately, my good man sheriff, for all of my somber inconveniences and losses as well. Justice I say, Justice! I want justice to be served now!"

Hearing the office door open, the sheriff looked up from his desk and stared firmly up at the huge fat beady-eyed man speaking before him, holding a gun pointed at the back of a man he did not recognize. Vinnie did not fit the description or look like the type of man the other man was describing to him. The sheriff had a pretty-good eye for people of faded glory, and this man did not fit that description. "What is your name, sir?" asked the sheriff of the man holding the gun to the back of the other. "I am the Duke! I see all, I hear all, and I know all!" The sheriff immediately pulled his gun from its holster and pointed it directly at the Duke. "You are both under arrest then until I can get to the bottom of this." "I am the Duke! You cannot arrest the Duke! I see all, I hear all, and I know all!"

Taking the Duke's gun carefully from his shaky hand, the sheriff spoke up very loud and clear, "Well then Mr. Duke, you must know it is also against the law to go around this country poisoning decent law-abiding citizens." The horrific thought of what he had done just the night before suddenly came back to haunt the Duke's very confused and debilitated mind. The thought of making a quick fortune off Vinnie and not fleeing to Boston had shadowed his good thinking of escaping to another country to live. He knew he was in more trouble now then he would have been if he had just left the little people in the wagon to fend for themselves and gone off to Boston alone on his new horse. "I do not go around this country poisoning perfectly healthy people, sir. I am the Duke! I see all! I hear all, and, I know all! I go around healing people of misfortune out of the goodness of my heart, not even hurting a small fly, the precious little creatures of God. I go around the countryside getting sick citizens of your fine country life, for a fee of course. I make and sell the highest quality of modern medicines there are to heal the very sick. I go around eradicating the many dreadful diseases on this earth by taking away the sicknesses from those who are helplessly diseased, and making them well. I eradicate freckles, mumps, and warts from everyone, my good honest sheriff, like yourself?"

"Who are you?" the sheriff asked as he turned away from the Duke and looked straight toward Vinnie. "I am Vinnie McDougall, sheriff. I run a livery stable and inn in the township of Greenfield, sir. I work for the Good Run Stagecoach Company out of Boston. I am contracted out to them for keeping their horses fed, shoed, and change teams for them when a stagecoach comes into my stable, sir." "How did you ever get mixed up with the likes of this Duke fellow?" "I stopped at a destroyed wagon out in the deep woods to see if I could be of any assistance to any of the occupants if any were still alive. Plain hap incense was to come across the wagon, by accident on the trail I was so leisurely enjoying out in the cool of forest on a hot day. During the tremendous winds of the thunderstorm last evening, the Dukes wagon crushed beyond repair by a huge fallen pine tree and the wagon was gone. I did not think I would find anyone alive inside. As a caring human being, I stopped to see if anyone inside was badly injured, and possibly try to help the best I could if there were any. Then this big brute of a bloke comes along all phony and loudmouthed as I am trying to get to anyone who might still be inside, and accused me of killing his horse and smashing up his wagon with a tree the lightning had struck. Then he had the nerve to accuse me of killing his poor little horse, the horses back all tattered open with flesh wounds from a bull whip as well. I believe he had done the work himself after seeing the shape his horse was in a week ago when I fixed a broken wheel for him back at my smithy shop, sir."

"Liar, he beat her to death himself, good sir sheriff. She was a tired old filly and was unable to pull my heavy load of wares any further in the muddy rutted road ahead. I left her safe, and sound, there in the middle of the woods with some hay in good health and harnessed to my wagon while I went to fetch another horse to help her. The one I purchased is standing right outside your door. My horse is-tied to hitching post, right alongside this crook's horse, which should belong to me now for bringing in this horse thief. The truth, good sheriff, is this. When I was gone in search of this other horse, this scoundrel of a villain came along, cruelly beating my poor tired Hannah to death with my own whip, mind you, the one I had left on the wagon. I had only to ask her gently, for she would do anything and everything for me I asked of her in a soft voice. Then this villainous scoundrel comes along and drops a huge pine tree down on both the wagon and the poor horse. He is nothing but a vicious scoundrel, I say to you sheriff! He is the one in need of being arrested locked up, and dealt severely with. You, my good man sheriff, cannot arrest me! I am the Duke! I see all, I hear all, and I know all!" The sheriff immediately put the two of them in behind bars in his jailhouse. He locked Vinnie in one cell and the Duke in another one.

Skip had formed such a good relationship with Vinnie that he could use Vinnie's eyes to see what was going on in the sheriff's office, and he could use his ears to hear every word spoken, as well. The situation at hand in the sheriff's office did not look promising for him or Vinnie to be heading back out into the forest to look for his missing parents real-soon. The gold in Skip's satchel began to moan and groan for no apparent reason. Placing his gold in his lap, it formed an arrow pointing toward the saddlebag resting on the Duke's horse saddle. Skip looked cautiously around to see that the coast was clear all around the horses and down the street. When it was, he jumped from Vinnie's horse's back to the Duke's horse's back making sure no one was around to spot him. He did not think it necessary to transpose as it was so close. Skip proceeded carefully looking into the Duke's saddlebags. He did not dare transpose inside the saddlebag in fear the Duke might have some poison or evil spell in them that had held his parents for so long. In them, Skip found the green-wired cage crushed by the pine tree. It was the same cage the Duke had been holding his father prisoner in all these years.

As Skip sat there staring down at the crinkled up metal, his pouch of gold began to hum out a lovely Irish melody. It was a melody so close to his heart that he felt the close warmness of Ireland all about him. What did this strange melody coming from his satchel of gold mean to him? Why was his gold coming out with this beautiful melody like a happy harp while he was standing on the back of the Duke's horse looking down into his saddlebags? Then a tiny reflection of sunlight reflected up at him from the scratch the Duke had made on the side of the cage with one of his metal coins from his pocket. The green cage was not made of iron at all, for the green cage was really made of shiny gold. He asked his gold what he should do next, but did not get a response from it that he had been looking for. The gold continued playing out its beautiful melody from his satchel. All that Skip was looking for was a change in the melody or something simple to show him what to do next, but there was no sign to him from his gold.

Skip took a coin from his satchel, and was going to scrape some of the green paint from off the golden cage. As soon as his gold piece touched the gold wire of the cage, a piece of the cage, with a loud thunderous pop, instantly turned into a bright shiny gold coin similar in shape of the gold coin of his own. He immediately poured out his entire pouch of tiny shiny golden coins from his pouch down into the Duke's saddlebag. Like a flash of lightning and an instant very loud clap of thunder, the gold coins from his pouch reacted simultaneously with his father's gold. The reaction caused by his gold touching his father's gold made a louder thunderous clap louder than a musket going off in one's ear.

The sheriff went bounding out from his office and the jailhouse door and into the street as fast as his feet would take him. He went into the street with his gun drawn for action, looking for the source of the two very explosive sounds that replicated the sound of gunshots. There was not a soul around. There were only the two horses that were jumping and twitching nervously around from the loud thunderous noise. The minute the gold reacted, Skip transposed to the safety of the jailhouse rooftop and out of sight. The sheriff did not see him looking down at him as he scanned the streets all around. He knew he had to protect his gold and the other gold in the Duke's saddlebag no matter what took place below. He knew the other gold must have belonged to his father or another fallen leprechaun. Seeing no one in or around the streets, the sheriff retreated, back inside to the quiet of his office and scratched his head. It must have been from another approaching storm. Leastwise he thought it would be quiet in his office.

"I demand, I demand you right now, sheriff, to bring me my saddlebags this very moment from my horse's saddle tied outside. Right now, I say sheriff!" The Duke, as usual, requested everything he wanted in life in a very loud abusive grumpy tone of voice. Vinnie was much nicer to the sheriff when he spoke to him. "Sir, all of my money and my belongings are in my saddlebags outside, sir. If you would not mind sheriff, when and if you go out to fetch his saddlebags, I would certainly appreciate it, if you were to fetch my saddlebags along with the Duke's, if you please, sir. Skip used his magical powers immediately taking all the gold from out of the Duke's saddlebags and transposed it all to the top of the roof with him. The gold formed into two neatly separate little piles. Skip's gold formed a pile in his lap, and the other pile of gold formed in a pile beside him on the rooftop.

Skip temporarily forgot all about Vinnie, and the predicament he was in, with His mind elsewhere, too busy staring down studying the two piles of gold before him. He was truly speculating who might the other pile of gold belonged to. He had a very good idea but not really knowing for certain, if it had been his father's gold or some other unfortunate leprechaun's gold. He requested the help of his gold again, as if it would just come out and talk to him. This time the gold in his lap did not talk he had hoped it might, but pointed directly to the pile of gold sitting beside of him on the rooftop. The pile turned itself into an arrow and pointed back across the town where he and Vinnie had just come from at the mountain. This arrow looked strange like his, for there was a similar piece of his golden arrow missing, quite similar to his own. Skip knew why his two pieces of gold were missing from his arrow when it formed, but was confused to why the other pile of gold also had a single piece of its golden arrow missing from it. He concentrated as hard he could on the other pile of gold, hoping it was one of his parent's satchels of gold. He did not know the pile of gold he had cried for in his own satchel, was once his mothers. Skip spotted the two of them sitting high on a mountaintop and hunkered down together looking out over a cleft of rocks. They seem to be gazing off in the far distance over the treetops eastward toward the ocean. Skip could barely make out the faint skyline of Boston's buildings sticking up in the horizon.

Reluctantly the sheriff, because of Vinnie's nice manners, did go out and get the saddlebags from the horses. He handed the saddlebags to the Duke cautiously through the opening in the bars he used to feed his prisoners. Then the sheriff turned and went to Vinnie's cell and handed him his saddlebags cautiously through the bars as well. Before the sheriff had handed either the Duke or Vinnie their saddlebags, he carefully scanned the insides of them, searching their belongings to make sure there was not possibly a handgun or some other type of weapon neatly hidden inside. "My good sheriff," the Duke bellowed out as usual, what had you gone and done with my gold?" "There was no gold in your saddlebags, Mr. Duke." "The crushed green cage was my gold." "There was no green cage in either side of your saddlebags."

"My good man sheriff, you are as much of a thief as that scoundrel you are securely harboring in the cell next to me. You are nothing but a crook, a crooked man of the law, and a thief yourself. You are nothing but a liar. I demand my gold from you this instant or you'll will, too, force me to have you arrested along with that scoundrel next to me." The sheriff was completely appalled with the Duke's sudden actions along with the horrific verbal abuse dished out at him all at the same time by the Duke. He knew the man must be a lunatic, a mad man, and insane as there had been no gold or wire cage in the Duke's saddlebags.

Soon a telegram came into the sheriff's office from his friend the sheriff of Greenfield. After reading the telegram, he turned to Vinnie with the keys to the cell in hand and unlocked his cell. "Mr. McDougall, sir, you are free to go. I received good word about you from the sheriff in Greenfield, and I am very sorry for any inconvenience he and I may have caused you. May I call upon you one day as a material witness in the near future if need be?" "I would be delighted to be a material witness for you too, sir. He is not a nice man." With saying those few words, Vinnie picked up his saddlebags from off the bunk in the cell and left the confines of the sheriff's office immediately in search of Skip.

"You are letting him escape, you fool! This murderer killed the horse and the very one who destroyed the wagon. You are letting a guilty man escape, sir. You are as much a crook as he is, Sheriff. You two are in-cahoots with one another, to share the gold the two of you have stolen from me. I will have the two of you tried and prosecuted for the real crooks you really are. You two will spend the rest of your living days behind steel bars in prison. I will see to it myself! I know, for I am the Duke. I see all I hear all, and I know all!" The Duke was a screaming mad man ranting and raving ludicrously at the top of his bold vicious voice about his gold the sheriff had stolen from him while Vinnie secured his saddlebags to his saddle. Mounting his horse, Vinnie slowly turned his mount easterly and slowly rode away in the direction of Wachusett Mountain.

CHAPTER FORTY

The Second Pouch of Gold

"Skip, Skip, where are you, Skip?" "I'm right here, Vinny." Vinny hearing Skip looked down to his right behind his saddle to his saddlebags. Skip was in there looking up at him. He was speaking out of the flap of the saddlebag where he had stayed hidden before. "I know where my mother and father are, Vinnie. I could see them in my vision; they are just fine and all right for the time being. They are sitting all alone on top of the mountain. We must hurry Vinny. Let us get going Vinnie. It will be way after dark before we can get back there if you do not hurry. We need to hurry so we can help them. We must move quickly. Hurry, Hurry, Hurry!"

The light of day was quickly passing by for them, for Vinny held so long in the sheriff's office, waiting for the telegram to arrive from Greenfield. The sheriff had to check out Vinny's story and verify he was living and owning the livery stable in Greenfield. He softly nudged his horse forward into a light trot to make up for precious lost time and then into a full gallop for a short time. The dark of night would soon befall them, and the first shade of darkness was quickly casting its shadow over them when they finally reached the site of the Duke's destroyed wagon in the wild of the woods. Everything at the site of the destroyed wagon still looked the same. The horse still laid hitched to the destroyed wagon, and not been torn apart by any wild animals of the forest yet. They quickly made up camp and had a fire ablaze near the rear of the wagon for the night. They both hoped Skip's parents were not very far away, and by chance might see the light from the campfire they had just made.

When they first arrived at the wagon site, Skip wanted immediately too start the desperate search for his parents. Then Vinnie insisted he help him find some dry kindling wood from fallen trees and get the campfire going first. It turned out to be a good thing that they had set up camp first, as the pitch black of night was now totally upon them. As soon as the fire flickered alive, the wicked sounds of the banshee's dreaded voice started singing her song of death that filled the dry dark night air with fright. Her song they heard coming closer and closer by flying in circles it seemed around the mountain. The fright of her singing covered poor Skip and Vinnie's weary faces. They just stared at one another as they stood in the light of the campfire. Skip was scared to death for the safety of his parents, and did not care about his own, as they were all alone on the top of the mountain without any magic for their own protection. He pulled off his heavy satchel of gold that had his and his father's gold mixed together with his own. The mixture of them caused him to have yet another vision, the clearest one he had ever had of his parents. The strength of both piles of gold made his vision of his mother and father seem as if they were standing right there next to them by the fire.

Skip could see his parents snuggled up tightly together by a large cluster of great protruding rocks. Where on the mountaintop where they, he wondered? Skip looked past the two of them to see what was near or close around them. They were very close to the top of the mountain, for Skip could see hundreds of pleasant bright glittering stars ablaze shining in the heavens above them, and the bright moon just cresting up over the horizon. He also saw something very menacing approaching them in the dark of night. A long dark black looking shadow of a figure was slithering along on the ground, creeping along the stone surface of rock with its legs stuck closely to the ground beneath its body as it approached. Then there came the cry of the banshee heard for miles around the mountain. She had finally found the two of them unprotected without any place to run or hide and without their magical powers to protect them from the likes of the she-devil of death. They were doomed!

With all of his might, Skip picked up all of the gold and clutched it tightly in his arms. He concentrated with all of his mental and magical powers on the banshee for he thought she was crawling along the ground to claim her prize. He stood standing beside Vinnie looking worried as sweat ran down his worried face. Suddenly a massive musclebound mountain lion lay crouched down beside Skip and Vinnie ready to pounce on some poor unsuspecting creature. Vinnie jumped back away from the creature and almost fell headfirst into the fire as he grabbed frantically for a burning branch from within the fire. The mountain lion was as frightened as the two of them. Not knowing what had just happened, it took off leaping over Skip and into the blackness of the night and was gone. "What on earth are you trying to do, Skip, get the two of us killed?" Vinnie yelled out at Skip with a very loud, very nervous quiver in his low voice, "I am trying to bring my parents here so they will be all right and safe". "Well, be more careful next time will you lad, or you shall get us both eaten alive."

Skip lost the vision of his parents for a split second the mountain lion arrived in camp. He had to concentrate again for the vision of his parents to return. There they were huddled tighter together now than before still looking over to where the huge cat had just been. They had seen it come and had no place left to hide. The two of them figured the mountain lion was some form of the wicked banshee coming to take them both away to the other side of life.

He concentrated extremely hard and very cautiously this time using all of his magical powers strictly on his mother. He figured he had more of a chance by transposing one at a time to the safety of the campfire than trying to transpose both at the same time. Skip was very glad he had summoned a cat to the campfire instead of the dreaded banshee. He did not know what he was going to do with her if it had been her. He just wanted to protect his mother and father standing there hunkered down and huddled up tight beside Skip and holding tightly to his arm. Seeing Vinnie standing there before her by the fire caused her to scream and caused Skip to fall over backwards. For a split second, he thought the mountain lion had returned. Skip's mother fell over the other way after seeing Skip and Vinnie standing beside her, scared to death of the two strangers that stood there before her. She knew it had to be black magic that took her away from her husband's side.

Then there came the screams of the deadly banshee's song of death again echoing through the warm night air and around the mountaintop.

All of the sudden, Skip's poor frightened mother felt the closeness of her loving son, Skip. She somehow knew the short stranger standing there beside her now with his full-grown beard must be her own son. She remembered Vinnie somewhere in the back of her mind. Skip quickly closed his eyes once again to concentrate on his father this time. In his vision, his poor frightened father was backing away from yet another mountain lion on the mountaintop coming at him from another direction as he walked away from the cleft of rocks in search of his wife. He thought the banshee they had both been watching had somehow taken her away to the other side of life, but he was not sure of it. He was backing away from another banshee by looking side to side frantically and calling out to his wife. He was slowly backing away from the two very black shiny diamond shaped eyes that sparkled like diamonds in the night from the new full moon in the sky. He could see the sparkly eyes very clearly in the darkness as they approached him slithering along in a smooth slow motion way.

When the big cat pounced forward toward his father, Skip concentrated with all his might. His father appeared out of nowhere like his mother had, but had the astonishing look of death written all across his face. He was falling over backwards to the ground when he appeared as if someone or something had just pushed him off his feet. "I see her", he screamed, "I see her, I see the banshee and her dreaded teeth of death!" He screamed out again as he landed on his back knowing he was safe. "She was screaming in my face and laughing at me with her teeth clicking and clacking and smiling at me." Picking himself up off the ground, his father jumped aside and ran straight to the side of his wife. He hugged her with all of his might, being very glad she was still very much alive and safe. "I will not let the likes of these two bug you, my love. What do the likes of you two blokes want with us anyway? We have no money, and we have no gold, "Skip's father stepped up in front of his wife to protect her as he should. "I have none of my powers left to grant you any wishes, so please let us be." He begged for their freedom. "Please let us go and be off with you." "It is Skip, Pa. It is our son, Skip, you foolish old man." Looking at Skip, his father did not recognize him to be his son and did not feel the closeness that his mother felt for her son. "Who is this mortal standing beside you then if you are our son? Does this mortal have all of your gold like the Duke has mine?"

"If he was to have my gold, Pa, you and Mother would not be standing here all safe and sound, now would you, Pa?" "Skip saved us, Pa. Our little boy has come all this way to America and saved our lives from the Duke." "He is not my son, and he is not your son either, you foolish old woman. My son is but a wee little lad, woman. This is no wee lad for he is but a young man, and not our wee son." Skip spoke up, "It has been a very long time, Pa, has it not since you last saw me? Father, I am your wee little boy, Skip." Tears welled up in Skip's loving heartfelt eyes. "Do not cry, my son, if you are my son, not in front of this mortal anyway. Your tears will turn to, well they will turn to, just do not cry in front of this mortal." Skip picked up his satchel of gold. "My tears might turn to gold, Pa, tears of gold." "Yes son, show your gold to that mortal there, and he will take it all away from you and your powers will be lost as well.

"This here mortal standing beside me has a name, Pa. His name is Vinnie, Pa, Mr. Vinnie McDougall. He helped us save you and Ma's life, Pa! You owe him your satchel of gold for helping me save your life." "I have no gold of my own any longer, son. The only piece of gold I have left is this mere old green broken lock made from my gold. The rest of the gold is still in the wagon in the form of a wire cage, and I do not know how to get it back so I might be able to use its powers again. By the looks of the wagon all pulled apart, I would say the Duke has come back and claimed all my gold for himself again. He had a cage of my gold made just to hold me prisoner in. The Duke knew I could not break the magic powers of my own gold. All my wonderful powers were lost forever, while trapped inside. The painted golden cage would get hot and burn should I touch it. When he threw the flinging it and me across the back of the wagon so hard, he broke the lock and the spell he had upon me. He was the only one who could break the spell, but he didn't know it when the lock broke and set me free."

"Your ma, the strong little lady she is, lifted up the cage all by herself just in the nick of time as the lightning bolt hit the tree. The cage door sprung open to free his prisoner, and picking up the broken lock just before leaving the wagon as the big tree came crashing down through it demolished it. Your ma here is the one who saved my life. Your Mom, she should get the all the gold, but the Duke is probably off with it right now as we speak. Sure as we are all talking here, he is off looking for the two of us right now. We were his two biggest attractions of his phony medicine show. He has the rest of my gold, and I shall never see it again." "No, Pa, the rest of your gold is right here in my pouch along with my own." Taking his satchel from his side, Skip poured out all the gold he had onto the ground below. Skip's gold stayed in one neat pile while his father's pile formed the shape of an arrow pointing in the direction of the green lock in his father's hand. "Give me your green lock of gold, Pa." His father was reluctant to hand his golden lock over to his son. "Give it to your boy, Pa." Listening to his wife, he reluctantly handed Skip the golden lock and placed it at the tip of the golden arrow. When the lock of gold touched the point of the arrow and the two pieces of gold touched one another, the green lock burst into the shape of the other golden coins, finishing the point of the arrow. The green paint had turned to dust and the green lock turned a bright shiny gold to match the rest of the golden arrow. Then the arrow turned back into a neat little pile of gold like Skip's gold had. "Here, this is all of your gold, Pa." "All of it?" "Now what on earth are you going to do with it now, Pa," asked Skip. He was hoping his father would do the right thing by freely presenting his satchel of gold to Vinnie and happy that he helped Skip save his life. It was the law of the leprechaun and his solemn obligation to do just that. Skip's father knew it was the way as well. As soon as he reached down and picked up his satchel of gold, poof he was gone.

Skip's mother spoke up. "Just like you, Pa, to do something like that, the wrong thing at the right time." Skip suddenly sensed something very strange and wrong taking place, and quickly reached out and took hold of his mother's hand. Unexpectedly, he felt a great surge of power trying to take Mom away from him. The more the strong power tried to take his mother away, the more Skip resisted it with all his might. His father was trying his hardest to take his mother away from him again and into the dark of the forest to hide there with him. He had his gold and all of his powers back again, and was trying with all of his might to use it one more time to reclaim his wife. He wanted her back in the worst-way, and Skip needed his mother more now than he had ever needed her before. Skip held tightly with all his might onto the one he so loved the most of anything else in all-the world.

"You cannot have her, Pa! She is going to stay right here with me Pa! You took her away from me once before, but you cannot do it to me again. You cheated me once before, your own son, Pa! You went and took her away from me for many years when I needed her the most, and you took yourself away from me as well when you left. I love the two of you very much, Pa, but if you want to go, then goodbye, but you cannot have her back this time. She is all mine! I need you, too, Pa. I missed-out, on a lot things Pa by not having you around when I was but a wee little lad. You cannot have her unless she wants to go. I have all of her powers now, Pa. If she wants to stay, she will stay; not any the powers of the world will match our powers combined. So if you want to go, go and be gone with you, for good!"

Skip's hand that was holding his mother's hand with was on fire with pain. He tried desperately to hold his mother there and keep her safe from leaving. His father's powers were great, but not great enough. His mother did not see how much pain Skip was going through because she could not feel the pain her son or husband where experiencing at the same time. All she could see was the deep love in her son's eyes for her as he stared back at her while talking to his father with a grimaced face of pain and love all at the same time. Skip reached down for his gold knowing very well if he held it firmly in his control, he would have more power than his father would. Soon as the gold in the pile touched his fingertips, the severe burning pain in his hand vanished. Simultaneously, the three standing by the campfire heard an excruciating cry of pain echoing out from the darkness in the woods.

"I love you, Pa," said Skip. "Please come back as we both need you now and want you to come home to Ireland with us. Mother will be brokenhearted without you after all these years. You must keep the ways of our people if you wish to be a good leprechaun. It is your fiduciary duty to act like an honest to goodness customs-abiding leprechaun. You must give all of your gold to Vinnie. He helped save your life, and you owe it to him." Skip's father called back to him from deep in the woods. "I will suffer the loss of my special powers again if I give up my gold to anyone and will not be able to do the good things leprechauns should do." "You did not do them right before so what makes you so sure you will do the right thing again in the future? You drank the evil tonic did you not, and you took away the freedom from yourself and your wife, never mind your so. You never did practice good leprechaun deeds before when you had all of your special powers. If you keep your gold for yourself and regain all of your powers, you will probably go and do the same bad things you did before all over again anyway. Give your gold to Vinnie, Pa, and come home to Ireland with us. I promise you I will take good care of you and Mother."

Several very long, slow agonizing minutes passed by for the three of them, especially for Skip. Vinnie, Skip, and Skip's mother stood patiently by the fire waiting for an answer from his father. They stood there waiting patiently for his father to say or do something very drastic. He held tight to his mother's hand and knew very well from his father's past poor reputation, that he just might try something very funny and out of the ordinary if he did not hold her tight. Then out of the deep darkness of the forest, his father appeared. He walked up to Vinnie, bowed down politely to him, and quickly placed all of his gold at Vinnie's feet. He then backed away very quickly from Vinnie as if not wanting to be seen and in a quick panic. "Here is my gold, Mr. Vinny McDougall, sir!" "Hand it over to him the right way, Pa! You know the proper way. Hand it over to him by your own hands!"

His father knowingly and very hesitantly bent down and slowly picked up his satchel of gold. He did so begrudgingly ever so slow and looked side to side with a frown across his face as if caught with his hands in the cookie jar. With each slow movement, he was constantly thinking of what he might do next to get out of handing Vinnie the gold finally without any recourse insight, he handed his satchel of gold over to Vinnie.

Skip's father was a very smart leprechaun and knew their ways. He knew if he did not hand the gold to Vinnie with his own two hands that in the future he could take it back from Vinnie at any time he wished. By handing the gold to Vinnie with his own two hands, it formed a valued seal between the two of them, never be broken; unless of course Vinnie wanted to freely hand back Skips fathers gold to him. Then and only then, could the special powers as a leprechaun and his gold be restored to him. "Did this here Mr. McDougall friend of yours save your life too, son? Do you have to give this here mortal Mr. McDougall all of your gold as well?" "No not yet do not have to give him any of my gold, but I did promise him a wish though. When I gave him a piece of my gold to hold onto as a token of friendship, I promised him a wish when I returned."

"You gave a mortal a piece of your leprechaun gold? What is the matter with your brains, son? Have you gone daft and lost your mind? You just cannot go around giving your leprechaun gold and powers away everyone you know. You will lose all of your special powers if you do such a foolish thing." "I know that, Pa, I know that now." "Then why did you do it in the first place?" "The reason is I had no mother or father to teach me any different. You two were gone far away remember? Grandma Broom and Grandpa Hair had said something about my gold once to me, but I was too young to care and did not listen to them because they were not my true parents. Vinnie McDougall here is a friend. That is why I gave him a piece of my special gold just to hold."

"Leprechauns do not have mortals for their friends, son. Leprechauns only have themselves to be friendly with and not to any cantankerous sneaky mortals like him. Your grandfather will have his way with you and will pull out every-last strand of hair on your daffy head one by one, when he finds out you have a mortal for a friend Skip. Leprechauns he would laugh having people for friends, huh, why that is unheard of. The mortals will steal you blind, Son. You just cannot go around trusting any of the. Why they are the most cantankerous, mischievous, and argumentative pranksters and liars of them all." "We are, are we not, Pa, exactly what you said about the mortals," he began to laugh a powerful laugh aloud. Vinnie saw the humor in it, as did Skip's mother, and they all began to laugh almost uncontrollably while Skip's father stood there without a clue to what Skip had just insinuated. "Why, what is so funny about that? Why he tricked me out of gold and power did him not?" "No, Pa, he did not, he helped to save your life by helping find you and save mother's life, too. We owe him a whole bunch more than just a pouch of leprechaun gold. I am not quite sure of what we owe him, but it is certainly a heck of a lot more than gold alone." "Then why can I not have my gold back?" "Because it is the way of the leprechauns, Pa, that is why".

CHAPTER FORTY-ONE

The Little Coach

"I am tired," Skip said with a grunt, "enough of this foolish malarkey about your gold." Skip turned and looked at the wrecked wagon lay strewn all about on the ground before them and raised his hands high above his head. He was saying a few words to a spell, and the pieces of strewn broken wood from the destroyed wagon flew up into the magical night air. The campfire illuminated many small swirling fragmented pieces of wagon like a small tornado of floating toothpicks high above the glow of fire. To Vinnie's amazing surprise, as all the fragmented pieces of wood came together as a whole, they formed themselves into the shape of a small stagecoach. Miniature in size compared to a full-size stagecoach, but just right for Skip, his mother, and his father to ride in. A comfortable seat he formed on top of the coach for Vinnie up front so he could drive it home to Greenfield.

The four of them all settled down by the fire after Vinnie's stoked it with more fallen wood from the forest they had gathered, and made sure his horse was safe and secure for the night. When daybreak arrived after a pleasant night's sleep by the fire, the four of them packed up what clothing Skip's parents wanted to salvage from the wrecked wagon. They were off down the beaten path on their slow journey toward Greenfield. Vinnie knew by being gone for only a couple of days that he needed to get back to the stable and inn, where he needed to be. He was sure Becky and Bernice would be worried sick about him after hearing from the sheriff of Westminster, and wondering what kind of mischievous trouble he and Skip had gotten themselves into this time. Vinnie drove the miniature stagecoach right through the small township of Westminster and past the sheriff's office. He could still hear the Duke ranting and raving about the sheriff being a crook and stealing all of his gold. He then drove it through the small township of South Gardner and several other small communities along the way. People looked in awe as Vinnie drove the miniature stagecoach by. He waved to all the good happy folk all along the way, especially to the children. People of the area had never seen such a magnificent replica of a large stagecoach before. When the town's people of the several small rural establishments came out alongside the coach to have a look inside, he would tell them it did not open. He said it was only for show, and the doors and windows on it made to remain closed. When the coast was clear, though, Skip had made a flexible wooden shades in order to be opened when Vinnie told him it was safe to view out and take in the beautiful scenery surrounding them along the country way.

It was late in the afternoon when Vinnie came rolling into Greenfield with his miniature stagecoach and his three tiny guests. Bernice and Becky were sitting on the front porch waiting for them to arrive, when Vinnie finally pulled his one horse stagecoach around the corner and upfront of the house. He waved cheerfully to the two of them with a wonderful smile painted across his happy face, and then went out back of the inn to the stable with the coach and his passengers. Bernice and Becky had been expecting them to come along at any moment as word had come to them by way of several stagecoach drivers who had passed them along the way to Greenfield. The drivers told the girls that Vinnie was driving a miniature stagecoach, and laughed as they told Bernice and Becky that he was trying to put the big stagecoach lines out of business. They could not believe their eyes when Vinnie finally pulled up in front of them. They had never seen such a beautiful coach, even a big stagecoach, made so well or as beautifully handcrafted shiny and polished, as this miniature coach ever made, to sparkle and shine.

"What in tarnation are you all doing now, Mr. Vincent McDougall?" Bernice said very loud with a smile on her face. "Gone off for a couple of days to play?" The work around here is building up as we speak, and you have the nerve to come back home with that contraption. I thought you and that Skip leprechaun friend of yours were both off trying to save his parents or something." Bernice sounded mad when she first spoke to Vinnie, though she was quite impressed with the bright brand new sparkling miniature stagecoach sitting in her stable's yard.

Skip opened the wooden shades when Bernice approached the miniature stagecoach. She gasped for a breath of air with wonderment on her face and nearly fell over backwards to the ground when she first spotted the three little leprechauns peeking their little heads out at her, all tucked safely away, and hidden comfortably inside. She turned and went straight toward the kitchen entrance of the inn without saying another word to Vinnie.

"You just cannot trust those mortals, Son. She is another one that will take your gold from you. Just you wait and see. I know it, for I can see it. She has that no good looking shiftiness in her eyes as well as that there Mr. McDougall friend of yours." Becky came quickly out and off the porch to greet Vinnie as Bernice passed her by. When they passed, Bernice looked funny at Becky, but did not say a word to her. She walked right on by with her head hung down shaking it from side to side and mumbling to herself.

"Close the shade, Son, close the shade! Here comes another one of those untrustworthy mortals." Skip just held the shade wide-open for Becky to peek inside as she asked Vinnie if everything had gone all right for them. She waved to Skip and his family, and he told Vinnie about the local sheriff of Greenfield who had come out all the way to the stagecoach inn that very afternoon looking for him. It seems a sheriff from down east somewhere needed Vinnie to come back and testify about some Duke called the medicine man. The sheriff had also requested Vinnie to wire him directions to where to find the Dukes crushed wagon and dead horse.

Vinnie just stared down at Skip after hearing this news and looked rather pale as he spoke. "What do we do now, Skip?" Skip took his mother and father from the miniature stagecoach safely into the house section of the inn. Bernice prepended neither Skip nor his parents were even there in the same room with her. She pretended as if they were fragments of her wild imagination playing little old tired tricks of age on her elderly mind. Becky came right along in with them and stayed with Skip's mother and father, while he and Vinnie went out back to the barn with the miniature stagecoach in tow.

CHAPTER FORTY-TWO

Trouble Brewing

"Vinnie," Skip said, "I need to borrow your satchel of gold for just a wee minute. I promise you a leprechaun's promise that I will give it right back to you when I am finished." Skip took his gold pouch and put the two piles of gold together as one. Skip next held the gold in both his hands concentrating as hard he possibly could on the site of the shambled tree covered wagon. He stared methodically at the miniature stagecoach in the barn with them with all his mental thought and ability. The miniature stagecoach instantly vanished into thin air, disappearing right before Vinnie and Skip's eyes. When Skip had finished his precise concentration on making the stagecoach disappear, he made a vision appear to him of the Duke's destroyed shambled wagon. The wagon lay crushed beneath the huge pine tree with broken tonic bottles strewn all about. The poor whipped and abused horse laying on the ground, still hooked up to the front of the wagon as she always had been. Skip tore open the canvas top of the wagon as if someone had tried to see inside to see if anyone was still alive, or trapped inside in need of medical help, so the sheriff could tell Vinnie had tried to help someone inside if he could have.

The next day Vinnie would go off to the sheriff's office in Greenfield and have the sheriff send a telegram to the sheriff's office in Westminster. Vinnie would give the sheriff the precise location where they could find the crushed wagon. Vinnie would forget all about the Duke ever retaliating against him forever. When the sheriff takes his men out to look at the wagon as a witness along with the Duke, the

Duke would surely tell the sheriff that Vinnie had taken the tree off the wagon all by himself after he had made the tree fall upon it. He would then proceed to tell the sheriff and his men just how Vinnie must have put the poison in the bottle with his medicine that killed poor old Mr. Bristol. For he is the Duke, the one who sees all, the one who hears all, and the one who does not know how to treat his beast or fellow human beings! The search party would uncover the truth about poor old Mr. Bristol's death. As for the other two people who were supposed to be with him in the wagon, well, there was no one around when he first discovered the crushed wagon. That was the truth, and that is why he looked inside to see if anyone was in there. Who would believe the Duke's wild story anyway? Leprechauns, Mr. McDougall stole his precious little leprechauns. Leprechauns that vanish into thin air, Vinnie laughed a hearty laugh. Then the Duke would tell the sheriff that Vinnie must have had his leprechaun friends put the tree back on top of the wagon to make him look bad. Vinnie laughed again.

Skip and his parents stayed at the inn hiding in the attic making it their temporary home for quite some time. His mother made a bed for herself and her husband out of spare blankets as Skip had made from the many blankets Bernice had stored there for her guests. Skip led his mother and father to the bed he had slept on for the past long year or so. The three of them would transpose up and down the stairs to eat at meal times with Bernice and Vinnie when the inn had no company or guests eating at the table except for Becky. Otherwise, the three of them would eat their meals up in the attic.

Skip stayed busy helping Vinnie with his many chores in the barn. Vinnie finally had to tell Skip to stop helping him do everything all of the time. He explained to him how he would forget how to do many things he needed to remember himself and what would he do when Skip and his family returned to Ireland? His body's muscles would be limp and his mind so soft that nothing would ever get done on time around the stable, and everyone around would suffer. Skip's family stayed at the inn with Vinnie and Bernice until word of a ship sailing for Ireland came along to carry them all back home again. Then and only then would Skip and his mother and father straight away off to Boston, on the first trek of their long way back home to Ireland.

Vinnie McDougall became a well-known celebrity in the area around Greenfield as the fastest stable man alive. He was becoming known statewide for his outstanding ability to change a team of tired out stagecoach horses for a fresh team in only a couple of minutes all by himself. Working hands at other stagecoach stops across the region tried to beat his record time, and the drivers of the stagecoaches would just laugh at them when they failed. What would Vinnie ever do when Skip returned to Ireland? Probably tell everyone around that the pace was just too fast for an aging older man such as himself to continue, and tell everyone he was slowing down just to save his health and to live a longer more enjoyable life. Becky became more deeply in love with Vinnie. His kindness around the children when they got off the coaches, the way he helped everyone, and for keeping a special secret that they all hid up in the attic of the inn. She was ready to wed him as soon as he built up enough courage to ask her. She was ready to raise a family with him and live at the inn with him and Bernice. Vinnie had shown both Becky and Bernice what kind of a man he really was. Bernice held Charles' thoughts of Vinnie as close to her heart as a son would be to her heart. Becky did not care if Bernice lived with them at the inn until the day she died, as Becky thought of Bernice as Vinnie's mother, and so did Vinnie.

It had been a long time coming, but finally one-day word came to the Inn of a ship sailing into Boston Harbor. On her departure, she would be sailing straight towards Ireland. She would be arriving in Boston soon and would be leaving for Ireland in just a few days after a short stay in Boston to unload some cargo and reload more to bring to Ireland. Skip was in high spirits and was extra anxious now than ever before to be heading home back to Ireland. Skip just could not wait to see his grandparents again. He was thrilled to the point of tears in his young caring eyes and with great joy in his heart of hearing about the ship. Grandma Broom and Grandpa Hair wore heavily on Skip's caring troubled mind. He had been worried sick, for some time now, that something awful might happen to one or both of them while he was away. He jumped up and down with joy when Vinnie told him the good news. He spun around in midair doing somersaults all across the barn floor and sang a song of joy. "What wish do you want me to grant you there, Mr. Vinnie McDougall, sir?" "I do not know, Skip." "A promise is a promise you know, Vinnie. Do you want my gold?" Skip asked timidly. "No", said Vinnie. What a relief those few precious words were to Skip's aching ears. At least he did not have to give up his gold at this young time in his life retaining all his special powers.

"I do have a wish, my friend. A wish I want you to grant to me." Skip broke out into a cold sweat. "I have a wish I want you to grant to me without any trickery." Skip only wished he had enough special powers in him without his two missing pieces of gold to grant Vinnie a very special wish he was ready to request of him. "My wish is this, Skip, let me see now, what I want, well. The wish I want you to grant me is this. I want", Skip started to sweat profusely, "I want you to grant to me. I want you to grant a wish that your family will have a safe voyage back home to Ireland, and you do not get yourself into any trouble in the meantime. That is, you don't cause any more trouble to anyone until after you and your parents get back home to Ireland and safely to your Grandma Broom and Grandpa Hair's house."

"That is the only special wish you want me to grant you, Mr. Vinnie McDougall? A wish that we shall all have a safe voyage home, and that I should not use my special powers till I get back home to my Grandma Broom and my Grandpa Hair's house, that's all?" "Yes, that is all Skip." "Are you sure there is nothing else in the whole wide world you would not like to ask of me other than that wish?" "No, that is all. That is the wish I want you to grant me." A sudden feeling of swift anxiety filled Skip's trying veins. The more he thought about the wish, the more he felt very uncomfortable with it. "That is a real hard wish for me to grant you, Mr. Vinnie McDougall, sir. I have to behave and I cannot get into any trouble. I have to." "Can I have my wish or not have my wish, Skip?" "Why yes, your wish is granted."

Skip walked away from Vinnie mumbling and grumbling to himself, not sure, he would be able to keep such a special wish for Vinny. "Behave myself only until I get back home to Grandma and

Grandpa's house, right?" "That is right, Skip." Skip walked away slowly again, and zap, he was back in front of Vinnie again with doubt written all over his face. "Not even a teeny tiny teensy little prank, Vinnie?" "No, not even one little prank." Skip went away this time thinking to himself how he might ever possibly keep Vinnie's wish. Zap, Skip was back in front of Vinnie's face once again, as Vinnie was trying to get his work done. "What if I should mess up just once, Vinnie, just one time?" "Then I shall want all of your gold." "Ok, ok, a wish is a wish. The wish granted then, I will not do a single prank until I get back home to Grandma Broom's home in Ireland. Then I can, right, Vinnie?" "Right, Skip, now go away, I have work to do." "Would you like me to help you do some of your chores today, Vinnie?" "No, if you go around doing everything for me, Skip, I will forget how to do it all myself. Now go away with you, please!" "How's about a new house Vinny, a new barn built out back the stable? What about a new anvil for your forge or a new forge?" Vinnie looked at Skip, deep right into Skip's sparkling bright green eyes. "Boy, that pouch you have tied there around your waist sure looks mighty good right about now!" Skip took one deep quick look at Vinnie's stern looking face with a grimaced smile upon his little face. "Your wish is granted, Vinnie." Poof, Skip was gone, stayed hidden from Vinnie's view for the remainder of the day while sitting up in the attic in a far corner feeling sorry for himself, and talking to himself about the wish he had just granted his mortal friend.

He was so troubled with it that he had to confer with his parents about this very special wish Vinnie had requested of him and what he ought to do about it. "How am I supposed to grant Vinnie this special awkward kind of wish of his? My veins are boiling hot with anxiety. I have a terrible desire necessity to go outdoors and be as mischievous as I can be. I just want to play as many dirty little pranks and tricks on someone, and I cannot stand this wish I have granted him." "Vinnie will have this satchel of gold before I know it. What can I do?" "I told you, Son, did I not tell you that Mr. Vinnie McDougall fellow is just like all the other bad mortals on this earth. They just cannot be trusted. Mortals are born crafty creatures of dishonesty and trickery. They will all take your gold from you by making you grant them a wish you just cannot possibly keep.

That Mr. McDougall mortal is no better than that slithering moral snake, the Duke. All he wants from you is your gold." Skip's mother jumped up and down, stomping and stamping her feet. She was very exasperated with the two of them by reminiscing over past mortals and comparing them to Vinnie. "The likes of you two, Vinny McDougall is a trustworthy proud mortal, someone for the two of you to look up to. He helped save our lives from the banshee, did he not?" "Vinny stole my gold, that's what he did, did him not"? Skips father yelled out.

"You are a foolish, selfish, and inconsiderate, and I do not know what kind of leprechaun you really are. I don't know what I ever saw in you in the first place when I first wanted to marry you, for you are just a foolish old inconsiderate leprechaun." Skip's mother turned away from the two of them and sobbed relentlessly like a baby as she rested her saddened face in her little hands, and cried. "I can really do it, Mother. A promise is a promise, Mother, is it not? A wish is a wish granted. I will get the three of us home safely to Ireland as I have promised Vinnie. I will keep the wish that I have granted him. I can do it! Vinnie McDougall does not truly want my gold because he told me that himself several times already. He said he is making his fortune in gold the old-fashioned way by doing his smithy work and running the stable. He will not even let me help him anymore around here with his work. I will keep my promise and the wish I promised to Vinnie that he could have."

CHAPTER FORTY-THREE

Time to Leave

Peeking out the special wooden slots that Skip had prepared for them, they watched the countryside as it slowly went by. Vinnie rode shotgun upfront with the driver on board the stagecoach taking the three leprechauns to Boston for their long voyage back home to Ireland. Vinnie constantly glanced back over his left shoulder to make sure the three special trunks he brought along for the ride were traveling comfortably and securely on top of the stagecoach. The unique occupants of one very special trunk were busy watching Vinnie and the driver as well as the beautiful scenery around them.

Skip could not help but observe a lone bull standing all by its lonesome out in the pasture minding its own business lazily grazing on tender shoots of grass. In a pasture all by itself, Skip had the urge to play a prank on the big bull. "No," Skip thought very grueling to himself. "A promise is a promise, and a wish is a wish to keep!" He repeatedly had to toss these special few words over again in his mischievous craving mind so that he would not make a single mistake and lose his valued satchel of gold and many strengths of power to Vinnie.

They arrived late in the day at the Trinity House. Skip knew it would be the finest place in Boston to spend the last night of his grand adventure in the new world. Vinnie went straight away to the front desk and persuaded the night clerk to rent him the same old room he and Skip had shared their first several days together. With his trunks safely placed in a rented room and opened, Vinnie sat down on the four-poster bed with his three little friends. The three talked all about Ireland. How nice it will be for the three of them to be back home in Ireland. Vinnie told them that he was home now. He explained to them that he had Becky and Bernice now, and in the near future, he and Becky would be married and start a family all their own. "You know, Skip, I hope if Becky and I ever had a son that he will be as brave a young lad and as dedicated to his parents as you are to yours."

Skip quickly jumped up from sitting and flew across the bed, and gave Vinnie a huge loving hug like one brother would to another. "Skip" his father yelled out at him, "you stop doing that immediately, Son. Leprechauns cannot and do not show compassion to one another, never mind to mortals of any kind. It just is not right to show your feelings like that to anyone, especially a mortal. They are supposed to be our enemies." Skip's mother got up right away and went to hug Vinnie as well. "You are wrong, Pa," Skip said. Leprechauns do have compassion, and should show it more often than they do. We should be happy with our sensitive side of feelings and show them all to whomever we want to. Where is it written Pa, leprechauns cannot have compassion or show their feelings and love for one another, or to mortals for that fact? Where, Pa, where is it written?"

Skip's father sat on the edge of the bed kicking his feet and searching his mind for an answer to Skip's unsuspecting question. Not knowing what to give for an answer, he spoke up. "I guess you are right, my son. We should show our feelings a little more often than we do. I guess I have always hidden my true feelings from you since you saved us. Once I had compassion, did I not, Ma, when I was a younger leprechaun?" He stuck out his hand for Vinnie to shake and he shook it. "Thank you, Vinnie, for what you have done for us and for my boy, Skip." Skip became extremely excited when his father and Vinnie finally becoming friends. He just had to make a devilfish dance on someone's plate to celebrate the night. He had to show his mother, father, and especially Vinnie just how much fun it really was to make this happen.

"Vinnie, I know I have made you a promise and a wish which I shall honor, but may I please play one last little prank just this once for you all to watch, and make a devilfish dance for you, my mom, and my dad?" Vinnie chuckled, and then laughed right out loud. "Just the one wee little prank Skip, that is all. I must be seated next to the table you are playing your prank, and not a bad prank either. Only the devilfish prank, Skip." Looking through Vinnie's eyes as he entered the dining hall door, Skip saw that the shelf above the hall was empty of obstacles, which could fall down onto the tables below. The manager had all the decorative objects removed from the shelf after Skip had knocked down the big vase placed there for exhibit. He transposed the three of them to the narrow shelf.

With a blink of an eye, Skip addressed the three of them like little mannequins watching the two sitting at the little table across the hall above the baby grand piano. Amazingly, a large colossal devilfish the size of a serving platter came bounding out of the inn's kitchen lay a big bright red steamy Lobster on a waiter's tray. The lobster was ready to serve to a very hungry customer with a very big appetite. Vinnie sat seated in a far-off corner right next to an old scruffy sailor drinking his fill from his second carafe of rum. Skip chuckled out-loud at the site of the old sailor. The young waiter delivered the huge crustacean to the table right next to Vinnie. Low and behold, it was the same old glutton of a sailor who Skip had first made the devilfish dance for the first time he and Vinnie were at the Trinity House.

What luck, Skip thought to himself, when the young waiter came cheerfully sauntering across the dining hall floor smiling cheerfully with the patrons great looking meal on his platter. The grumpy old sailor was as rude as rude could be to the poor young waiter who was serving him. "Put it down right now, right here mate. Now! Now go get me another carafe of rum instantly for I am as thirsty as dry sand down to my barnacles." As soon as the young lad turned to leave, Vinnie's eyes grew to be as big as saucers, and he joyfully began to laugh out-loud. The devilfish on the sultry old sailor's plate behind the waiter stood up on its tail, bowed down to the drunken old sailor, and laid itself back down on his plate. The drunken old sailor turned to see if anyone else in the dining hall had seen, the devilfish bow down to him, especially after hearing Vinnie laugh so vibrantly. Vinnie quickly turned his head away from the sailor while still smiling and chuckling to himself. He looked off in the direction of another table for a split second, and returned his attention to the sailor as soon as the sailor turned his head. The drunken old sailor reached out again to take ahold of his lobster to break it in half and start to eat it, but the lobster again stood up and started shaking one of its huge colossal claws at him. It looked as if it was giving him the dickens for trying to eat him. It laid back down on the platter as the old man swiftly took his hands back. Vinnie laughed harder out-loud, of course, trying to cover his mouth so he would not make a scene. His stomach hurt from trying not to laugh out, and his face turned a crimson red as he turned away from the humorous site-taking place right next to him until he could compose himself once again.

The hilarious look frown on the old sailor's face could have painted a thousand pictures, Vinnie thought. The drunken sailor screamed at the young waiter, who was going off to fetch him another carafe of wine, to stop and return at once. The poor waiter had not quite got as far away as the kitchen door when the old grouch called out to him. He quite vividly remembered the old sailor from the last time he was in the Trinity's dining room over a year ago. It had been his first day as a waiter at the Trinity House and he assured the sailor as he had the last time that this lobster on his plate was quite well cooked and very much dead. The young lad was angered at the situation at hand the young waiter took the lobster from off the sailor's plate, broke off his two front claws, and laid it back down on the tray for the sailor to eat. As soon as the waiter turned to leave, he appeared with his meal of steak, potatoes, bread, and a nip of scotch. He politely placed the meal down in front of him making very sure he needed nothing else before he turned and walked away. Suddenly Vinnie's steak stood up on its edge and bowed down to him and Vinnie laughed out-loud.

Seeing Vinnie's steak get up and bow down to him was just too much for the poor old drunk sitting across from him to take. The sailor immediately pushed out his chair, got up roughly from his table, and headed for the exit door. Vinnie again was not able to control himself at the funny situation at hand, and laughed vibrantly out-loud. The old sailor rushed briskly past him sputtering to himself about never going to drink another pint of ale ever again. Vinnie looked up at the ledge above to see his little friends, but they had already finished. Vinnie ate his meal while chuckling to himself about the old sailor and the way Skip had made the devilfish act, then returned to his room for the night. The four of them laughed late into the evening about the devilfish, and Vinnie made him promise to keep his word about his wish.

In the early morning hours at the first crack of daylight, the four of them were off down the road to the harbor. They were safely away in their special travel trunk and were busy looking out their special little peepholes at the sites of Boston. Skip became extremely excited when he first saw the ship they were about to sail on back home to Ireland. She looked very ready for their passage back home to Ireland, and he was bubbling over with joy knowing he was really going home. The ship looked very familiar to him with her tall slender streamlined build as they rounded the corner of the boardwalk, and down the pier. He looked up at her bow with her neatly handcrafted shimmer glistening bright green like emeralds in the early morning sunlight.

CHAPTER FORTY-FOUR

The Shamrock

She was the beautiful Shamrock! Skip felt in his heart that this would be a most pleasant voyage back home to Ireland for the three of them. Skip knew this ship firsthand for it traveled the rolling waves of the sea like a butterfly gliding gently on a soft breeze as it floated on air. He immediately looked at her front jib sail's mast. Memories of the foolish whale seen on board her came back instantly to his mind like a magnetic nightmare. There would be no more dangerous pranks played until Skip got back home, and even then, they would not, get hurt by them.

Vinnie went straight away to see the captain of the Shamrock when they first boarded her. The captain remembered Vinnie very well and greeted him favorably, for Vinnie had helped him save his vessel. He purchased a private cabin from the captain for the long voyage just for his prize trunks and their belongings. Orders were the cabin was not to be opened by anyone until they arrived safely back in Dublin. Then the trunks stored there, delivered to a very special address, just outside of Dublin Town. With a good swap of silver and a hearty handshake, the captain assured Vinnie that the trunks would find at their destinations in one piece. The captain had assured Vinnie the cabin would stay locked until the end of the voyage. These chests never opened except by the ones delivered too. Being a man of his word, the captain assured Vinnie he would personally deliver his trunks to their proper destination. The private cabin would be like a special cargo hold for a very special precious cargo. The captain was quite curious about the contents of the trunks, but well paid by Vinny the Captain would most likely not break his word.

Going into the private cabin with his trunks, Vinnie closed the door tightly behind him and sat down on the chair at the little desk. Looking up at the ceiling, he saw the oil lamp he had Billy place there above the desk just for him. Skip, his mother, and father came out of hiding from their trunks and sat down on the bunk next to Vinnie. "Remember, Skip, you must remember my wish? If you break it, I want all of your gold." Skip nodded his head up and down saying yes. "I want all of you to have a happy and safe voyage back home to Ireland now. No pranks or funny business, until you all reaches your grandparents' home. Right, remember that, Skip?" "Yes, sir, Mr. McDougall", Skip replied with a serious look on his little face.

"Will we ever see one another again, Vinnie," Skip asked. "Probably not, Skip, only if you come back to visit me in the new country. As I have said to you before, I have found for myself a new land, and a new life in this wonderful Country. This country is my new home now, Skip. Someday I may come back to Ireland for a wee visit. I do not think I shall at any time very soon, but maybe. If I do come back home again to Ireland, I promise Skip I will be sure to try my hardest to find you out by farmer Prendergast's farm. I will call out your name Skip vert loud, as loud as I can, you will know it is me if I come Skip". Vinnie said his last goodbyes to the three of them and they hugged. Both Skip and his mother gave Vinnie great big tight loving hugs, but his father took Vinnie's hand and shook it with a good firm meaningful grip instead. Vinnie smiled and waved goodbye as he turned and closed the door quickly behind him. With tears in his eyes, he left the ship. Vinnie felt as though he was losing another member of his family, and Skip felt the same way when he locked the cabin door behind Vinnie when he left the ship.

Skip could sense Vinnie's closeness even after he departed the gangplank of the ship. He was not very far away Skip felt, and he was not. He was standing on the dock of the bay when the Captain of the Shamrock hollered to his crew to release the ship's tie-down lines as the ship set sail. He sensed a significant sadness in his lonely heart for

Vinnie. He felt he was losing his only true friend and soulmate. The dreadful pain Skip was feeling in his heart was real, and it hurt worse than being homesick. It felt like nothing else he had ever experienced and wondered if the pain would ever go away. Maybe in time it would heal itself, but it was real and as painful as could be. Grandma Broom and Grandpa Hair explained to him that his parents were never going to come back home to be with him ever again. Several small tears fell from his saddened eyes dampening his little hand as he tried to wipe them so his father would not see them. His mother saw a tiny tear trickle softly down his little cheek, and she put her loving arms around him to comfort him. She held him gently in her grasp knowing just what he was experiencing deep down inside his hurting loving heart. She whispered gently in her little boy's ear, "He is a good friend, Skip, you shall never lose him as he will always be living in your heart, the same way you are living in his." Skip could not be any happier with his life now with his loving mother's warm hands holding him tight while feeling her loving arms softly wrapped around him once again. This is why he had ventured off to Dublin Town in the first place, and now it has all come to fruition for him, well worth getting drunk and ending up in America in Vinnie's trunk.

Captain Drake yelled out to his crew to set the Shamrock's sails to sail, and she began to slowly, leave her berth. Skip's only wish since he had left home was now coming true for him. He was disembarking the port of Boston for the open sea to return home to Ireland. Not only is one wish coming true, but also two having his mother and father with him was all he ever wanted before in the whole wide world. He knew he might never see Vinnie again, so one last goodbye to Vinnie was in store before they left port, and of the Shamrock was out of sight of land. Skip just had to see if Vinnie really cared as much for him as he said he did, and was watching the ship leave the port of Boston. He did not want to see him in a vision, but wanted to see him in person if Vinnie cared as much about him, as he cared about him. Skip transposed to the beam out in the scully way, then beneath the grate in the deck. Looking up and seeing that it was empty, he transposed to the empty crow's nest high above. Sure enough, Vinnie could be seen by Skip's eyes standing alone, a little sad perhaps, on the dock of Boston's bay wondering if he would ever see his little friend again. He watched as the Shamrock pulled slowly away from her berth. With her sails filled full of air from the strong wind behind her, she began pulling away into the brightness of the early morning sunrise partially blinding Vinnie as he looked for his little friend possibly up in the crow's nest of the ship waving goodbye. Skip waved to Vinnie from high above the Shamrock, perched high up on her tallest mast. Vinnie waved a hearty hand at the departing Shamrock. Not really seeing Skips' little hand waving back at him, he turned and slowly walked away sad and glad all at the very same time. Vinnie was glad Skip was going home, but had formed a brotherly sort of friendship with the little leprechaun that a mortal should have never formed. Skip wondered if Vinnie had really seen his little hand waving to him. Looking down to the deck far below, Skip could see the metal strap once more that Vinnie had so meticulously forged in the ship's galley's kitchen stove to secure the two halves of the broken jib mast back together. Oh, what a terrible day that was, he thought back to himself. Instantly, the wish he had given Vinnie came ringing and echoing into his little head like the ringing of a ship's bell. No jokes, no pranks, and a safe voyage home, this wish would be much harder for him to keep, but he would do it for himself and particularly for his loving mother and his dear friend in Vinnie.

CHAPTER FORTY-FIVE

Billy the Cabin Boy

Skip spotted Billy the cabin boy from high above down on the ship's main deck far below while looking back toward Boston. Billy looked dreadfully different now, than he had before when Skip last saw him, and when they had spent those last two nights together aboard the Shamrock. He was now skinny as a whittled down gauntly looking toothpick, and his eyes were sunken into his tired looking face. It looked like he had not had a good night's sleep in more than a year, and the clothes on his back were extremely baggy on him. He sure was not the same little jolly cabin boy he once remembered him to be at the end of their last voyage together. Maybe he would try conversing with him later on, in the long voyage or maybe when they were much closer to Ireland. For some reason, Skip felt uneasy about striking up his friendship again this early in the trip. Maybe it was his leprechaun intuition or something similar to that, but he did not know if he could trust him anymore, seeing him in this awful way. He wondered how he was going to get his two pieces of gold back to complete his satchel along with their precious powers held in them. He had so happily given them to Billy to keep or was it to hold as a token or whatever the circumstance. Billy had possession of them now, or at least he hoped he still had them. Somehow, before the end of the voyage, Skip knew he had to get Billy to hand him back his two gold coins.

Back to the safety of the crossbeam in the scully way, Skip went in a flash. He had finally learned how properly too transpose with the swaying of the ship on the rolling water. He transposed back to the safety of the cabin Vinnie so specially and generously arranged for them to travel in. Seeing his mother and father safely sitting on the bunk, he told them all about Vinnie. How Vinny waved goodbye to them from the dock as he turned for home, and left the dock behind. After a while, Skip transposed to the hold of the ship where he had made his home on his first long voyage to America. There were his two little ship friends, the ship's rats running loosely around the hold of the ship lay half filled up with green tobacco leaves, and spices probably picked up in the far off lands of the West Indies. Where were the kegs of rum he thought, what was anyone going to do with a ship full of useless green leaves that smelled sweet, eat them. Skip picked up one of the sweet smelling leaves up and began to chew on it as if he was going to eat it. The leaf had a disgusting foul revolting taste to it, so he spat it out and threw down the remainder of the leaf to the floor. No wonder, that old sailor wanted to spit that stuff out into the spittoon where this whole fiasco of an adventure began for him. He could not imagine anyone liking these leaves for any reason except possibly to make a hemp rope out of the substance of the leaf. Skip transposed back to the cabin to be with his parents. His mother was concerned that he was possibly breaking the very wish he had granted any just days before and was violating his true leprechaun rules. "You remember Vinnie's wish, don't you, Son?" "Yes, Mother, I do. A promise is a promise, and a wish is a wish. I will not break his wish nor my promise to him. I swear to it on the crowned jewels of the King of the Leprechauns!"

Bernice, Vinny, and Becky had meticulously packed a couple of huge trunks full of food and beverage for the long voyage for Skip and his family. One trunk was full of their clothes, blankets, and pillows Bernice had made and packed for them. Bernice was more than happy when the three of them left her inn. They made her extremely nervous by appearing out of thin air in the middle of the kitchen when the three of them showed up for their morning, midday, and evening meals. Bernice was afraid they might somehow show up when she had some unexpected guests sitting at the table for dinner. Surely, Bernice would miss the way Skip always helped after the meals, and cleaned up the dinner dishes, pot, and pans. Skip's magic sure did make cleaning up around the inn much easier than before. Vinnie would definitely miss the way Skip helped him out around the stable and farm. He made the changing of horses for the stagecoaches way too easy, and now it would take him almost half an hour instead of just a couple of minutes to change out one tired team of horses for a fresh new team. His record time for changing out teams of horses would soon disappear for good. Besides he was getting older now, and the fast pace was getting to him, he would tell the different teamsters when they question this time in changing out the horses.

CHAPTER FORTY-SIX

The Locked Cabin

Billy knocked at the cabin door where Skip and his parents were staying. The ship's captain, Captain Drake neglected to inform Billy the way he should have not to bother with cabin number four. "Cabin boy here, Whales oil and wicks for your lamps". "We need none at this time, thank you," Skip said. Deepening and disguising his voice so Billy would not recognize it. His voice had already deepened with the growing of his beard and sideburns. Billy just walked away not giving it any thought the lamps in cabin number 4 having been filled, the day before. For the next several days, Skip took the whale oil and wicks they needed from Billy's supplies without him ever knowing they went missing. He had not changed his mind about talking to Billy for the meantime, and did not want to run into Billy on this voyage. He was particularly concerned about Billy because he had drastically changed. Billy questioned his own thoughts as to why the person or persons in the cabin and did not want them to run out of whale oil for their lamps. He figured whoever it was hiding in the cabin must be as afraid of the pirates on the open sea as he was. Maybe that was why they stayed hidden and locked away in their cabin all the while. He thought it was very strange, and thought to himself after a couple of days that he might have to have a word to the captain about this matter.

CHAPTER FORTY-SEVEN

Cherubs

Strange sounds came echoing up through the hull of the ship as the Shamrock glided across the water. It sounded much like a bunch of cherubs playing a melody on lovely harps beneath the ship in the sea. Perhaps it was a few mermaids playing on their harps, Skip thought, and then he remembered the whales that had swam alongside the Shamrock with them. How could he have ever possibly forgotten about the whales? He could hear them and feel them on the bottom of the ship as they came up close beneath it, and could feel one or two of them rubbing their barnacle-laden backs up against the hull and main beam. They did this to rub and scrape away the many calcified barnacles and leeches that may have attached themselves to their backs. The lovely sounds of cherubs soon turned to a gruesome sound of rocks scraping hard up against the wooden hull. The awful sound of grinding wooden shells made goosebumps rise up on his tiny back. The sound was the same as someone dragging their very sharp fingernails across a hardened blackboard.

He sat there with his parents in the cabin and enjoying the many sounds around them. They enjoyed the sound of the wind, the water splashing, the whales singing, and the different sounds of the sea in general. He sat there explaining to them just how he had met Vinnie in the first place on the streets of Dublin Town that dreadful rainy day. It was a day when he should have been safely home with Grandma Broom and Grandpa Hair. Skip sure hoped his Grandparents, were both safe, and sound back home in their Tree House. He told them the reason he had been out searching the main streets and back alleys of Dublin Town was to look for them and wanted to bring them both back home safe and sound. He figured his grandparents should have gone looking for them, but they did not. "Grandma should have found the two of you in her travels for food, or certainly Grandpa should have been able to find you. They told me they didn't have the powers to find you, so I went looking for you all by myself." He explained how he had gone into Mrs. Mosher's pub and had taken part in some of the evil tonics the way his dad had done that dreadful day when the Duke had captured him and his mother. Then he explained how he had followed Vinnie to the boarding house pub, and became polecat drunk and ended up in his trunk. He thought Vinnie was going to lead him to the mysterious secrets of making gold for himself because he did not know how he was going to get his own satchel of gold at that time.

There were so many stories that he wanted to tell them. He told them how he fell asleep in Vinnie's trunk and became a stowaway in this very cabin they were now safely sailing. He told them of his many travels with Vinnie around the new world until they finally settled down in Greenfield. The rest of the story he told was obvious. Skip's father asked Skip about his gold. He wanted to know how he knew of its many powers. He told him he did not know the many powers of his gold yet, never taught them nor told about them. Then his father said he would teach him the powers of his gold. "Give to me your gold, Son, and I shall teach the powers to you." "No," cried out Skip's mother. "No, definitely do not! Do not ever give your father your gold. Do not you go tricking your own son Pa, your own son into giving up his precious gold! You, Jeffrey B. O'Brien, are no better a leprechaun than that mortal bloke, the Duke, is of being a kind human being, for you are nothing but a scoundrel yourself. You never give up your gold to anyone, Skip, no matter who it is or who wants to hold it just to see how it feels. Your gold will then become theirs instantly. No matter, you ever want to get it back or not, it will always be theirs to keep. If they have some of your gold and use its special powers, you will definitely never get it all back again unless of course they voluntarily hand it back to you or you can trick them into giving it back to you. It is a good thing mortals do not know or understand this or they would take great advantage of us leprechauns all of the time. "Skip felt terrible hearing these words from his mother. He had given Billy some of his gold as a gift and now only hoped he could get it back with all of its powers still attached within it. He had not really given it to Billy directly, or had he. He had just laid it beneath Billy's pillow for safekeeping. He did not quite dare tell his parents what he had done with the two pieces.

The weather for several days had been calm, but the seas must be getting ready to turn rough, Skip thought. He could hear the sounds of thunder rumbling in the sky not far from the ship. It was a strange time of year for a thunderstorm to form in the north Atlantic sea, he thought, even more peculiar was the several claps of thunder all at the same time so close together. He sprang to his feet looking extremely frightened and very serious. His mother looked at him in a very strange way sensing something was amiss with his strange look. This was not the sound of an early summer's approaching thunderstorm, but the sound of cannons firing at them from far off in the distance. Skip's heart went racing instantaneously up into the top of his throat. He screamed, "Pirates, the pirates are shooting at us!"

Skip instantly transposed from the cabin and to the crossbeam in the scully way, and then to the opening in the deck. He transposed straightaway up to the crow's nest high atop the main mast and sat perched there looking out over the ocean. He could not make out the ship that was approaching them by the colors she was flying, but she was definitely a pirate ship. As a warring vessel, she was firing on the Shamrock with all her cannons from her port side. Her crew of scallywags got her cannons to roar out again at the Shamrock. Using the light of the bright moon above for their lantern, the pirate ship Lady, very light on the water's surface, bared down on the heavily loaded Shamrock. She was cutting across the path of the Shamrock's bow and coming at her from the southeast. The pirate ship had the wind at her back giving her an unfair advantage over the Shamrock. The Shamrock was having a hard time to cut an angle into the waves of the ocean and into the wind to keep her course for Ireland true. This caused her to go against the wind and not with it, and against the rolling waves. Her sails were half-full of air keeping her from listing, as she cut sideways against the wind, and into the line of the swift Gulf Stream. Streamlining against her side, the pirate ship was bearing down on the Shamrock from its port side as she blasted out yet another volley of cannon fire. This time the cannonballs were only a few rods away from striking the Shamrock. Skip did not know quite what to do next, but he thought of Vinnie's wish. No pranks, no jokes, and have a safe voyage home. These were neither jokes nor pranks for these pirates meant real life- threatening business. They were shooting hot iron cannonballs at the ship and might board her and take her treasures away from her if she had any. What should he do, use the magical powers of his gold, and lose it all to any, or not use the power of it, and lose it all to the rogue pirates anyway. It did not take Skip long to make up his mind. He would rather give up all of his gold if necessary then give up his life or gold to the dirty pirates. "Have a safe voyage home." Those were the exact words Vinnie had said for him to do. Have a safe voyage.

The next round of cannonballs came flying through the air toward the Shamrock from the pirate ship, as the front jib mast of the Shamrock's forward sail came crashing down to the deck, the same way it had come down when the whale that Skip had placed on the deck had smashed it down. The cannonball took down the jib mast Vinnie had made the metal sleeve to wrap around it. Seeing this take place, got Skip's emotions all fire up wondering what he should do next. He made up his mind to have a safe voyage and would have to use all his very special powers to do so. No jokes, no pranks, no shenanigans, this was not going to be for the fun of it to appease himself. If he had to give up all his gold to Vinnie, he would do so willingly. Another volley of cannonballs came flying through the air at them. Skip held his satchel of gold tight and concentrated as high as he could on the flying steel balls. He had to make Vinnie's wish come true for him, his father, and especially his mother. When the next volley of cannonballs fired, he sent the lot of them back to where they had come; right smack dab back down into the middle of the cannon barrels from which they had been fired. When they went back down the tubes of the cannons, they exploded into a million pieces sending metal shrapnel everywhere like fireworks about the pirate ship. When the Pirate ship came around on the Shamrock, she was readying herself by preparing the cannons on her starboard side to fire. She was angry for what had just happened to her and was getting ready to finish blowing the Shamrock up, and sinking her. The crew of the Shamrock was just barely getting her few cannons ready to fire back at the scoundrels, when the Shamrock's crew, were finally able to fire her first set of cannonball fire. Skip guided the balls into the paths of the pirate ship's second round of cannonballs coming in at them and struck them all in midair. They all exploded in a most brilliant display of bright lights and sparkled like lightning, lighting up the blackened sky above the sea.

Was it a vision or was it a premonition or just the thought of the Shamrock sinking in the deep of the sea that worried the daylights out of Skip. In his subconscious mind, seeing everyone drowning on the Shamrock as the ship went down, sent cold chills up and down his tiny spine and caused him to not give a damn one single bit one way or the other if he was to lose all of this, now was the time for great measures to be dealt with, immediately. precious gold to Vinnie or not. Dealing with these hostile menacing pirates of the sea was the most important job at hand and nothing else mattered. Previous enlightening magical words spoken to him by his Grandma Broom came straight to his quick spinning mind. "Do not pick up anything into the air so far that you cannot put it back down safely and gently. You could break it. Do not attempt to catch anything in your hand either as you may get hurt. Skip laughed. He used his new magical powers of his gold in his pouch to enhance his youthful magic. With it, he lifted the pirate ship up into the air high above the surface of the sea and then let it fall. Without using his control of it, the pirate ship went crashing back down into the sea. Down, down, and down the ship went beneath the surface of the water. Then like a whale breaking the surface of the sea, it shot back up out of the water and came to rest on the water's surface looking more like a cork bouncing on top of the water's surface on a fishing line rather than a pirate ship of war.

There were many untrustworthy mangy pirates afloat on the water scattered everywhere in the salty brine and swimming for their lives. They had no idea what had just happened to them or their ship and neither did the crew of the Shamrock. It must have been an explosion deep in the hole aboard the pirate's vessel, thought the crew and passengers of the Shamrock. The small tidal wave caused by the sinking and reappearance of the pirate ship, pushed the Shamrock out of harm's way, and onto a safe course northeasterly, bound again with full sails and fresh air at her back. The Shamrock was now under full power again except for the fractured fallen jib mast.

The very thought of losing his precious gold came back to Skip for less than a split second. Then he let it go with a smile on his face knowing that he had let Vinnie's special wish come true for the moment. He could not have made it come true without using his very special powers. These were not acts of the tomfoolery prankster out having fun. These were very desperate acts of a very desperate leprechaun. Skip did not know what to do to fulfill a special wish he had made to a friend, even if that friend was a very special mortal. Without-delay, Skip returned to his cabin below deck, just in time to hear a loud knocking and a rapid banging at their cabin door. "Henry, Henry, Henry are you in there"? Skip, instantly recognized the voice at the door, that of Billy. "I know it is you in there, Henry. Please let me in., please?" "Who is that at the door, Skip? Who is Henry, some other mortal friend of yours, I suppose", asked Skip's father angrily. "My name, Pa, is Henry to that young lad standing outside the door." "Who else Skip who else have you gone and befriended on board this bloody vessel? Are you not a leprechaun for crying out-loud, and if you are, why do you not act like one? You are not supposed to go around befriending mortals of any kind whether young or old, on board a ship, or on the land. You are only supposed to play tricks, pull pranks, and any other tomfoolery you can on them. What have you gone and done this time? Don't you have any leprechaun morals in you at all?"

Skip quickly hid his parents in separate trunks, and slid them magically beneath the bunk and opened the door to the cabin. Quickly Billy scurried in from the empty scully way and closed the door firmly behind him. "I thought it must be you in here, Henry. I thought it the instant the pirate ship went floating off into the air and then came crashing back down into the sea again. When the cannonballs all exploded in midair, I knew it must be you, who did it for us again, Henry. From that very moment on, I just knew you had to be on board the Shamrock again somewhere." Billy had his old familiar smile back on his face the happy look Skip remembered when he first met him before. His face now was almost skeletal with a gauntly looking happy smile on his face. "What is your problem, Billy?" Skip asked. "You smile but yet you look so sad and very sick." "Sick yelled out Skip's father from within the first trunk beneath the bed. Billy's eyes became large when hearing Skip father's voice come echoing out from beneath the bunk. "Who do you have stuck in the trunk, Henry, a prisoner from the pirate ship, the pirate ship's captain, or a hostage of some kind from the ship?" "Can you keep a secret for me Billy? You have promised me you will first." "If you can keep the pirate ships away from the Shamrock, I can keep a whole pirate ship full of secrets for you Henry."

Making sure, the cabin door securely locked; Skip pointed his finger towards the trunks hidden beneath the bunk. They both slid out from beneath the bunk and their lids flew softly open. Billy sucked in a huge deep breath of air out of pure astonishment when he first saw Skip's mother and then again when he saw his father. "More leprechauns, Billy said. Skip said, "Shhhhh, Billy, not so loud so someone can hear you, whisper-softly. Others on board might hear you." "No, not anymore, I am not a leprechaun. I have no more of my gold, and without it I have no more of my super magical powers left either, thanks to your no good friend Henry over there." Skip's father immediately pointed a sly finger at Skip, along with a sly bad-mannered attitude on his grumpy looking face. "He there made me give it all away, he did. He is your leprechaun. Skip's mother poked her husband hard in the ribs with the point of her elbow. "Shush, Pa, you have given all of your gold to Mr. McDougall all by yourself. Your son had nothing to do with it, as it is the way of the leprechauns.

Billy found a seat by closing the lids to the two trunks Skip's mother and father had been hiding. "These two little people here are your mother and your father, Henry? I just cannot believe it. Boy, how I miss my mother, my brothers, and my sisters, too. I just cannot wait to get back there just to see them all once again. Many times the Shamrocks been chased by pirate ships, and has not been fun for us when it happens. Since we were last together Henry, it really has not been much fun to be chased all over the place and shot at so many times by this bunch of dreaded buccaneers. That is why I am so sick because of the dreadful pirates. I cannot eat and I cannot sleep at night anymore. The whole idea of getting caught by any of them scares me half to death just to think that one of these days a lucky pirate ship might out sail us and catch us on the open sea. The very thought Billy said of not being able to see mom and the kids again worries me half to death. To leave them all for another whole year or two after we make this port of call in Dublin Town makes me sicker and sicker all of the time, too, but even more now than before."

"I have but one more year to serve on the Shamrock before the house is paid for. Then and only then maybe I will not have to go out to sea aboard the ship any longer to earn this weak wage to help out my poor mom and the kids. Boy, I cannot wait to see my mom when I get home. I did not realize how lonely you could get out here on the sea, all by your lonesome. My, Pa always said the sea was no place for a smart young lad such as myself, or a young married bloke to go out to sea to make a hearty living. Better to be a good poor happy young farmer than to be a rich old lonely sailor, he said."

"Well, why are not you back home farming with your pa, son," Skip's father yelled out sarcastically. Skip jumped up from the chair and shook his index finger aggressively in his father's face and shook his head side to side shouting, "his father is gone, Pa, that is why he is not home farming. He died working hard, not like you, out at sea while trying to make a good living for Billy and his family. You should be real proud of your mouth, Pa." "I am truly sorry for what I said Billy, Skip's father said, as he bowed his head in shame.

Suddenly Skip disappeared from the cabin and so did the trunk that Billy had sat on. Billy fell flat onto the cabin floor with a great surprised look on his face. He started to pick himself up off the floor, and wondered what had just happened to the trunk and to Skip as well. Skip suddenly returned with the trunk almost as fast as he had disappeared with it even before for Billy had time to pick himself up off the floor. The big trunk was dripping wet with Seawater all over it same as was Skip. "Sorry, I needed to take your trunk for a wee second. I should have told you to get up for a second because I was going to need it." With a blink of his eyes, Skip, the floor, and the trunk in the cabin were all dry again.

"Where about Dublin Town, do you and your family live, Billy"? Skip wanted to know. "We live on McDuff Road leading out of Dublin Town, out towards Chambers town. Number 20 McDuff Road. It is nothing fancy, mind you Henry, just a mere roof over our heads. Billy said his family belongs to the lower class of people in Ireland, for most folk around Dublin Town call us poor folks. Just happy to be alive that is all, and getting by is all we want, just poor happy folk living the best we can. There is nothing of value in our home for a leprechaun to take, or to be happy stealing. We have no gold or silver to steal." "Leprechauns do not get their gold by stealing it, Billy. They earn every bit of it all by themselves crying for it, year after year." His father looked fearfully toward Skip when he said that, and Skip said no more.

"Captain Drake says only two more days until we reach the port of Dublin Town. I sure hope we don't see any more of those pesky pirates out here, Henry?" "I assure you, Billy, those pirates we left behind us will not be bothering any ship any time soon, if ever!" What did Skip know about the pirates that no one else in the cabin knew? Billy heard his name called out loudly above on deck by the captain. He excused himself, left quickly, and locked the door behind him. The captain was concerned making sure everyone on board the Shamrock was accounted for; especially after the pirate ship attacked them. The ship had minor damage to her bow where the cannonball had hit and ripped through the front jib's mast, tearing down the front Jib. The captain was extremely concerned about Billy, as he may have been standing right there beside the mast when the cannonball struck it. The captain knew he loved to stand up front of the jib when he was not busy looking out for pirate ships up in the crow's nest. The front railing where Billy so often stood was gone as well as the front jib, so more than one lucky cannonball must have reached the Shamrock.

Billy came back the next night to visit with Skip and his parents when his work was completed. He told them all about the story of his lonely life living aboard the Shamrock for the past year and a couple of months. Billy told all about the many ports the Shamrock had visited in the last two years, and how they had sailed around the world. They had visited the West Indies and the South and North America. On and on through the night, Billy talked about his many adventures. He told them about the several pirate ships that attempted to capture them on the open sea, and how the Shamrock had quickly outrun them except for this last one, which they Shamrock was not prepared for on such a windy rough sea quiet moonlit night. Billy said he knew one day his luck and the luck of the Shamrock would run out for them, and they would not be able to outrun one of the many pirate ships floating wildly upon the sea. Billy was afraid he would be captured one day, afraid they would all have to walk the dreaded gangplank to their deaths, and may never be able to see his family again.

Halfway through the night, Skip took over the storytelling and told of his adventures in the new world to Billy. He told him how Vinnie had helped him save his parents lives, and how he had traveled all the way to Boston to stop him before he sailed for Ireland. How Vinnie left without him, and he had to travel all by himself all the way back to Greenfield. He told him every little detail of his adventure that he could possibly think of; and most of all, how he had beaten away the banshee with his powers and some of his father's powers all by himself. Using the power of his magic along with his new wisdom, Skip retrieved the last two precious missing pieces of gold from Billy. Now that his power was all complete, the urge drew to an honest strength to play tomfoolery tricks, hooliganism and pranks on all mortals, the beasts of the farms, and the many prey of the earth as it grew tenfold. All his gold and powers put together as one in his tiny gold pouch.

During the last night, Skip promised Billy that he would give him something very special and more precious than the gold he had lent him for luck. A gift so special it should forever seal their true friendship, and last Billy a lifetime. Skip promised him that tomorrow or the next day, he would receive this very special gift before the day came to its end. "Until tomorrow", said Billy then turned and went out the cabin door and closed it tightly behind him. Skip was so excited to be so close to home, and he just could not wait to see Grandma and Grandpa once again. Just a little tug or a very hard yanks his hair by his Grandpa Hair, or a swift switch on his pants with a broomstick by his Grandma Broom. Oh, how nice it will be to see the two of them again. Would either of them even recognize him all grown up now especially with his beard covering his face? Oh, how he so hoped they would remember him.

"Land ho" came a loud call down to the deck hands below from a sailor stationed high up in the crow's nest. Skip shot to the beam in the scully way and to the grated hole in the deck where he could look up toward the crow's nest. The sailor who had just been in the crow's nest on his watch was now coming down to help the crew prepare the Shamrock for docking. He could see the sailor carefully descending the rope ladder to the deck one hand and foot at a time. In a flash, Skip found himself sitting high in the crow's nest above the Shamrock happily looking out over the sea toward home, toward Ireland. Oh what a beautiful place to call home he thought. The land was as green as an emerald stone. Her rolling coastline of cliffs pleased Skip's vision, and the smell of her green grass filled his nostrils with a pleasant aroma of his homeland. He had not smelled as sweet a lovely smell in a very long time, and it sure felt good to be almost home. The high cliffs to the north and the sweet dream of her land almost made Skip cry with pleasure from seeing her beauty once again.

His growing urge to play just one silly prank on someone or something was growing and growing more intense by the passing minute. It seemed to grow even stronger the closer they got to land. It would not be too long now before he could play his first silly prank on someone again. The energy was building so strong deep inside of him, that Skip wanted to burst at the seams. No pranks, no tricks, a promise is a promise, a wish is a wish. He kept repeating this phrase over, and over in his mind. He wondered if what he had already done to the pirate ship during and after their encounter would be valid as a prank against him. Would the stripping of the pirate ship of her sails and other belongings be enough for him to lose his precious golden powers to Vinnie? He thought it was not a promise broken, but a promise kept. Vinnie was thousands of kilometers away anyway, and he had not mentioned it to anyone. No one would ever tell Vinnie what happened to the Shamrock on the high seas on their long voyage home to Ireland. It was Vinnie's wish of a safe voyage home anyway. Skip decided he had done the right thing and would not worry about his precious gold any longer.

When the Shamrock came softly up against her berth at the dock in Dublin, Skip transposed himself and his parents to a safe location onshore. Several chests that were in the cabin could be safely loaded onto a wagon for the short ride home. Timothy Barron's farm was right next door to the Prendergast farm just outside of Dublin. Only four of the five trunks Vinnie had put into the cabin, the men placed on-board the same wagon. Seeing the trunks safely on the wagon, Skip transposed himself and his parents back into one of the four huge trunks for their short ride home.

CHAPTER FORTY-EIGHT

Leprechaun Trickery

Billy became miserably depressed when he realized he had missed saying goodbye to his leprechaun friend and his family. Skip had promised he would say goodbye, he thought, and would leave him a gift to remember them all by. He guessed Henry did not really mean what he had thought he said. He was a leprechaun, and leprechauns were known to make false promises, and fool people all of the time. He was very sad about Skip, but overly pleased to have his feet back on good old Irish soil again. Soon he would see his mother, brothers, and sisters once again.

Peeking out the holes of their trunk and riding along in the back of the wagon, Dublin Town had changed quite significantly for his parents since they had last seen her busy streets. It must have been several long years or so since they last saw the streets of Dublin. Skip's mother felt as if she was coming home to a city she did not know any longer. Everything around Dublin Town seemed to have changed in color, storefronts, and structure. Skip, on the other hand, felt right at home being back in Dublin Town. Things did not seem to have changed very much for Skip from his short time away. The sound of the horses' hooves and steel horseshoes clicking along the cobblestone streets made Skip extremely cheerful, and could not be any the more happier than to be back home again. Just the same, he did think it was strange that some of the building's storefronts had changed a tad. Listening to his parents talk about how different everything looked to them, made Skip see the very slightest of differences in everything in and around Dublin Town.

CHAPTER FORTY-NINE

Billy's Home

"Billy's home, Billy's home", came shouts from his brothers and sisters as they all came running down the sidewalk to greet him back home from his long time out at sea. His little sister, Megan, had been sitting on the front porch all day just waiting for her big brother to come strolling home from the wharf. Word of mouth had come to Billy's family that the ship he was on would be docking in port. Little Megan did not even want to eat her lunch. She was so excited when she saw Billy first walking up the lonely street carrying his gunnysack slung over his right shoulder. He also, like the tradition of his father, was carrying a handbag in his left hand full of treats for the kids when he came walking home after a long time out fishing. His big sister and the small ones covered him with loving hugs and kisses while his brothers fought to carry his heavy gunnysack and other bag the rest of the way up the hill to the house for him. His mother stood tall and proud of her hero boy and half crying while standing in the doorway of their home that Billy so unselfishly was helping her to provide for them. When he finally came onto the front porch to greet her at the door, she was softly but openly weeping. She gently threw her loving arms around her elder son, the one she wept for and had so unselfishly surrendered his youthful life so dearly for her and her needy children. She clung tight to him as if he had just returned home from a dreadful war, and been wounded in battle. He looked the part of a tired out soldier who had gone through hell losing much of his weight. He was pale white when she saw him coming across the porch, and she did not know why, for his unhealthy looks caused by the fright of worrying about the pirates, and their deadly ways bout them. He was thin and sickly looking from staying hidden when he could. His caring mother cried out in pain of loving anguish for the way he looked as she studied her elder child. His young responsible manner had made it possible for the family to stay together as one unit. His small wages paid for everything his mother could not afford but needed above her poor wages from working at Mrs. Mosher's Tavern.

Billy kept his mother, brothers, and sisters up to the wee hours of the early next morning. He was enjoying telling his family all his fabulous stories of the many adventures He had aboard his ship the Shamrock, and where they had sailed to around the world. He liked telling them about the many pirate ships, watching as their eyes bulged out in fear listening to tales of the ships trying to attack them out on the seven seas of the world. He especially enjoyed telling them all about Henry, his leprechaun friend who had protected the Shamrock from the very first and last pirate ship attack. "Now don't you go filling these young ones' little heads full of fairy dust with all those wild tall tales of leprechauns and their golden legends of gobbledygook? They are nothing but old wives' tales to children, and this nonsense of talking all about things that did no really happen and best not talked about at all. The young ones just might think and believe your wild tales if they think you are really telling them the truth. Time for bed everyone. It is well past everyone's bedtime. Now scoot and off to bed with the lot of you."

CHAPTER FIFTY

The Gift from Henry

Everyone was fast asleep when there came a loud knocking at Billy's front door. It woke his mother up from a deep sound sleep, which she had not experienced since Billy first went sailing off. "Billy, there are some gentlemen here at the front door from the ship looking for you." When he came to the front door, the captain of the Shamrock, Captain Drake, was standing tall and proud in the middle of the small doorway. "Why, Billy, do you live here?" "Yes, sir, Captain." "I have a trunk here for the man of the house at this very address, sent all the way from America. The gentle man left notes in the cabin that I should deliver this big chest in person to this very address, for a fee of course which the person paid. The Shamrock sets sail in three days if the jib mast is fixed and the handrails repaired. See you on board Billy". "Yes, sir, Captain, three days until we sail."

He could not imagine that anyone knew him or his family from way across the sea in America. Then Billy remembered seeing this very trunk once before. This trunk is the very same trunk I had been sitting on in Henry's cabin after the pirate ship had attacked the Shamrock. The same one Henry had taken out from beneath his hind end when they both disappeared from the cabin and let him fall flat on the floor on the seat of his pants. Henry had returned with it all soaking wet along with himself. There sitting on the lid of the chest fastened to its cover was a small Shamrock carved out of wood with Skip's name "Henry" engraved on it. Billy quickly broke open the seal that the captain had placed on the chest at the beginning of the voyage. No wonder it took two of the biggest and strongest men on board the Shamrock to carry it. When he opened the chest, he could not believe the site that hurt his and his mother's eyes. The chest was full, full to its top with gold coins, rubies, diamonds, and silver. He would never have to go back out to see ever again to earn money for his family. He could stay home forever with his mother, brothers, and sisters and his loving family would never be without financial security for life. They had enough money now to purchase plenty of food to eat, and to fix up the home they all lived in the way they wanted. Billy smiled. "This gift is from my friend the leprechaun." Billy's mother did not say a single word about leprechauns to anyone ever again. She just stood there staring down in awe at the chest that glittered back into her misty happy eyes. Skip had kept his promise to Billy; therefore, he would never forget him for the rest of his life. He would think about his little friend, Henry the leprechaun, for the rest of his life or until they met again, possibly someday in the far-off future.

CHAPTER FIFTY-ONE

Reunited With Their Daughter

Transposing the three of them from the safety of the trunks to a nice secluded hiding place along the edge of the roadway, the three little leprechauns watched as the wagon that had transported them home to Grandma Broom and Grandpa Hair's carried the trunks off down the road toward the Timothy Barren's farm just past farmer Prendergast's farmstead. Down the narrow path, they all ran toward the clump of trees that grew beside the pond near the meadow. Skip hid his mother and father behind a thicket of brush growing in and beneath the tree. He proceeded right up to the front door of his grandparent's house hidden safely in and beneath the roots of the big old tall tree. Skip pounded frantically on his grandparents front wooden door, as hard as he possibly could, making it rattle like it was going to fall right off its hinges, the very same bothersome way he had always done before to get his grandparents all fired up and upset with him when he came home usually later then he should have. Gradually with great care, the small wooden-framed door slowly opened up. Skip's grandparents could not believe their old saddened eyes when they cast them upon their long lost grandson. "We thought you were dead, Skip. We thought the mortals had taken you away just like they had done to your parents." Tears of happiness filled their saddened eyes as the three laughed, hugged, and kissed.

"I brought my mom and my pa home with me, Grandma. I saved them all by myself, I did!" His grandparents looked quickly over Skip's shoulders to see where their long-lost daughter might be. The path behind him leading out to the roadway was clear with not one single sign of anyone in sight. His grandfather immediately reached right up, and grabbed a large lock of Skip's hair and gave it a hardy yank. The sudden pain of surprise felt good to Skip he thought, so he laughed. "You will never change your dang poor ways, will you, Skip. It is not nice to lie to us especially to your grandmother that way." Skip's mother could see her parents becoming angry and hurt by his silly shenanigans so they came rushing out from hiding behind the bushes. Grandpa was the first one to observe his long-lost daughter come running out and rushed quickly past Skip and out the front door to welcome her back home. He hugged and kissed her while streams of cheerful tears ran flowing down both of their cheeks. Grandma rushed over to her and hugged her daughter and husband together. Skip felt like he had done the best wide-world prank this time. He had saved his parents from the evil mortal devil himself, the Duke.

Skip yelled to everyone on the stoop that were hugging and kissing. "Hey everyone, I have some very important business to attend to down in the field. I shall be right back in a flash." No one was listening to Skip they were way too busy giving hugs and kisses to one another. He quickly transposed down the pathway to the side of Prendergast's field where he used to play. Then he transposed into the middle of the pasture and up into the lone tall old tree. He perched himself high up on one of its small branches as he looked happily down toward the green grass below. He then began to laugh out-loud and sing joyfully to himself. Out in the field below him, grazing on the fresh green grasses of the field, stood the same old mighty bull he used to play his first childhood pranks on when he was a very young testy leprechaun. Oh, how lucky Skip felt to be back home in Ireland again, but the urge to play silly pranks grew even deeper inside now. Jumping down to the green grassy ground below, he began making all kinds of silly little noises as he called out to the old bull who was grazing slothfully in farmer Prendergast's field, "Hey ye bull! I am home?" **I AM HOME!**

THE END

OTHER WORKS BY L. S. WOOD

EARTH LOST WITHOUT POWER

Greedy individuals took over Russia and produced Neutron bombs to try to take over the Earth. They produce thousands of them and place them into orbit around the Earth in multi headed missiles. Each missile had a faulty failsafe device onboard so no nation could enter space to retrieve the many missiles and unarm the many warheads held in their nose cones. When space particles from a passing Comet passed the Earth, they triggered the entire fleet of missiles to return to Earth, and destroy whatever was in their path. Knowing they had no control over their missiles, and where they were going, they pushed the panic button to destroy the missiles, but it was too late. The missiles had already entered the Earth's atmosphere when they pushed the button to destroy them. Life on Earth would never be the same until the Earth was able to take back what the billions of neutrons took away from it. Electricity around the globe was gone. Planes fell from the sky, and everything run by electricity came to a standstill. Many thousands of people lost their lives when this creature in the sky took away their electrical impulses making their hearts beat, and their lungs to breath. The Earth was lost without power to make lightning in its sky and its thunder heard round the world, would no longer be heard again, until the Earth took back control of its atmosphere, and magnetism.

CHIEF WHITE EAGLE
The last free Abnaki Indian

Chief White Eagle is the first of a series of books from his birth into the world, living in a small tribe of Abnaki Indians, living in the State of Vermont until his death. The many good and sorrowful adventures he faced growing up trying to avoid capture by the white man. With the loss of his young bride and son too small pox, he leaving the reservation the white man had placed the tribe on. He left because of a promise to his wife, he would return to their old village by cover of night along the roadway and woods by day to bury her and their infant son in a meadow they had promised each other when they were small they would return too. White Eagle having unknowingly been vaccinated against the smallpox by a Cow with cow pox when milking it as a young boy, he would not die, and would spend the rest of his years living in a large cave he had found near the old village as a boy. He saved a Bald Eagle with a broken wing from a fox, and nurtured it back to health. He saved a young white boy from stepping off a cliff to his death in a blinding rainstorm, and formed a lifelong friendship between the two lasted until his Death.

L. S. Wood lives in Winchendon Massachusetts with his lovely wife Rebecca of more than 50 wonderful years. They have two lovely children, Scott and Jennifer. His five grandchildren keep him very busy, but he loves it. He graduated from Mount Wachusett Community College and attended Fitchburg State University. He worked for a bank, then for industry, then started a real estate and construction business for his family, and built many homes around New England. He has written many children's books, science fiction, love stories, and more. He has many handwritten ones sitting on shelves, and in file cabinets, not yet been published. Due to family and friend pressuring into sharing his works with the world, he is now just longing to publish and share his works with the world. He hopes everyone will enjoy his books as much as he has enjoyed writing them.

THE BROKENHEARTED LEPRECHAUN

SKIP INTO TROUBLE

By L. S. WOOD

LARRY S WOOD at beclarwood@comcast.net